S0-BZG-688

"SENSUOUS, THRILLING, WONDERFUL!"
Houston Chronicle

"Anne Rice is a writer who follows a hidden path . . . into an unfamiliar world. But if you surrender and go with her on her eerie journey, you will find that you have surrendered to enchantment, as if in a voluptuous dream."
Boston Globe

"UNUSUALLY MOVING."
Miami Herald

"A chilling, thought-provoking tale, beautifully frightening, sensuous, and utterly unnerving."
Hartford Courant

"A COLOSSAL NOVEL

. . . AN UNMITIGATED TERROR TRIP NOT MEANT FOR THE WEAK OF HEART.

Seldom before has this mythical being been so explored and exposed. The imaginative plot plunges you into the world of the undead and leads you on a journey that begins in the New Orleans of 200 years ago. Caught in undesired immortality, the author's pathetic and nameless vampire gives a first person account of his past. His ghastly initiation into the netherworld is as mesmeric as is the discovery he is not alone in the nightly search for warm fresh blood. Lurking in the dark corners of the night are more of his kind—many more—a community of the undead roaming the near vacant streets of every city. Unable to control his desires and longing for death, the vampire travels through the years lonely, yet not alone. For there is Lestat, his tutor and initiator in this new existence. And there is Claudia, the vampire who will always retain the body of a child though her mind and passions continue to grow . . .

A BONAFIDE BLOCKBUSTER . . . AUDACIOUS, EROTIC, AND UNFORGETTABLE!"

The Cincinnati Enquirer.

"THRILLING . . . STRIKINGLY ORIGINAL."
New York Post

"Sensational and fantastic . . . woven with uncanny magic . . . INTERVIEW WITH THE VAMPIRE is hypnotically poetic in tone, rich in sensory imagery and dense with the darkness that lies behind the veil of human thought."
St. Louis Post-Dispatch

"EXCITEMENT AND HORROR!"
The Kansas City Star

"From the beginning we are seduced, hypnotized by the voice of the vampire . . . a masterful suspense story . . . that plumbs the deepest recesses of human sensuality."
Chicago Tribune Book World

INTERVIEW WITH THE VAMPIRE

A NOVEL BY

ANNE RICE

BALLANTINE BOOKS • NEW YORK

*For Stan Rice, Carole Malkin,
and Alice O'Brien Borchardt*

Copyright © 1976 by Anne O'Brien Rice

All rights reserved under International and Pan-American
Copyright Conventions. Published in the United States by
Ballantine Books, a division of Random House, Inc., New
York, and simultaneously in Canada by Random House of
Canada Limited, Toronto.

Library of Congress Catalog Card Number: 75-36792

ISBN 0-345-33197-4

This edition published by arrangement with
Alfred A. Knopf, Inc.

Manufactured in the United States of America

First Ballantine Books Edition: May 1977
Eleventh Printing: November 1985

First Canadian Printing: May 1977

PART I

I SEE . . ." said the vampire thoughtfully, and slowly he walked across the room towards the window. For a long time he stood there against the dim light from Divisadero Street and the passing beams of traffic. The boy could see the furnishings of the room more clearly now, the round oak table, the chairs. A wash basin hung on one wall with a mirror. He set his brief case on the table and waited.

"But how much tape do you have with you?" asked the vampire, turning now so the boy could see his profile. "Enough for the story of a life?"

"Sure, if it's a good life. Sometimes I interview as many as three or four people a night if I'm lucky. But it has to be a good story. That's only fair, isn't it?"

"Admirably fair," the vampire answered. "I would like to tell you the story of my life, then. I would like to do that very much."

"Great," said the boy. And quickly he removed the small tape recorder from his brief case, making a check of the cassette and the batteries. "I'm really anxious to hear why you believe this, why you . . ."

"No," said the vampire abruptly. "We can't begin that way. Is your equipment ready?"

"Yes," said the boy.

"Then sit down. I'm going to turn on the overhead light."

"But I thought vampires didn't like light," said the boy. "If you think the dark adds to the atmosphere . . ." But then he stopped. The vampire was watching him with his back to the window. The boy could make out nothing of his face now, and something about the still figure there distracted him. He started to say something again but he said nothing. And then he sighed with relief when the vampire moved towards the table and reached for the overhead cord.

At once the room was flooded with a harsh yellow light. And the boy, staring up at the vampire, could not repress a gasp. His fingers danced backwards on the table to grasp the edge. "Dear God!" he whispered, and then he gazed, speechless, at the vampire.

The vampire was utterly white and smooth, as if he were sculpted from bleached bone, and his face was as seemingly inanimate as a statue, except for two brilliant green eyes that looked down at the boy intently like flames in a skull. But then the vampire smiled almost wistfully, and the smooth white substance of his face moved with the infinitely flexible but minimal lines of a cartoon. "Do you see?" he asked softly.

The boy shuddered, lifting his hand as if to shield himself from a powerful light. His eyes moved slowly over the finely tailored black coat he'd only glimpsed in the bar, the long folds of the cape, the black silk tie knotted at the throat, and the gleam of the white collar that was as white as the vampire's flesh. He stared at the vampire's full black hair, the waves that were combed back over the tips of the ears, the curls that barely touched the edge of the white collar.

"Now, do you still want the interview?" the vampire asked.

The boy's mouth was open before the sound came out. He was nodding. Then he said, "Yes."

The vampire sat down slowly opposite him and, leaning forward, said gently, confidentially, "Don't be afraid. Just start the tape."

And then he reached out over the length of the table. The boy recoiled, sweat running down the sides of his face. The vampire clamped a hand on the boy's shoulder and said, "Believe me, I won't hurt you. I want this opportunity. It's more important to me than you can realize now. I want you to begin." And he withdrew his hand and sat collected, waiting.

It took a moment for the boy to wipe his forehead and his lips with a handkerchief, to stammer that the microphone was in the machine, to press the button, to say that the machine was on.

"You weren't always a vampire, were you?" he began.

"No," answered the vampire. "I was a twenty-five-year-old man when I became a vampire, and the year was seventeen ninety-one."

The boy was startled by the preciseness of the date and he repeated it before he asked, "How did it come about?"

"There's a simple answer to that. I don't believe I want to give simple answers," said the vampire. "I think I want to tell the real story. . . ."

"Yes," the boy said quickly. He was folding his handkerchief over and over and wiping his lips now with it again.

"There was a tragedy . . ." the vampire started. "It was my younger brother. . . . He died." And then he stopped, so that the boy cleared his throat and wiped at his face again before stuffing the handkerchief almost impatiently into his pocket.

"It's not painful, is it?" he asked timidly.

"Does it seem so?" asked the vampire. "No." He shook his head. "It's simply that I've only told this story to one other person. And that was so long ago. No, it's not painful. . . .

"We were living in Louisiana then. We'd received a land grant and settled two indigo plantations on the Mississippi very near New Orleans. . . ."

"Ah, that's the accent . . ." the boy said softly.

For a moment the vampire stared blankly. "I have an accent?" He began to laugh.

And the boy, flustered, answered quickly. "I noticed it in the bar when I asked you what you did for a living. It's just a slight sharpness to the consonants, that's all. I never guessed it was French."

"It's all right," the vampire assured him. "I'm not as shocked as I pretend to be. It's only that I forget it from time to time. But let me go on. . . ."

"Please . . ." said the boy.

"I was talking about the plantations. They had a great deal to do with it, really, my becoming a vampire. But I'll come to that. Our life there was both luxurious and primitive. And we ourselves found it extremely attractive. You see, we lived far better there than we could have ever lived in France. Perhaps the sheer wilderness of Louisiana only made it seem so, but seeming so, it was. I remember the imported furniture that cluttered the house." The vampire smiled. "And the harpsichord; that was lovely. My sister used to play it. On summer evenings, she would sit at the keys with her back to the open French windows. And I can still remember that thin, rapid music and the vision of the swamp rising beyond her, the moss-hung cypresses floating against the sky. And there were the sounds of the swamp, a chorus of creatures, the cry of the birds. I think we loved it. It made the rosewood furniture all the more precious, the music more delicate and desirable. Even when the wisteria tore the shutters off the attic windows and worked its tendrils right into the whitewashed brick in less than a year. . . . Yes, we loved it. All except my brother. I don't think I ever heard him complain of anything, but I knew how he felt. My father was dead then, and I was head of the family and I had to defend him constantly from my mother and sister. They wanted to take him visiting, and to New Orleans for parties, but he hated these things. I think he stopped going altogether before he was twelve. Prayer was what mattered to him, prayer and his leatherbound lives of the saints.

"Finally I built him an oratory removed from the house, and he began to spend most of every day there and often the early evening. It was ironic, really. He was so different from us, so different from everyone, and I was so regular! There was nothing extraordinary about me whatsoever." The vampire smiled.

"Sometimes in the evening I would go out to him and find him in the garden near the oratory, sitting absolutely composed on a stone bench there, and I'd tell him my troubles, the difficulties I had with the slaves, how I distrusted the overseer or the weather or my brokers . . . all the problems that made up the length and breadth of my existence. And he would listen, making only a few comments, always sympathetic, so that when I left him I had the distinct impression he had solved everything for me. I didn't think I could deny him anything, and I vowed that no matter how it would break my heart to lose him, he could enter the priesthood when the time came. Of course, I was wrong." The vampire stopped.

For a moment the boy only gazed at him and then he started as if awakened from deep thought, and he floundered, as if he could not find the right words. "Ah . . . he didn't want to be a priest?" the boy asked. The vampire studied him as if trying to discern the meaning of his expression. Then he said:

"I meant that I was wrong about myself, about my not denying him anything." His eyes moved over the far wall and fixed on the panes of the window. "He began to see visions."

"Real visions?" the boy asked, but again there was hesitation, as if he were thinking of something else.

"I didn't think so," the vampire answered. "It happened when he was fifteen. He was very handsome then. He had the smoothest skin and the largest blue eyes. He was robust, not thin as I am now and was then . . . but his eyes . . . it was as if when I looked into his eyes I was standing alone on the edge of the world . . . on a windswept ocean beach. There was nothing but the soft roar of the waves. Well," he said, his eyes still fixed on the window panes, "he began to see visions. He only hinted at this at first, and he stopped taking his meals altogether. He lived in the oratory. At any hour of day or night, I could find him on the bare flagstones kneeling before the altar. And the oratory itself was neglected. He stopped tending the candles or changing the altar cloths or even sweeping out the leaves. One night I became really alarmed when I stood in the rose arbor watching him for one solid hour, during which he never moved from his knees and never once lowered his arms, which he held outstretched in the form of a cross. The slaves all thought he was mad." The vampire raised his eyebrows in wonder. "I was convinced that he was only . . . overzealous. That in his love for God, he had perhaps gone too far. Then he told me about the visions. Both St. Dominic and the Blessed Virgin Mary had come to him in the oratory. They had told him he was to sell all our property in Louisiana, everything we owned, and use the money to do God's work in France. My brother was to be a great religious leader, to return the country to its former fervor, to turn the tide against atheism and the Revolution. Of course, he had no money of his own. I was to sell the plantations and our town houses in New Orleans and give the money to him."

Again the vampire stopped. And the boy sat motionless regarding him, astonished. "Ah . . . excuse me," he whispered. "What did you say? Did you sell the plantations?"

"No," said the vampire, his face calm as it had been from the start. "I laughed at him. And he . . . he became incensed. He insisted his command came from the Virgin herself. Who was I to disregard it? Who indeed?" he asked softly, as if he were thinking of this again. "Who indeed? And the more he tried to convince me, the more I laughed. It was nonsense, I told him, the product of an immature and even morbid mind. The oratory was a mistake, I said to him; I would have it torn down at once. He would go to school in New Orleans and get such inane notions out of his head. I don't remember all that I said. But I remember the feeling. Behind all this contemptuous dismissal on my part was a smoldering anger and a disappointment. I was bitterly disappointed. I didn't believe him at all."

"But that's understandable," said the boy quickly when the vampire paused, his expression of astonishment softening. "I mean, would anyone have believed him?"

"Is it so understandable?" The vampire looked at the boy. "I think perhaps it was vicious egotism. Let me explain. I loved my brother, as I told you, and at times I believed him to be a living saint. I encouraged him in his prayer and meditations, as I said, and I was willing to give him up to the priesthood. And if someone had told me of a saint in Arles or Lourdes who saw visions, I would have believed it. I was a Catholic; I believed in saints. I lit tapers before their marble statues in churches; I knew their pictures, their symbols, their names. But I didn't, couldn't believe my brother. Not only did I not believe he saw visions, I couldn't entertain the notion for a moment. Now, why? Because he was my brother. Holy he might be, peculiar most definitely; but Francis of Assisi, no. Not *my* brother. No brother of mine could be such. That is egotism. Do you see?"

The boy thought about it before he answered and then he nodded and said that yes, he thought that he did.

"Perhaps he saw the visions," said the vampire.

"Then you . . . you don't claim to know . . . now . . . whether he did not not?"

"No, but I do know that he never wavered in his conviction for a second. That I know now and knew then the night he left my room crazed and grieved. He never wavered for an instant. And within minutes, he was dead."

"How?" the boy asked.

"He simply walked out of the French doors onto the gallery and stood for a moment at the head of the brick stairs. And then he fell. He was dead when I reached the bottom, his neck broken." The vampire shook his head in consternation, but his face was still serene.

"Did you see him fall?" asked the boy. "Did he lose his footing?"

"No, but two of the servants saw it happen. They said that he had looked up as if he had just seen something in the air. Then his entire body moved forward as if being swept by a wind. One of them said he was about to say something when he fell. I thought that he was about to say something too, but it was at that moment I turned away from the window. My back was turned when I heard the noise." He glanced at the tape recorder. "I could not forgive myself. I felt responsible for his death," he said. "And everyone else seemed to think I was responsible also."

"But how could they? You said they saw him fall."

"It wasn't a direct accusation. They simply knew that something had passed between us that was unpleasant. That we had argued minutes before the fall.

The servants had heard us, my mother had heard us. My mother would not stop asking me what had happened and why my brother, who was so quiet, had been shouting. Then my sister joined in, and of course I refused to say. I was so bitterly shocked and miserable that I had no patience with anyone, only the vague determination they would not know about his 'visions.' They would not know that he had become, finally, not a saint, but only a . . . fanatic. My sister went to bed rather than face the funeral, and my mother told everyone in the parish that something horrible had happened in my room which I would not reveal; and even the police questioned me, on the word of my own mother. Finally the priest came to see me and demanded to know what had gone on. I told no one. It was only a discussion, I said. I was not on the gallery when he fell, I protested, and they all stared at me as if I'd killed him. And I felt that I'd killed him. I sat in the parlor beside his coffin for two days thinking, I have killed him. I stared at his face until spots appeared before my eyes and I nearly fainted. The back of his skull had been shattered on the pavement, and his head had the wrong shape on the pillow. I forced myself to stare at it, to study it simply because I could hardly endure the pain and the smell of decay, and I was tempted over and over to try to open his eyes. All these were mad thoughts, mad impulses. The main thought was this: I had laughed at him; I had not believed him; I had not been kind to him. He had fallen because of me."

"This really happened, didn't it?" the boy whispered. "You're telling me something . . . that's true."

"Yes," said the vampire, looking at him without surprise. "I want to go on telling you." But as his eyes passed over the boy and returned to the window, he showed only faint interest in the boy, who seemed engaged in some silent inner struggle.

"But you said you didn't know about the visions, that you, a vampire . . . didn't know for certain whether . . ."

"I want to take things in order," said the vampire, "I want to go on telling you things as they happened.

No, I don't know about the visions. To this day." And again he waited until the boy said:

"Yes, please, please go on."

"Well, I wanted to sell the plantations. I never wanted to see the house or the oratory again. I leased them finally to an agency which would work them for me and manage things so I need never go there, and I moved my mother and sister to one of the town houses in New Orleans. Of course, I did not escape my brother for a moment. I could think of nothing but his body rotting in the ground. He was buried in the St. Louis cemetery in New Orleans, and I did everything to avoid passing those gates; but still I thought of him constantly. Drunk or sober, I saw his body rotting in the coffin, and I couldn't bear it. Over and over I dreamed that he was at the head of the steps and I was holding his arm, talking kindly to him, urging him back into the bedroom, telling him gently that I did believe him, that he must pray for me to have faith. Meantime, the slaves on Pointe du Lac (that was my plantation) had begun to talk of seeing his ghost on the gallery, and the overseer couldn't keep order. People in society asked my sister offensive questions about the whole incident, and she became an hysteric. She wasn't really an hysteric. She simply thought she ought to react that way, so she did. I drank all the time and was at home as little as possible. I lived like a man who wanted to die but who had no courage to do it himself. I walked black streets and alleys alone; I passed out in cabarets. I backed out of two duels more from apathy than cowardice and truly wished to be murdered. And then I was attacked. It might have been anyone—and my invitation was open to sailors, thieves, maniacs, anyone. But it was a vampire. He caught me just a few steps from my door one night and left me for dead, or so I thought."

"You mean . . . he sucked your blood?" the boy asked.

"Yes," the vampire laughed. "He sucked my blood. That is the way it's done."

"But you lived," said the young man. "You said he left you for dead."

"Well, he drained me almost to the point of death, which was for him sufficient. I was put to bed as soon as I was found, confused and really unaware of what had happened to me. I suppose I thought that drink had finally caused a stroke. I expected to die now and had no interest in eating or drinking or talking to the doctor. My mother sent for the priest. I was feverish by then and I told the priest everything, all about my brother's visions and what I had done. I remember I clung to his arm, making him swear over and over he would tell no one. 'I know I didn't kill him,' I said to the priest finally. 'It's that I cannot live now that he's dead. Not after the way I treated him.'

" 'That's ridiculous,' he answered me. 'Of course you can live. There's nothing wrong with you but self-indulgence. Your mother needs you, not to mention your sister. And as for this brother of yours, he was possessed of the devil.' I was so stunned when he said this I couldn't protest. The devil made the visions, he went on to explain. The devil was rampant. The entire country of France was under the influence of the devil, and the Revolution had been his greatest triumph. Nothing would have saved my brother but exorcism, prayer, and fasting, men to hold him down while the devil raged in his body and tried to throw him about. 'The devil threw him down the steps; it's perfectly obvious,' he declared. 'You weren't talking to your brother in that room, you were talking to the devil.' Well, this enraged me. I believed before that I had been pushed to my limits, but I had not. He went on talking about the devil, about voodoo amongst the slaves and cases of possession in other parts of the world. And I went wild. I wrecked the room in the process of nearly killing him."

"But your strength . . . the vampire . . . ?" asked the boy.

"I was out of my mind," the vampire explained. "I did things I could not have done in perfect health. The scene is confused, pale, fantastical now. But I do remember that I drove him out of the back doors of the house, across the courtyard, and against the brick wall of the kitchen, where I pounded his head until I nearly killed him. When I was subdued finally, and exhausted then almost to the point of death, they bled me. The fools. But I was going to say something else. It was then that I conceived of my own egotism. Perhaps I'd seen it reflected in the priest. His contemptuous attitude towards my brother reflected my own; his immediate and shallow carping about the devil; his refusal to even entertain the idea that sanctity had passed so close."

"But he did believe in possession by the devil."

"That is a much more mundane idea," said the vampire immediately. "People who cease to believe in God or goodness altogether still believe in the devil. I don't know why. No, I do indeed know why. Evil is always possible. And goodness is eternally difficult. But you must understand, possession is really another way of saying someone is mad. I felt it was, for the priest. I'm sure he'd seen madness. Perhaps he had stood right over raving madness and pronounced it possession. You don't have to see Satan when he is exorcised. But to stand in the presence of a saint . . . To believe that the saint has seen a vision. No, it's egotism, our refusal to believe it could occur in our midst."

"I never thought of it in that way," said the boy. "But what happened to you? You said they bled you to cure you, and that must have nearly killed you."

The vampire laughed. "Yes. It certainly did. But the vampire came back that night. You see, he wanted Pointe du Lac, my plantation.

"It was very late, after my sister had fallen asleep. I can remember it as if it were yesterday. He came in from the courtyard, opening the French doors without a sound, a tall fair-skinned man with a mass of blond hair and a graceful, almost feline quality to his movements. And gently, he draped a shawl over my sister's eyes and lowered the wick of the lamp. She dozed there beside the basin and the cloth with which she'd bathed my forehead, and she never once stirred under that shawl until morning. But by that time I was greatly changed."

"What *was* this change?" asked the boy.

The vampire sighed. He leaned back against the

chair and looked at the walls. "At first I thought he was another doctor, or someone summoned by the family to try to reason with me. But this suspicion was removed at once. He stepped close to my bed and leaned down so that his face was in the lamplight, and I saw that he was no ordinary man at all. His gray eyes burned with an incandescence, and the long white hands which hung by his sides were not those of a human being. I think I knew everything in that instant, and all that he told me was only aftermath. What I mean is, the moment I saw him, saw his extraordinary aura and knew him to be no creature I'd ever known, I was reduced to nothing. That ego which could not accept the presence of an extraordinary human being in its midst was crushed. All my conceptions, even my guilt and wish to die, seemed utterly unimportant. I completely forgot *myself!*" he said, now silently touching his breast with his fist. "I forgot myself totally. And in the same instant knew totally the meaning of possibility. From then on I experienced only increasing wonder. As he talked to me and told me of what I might become, of what his life had been and stood to be, my past shrank to embers. I saw my life as if I stood apart from it, the vanity, the self-serving, the constant fleeing from one petty annoyance after another, the lip service to God and the Virgin and a host of saints whose names filled my prayer books, none of whom made the slightest difference in a narrow, materialistic, and selfish existence. I saw my real gods . . . the gods of most men. Food, drink, and security in conformity. Cinders."

The boy's face was tense with a mixture of confusion and amazement. "And so you decided to become a vampire?" he asked. The vampire was silent for a moment.

"Decided. It doesn't seem the right word. Yet I cannot say it was inevitable from the moment that he stepped into that room. No, indeed, it was not inevitable. Yet I can't say I decided. Let me say that when he'd finished speaking, no other decision was possible for me, and I pursued my course without a backward glance. Except for one."

"Except for one? What?"

"My last sunrise," said the vampire. "That morning, I was not yet a vampire. And I saw my last sunrise.

"I remember it completely; yet I do not think I remember any other sunrise before it. I remember the light came first to the tops of the French windows, a paling behind the lace curtains, and then a gleam growing brighter and brighter in patches among the leaves of the trees. Finally the sun came through the windows themselves and the lace lay in shadows on the stone floor, and all over the form of my sister, who was still sleeping, shadows of lace on the shawl over her shoulders and head. As soon as she was warm, she pushed the shawl away without awakening, and then the sun shone full on her eyes and she tightened her eyelids. Then it was gleaming on the table where she rested her head on her arms, and gleaming, blazing, in the water in the pitcher. And I could feel it on my hands on the counterpane and then on my face. I lay in the bed thinking about all the things the vampire had told me, and then it was that I said good-bye to the sunrise and went out to become a vampire. It was . . . the last sunrise."

The vampire was looking out the window again. And when he stopped, the silence was so sudden the boy seemed to hear it. Then he could hear the noises from the street. The sound of a truck was deafening. The light cord stirred with the vibration. Then the truck was gone.

"Do you miss it?" he asked then in a small voice.

"Not really," said the vampire. "There are so many other things. But where were we? You want to know how it happened, how I became a vampire."

"Yes," said the boy. "How did you change, exactly?"

"I can't tell you exactly," said the vampire. "I can tell you about it, enclose it with words that will make the value of it to me evident to you. But I can't tell you exactly, any more than I could tell you exactly what is the experience of sex if you have never had it."

The young man seemed struck suddenly with still another question, but before he could speak the vampire went on. "As I told you, this vampire Lestat, wanted the plantation. A mundane reason, surely, for granting me a life which will last until the end of the world; but he was not a very discriminating person. He didn't consider the world's small population of vampires as being a select club, I should say. He had human problems, a blind father who did not know his son was a vampire and must not find out. Living in New Orleans had become too difficult for him, considering his needs and the necessity to care for his father, and he wanted Pointe du Lac.

"We went at once to the plantation the next evening, ensconced the blind father in the master bedroom, and I proceeded to make the change. I cannot say that it consisted in any one step really—though one, of course, was the step beyond which I could make no return. But there were several acts involved, and the first was the death of the overseer. Lestat took him in his sleep. I was to watch and to approve; that is, to witness the taking of a human life as proof of my commitment and part of my change. This proved without doubt the most difficult part for me. I've told you I had no fear regarding my own death, only a squeamishness about taking my life myself. But I had a most high regard for the life of others, and a horror of death most recently developed because of my brother. I had to watch the overseer awake with a start, try to throw off Lestat with both hands, fail, then lie there struggling under Lestat's grasp, and finally go limp, drained of blood. And die. He did not die at once. We stood in his narrow bedroom for the better part of an hour watching him die. Part of my change, as I said. Lestat would never have stayed otherwise. Then it was necessary to get rid of the overseer's body. I was almost sick from this. Weak and feverish already, I had little reserve; and handling the dead body with such a purpose caused me nausea. Lestat was laughing, telling me callously that I would feel so different once I was a vampire that I would laugh, too. He was wrong about that. I never laugh at death, no matter how often and regularly I am the cause of it.

"But let me take things in order. We had to drive up the river road until we came to open fields and leave the overseer there. We tore his coat, stole his money, and saw to it his lips were stained with liquor. I knew his wife, who lived in New Orleans, and knew the state of desperation she would suffer when the body was discovered. But more than sorrow for her, I felt pain that she would never know what had happened, that her husband had not been found drunk on the road by robbers. As we beat the body, bruising the face and the shoulders, I became more and more aroused. Of course, you must realize that all this time the vampire Lestat was extraordinary. He was no more human to me than a biblical angel. But under this pressure, my enchantment with him was strained. I had seen my becoming a vampire in two lights: The first light was simply enchantment; Lestat had overwhelmed me on my deathbed. But the other light was my wish for self-destruction. My desire to be thoroughly damned. This was the open door through which Lestat had come on both the first and second occasion. Now I was not destroying myself but someone else. The overseer, his wife, his family. I recoiled and might have fled from Lestat, my sanity thoroughly shattered, had not he sensed with an infallible instinct what was happening. Infallible instinct . . ." The vampire mused. "Let me say the powerful instinct of a vampire to whom even the slightest change in a human's facial expression is as apparent as a gesture. Lestat had preternatural timing. He rushed me into the carriage and whipped the horses home. 'I want to die,' I began to murmur. 'This is unbearable. I want to die. You have it in your power to kill me. Let me die.' I refused to look at him, to be spellbound by the sheer beauty of his appearance. He spoke my name to me softly, laughing. As I said, he was determined to have the plantation."

"But would he have let you go?" asked the boy. "Under any circumstances?"

"I don't know. Knowing Lestat as I do now, I would say he would have killed me rather than let me go. But this was what I wanted, you see. It didn't matter. No, this was what I thought I wanted. As soon as we reached the house, I jumped down out of the carriage and walked, a zombie, to the brick stairs where my brother had fallen. The house had been unoccupied for months now, the overseer having his own cottage, and the Louisiana heat and damp were already picking apart the steps. Every crevice was sprouting grass and even small wildflowers. I remember feeling the moisture which in the night was cool as I sat down on the lower steps and even rested my head against the brick and felt the little wax-stemmed wildflowers with my hands. I pulled a clump of them out of the easy dirt in one hand. 'I want to die; kill me. Kill me,' I said to the vampire. 'Now I am guilty of murder. I can't live.' He sneered with the impatience of people listening to the obvious lies of others. And then in a flash he fastened on me just as he had on my man. I thrashed against him wildly. I dug my boot into his chest and kicked him as fiercely as I could, his teeth stinging my throat, the fever pounding in my temples. And with a movement of his entire body, much too fast for me to see, he was suddenly standing disdainfully at the foot of the steps. 'I thought you wanted to die, Louis,' he said."

The boy made a soft, abrupt sound when the vampire said his name which the vampire acknowledged with the quick statement, "Yes, that is my name," and went on.

"Well, I lay there helpless in the face of my own cowardice and fatuousness again," he said. "Perhaps so directly confronted with it, I might in time have gained the courage to truly take my life, not to whine and beg for others to take it. I saw myself turning on a knife then, lauguishing in a day-to-day suffering which I found as necessary as penance from the confessional, truly hoping death would find me unawares and render me fit for eternal pardon. And also I saw myself as if in a vision standing at the head of the stairs, just where my brother had stood, and then hurtling my body down on the bricks.

"But there was no time for courage. Or shall I say, there was no time in Lestat's plan for anything but his plan. 'Now listen to me, Louis,' he said, and he lay down beside me now on the steps, his movement so graceful and so personal that at once it made me think of a lover. I recoiled. But he put his right arm around me and pulled me close to his chest. Never had I been this close to him before, and in the dim light I could see the magnificent radiance of his eye and the unnatural mask of his skin. As I tried to move, he pressed his right fingers against my lips and said, 'Be still. I am going to drain you now to the very threshold of death, and I want you to be quiet, so quiet that you can almost hear the flow of blood through your veins, so quiet that you can hear the flow of that same blood through mine. It is your consciousness, your will, which must keep you alive.' I wanted to struggle, but he pressed so hard with his fingers that he held my entire prone body in check; and as soon as I stopped my abortive attempt at rebellion, he sank his teeth into my neck."

The boy's eyes grew huge. He had drawn farther and farther back in his chair as the vampire spoke, and now his face was tense, his eyes narrow, as if he were preparing to weather a blow.

"Have you ever lost a great amount of blood?" asked the vampire. "Do you know the feeling?"

The boy's lips shaped the word *no*, but no sound came out. He cleared his throat. "No," he said.

"Candles burned in the upstairs parlor, where we had planned the death of the overseer. An oil lantern swayed in the breeze on the gallery. All of this light coalesced and began to shimmer, as though a golden presence hovered above me, suspended in the stairwell, softly entangled with the railings, curling and contracting like smoke. 'Listen, keep your eyes wide,' Lestat whispered to me, his lips moving against my neck. I remember that the movement of his lips raised the hair all over my body, sent a shock of sensation through my body that was not unlike the pleasure of passion. . . ."

He mused, his right fingers slightly curled beneath his chin, the first finger appearing to lightly stroke it. "The result was that within minutes I was weak to paralysis. Panic-stricken, I discovered I could not even will myself to speak. Lestat still held me, of course, and his arm was like the weight of an iron bar. I felt his teeth withdraw with such a keenness that the two puncture wounds seemed enormous, lined with pain. And now he bent over my helpless head and, taking his right hand off me, bit his own wrist. The blood flowed down upon my shirt and coat, and he watched it with a narrow, gleaming eye. It seemed an eternity that he watched it, and that shimmer of light now hung behind his head like the backdrop of an apparition. I think that I knew what he meant to do even before he did it, and I was waiting in my helplessness as if I'd been waiting for years. He pressed his bleeding wrist to my mouth, said firmly, a little impatiently, 'Louis, drink.' And I did. 'Steady, Louis,' and 'Hurry,' he whispered to me a number of times. I drank, sucking the blood out of the holes, experiencing for the first time since infancy the special pleasure of sucking nourishment, the body focused with the mind upon one vital source. Then something happened." The vampire sat back, a slight frown on his face.

"How pathetic it is to describe these things which can't truly be described," he said, his voice low almost to a whisper. The boy sat as if frozen.

"I saw nothing but that light then as I drew blood. And then this next thing, this next thing was . . . sound. A dull roar at first and then a pounding like the pounding of a drum, growing louder and louder, as if some enormous creature were coming up on one slowly through a dark and alien forest, pounding as he came, a huge drum. And then there came the pounding of another drum, as if another giant were coming yards behind him, and each giant, intent on his own drum, gave no notice to the rhythm of the other. The sound grew louder and louder until it seemed to fill not just my hearing but all my senses, to be throbbing in my lips and fingers, in the flesh of my temples, in my veins. Above all, in my veins, drum and then the other drum; and then Lestat pulled his wrist free suddenly, and I opened my eyes and checked myself in a moment of reaching for his wrist, grabbing it, forcing it back to my mouth at all costs; I checked myself because I realized that the drum was my heart, and the second drum had been his." The vampire sighed. "Do you understand?"

The boy began to speak, and then he shook his head. "No . . . I mean, I do," he said. "I mean, I . . ."

"Of course," said the vampire, looking away.

"Wait, wait!" said the boy in a welter of excitement. "The tape is almost gone. I have to turn it over." The vampire watched patiently as he changed it.

"What happened then?" the boy asked. His face was moist, and he wiped it hurriedly with his handkerchief.

"I saw as a vampire," said the vampire, his voice now slightly detached. It seemed almost distracted. Then he drew himself up. "Lestat was standing again at the foot of the stairs, and I saw him as I could not possibly have seen him before. He had seemed white to me before, starkly white, so that in the night he was almost luminous; and now I saw him filled with his own life and own blood: he was radiant, not luminous. And then I saw that not only Lestat had changed, but all things had changed.

"It was as if I had only just been able to see colors and shapes for the first time. I was so enthralled with the buttons on Lestat's black coat that I looked at nothing else for a long time. Then Lestat began to laugh, and I heard his laughter as I had never heard anything before. His heart I still heard like the beating of a drum, and now came this metallic laughter. It was confusing, each sound running into the next sound, like the mingling reverberations of bells, until I learned to separate the sounds, and then they overlapped, each soft but distinct, increasing but discrete, peals of laughter." The vampire smiled with delight. "Peals of bells.

" 'Stop looking at my buttons,' Lestat said. 'Go out there into the trees. Rid yourself of all the human waste in your body, and don't fall so madly in love with the night that you lose your way!'

"That, of course, was a wise command. When I saw the moon on the flagstones, I became so enamored with it that I must have spent an hour there. I passed my brother's oratory without so much as a thought of him, and standing among the cottonwood and oaks, I heard the night as if it were a chorus of whispering women, all beckoning me to their breasts. As for my body, it was not yet totally converted, and as soon as I became the least accustomed to the sounds and sights, it began to ache. All my human fluids were being forced out of me. I was dying as a human, yet completely alive as a vampire; and with my awakened senses, I had to preside over the death of my body with a certain discomfort and then, finally, fear. I ran back up the steps to the parlor, where Lestat was already at work on the plantation papers, going over the expenses and profits for the last year. 'You're a rich man,' he said to me when I came in. 'Something's happening to me,' I shouted.

" 'You're dying, that's all; don't be a fool. Don't you have any oil lamps? All this money and you can't afford whale oil except for that lantern. Bring me that lantern.'

" 'Dying!' I shouted. 'Dying!'

" 'It happens to everyone,' he persisted, refusing to help me. As I look back on this, I still despise him for it. Not because I was afraid, but because he might have drawn my attention to these changes with reverence. He might have calmed me and told me I might watch my death with the same fascination with which I had watched and felt the night. But he didn't. Lestat was never the vampire I am. Not at all." The vampire did not say this boastfully. He said it as if he would truly have had it otherwise.

"*Alors,*" he sighed. "I was dying fast, which meant that my capacity for fear was diminishing as rapidly. I simply regret I was not more attentive to the process. Lestat was being a perfect idiot. 'Oh, for the love of hell!' he began shouting. 'Do you realize I've made no provision for you? What a fool I am.' I was tempted to say, 'Yes, you are,' but I didn't. 'You'll have to bed down with me this morning. I haven't prepared you a coffin.' "

The vampire laughed. "The coffin struck such a chord of terror in me I think it absorbed all the capacity for terror I had left. Then came only my mild alarm at having to share a coffin with Lestat. He was in his father's bedroom meantime, telling the old man good-bye, that he would return in the morning. 'But where do you go, why must you live by such a schedule!' the old man demanded, and Lestat became impatient. Before this, he'd been gracious to the old man, almost to the point of sickening one, but now he became a bully. 'I take care of you, don't I? I've put a better roof over your head than you ever put over mine! If I want to sleep all day and drink all night, I'll do it, damn you!' The old man started to whine. Only my peculiar state of emotions and most unusual feeling of exhaustion kept me from disapproving. I was watching the scene through the open door, enthralled with the colors of the counterpane and the positive riot of color in the old man's face. His blue veins pulsed beneath his pink and grayish flesh. I found even the yellow of his teeth appealing to me, and I became almost hypnotized by the quivering of his lip. 'Such a son, such a son,' he said, never suspecting, of course, the true nature of his son. 'All right, then, go. I know you keep a woman somewhere; you go to see her as soon as her husband leaves in the morning. Give me my rosary. What's happened to my rosary?' Lestat said something blasphemous and gave him the rosary. . . ."

"But . . ." the boy started.

"Yes?" said the vampire. "I'm afraid I don't allow you to ask enough questions."

"I was going to ask, rosaries have crosses on them, don't they?"

"Oh, the rumor about crosses!" the vampire laughed. "You refer to our being afraid of crosses?"

"Unable to look on them, I thought," said the boy.

"Nonsense, my friend, sheer nonsense. I can look on anything I like. And I rather like looking on crucifixes in particular."

"And what about the rumor about keyholes? That you can . . . become steam and go through them."

"I wish I could," laughed the vampire. "How positively delightful. I should like to pass through all manner of different keyholes and feel the tickle of their peculiar shapes. No." He shook his head. "That is, how would you say today . . . bullshit?"

The boy laughed despite himself. Then his face grew serious.

"You mustn't be so shy with me," the vampire said. "What is it?"

"The story about stakes through the heart," said the boy, his cheeks coloring slightly.

"The same," said the vampire. "Bull-shit," he said, carefully articulating both syllables, so that the boy smiled. "No magical power whatsoever. Why don't you smoke one of your cigarettes? I see you have them in your shirt pocket."

"Oh, thank you," the boy said, as if it were a marvellous suggestion. But once he had the cigarette to his lips, his hands were trembling so badly that he mangled the first fragile book match.

"Allow me," said the vampire. And, taking the book, he quickly put a lighted match to the boy's cigarette. The boy inhaled, his eyes on the vampire's fingers. Now the vampire withdrew across the table with a soft rustling of garments. "There's an ashtray on the basin," he said, and the boy moved nervously to get it. He stared at the few butts in it for a moment, and then, seeing the small waste basket beneath, he emptied the ashtray and quickly set it on the table. His fingers left damp marks on the cigarette when he put it down. "Is this your room?" he asked.

"No," answered the vampire. "Just a room."

"What happened then?" the boy asked. The vampire appeared to be watching the smoke gather beneath the the overhead bulb.

"Ah . . . we went back to New Orleans posthaste," he said. "Lestat had his coffin in a miserable room near the ramparts."

"And you did get into the coffin?"

"I had no choice. I begged Lestat to let me stay in the closet, but he laughed, astonished. 'Don't you know what you are?' he asked. 'But is it magical? Must it have this shape?' I pleaded. Only to hear him laugh again. I couldn't bear the idea; but as we argued, I realized I had no real fear. It was a strange realization. All my life I'd feared closed places. Born and bred in French houses with lofty ceilings and floor-length

windows, I had a dread of being enclosed. I felt uncomfortable even in the confessional in church. It was
a normal enough fear. And now I realized as I protested to Lestat, I did not actually feel this anymore. I
was simply remembering it. Hanging on to it from
habit, from a deficiency of ability to recognize my
present and exhilarating freedom. 'You're carrying on
badly,' Lestat said finally. 'And it's almost dawn. I
should let you die. You will die, you know. The sun
will destroy the blood I've given you, in every tissue,
every vein. But you shouldn't be feeling this fear at all.
I think you're like a man who loses an arm or a leg
and keeps insisting that he can feel pain where the
arm or leg used to be.' Well, that was positively the
most intelligent and useful thing Lestat ever said in my
presence, and it brought me around at once. 'Now, I'm
getting into the coffin,' he finally said to me in his
most disdainful tone, 'and you will get in on top of me
if you know what's good for you.' And I did. I lay
face-down on him, utterly confused by my absence of
dread and filled with a distaste for being so close to
him, handsome and intriguing though he was. And he
shut the lid. Then I asked him if I was completely
dead. My body was tingling and itching all over. 'No,
you're not then,' he said. 'When you are, you'll only
hear and see it changing and feel nothing. You should
be dead by tonight. Go to sleep.' "

"Was he right? Were you . . . dead when you woke
up?"

"Yes, changed, I should say. As obviously I am
alive. My body was dead. It was some time before it
became absolutely cleansed of the fluids and matter it
no longer needed, but it was dead. And with the realization of it came another stage in my divorce from
human emotions. The first thing which became apparent to me, even while Lestat and I were loading the
coffin into a hearse and stealing another coffin from a
mortuary, was that I did not like Lestat at all. I was
far from being his equal yet, but I was infinitely closer
to him than I had been before the death of my body. I
can't really make this clear to you for the obvious
reason that you are now as I was before my body died.

You cannot understand. But before I died, Lestat was absolutely the most overwhelming *experience* I'd ever had. Your cigarette has become one long cylindrical ash."

"Oh!" The boy quickly ground the filter into the glass. "You mean that when the gap was closed between you, he lost his . . . spell?" he asked, his eyes quickly fixed on the vampire, his hands now producing a cigarette and match much more easily than before.

"Yes, that's correct," said the vampire with obvious pleasure. "The trip back to Pointe du Lac was thrilling. And the constant chatter of Lestat was positively the most boring and disheartening thing I experienced. Of course as I said, I was far from being his equal. I had my dead limbs to contend with . . . to use his comparison. And I learned that on that very night, when I had to make my first kill."

The vampire reached across the table now and gently brushed an ash from the boy's lapel, and the boy stared at his withdrawing hand in alarm. "Excuse me," said the vampire. "I didn't mean to frighten you."

"Excuse *me*," said the boy. "I just got the impression suddenly that your arm was . . . abnormally long. You reach so far without moving!"

"No," said the vampire, resting his hands again on his crossed knees. "I moved forward much too fast for you to see. It was an illusion."

"You moved forward? But you didn't. You were sitting just as you are now, with your back against the chair."

"No," repeated the vampire firmly. "I moved forward as I told you. Here, I'll do it again." And he did it again, and the boy stared with the same mixture of confusion and fear. "You still didn't see it," said the vampire. "But, you see, if you look at my outstretched arm now, it's really not remarkably long at all." And he raised his arm, first finger pointing heavenward as if he were an angel about to give the Word of the Lord. "You have experienced a fundamental difference between the way you see and I see. My gesture appeared slow and somewhat languid to me. And the sound of my finger brushing your coat was quite audible. Well, I didn't mean to frighten you, I confess. But perhaps you can see from this that my return to Pointe du Lac was a feast of new experiences, the mere swaying of a tree branch in the wind a delight."

"Yes," said the boy; but he was still visibly shaken. The vampire eyed him for a moment, and then he said, "I was telling you . . ."

"About your first kill," said the boy.

"Yes. I should say first, however, that the plantation was in a state of pandemonium. The overseer's body had been found and so had the blind old man in the master bedroom, and no one could explain the blind old man's presence. And no one had been able to find me in New Orleans. My sister had contacted the police, and several of them were at Pointe du Lac when I arrived. It was already quite dark, naturally, and Lestat quickly explained to me that I must not let the police see me in even minimal light, especially not with my body in its present remarkable state; so I talked to them in the avenue of oaks before the plantation house, ignoring their requests that we go inside. I explained I'd been to Pointe du Lac the night before and the blind old man was my guest. As for the overseer, he had not been here, but had gone to New Orleans on business.

"After that was settled, during which my new detachment served me admirably, I had the problem of the plantation itself. My slaves were in a state of complete confusion, and no work had been done all day. We had a large plant then for the making of the indigo dye, and the overseer's management had been most important. But I had several extremely intelligent slaves who might have done his job just as well a long time before, if I had recognized their intelligence and not feared their African appearance and manner. I studied them clearly now and gave the management of things over to them. To the best, I gave the overseer's house on a promise. Two of the young women were brought back into the house from the fields to care for Lestat's father, and I told them I wanted as much privacy as possible and they would all of them be rewarded not only for service but for leaving me and

Lestat absolutely alone. I did not realize at the time that these slaves would be the first, and possibly the only ones, to ever suspect that Lestat and I were not ordinary creatures. I failed to realize that their experience with the supernatural was far greater than that of white men. In my own inexperience I still thought of them as childlike savages barely domesticated by slavery. I made a bad mistake. But let me keep to my story. I was going to tell you about my first kill. Lestat bungled it with his characteristic lack of common sense."

"Bungled it?" asked the boy.

"I should never have started with human beings. But this was something I had to learn by myself. Lestat had us plunge headlong into the swamps right after the police and the slaves were settled. It was very late, and the slave cabins were completely dark. We soon lost sight of the lights of Pointe du Lac altogether, and I became very agitated. It was the same thing again: remembered fears, confusion. Lestat, had he any native intelligence, might have explained things to me patiently and gently—that I had no need to fear the swamps, that to snakes and insects I was utterly invulnerable, and that I must concentrate on my new ability to see in total darkness. Instead, he harassed me with condemnations. He was concerned only with our victims, with finishing my initiation and getting on with it.

"And when we finally came upon our victims, he rushed me into action. They were a small camp of runaway slaves. Lestat had visited them before and picked off perhaps a fourth of their number by watching from the dark for one of them to leave the fire, or by taking them in their sleep. They knew absolutely nothing of Lestat's presence. We had to watch for well over an hour before one of the men—they were all men—finally left the clearing and came just a few paces into the trees. He unhooked his pants now and attended to an ordinary physical necessity; and as he turned to go, Lestat shook me and said, 'Take him.'" The vampire smiled at the boy's wide eyes. "I think I was about as horrorstruck as you would be," he said. "But I didn't know then that I might kill animals instead of humans. I said quickly I could not possibly take him. And the slave heard me speak. He turned, his back to the distant fire, and peered into the dark. Then quickly and silently, he drew a long knife out of his belt. He was naked except for the pants and the belt, a tall, strong-armed, sleek young man. He said something in the French patois, and then he stepped forward. I realized that, though I saw him clearly in the dark, he could not see us. Lestat stepped in back of him with a swiftness that baffled me and got a hold around his neck while he pinned his left arm. The slave cried out and tried to throw Lestat off. He sank his teeth now, and the slave froze as if from snakebite. He sank to his knees, and Lestat fed fast as the other slaves came running. 'You sicken me,' he said when he got back to me. It was as if we were black insects utterly camouflaged in the night, watching the slaves move, oblivious to us, discover the wounded man, drag him back, fan out in the foliage searching for the attacker. 'Come on, we have to get another one before they all return to camp,' he said. And quickly we set off after one man who was separated from the others. I was still terribly agitated, convinced I couldn't bring myself to attack and feeling no urge to do so. There were many things, as I mention, which Lestat might have said and done. He might have made the experience rich in so many ways. But he did not."

"What could he have done?" the boy asked. "What do you mean?"

"Killing is no ordinary act," said the vampire. "One doesn't simply glut oneself on blood." He shook his head. "It is the experience of another's life for certain, and often the experience of the loss of that life through the blood, slowly. It is again and again the experience of that loss of my own life, which I experienced when I sucked the blood from Lestat's wrist and felt his heart pound with my heart. It is again and again a celebration of that experience; because for vampires that is the ultimate experience." He said this most seriously, as if he were arguing with someone who held a different view. "I don't think Lestat ever appreciated that, though how he could not, I don't know. Let me say he appreciated something, but very little, I think, of what there is to know. In any event, he took no pains to remind me now of what I'd felt when I clamped onto his wrist for life itself and wouldn't let it go; or to pick and choose a place for me where I might experience my first kill with some measure of quiet and dignity. He rushed headlong through the encounter as if it were something to put behind us as quickly as possible, like so many yards of the road. Once he had caught the slave, he gagged him and held him, baring his neck. 'Do it,' he said. 'You can't turn back now.' Overcome with revulsion and weak with frustration, I obeyed. I knelt beside the bent, struggling man and, clamping both my hands on his shoulders, I went into his neck. My teeth had only just begun to change, and I had to tear his flesh, not puncture it; but once the wound was made, the blood flowed. And once that happened, once I was locked to it, drinking . . . all else vanished.

"Lestat and the swamp and the noise of the distant camp meant nothing. Lestat might have been an insect, buzzing, lighting, then vanishing in significance. The sucking mesmerized me; the warm struggling of the man was soothing to the tension of my hands; and there came the beating of the drum again, which was the drumbeat of his heart—only this time it beat in perfect rhythm with the drumbeat of my own heart, the two resounding in every fiber of my being, until the beat began to grow slower and slower, so that each was a soft rumble that threatened to go on without end. I was drowsing, falling into weightlessness; and then Lestat pulled me back. 'He's dead, you idiot!' he said with his characteristic charm and tact. 'You don't drink after they're dead! Understand that!' I was in a frenzy for a moment, not myself, insisting to him that the man's heart still beat, and I was in an agony to clamp onto him again. I ran my hands over his chest, then grabbed at his wrists. I would have cut into his wrist if Lestat hadn't pulled me to my feet and slapped my face. This slap was astonishing. It was not painful in the ordinary way. It was a sensational shock of another sort, a rapping of the senses, so that I spun in confusion and found myself helpless and staring, my back against a cypress, the night pulsing with insects in my ears. 'You'll die if you do that,' Lestat was saying. 'He'll suck you right down into death with him if you cling to him in death. And now you've drunk too much, besides; you'll be ill.' His voice grated on me. I had the urge to throw myself on him suddenly, but I was feeling just what he'd said. There was a grinding pain in my stomach, as if some whirlpool there were sucking my insides into itself. It was the blood passing too rapidly into my own blood, but I didn't know it. Lestat moved through the night now like a cat and I followed him, my head throbbing, this pain in my stomach no better when we reached the house of Pointe du Lac.

"As we sat at the table in the parlor, Lestat dealing a game of solitaire on the polished wood, I sat there staring at him with contempt. He was mumbling nonsense. I would get used to killing, he said; it would be nothing. I must not allow myself to be shaken. I was reacting too much as if the 'mortal coil' had not been shaken off. I would become accustomed to things all too quickly. 'Do you think so?' I asked him finally. I really had no interest in his answer. I understood now the difference between us. For me the experience of killing had been cataclysmic. So had that of sucking Lestat's wrist. These experiences so overwhelmed and so changed my view of everything around me, from the picture of my brother on the parlor wall to the sight of a single star in the topmost pane of the French window, that I could not imagine another vampire taking them for granted. I was altered, permanently; I knew it. And what I felt, most profoundly, for everything, even the sound of the playing cards being laid down one by one upon the shining rows of the solitaire, was respect. Lestat felt the opposite. Or he felt nothing. He was the sow's ear out of which nothing fine could be made. As boring as a mortal, as trivial and unhappy as a mortal, he chattered over the game, belittling my experience, utterly locked against the possibility of any experience of his own. By morning, I realized that I was his complete superior and I had been sadly cheated in having him for a teacher. He must guide me through the necessary lessons, if there were any more real lessons, and I must tolerate in him a frame of mind which was blasphemous to life itself. I felt cold towards him. I had no contempt in superiority. Only a hunger for new experience, for that which was beautiful and as devastating as my kill. And I saw that if I were to maximize every experience available to me, I must exert my own powers over my learning. Lestat was of no use.

"It was well past midnight when I finally rose out of the chair and went out on the gallery. The moon was large over the cypresses, and the candlelight poured from the open doors. The thick plastered pillars and walls of the house had been freshly whitewashed, the floorboards freshly swept, and a summer rain had left the night clean and sparkling with drops of water. I leaned against the end pillar of the gallery, my head touching the soft tendrils of a jasmine which grew there in constant battle with a wisteria, and I thought of what lay before me throughout the world and throughout time, and resolved to go about it delicately and reverently, learning that from each thing which would take me best to another. What this meant, I wasn't sure myself. Do you understand me when I say I did not wish to rush headlong into experience, that what I'd felt as a vampire was far too powerful to be wasted?"

"Yes," said the boy eagerly. "It sounds as if it was like being in love."

The vampire's eyes gleamed. "That's correct. It is like love," he smiled. "And I tell you my frame of mind that night so you can know there are profound differences between vampires, and how I came to take a different approach from Lestat. You must understand I did not snub him because he did not appreciate his experience. I simply could not understand how such feelings could be wasted. But then Lestat did something which was to show me a way to go about my learning.

"He had more than a casual appreciation of the wealth at Pointe du Lac. He'd been much pleased by the beauty of the china used for his father's supper; and he liked the feel of the velvet drapes, and he traced the patterns of the carpets with his toe. And now he took from one of the china closets a crystal glass and said, 'I do miss glasses.' Only he said this with an impish delight that caused me to study him with a hard eye. I disliked him intensely! 'I want to show you a little trick,' he said. 'That is, if you like glasses.' And after setting it on the card table he came out on the gallery where I stood and changed his manner again into that of a stalking animal, eyes piercing the dark beyond the lights of the house, peering down under the arching branches of the oaks. In an instant, he had vaulted the railing and dropped softly on the dirt below, and then lunged into the blackness to catch something in both his hands. When he stood before me with it, I gasped to see it was a rat. 'Don't be such a damned idiot,' he said. 'Haven't you ever seen a rat?' It was a huge, struggling field rat with a long tail. He held its neck so it couldn't bite. 'Rats can be quite nice,' he said. And he took the rat to the wine glass, slashed its throat, and filled the glass rapidly with blood. The rat then went hurtling over the gallery railing, and Lestat held the wine glass to the candle triumphantly. 'You may well have to live off rats from time to time, so wipe that expression off your face,' he said. 'Rats, chickens, cattle. Travelling by ship, you damn well better live off rats, if you don't wish to cause such a panic on board that they search your coffin. You damn well better keep the ship clean of rats.' And then he sipped the blood as delicately as if it were burgundy. He made a slight face. 'It gets cold so fast.'

" 'Do you mean, then, we can live from animals?' I asked.

" 'Yes.' He drank it all down and then casually threw the glass at the fireplace. I stared at the fragments. 'You don't mind, do you?' He gestured to the broken glass with a sarcastic smile. 'I surely hope you don't, because there's nothing much you can do about it if you do mind.'

" 'I can throw you and your father out of Pointe du Lac, if I mind,' I said. I believe this was my first show of temper.

" 'Why would you do that?' he asked with mock alarm. 'You don't know everything yet . . . do you?' He was laughing then and walking slowly about the room. He ran his fingers over the satin finish of the spinet. 'Do you play?' he asked.

"I said something like, 'Don't touch it!' and he laughed at me. 'I'll touch it if I like!' he said. 'You don't know, for example, all the ways you can die. And dying now would be *such* a calamity, wouldn't it?'

" 'There must be someone else in the world to teach me these things,' I said. 'Certainly you're not the only vampire! And your father, he's perhaps seventy. You couldn't have been a vampire long, so someone must have instructed you. . . .'

" 'And do you think you can find other vampires by yourself? They might see you coming, my friend, but you won't see them. No, I don't think you have much choice about things at this point, friend. I'm your teacher and you need me, and there isn't much you can do about it either way. And we both have people to provide for. My father needs a doctor, and then there is the matter of your mother and sister. Don't get any mortal notions about telling them you are a vampire. Just provide for them and for my father, which means that tomorrow night you had better kill fast and then attend to the business of your plantation. Now to bed. We both sleep in the same room; it makes for far less risk.'

" 'No, you secure the bedroom for yourself,' I said. 'I've no intention of staying in the same room with you.'

"He became furious. 'Don't do anything stupid, Louis. I warn you. There's nothing you can do to defend yourself once the sun rises, nothing. Separate rooms mean separate security. Double precautions and double chance of notice.' He then said a score of things to frighten me into complying, but he might as well have been talking to the walls. I watched him intently, but I didn't listen to him. He appeared frail and stupid to me, a man made of dried twigs with a thin, carping voice. 'I sleep alone,' I said, and gently put my hand around the candle flames one by one. 'It's almost morning!' he insisted.

" 'So lock yourself in,' I said, embracing my coffin, hoisting it and carrying it down the brick stairs. I could hear the locks snapping on the French doors above, the swoosh of the drapes. The sky was pale but still sprinkled with stars, and another light rain blew now on the breeze from the river, speckling the flagstones. I opened the door of my brother's oratory, shoving back the roses and thorns which had almost sealed it, and set the coffin on the stone floor before the priedieu. I could almost make out the images of the saints on the walls. 'Paul,' I said softly, addressing my brother, 'for the first time in my life I feel nothing for you, nothing for your death; and for the first time I feel everything for you, feel the sorrow of your loss as if I never before knew feeling.' You see . . ."

The vampire turned to the boy. "For the first time now I was fully and completely a vampire. I shut the wood blinds flat upon the small barred windows and bolted the door. Then I climbed into the satin-lined coffin, barely able to see the gleam of cloth in the darkness, and locked myself in. That is how I became a vampire."

AND THERE YOU WERE," said the boy after a pause, "with another vampire you hated."

"But I had to stay with him," answered the vampire. "As I've told you, he had me at a great disadvantage.

He hinted there was much I didn't know and must know and that he alone could tell me. But in fact, the main part of what he did teach me was practical and not so difficult to figure out for oneself. How we might travel, for instance, by ship, having our coffins transported for us as though they contained the remains of loved ones being sent here or there for burial; how no one would dare to open such a coffin, and we might rise from it at night to clean the ship of rats—things of this nature. And then there were the shops and businessmen he knew who admitted us well after hours to outfit us in the finest Paris fashions, and those agents willing to transact financial matters in restaurants and cabarets. And in all of these mundane matters, Lestat was an adequate teacher. What manner of man he'd been in life, I couldn't tell and didn't care; but he was for all appearances of the same class now as myself, which meant little to me, except that it made our lives run a little more smoothly than they might have otherwise. He had impeccable taste, though my library to him was a 'pile of dust,' and he seemed more than once to be infuriated by the sight of my reading a book or writing some observations in a journal. 'That mortal nonsense,' he would say to me, while at the same time spending so much of my money to splendidly furnish Pointe du Lac, that even I, who cared nothing for the money, was forced to wince. And in entertaining visitors at Pointe du Lac—those hapless travellers who came up the river road by horseback or carriage begging accommodations for the night, sporting letters of introduction from other planters or officials in New Orleans—to these he was so gentle and polite that it made things far easier for me, who found myself hopelessly locked to him and jarred over and over by his viciousness."

"But he didn't harm these men?" asked the boy.

"Oh yes, often, he did. But I'll tell you a little secret if I may, which applies not only to vampires, but to generals, soldiers, and kings. Most of us would much rather see somebody die than be the object of rudeness under our roofs. Strange . . . yes. But very true, I assure you. That Lestat hunted for mortals every night,

I knew. But had he been savage and ugly to my family, my guests, and my slaves, I couldn't have endured it. He was not. He seemed particularly to delight in the visitors. But he said we must spare no expense where our families were concerned. And he seemed to me to push luxury upon his father to an almost ludicrous point. The old blind man must be told constantly how fine and expensive were his bed jackets and robes and what imported draperies had just been fixed to his bed and what French and Spanish wines we had in the cellar and how much the plantation yielded even in bad years when the coast talked of abandoning the indigo production altogether and going into sugar. But then at other times he would bully the old man, as I mentioned. He would erupt into such rage that the old man whimpered like a child. 'Don't I take care of you in baronial splendor!' Lestat would shout at him. 'Don't I provide for your every want! Stop whining to me about going to church or old friends! Such nonsense. Your old friends are dead. Why don't you die and leave me and my bankroll in peace!' The old man would cry softly that these things meant so little to him in old age. He would have been content on his little farm forever. I wanted often to ask him later, 'Where was this farm? From where did you come to Louisiana?' to get some clue to that place where Lestat might have known another vampire. But I didn't dare to bring these things up, lest the old man start crying and Lestat become enraged. But these fits were no more frequent than periods of near obsequious kindness when Lestat would bring his father supper on a tray and feed him patiently while talking of the weather and the New Orleans news and the activities of my mother and sister. It was obvious that a great gulf existed between father and son, both in education and refinement, but how it came about, I could not quite guess. And from this whole matter, I achieved a somewhat consistent detachment.

"Existence, as I've said, was possible. There was always the promise behind his mocking smile that he knew great things or terrible things, had commerce

with levels of darkness I could not possibly guess at.
And all the time, he belittled me and attacked me for
my love of the senses, my reluctance to kill, and the
near swoon which killing could produce in me. He
laughed uproariously when I discovered that I could
see myself in a mirror and that crosses had no effect
upon me, and would taunt me with sealed lips when
I asked about God or the devil. 'I'd like to meet the
devil some night,' he said once with a malignant smile.
'I'd chase him from here to the wilds of the Pacific.
I am the devil.' And when I was aghast at this, he
went into peals of laughter. But what happened was
simply that in my distaste for him I came to ignore
and suspect him, and yet to study him with a detached
fascination. Sometimes I'd find myself staring at his
wrist from which I'd drawn my vampire life, and I
would fall into such a stillness that my mind seemed
to leave my body or rather my body to become my
mind; and then he would see me and stare at me
with a stubborn ignorance of what I felt and longed
to know and, reaching over, shake me roughly out of
it. I bore this with an overt detachment unknown to
me in mortal life and came to understand this as a
part of vampire nature: that I might sit at home at
Pointe du Lac and think for hours of my brother's
mortal life and see it short and rounded in unfathom-
able darkness, understanding now the vain and sense-
less wasting passion with which I'd mourned his loss
and turned on other mortals like a maddened animal.
All that confusion was then like dancers frenzied in a
fog; and now, now in this strange vampire nature,
I felt a profound sadness. But I did not brood over
this. Let me not give you that impression, for brooding would have been to me the most terrible waste; but
rather I looked around me at all the mortals that I
knew and saw all life as precious, condemning all
fruitless guilt and passion that would let it slip through
the fingers like sand. It was only now as a vampire
that I did come to know my sister, forbidding her the
plantation for the city life which she so needed in
order to know her own time of life and her own
beauty and come to marry, not brood for our lost

brother or my going away or become a nursemaid for
our mother. And I provided for them all they might
need or want, finding even the most trivial request
worth my immediate attention. My sister laughed at
the transformation in me when we would meet at
night and I would take her from our flat out the
narrow wooden streets to walk along the tree-lined
levee in the moonlight, savoring the orange blossoms
and the caressing warmth, talking for hours of her
most secret thoughts and dreams, those little fantasies
she dared to tell no one and would even whisper to
me when we sat in the dim-lit parlor entirely alone.
And I would see her sweet and palpable before me, a
shimmering, precious creature soon to grow old, soon
to die, soon to lose these moments that in their in-
tangibility promised to us, wrongly . . . wrongly, an
immortality. As if it were our very birthright, which
we could not come to grasp the meaning of until this
time of middle life when we looked on only as many
years ahead as already lay behind us. When every
moment, every moment must be first known and then
savored.

"It was detachment that made this possible, a sublime loneliness with which Lestat and I moved through
the world of mortal men. And all material troubles
passed from us. I should tell you the practical nature
of it.

"Lestat had always known how to steal from victims chosen for sumptuous dress and other promising
signs of extravagance. But the great problems of
shelter and secrecy had been for him a terrible struggle.
I suspected that beneath his gentleman's veneer he
was painfully ignorant of the most simple financial
matters. But I was not. And so he could acquire cash
at any moment and I could invest it. If he were not
picking the pocket of a dead man in an alley, he was
at the greatest gambling tables in the richest salons of
the city, using his vampire keenness to suck gold and
dollars and deeds of property from young planters'
sons who found him deceptive in his friendship and
alluring in his charm. But this had never given him
the life he wanted, and so for that he had ushered

me into the preternatural world that he might acquire an investor and manager for whom these skills of mortal life became most valuable in this life after.

"But, let me describe New Orleans, as it was then, and as it was to become, so you can understand how simple our lives were. There was no city in America like New Orleans. It was filled not only with the French and Spanish of all classes who had formed in part its peculiar aristocracy, but later with immigrants of all kinds, the Irish and the German in particular. Then there were not only the black slaves, yet unhomogenized and fantastical in their different tribal garb and manners, but the great growing class of the free people of color, those marvellous people of our mixed blood and that of the islands, who produced a magnificent and unique caste of craftsmen, artists, poets, and renowned feminine beauty. And then there were the Indians, who covered the levee on summer days selling herbs and crafted wares. And drifting through all, through this medley of languages and colors, were the people of the port, the sailors of ships, who came in great waves to spend their money in the cabarets, to buy for the night the beautiful women both dark and light, to dine on the best of Spanish and French cooking and drink the imported wines of the world. Then add to these, within years after my transformation, the Americans, who built the city up river from the old French Quarter with magnificent Grecian houses which gleamed in the moonlight like temples. And, of course, the planters, always the planters, coming to town with their families in shining landaus to buy evening gowns and silver and gems, to crowd the narrow streets on the way to the old French Opera House and the Théâtre d'Orléans and the St. Louis Cathedral, from whose open doors came the chants of High Mass over the crowds of the Place d'Armes on Sundays, over the noise and bickering of the French Market, over the silent, ghostly drift of the ships along the raised waters of the Mississippi, which flowed against the levee above the ground of New Orleans itself, so that the ships appeared to float against the sky.

"This was New Orleans, a magical and magnificent place to live. In which a vampire, richly dressed and gracefully walking through the pools of light of one gas lamp after another might attract no more notice in the evening than hundreds of other exotic creatures —if he attracted any at all, if anyone stopped to whisper behind a fan, 'That man . . . how pale, how he gleams . . . how he moves. It's not natural!' A city in which a vampire might be gone before the words had even passed the lips, seeking out the alleys in which he could see like a cat, the darkened bars in which sailors slept with their heads on the table, great high-ceilinged hotel rooms where a lone figure might sit, her feet upon an embroidered cushion, her legs covered with a lace counterpane, her head bent under the tarnished light of a single candle, never seeing the great shadow move across the plaster flowers of the ceiling, never seeing the long white finger reached to press the fragile flame.

"Remarkable, if for nothing else, because of this, that all of those men and women who stayed for any reason left behind them some monument, some structure of marble and brick and stone that still stands; so that even when the gas lamps went out and the planes came in and the office buildings crowded the blocks of Canal Street, something irreducible of beauty and romance remained; not in every street perhaps, but in so many that the landscape is for me the landscape of those times always, and walking now in the starlit streets of the Quarter or the Garden District I am in those times again. I suppose that is the nature of the monument. Be it a small house or a mansion of Corinthian columns and wrought-iron lace. The monument does not say that this or that man walked here. No, that what he felt in one time in one spot continues. The moon that rose over New Orleans then still rises. As long as the monuments stand, it still rises. The feeling, at least here . . . and there . . . it remains the same."

The vampire appeared sad. He sighed, as if he doubted what he had just said. "What was it?" he asked suddenly as if he were slightly tired. "Yes, money. Lestat and I had to make money. And I was telling you that he could steal. But it was investment afterwards that mattered. What we accumulated we must use. But I go ahead of myself. I killed animals. But I'll get to that in a moment. Lestat killed humans all the time, sometimes two or three a night, sometimes more. He would drink from one just enough to satisfy a momentary thirst, and then go on to another. The better the human, as he would say in his vulgar way, the more he liked it. A fresh young girl, that was his favorite food the first of the evening; but the triumphant kill for Lestat was a young man. A young man around your age would have appealed to him in particular."

"Me?" the boy whispered. He had leaned forward on his elbows to peer into the vampire's eyes, and now he drew up.

"Yes," the vampire went on, as if he hadn't observed the boy's change of expression. "You see, they represented the greatest loss to Lestat, because they stood on the threshold of the maximum possibility of life. Of course, Lestat didn't understand this himself. I came to understand it. Lestat understood nothing.

"I shall give you a perfect example of what Lestat liked. Up the river from us was the Freniere plantation, a magnificent spread of land which had great hopes of making a fortune in sugar, just shortly after the refining process had been invented. I presume you know sugar was refined in Louisiana. There is something perfect and ironic about it, this land which I loved producing refined sugar. I mean this more unhappily than I think you know. This refined sugar is a poison. It was like the essence of life in New Orleans, so sweet that it can be fatal, so richly enticing that all other values are forgotten. . . . But as I was saying up river from us lived the Frenieres, a great old French family which had produced in this generation five young women and one young man. Now, three of the young women were destined not to marry, but two were young enough still and all depended upon the young man. He was to manage the plantation as I had done for my mother and sister;

he was to negotiate marriages, to put together dowries
when the entire fortune of the place rode precariously
on the next year's sugar crop; he was to bargain, fight,
and keep at a distance the entire material world for
the world of Freniere. Lestat decided he wanted him.
And when fate alone nearly cheated Lestat, he went
wild. He risked his own life to get the Freniere boy,
who had become involved in a duel. He had insulted
a young Spanish Creole at a ball. The whole thing was
nothing, really; but like most young Creoles this one
was willing to die for nothing. They were both willing
to die for nothing. The Freniere household was in an
uproar. You must understand, Lestat knew this perfectly. Both of us had hunted the Freniere plantation,
Lestat for slaves and chicken thieves and me for
animals."

"You were killing *only* animals?"

"Yes. But I'll come to that later, as I said. We both
knew the plantation, and I had indulged in one of the
greatest pleasures of a vampire, that of watching
people unbeknownst to them. I knew the Freniere
sisters as I knew the magnificent rose trees around my
brother's oratory. They were a unique group of
women. Each in her own way was as smart as the
brother; and one of them, I shall call her Babette,
was not only as smart as her brother, but far wiser.
Yet none had been educated to care for the plantation;
none understood even the simplest facts about its
financial state. All were totally dependent upon young
Freniere, and all knew it. And so, larded with their
love for him, their passionate belief that he hung the
moon and that any conjugal love they might ever
know would only be a pale reflection of their love for
him, larded with this was a desperation as strong as
the will to survive. If Freniere died in the duel, the
plantation would collapse. Its fragile economy, a life
of splendor based on the perennial mortgaging of the
next year's crop, was in his hands alone. So you can
imagine the panic and misery in the Freniere household the night that the son went to town to fight the
appointed duel. And now picture Lestat, gnashing his

teeth like a comic-opera devil because he was not going to kill the young Freniere."

"You mean then . . . that you *felt* for the Freniere women?"

"I felt for them totally," said the vampire. "Their position was agonizing. And I felt for the boy. That night he locked himself in his father's study and made a will. He knew full well that if he fell under the rapier at four A.M. the next morning, his family would fall with him. He deplored his situation and yet could do nothing to help it. To run out on the duel would not only mean social ruin for him, but would probably have been impossible. The other young man would have pursued him until he was forced to fight. When he left the plantation at midnight, he was staring into the face of death itself with the character of a man who, having only one path to follow, has resolved to follow it with perfect courage. He would either kill the Spanish boy or die; it was unpredictable, despite all his skill. His face reflected a depth of feeling and wisdom I'd never seen on the face of any of Lestat's struggling victims. I had my first battle with Lestat then and there. I'd prevented him from killing the boy for months, and now he meant to kill him before the Spanish boy could.

"We were on horseback, racing after the young Freniere towards New Orleans, Lestat bent on overtaking him, I bent on overtaking Lestat. Well, the duel, as I told you, was scheduled for four A.M. On the edge of the swamp just beyond the city's northern gate. And arriving there just shortly before four, we had precious little time to return to Pointe du Lac, which meant our own lives were in danger. I was incensed at Lestat as never before, and he was determined to get the boy. 'Give him his chance!' I was insisting, getting hold of Lestat before he could approach the boy. It was midwinter, bitter-cold and damp in the swamps, one volley of icy rain after another sweeping the clearing where the duel was to be fought. Of course, I did not fear these elements in the sense that you might; they did not numb me, nor threaten me with mortal shivering or illness. But vampires feel cold as acutely as humans, and the blood of the kill is often the rich, sensual alleviation of that cold. But what concerned me that morning was not the pain I felt, but the excellent cover of darkness these elements provided, which made Freniere extremely vulnerable to Lestat's attack. All he need do would be step away from his two friends towards the swamp and Lestat might take him. And so I physically grappled with Lestat. I held him."

"But towards all this you had detachment, distance?"

"Hmmm . . ." the vampire sighed. "Yes. I had it, and with it a supremely resolute anger. To glut himself upon the life of an entire family was to me Lestat's supreme act of utter contempt and disregard for all he should have seen with a vampire's depth. So I held him in the dark, where he spit at me and cursed at me; and young Freniere took his rapier from his friend and second and went out on the slick, wet grass to meet his opponent. There was a brief conversation, then the duel commenced. In moments, it was over. Freniere had mortally wounded the other boy with a swift thrust to the chest. And he knelt in the grass, bleeding, dying, shouting something unintelligible at Freniere. The victor simply stood there. Everyone could see there was no sweetness in the victory. Freniere looked on death as if it were an abomination. His companions advanced with their lanterns, urging him to come away as soon as possible and leave the dying man to his friends. Meantime, the wounded one would allow no one to touch him. And then, as Freniere's group turned to go, the three of them walking heavily towards their horses, the man on the ground drew a pistol. Perhaps I alone could see this in the powerful dark. But, in any event, I shouted to Freniere as I ran towards the gun. And this was all that Lestat needed. While I was lost in my clumsiness, distracting Freniere and going for the gun itself, Lestat, with his years of experience and superior speed, grabbed the young man and spirited him into the cypresses. I doubt his friends even knew what had happened. The pistol had gone off, the wounded man had collapsed, and I was tearing through the near-frozen marshes shouting for Lestat.

"Then I saw him. Freniere lay sprawled over the knobbed roots of a cypress, his boots deep in the murky water, and Lestat was still bent over him, one hand on the hand of Freniere that still held the foil. I went to pull Lestat off, and that right hand swung at me with such lightning speed I did not see it, did not know it had struck me until I found myself in the water also; and, of course, by the time I recovered, Freniere was dead. I saw him as he lay there, his eyes closed, his lips utterly still as if he were just sleeping. 'Damn you!' I began cursing Lestat. And then I started, for the body of Freniere had begun to slip down into the marsh. The water rose over his face and covered him completely. Lestat was jubilant; he reminded me tersely that we had less than an hour to get back to Pointe du Lac, and he swore revenge on me. 'If I didn't like the life of a Southern planter, I'd finish you tonight. I know a way,' he threatened me. 'I ought to drive your horse into the swamps. You'd have to dig yourself a hole and smother!' He rode off.

"Even over all these years, I feel that anger for him like a white-hot liquid filling my veins. I saw then what being a vampire meant to him."

"He was just a killer," the boy said, his voice reflecting some of the vampire's emotion. "No regard for anything."

"No. Being a vampire for him meant revenge. Revenge against life itself. Every time he took a life it was revenge. It was no wonder, then, that he appreciated nothing. The nuances of vampire existence weren't even available to him because he was focused with a maniacal vengeance upon the mortal life he'd left. Consumed with hatred, he looked back. Consumed with envy, nothing pleased him unless he could take it from others; and once having it, he grew cold and dissatisfied, not loving the thing for itself; and so he went after something else. Vengeance, blind and sterile and contemptible.

"But I've spoken to you about the Freniere sisters. It was almost half past five when I reached their plantation. Dawn would come shortly after six, but I was almost home. I slipped onto the upper gallery of their house and saw them all gathered in the parlor; they had never even dressed for bed. The candles burnt low, and they sat already as mourners, waiting for the word. They were all dressed in black, as was their at-home custom, and in the dark the black shapes of their dresses massed together with their raven hair, so that in the glow of the candles their faces appeared as five soft, shimmering apparitions, each uniquely sad, each uniquely courageous. Babette's face alone appeared resolute. It was as if she had already made up her mind to take the burdens of Freniere if her brother died, and she had that same expression on her face now which had been on her brother's when he mounted to leave for the duel. What lay ahead of her was nearly impossible. What lay ahead was the final death of which Lestat was guilty. So I did something then which caused me great risk. I made myself known to her. I did this by playing the light. As you can see, my face is very white and has a smooth, highly reflective surface, rather like that of polished marble."

"Yes," the boy nodded, and appeared flustered. "It's very . . . beautiful, actually," said the boy. "I wonder if . . . but what happened?"

"You wonder if I was a handsome man when I was alive," said the vampire. The boy nodded. "I was. Nothing structurally is changed in me. Only I never knew that I was handsome. Life whirled about me a wind of petty concerns, as I've said. I gazed at nothing, not even a mirror . . . especially not a mirror . . . with a free eye. But this is what happened. I stepped near to the pane of glass and let the light touch my face. And this I did at a moment when Babette's eyes were turned towards the panes. Then I appropriately vanished.

"Within seconds all the sisters knew a 'strange creature' had been seen, a ghostlike creature, and the two slave maids steadfastly refused to investigate. I waited out these moments impatiently for just that which I wanted to happen: Babette finally took a candelabrum from a side table, lit the candles and, scorning everyone's fear, ventured out onto the cold gallery alone to see what was there, her sisters hovering in the door like great, black birds, one of them crying that the brother was dead and she had indeed seen his ghost. Of course, you must understand that Babette, being as strong as she was, never once attributed what she saw to imagination or to ghosts. I let her come the length of the dark gallery before I spoke to her, and even then I let her see only the vague outline of my body beside one of the columns. 'Tell your sisters to go back,' I whispered to her. 'I come to tell you of your brother. Do as I say.' She was still for an instant, and then she turned to me and strained to see me in the dark. 'I have only a little time. I would not harm you for the world,' I said. And she obeyed. Saying it was nothing, she told them to shut the door, and they obeyed as people obey who not only need a leader but are desperate for one. Then I stepped into the light of Babette's candles."

The boy's eyes were wide. He put his hand to his lips. "Did you look to her . . . as you do to me?" he asked.

"You ask that with such innocence," said the vampire. "Yes, I suppose I certainly did. Only, by candlelight I always had a less supernatural appearance. And I made no pretense with her of being an ordinary creature. 'I have only minutes,' I told her at once. 'But what I have to tell you is of the greatest importance. Your brother fought bravely and won the duel—but wait. You must know now, he is dead. Death was proverbial with him, the thief in the night about which all his goodness or courage could do nothing. But this is not the principal thing which I came to tell you. It is this. You can rule the plantation and you can save it. All that is required is that you let no one convince you otherwise. You must assume his position despite any outcry, any talk of convention, any talk of propriety or common sense. You must listen to nothing. The same land is here now that was here yesterday morning when your brother slept above. Nothing is changed. You must take his place.

If you do not, the land is lost and the family is lost.
You will be five women on a small pension doomed
to live but half or less of what life could give you.
Learn what you must know. Stop at nothing until you
have the answers. And take my visitation to you to be
your courage whenever you waver. You must take the
reins of your own life. Your brother is dead.'

"I could see by her face that she had heard every
word. She would have questioned me had there been
time, but she believed me when I said there was not.
Then I used all my skill to leave her so swiftly I appeared to vanish. From the garden I saw her face
above in the glow of her candles. I saw her search
the dark for me, turning around and around. And then
I saw her make the Sign of the Cross and walk back
to her sisters within."

The vampire smiled. "There was absolutely no talk
on the river coast of any strange apparition to Babette
Freniere, but after the first mourning and sad talk of
the women left all alone, she became the scandal of
the neighborhood because she chose to run the plantation on her own. She managed an immense dowry for
her younger sister, and was married herself in another
year. And Lestat and I almost never exchanged
words."

"Did he go on living at Pointe du Lac?"

"Yes. I could not be certain he'd told me all I
needed to know. And great pretense was necessary.
My sister was married in my absence, for example,
while I had a 'malarial chill,' and something similar
overcame me the morning of my mother's funeral.
Meantime, Lestat and I sat down to dinner each night
with the old man and made nice noises with our knives
and forks, while he told us to eat everything on our
plates and not to drink our wine too fast. With dozens
of miserable headaches I would receive my sister in a
darkened bedroom, the covers up to my chin, bid her
and her husband bear with the dim light on account of
the pain in my eyes, as I entrusted to them large
amounts of money to invest for us all. Fortunately her
husband was an idiot; a harmless one, but an idiot, the

product of four generations of marriages between first cousins.

"But though these things went well, we began to have our problems with the slaves. They were the suspicious ones; and, as I've indicated, Lestat killed anyone and everyone he chose. So there was always some talk of mysterious death on the part of the coast. But it was what they saw of us which began the talk, and I heard it one evening when I was playing a shadow about the slave cabins.

"Now, let me explain first the character of these slaves. It was only about seventeen ninety-five, Lestat and I having lived there for four years in relative quiet, I investing the money which he acquired, increasing our lands, purchasing apartments and town houses in New Orleans which I rented, the work of the plantation itself producing little . . . more a cover for us than an investment. I say 'our.' This is wrong. I never signed anything over to Lestat, and, as you realize, I was still legally alive. But in seventeen ninety-five these slaves did not have the character which you've seen in films and novels of the South. They were not soft-spoken, brown-skinned people in drab rags who spoke an English dialect. They were Africans. And they were islanders; that is, some of them had come from Santo Domingo. They were very black and totally foreign; they spoke in their African tongues, and they spoke the French patois; and when they sang, they sang African songs which made the fields exotic and strange, always frightening to me in my mortal life. They were superstitious and had their own secrets and traditions. In short, they had not yet been destroyed as Africans completely. Slavery was the curse of their existence; but they had not been robbed yet of that which had been characteristically theirs. They tolerated the baptism and modest garments imposed on them by the French Catholic laws; but in the evenings, they made their cheap fabrics into alluring costumes, made jewelry of animal bones and bits of discarded metal which they polished to look like gold; and the slave cabins of Pointe du Lac were a foreign country, an African coast after dark, in which not even the coldest overseer would want to wander. No fear for the vampire.

"Not until one summer evening when, passing for a shadow, I heard through the open doors of the black foreman's cottage a conversation which convinced me that Lestat and I slept in real danger. The slaves knew now we were not ordinary mortals. In hushed tones, the maids told of how, through a crack in the door, they had seen us dine on empty plates with empty silver, lifting empty glasses to our lips, laughing, our faces bleached and ghostly in the candlelight, the blind man a helpless fool in our power. Through keyholes they had seen Lestat's coffin, and once he had beaten one of them mercilessly for dawdling by the gallery windows of his room. 'There is no bed in there,' they confided one to the other with nodding heads. 'He sleeps in the coffin, I know it.' They were convinced, on the best of grounds, of what we were. And as for me, they'd seen me evening after evening emerge from the oratory, which was now little more than a shapeless mass of brick and vine, layered with flowering wisteria in the spring, wild roses in summer, moss gleaming on the old unpainted shutters which had never been opened, spiders spinning in the stone arches. Of course, I'd pretended to visit it in memory of Paul, but it was clear by their speech they no longer believed such lies. And now they attributed to us not only the deaths of slaves found in the fields and swamps and also the dead cattle and occasional horses, but all other strange events; even floods and thunder were the weapons of God in a personal battle waged with Louis and Lestat. But worse still, they were not planning to run away. We were devils. Our power inescapable. No, we must be destroyed. And at this gathering, where I became an unseen member, were a number of the Freniere slaves.

"This meant word would get to the entire coast. And though I firmly believed the entire coast to be impervious to a wave of hysteria, I did not intend to risk notice of any kind. I hurried back to the plantation house to tell Lestat our game of playing planter was over. He'd have to give up his slave whip and golden napkin ring and move into town.

"He resisted, naturally. His father was gravely ill and might not live. He had no intention of running away from stupid slaves. 'I'll kill them all,' he said calmly, 'in threes and fours. Some will run away and that will be fine.'

" 'You're talking madness. The fact is I want you gone from here.'

" 'You want me gone! You,' he sneered. He was building a card palace on the dining room table with a pack of very fine French cards. 'You whining coward of a vampire who prowls the night killing alley cats and rats and staring for hours at candles as if they were people and standing in the rain like a zombie until your clothes are drenched and you smell like old wardrobe trunks in attics and have the look of a baffled idiot at the zoo.'

" 'You've nothing more to tell me, and your insistence on recklessness has endangered us both. I might live in that oratory alone while this house fell to ruin. I don't care about it!' I told him. Because this was quite true. 'But you must have all the things you never had of life and make of immortality a junk shop in which both of us become grotesque. Now, go look at your father and tell me how long he has to live, for that's how long you stay, and only if the slaves don't rise up against us!'

"He told me then to go look at his father myself, since I was the one who was always 'looking,' and I did. The old man was truly dying. I had been spared my mother's death, more or less, because she had died very suddenly on an afternoon. She'd been found with her sewing basket, seated quietly in the courtyard; she had died as one goes to sleep. But now I was seeing a natural death that was too slow with agony and with consciousness. And I'd always liked the old man; he was kindly and simple and made few demands. By day, he sat in the sun of the gallery dozing and listening to the birds; by night, any chatter on our part kept him company. He could play chess, carefully feeling each piece and remembering the entire state of the board with remarkable accuracy; and though Lestat would never play with him, I did often. Now he lay gasping for breath, his forehead hot and wet, the pillow around him stained with sweat. And as he moaned and prayed for death, Lestat in the other room began to play the spinet. I slammed it shut, barely missing his fingers. 'You won't play while he dies!' I said. 'The hell I won't!' he answered me. 'I'll play the drum if I like!' And taking a great sterling silver platter from a sideboard he slipped a finger through one of its handles and beat it with a spoon.

"I told him to stop it, or I would make him stop it. And then we both ceased our noise because the old man was calling his name. He was saying that he must talk to Lestat now before he died. I told Lestat to go to him. The sound of his crying was terrible. 'Why should I? I've cared for him all these years. Isn't that enough?' And he drew from his pocket a nail file, and, seating himself on the foot of the old man's bed, he began to file his long nails.

"Meantime, I should tell you that I was aware of slaves about the house. They were watching and listening. I was truly hoping the old man would die within minutes. Once or twice before I'd dealt with suspicion or doubt on the part of several slaves, but never such a number. I immediately rang for Daniel, the slave to whom I'd given the overseer's house and position. But while I waited for him, I could hear the old man talking to Lestat; Lestat, who sat with his legs crossed, filing and filing, one eyebrow arched, his attention on his perfect nails. 'It was the school,' the old man was saying. 'Oh, I know you remember . . . what can I say to you . . .' he moaned.

" 'You'd better say it,' Lestat said, 'because you're about to die.' The old man let out a terrible noise, and I suspect I made some sound of my own. I positively loathed Lestat. I had a mind now to get him out of the room. 'Well, you know that, don't you? Even a fool like you knows that,' said Lestat.

" 'You'll never forgive me, will you? Not now, not even after I'm dead,' said the old man.

" 'I don't know what you're talking about!" said Lestat.

"My patience was becoming exhausted with him, and the old man was becoming more and more agitated. He was begging Lestat to listen to him with a warm heart. The whole thing was making me shudder. Meantime, Daniel had come, and I knew the moment I saw him that everything at Pointe du Lac was lost. Had I been more attentive I'd have seen signs of it before now. He looked at me with eyes of glass. I was a monster to him. 'Monsieur Lestat's father is very ill. Going,' I said, ignoring his expression. 'I want no noise tonight; the slaves must all stay within the cabins. A doctor is on his way.' He stared at me as if I were lying. And then his eyes moved curiously and coldly away from me towards the old man's door. His face underwent such a change that I rose at once and looked in the room. It was Lestat, slouched at the foot of the bed, his back to the bedpost, his nail file working furiously, grimacing in such a way that both his great teeth showed prominently."

The vampire stopped, his shoulders shaking with silent laughter. He was looking at the boy. And the boy looked shyly at the table. But he had already looked, and fixedly, at the vampire's mouth. He had seen that the lips were of a different texture from the vampire's skin, that they were silken and delicately lined like any person's lips, only deadly white; and he had glimpsed the white teeth. Only, the vampire had such a way of smiling that they were not completely revealed; and the boy had not even thought of such teeth until now. "You can imagine," said the vampire, "what this meant.

"I had to kill him."

"You what?" said the boy.

"I had to kill him. He started to run. He would have alarmed everyone. Perhaps it might have been handled some other way, but I had no time. So I went after him, overpowering him. But then, finding myself in the act of doing what I had not done for four years, I stopped. This was a man. He had his bone-handle knife in his hand to defend himself. And I took it

from him easily and slipped it into his heart. He sank
to his knees at once, his fingers tightening on the
blade, bleeding on it. And the sight of the blood, the
aroma of it, maddened me. I believe I moaned aloud.
But I did not reach for him, I would not. Then I remember seeing Lestat's figure emerge in the mirror
over the sideboard. 'Why did you do this!' he demanded. I turned to face him, determined he would
not see me in this weakened state. The old man was
delirious, he went on, he could not understand what
the old man was saying. 'The slaves, they know . . .
you must go to the cabins and keep watch,' I managed to say to him. 'I'll care for the old man.'

" 'Kill him,' Lestat said.

" 'Are you mad!' I answered. 'He's your father!'

" 'I know he's my father!' said Lestat. 'That's why
you have to kill him. I can't kill him! If I could, I
would have done it a long time ago, damn him!' He
wrung his hands. 'We've got to get out of here. And
look what you've done killing this one. There's no
time to lose. His wife will be wailing up here in
minutes . . . or she'll send someone worse!' "

The vampire sighed. "This was all true. Lestat was
right. I could hear the slaves gathering around Daniel's
cottage, waiting for him. Daniel had been brave
enough to come into the haunted house alone. When
he didn't return, the slaves would panic, become a
mob. I told Lestat to calm them, to use all his power
as a white master over them and not to alarm them
with horror, and then I went into the bedroom and
shut the door. I had then another shock in a night of
shocks. Because I'd never seen Lestat's father as he
was then.

"He was sitting up now, leaning forward, talking to
Lestat, begging Lestat to answer him, telling him he
understood his bitterness better than Lestat did himself. And he was a living corpse. Nothing animated his
sunken body but a fierce will: hence, his eyes for
their gleam were all the more sunken in his skull, and
his lips in their trembling made his old yellowed mouth
more horrible. I sat at the foot of the bed, and, suffering to see him so, I gave him my hand. I cannot tell

you how much his appearance had shaken me. For when I bring death, it is swift and consciousless, leaving the victim as if in enchanted sleep. But this was the slow decay, the body refusing to surrender to the vampire of time which had sucked upon it for years on end. 'Lestat,' he said. 'Just for once, don't be hard with me. Just for once, be for me the boy you were. My son.' He said this over and over, the words, 'My son, my son'; and then he said something I could not hear about innocence and innocence destroyed. But I could see that he was not out of his mind, as Lestat thought, but in some terrible state of lucidity. The burden of the past was on him with full force; and the present, which was only death, which he fought with all his will, could do nothing to soften that burden. But I knew I might deceive him if I used all my skill, and, bending close to him now, I whispered the word, 'Father.' It was not Lestat's voice, it was mine, a soft whisper. But he calmed at once and I thought then he might die. But he held my hand as if he were being pulled under by dark ocean waves and I alone could save him. He talked now of some country teacher, a name garbled, who found in Lestat a brilliant pupil and begged to take him to a monastery for an education. He cursed himself for bringing Lestat home, for burning his books. 'You must forgive me, Lestat,' he cried.

"I pressed his hand tightly, hoping this might do for some answer, but he repeated this again. 'You have it all to live for, but you are as cold and brutal as I was then with the work always there and the cold and hunger! Lestat, you must remember. You were the gentlest of them all! God will forgive me if you forgive me.'

"Well, at that moment, the real Esau came through the door. I gestured for quiet, but he wouldn't see that. So I had to get up quickly so the father wouldn't hear his voice from a distance. The slaves had run from him. 'But they're out there, they're gathered in the dark. I hear them,' said Lestat. And then he glared at the old man. 'Kill him, Louis!' he said to me, his voice touched with the first pleading I'd ever heard in it. Then he bit down in rage. 'Do it!'

" 'Lean over that pillow and tell him you forgive him all, forgive him for taking you out of school when you were a boy! Tell him that now.'

" 'For what!' Lestat grimaced, so that his face looked like a skull. 'Taking me out of school!' He threw up his hands and let out a terrible roar of desperation. 'Damn him! Kill him!' he said.

" 'No!' I said. 'You forgive him. Or you kill him yourself. Go on. Kill your own father.'

"The old man begged to be told what we were saying. He called out, 'Son, son,' and Lestat danced like the maddened Rumpelstiltskin about to put his foot through the floor. I went to the lace curtains. I could see and hear the slaves surrounding the house of Pointe du Lac, forms woven in the shadows, drawing near. 'You were Joseph among your brothers,' the old man said. 'The best of them, but how was I to know? It was when you were gone I knew, when all those years passed and they could offer me no comfort, no solace. And then you came back to me and took me from the farm, but it wasn't you. It wasn't the same boy.'

"I turned on Lestat now and veritably dragged him towards the bed. Never had I seen him so weak, and at the same time enraged. He shook me off and then knelt down near the pillow, glowering at me. I stood resolute, and whispered, 'Forgive!'

"It's all right, Father. You must rest easy. I hold nothing against you," he said, his voice thin and strained over his anger.

"The old man turned on the pillow, murmuring something soft with relief, but Lestat was already gone. He stopped short in the doorway, his hands over his ears. 'They're coming!' he whispered; and then, turning just so he could see me, he said, 'Take him. For *God's sake!*'

"The old man never even knew what happened. He never awoke from his stupor. I bled him just enough, opening the gash so he would then die without feeding my dark passion. That thought I couldn't bear. I knew now it wouldn't matter if the body was found in this manner, because I had had enough of Pointe du Lac and Lestat and all this identity of Pointe du Lac's prosperous master. I would torch the house, and turn to the wealth I'd held under many names, safe for just such a moment.

"Meantime, Lestat was after the slaves. He would leave such ruin and death behind him no one could make a story of that night at Pointe du Lac, and I went with him. Always before, his ferocity was mysterious, but now I bared my fangs on the humans who fled from me, my steady advance overcoming their clumsy, pathetic speed as the veil of death descended, or the veil of madness. The power and the proof of the vampire was incontestable, so that the slaves scattered in all directions. And it was I who ran back up the steps to put the torch to Pointe du Lac.

"Lestat came bounding after me. 'What are you doing!' he shouted. 'Are you mad!' But there was no way to put out the flames. 'They're gone and you're destroying it, all of it.' He turned round and round in the magnificent parlor, amid his fragile splendor. 'Get your coffin out. You have three hours till dawn!' I said. The house was a funeral pyre."

"Could the fire have hurt you?" asked the boy.

"Most definitely!" said the vampire.

"Did you go back to the oratory? Was it safe?"

"No. Not at all. Some fifty-five slaves were scattered around the grounds. Many of them would not have desired the life of a runaway and would most certainly go right to Freniere or south to the Bel Jardin plantation down river. I had no intention of staying there that night. But there was little time to go anywhere else."

"The woman, Babette!" said the boy.

The vampire smiled. "Yes, I went to Babette. She lived now at Freniere with her young husband. I had enough time to load my coffin into the carriage and go to her."

"But what about Lestat?"

The vampire sighed. "Lestat went with me. It was his intention to go on to New Orleans, and he was

trying to persuade me to do just that. But when he
saw *I* meant to hide at Freniere, he opted for that also.
We might not have ever made it to New Orleans. It
was growing light. Not so that mortal eyes would have
seen it, but Lestat and I could see it.

"Now, as for Babette, I had visited her once again.
As I told you, she had scandalized the coast by remaining alone on the plantation without a man in the
house, without even an older woman. Babette's greatest
problem was that she might succeed financially only to
suffer the isolation of social ostracism. She had such a
sensibility that wealth itself mean nothing to her;
family, a line . . . this meant something to Babette.
Though she was able to hold the plantation together,
the scandal was wearing on her. She was giving up inside. I came to her one night in the garden. Not per-
mitting her to look on me, I told her in a most gentle
voice that I was the same person she'd seen before.
That I knew of her life and her suffering. 'Don't expect
people to understand it,' I told her. 'They are fools.
They want you to retire because of your brother's
death. They would use your life as if it were merely
oil for a proper lamp. You must defy them, but you
must defy them with purity and confidence.' She was
listening all the while in silence. I told her she was to
give a ball for a cause. And the cause to be religious.
She might pick a convent in New Orleans, any one,
and plan for a philanthropic ball. She would invite her
deceased mother's dearest friends to be chaperones and
she would do all of this with perfect confidence. Above
all, perfect confidence. It was confidence and purity
which were all-important.

"Well, Babette thought this to be a stroke of genius.
'I don't know what you are, and you will not tell me,'
she said. (This was true, I would not.) 'But I can only
think that you are an angel.' And she begged to see
my face. That is, she begged in the manner of such
people as Babette, who are not given to truly begging
anyone for anything. Not that Babette was proud. She
was simply strong and honest, which in most cases
makes begging . . . I see you want to ask me a question." The vampire stopped.

"Oh, no," said the boy, who had meant to hide it.

"But you mustn't be afraid to ask me anything. If I held something too close . . ." And when the vampire said this his face darkened for an instant. He frowned, and as his brows drew together a small well appeared in the flesh of his forehead over his left brow, as though someone had pressed it with a finger. It gave him a peculiar look of deep distress. "If I held something too close for you to ask about it, I would not bring it up in the first place," he said.

The boy found himself staring at the vampire's eyes, at the eyelashes which were fine black wires in the tender flesh of the lids.

"Ask me," he said to the boy.

"Babette, the way you speak of her," said the boy. "As if your feeling was special."

"Did I give you the impression I could not feel?" asked the vampire.

"No, not at all. Obviously you felt for the old man. You stayed to comfort him when you were in danger. And what you felt for young Freniere when Lestat wanted to kill him . . . all this you explained. But I was wondering . . . did you have a special feeling for Babette? Was it feeling for Babette all along that caused you to protect Freniere?"

"You mean love," said the vampire. "Why do you hesitate to say it?"

"Because you spoke of detachment," said the boy.

"Do you think that angels are detached?" asked the vampire.

The boy thought for a moment. "Yes," he said.

"But aren't angels capable of love?" asked the vampire. "Don't angels gaze upon the face of God with complete love?"

The boy thought for a moment. "Love or adoration," he said.

"What is the difference?" asked the vampire thoughtfully. "What is the difference?" It was clearly not a riddle for the boy. He was asking himself. "Angels feel love, and pride . . . the pride of The Fall . . . and hatred. The strong overpowering emotions of detached persons in whom emotion and will are one," he said finally. He stared at the table now, as though he were thinking this over, was not entirely satisfied with it. "I had for Babette . . . a strong feeling. It is not the strongest I've ever known for a human being." He looked up at the boy. "But it was very strong. Babette was to me in her own way an ideal human being. . . ."

He shifted in his chair, the cape moving softly about him, and turned his face to the windows. The boy bent forward and checked the tape. Then he took another cassette from his brief case and, begging the vampire's pardon, fitted it into place. "I'm afraid I did ask something too personal. I didn't mean . . ." he said anxiously to the vampire.

"You asked nothing of the sort," said the vampire, looking at him suddenly. "It is a question right to the point. I feel love, and I felt some measure of love for Babette, though not the greatest love I've ever felt. It was foreshadowed in Babette.

"To return to my story, Babette's charity ball was a success and her re-entry in social life assured by it. Her money generously underwrote any doubts in the minds of her suitors' families, and she married. On summer nights, I used to visit her, never letting her see me or know that I was there. I came to see that she was happy, and seeing her happy I felt a happiness as the result.

"And to Babette I came now with Lestat. He would have killed the Frenieres long ago if I hadn't stopped him, and he thought now that was what I meant to do. 'And what peace would that bring?' I asked. 'You call me the idiot, and you've been the idiot all along. Do you think I don't know why you made me a vampire? You couldn't live by yourself, you couldn't manage even the simplest things. For years now, I've managed everything while you sat about making a pretense of superiority. There's nothing left for you to tell me about life. I have no need of you and no use for you. It's you who need me, and if you touch but one of the Freniere slaves, I'll get rid of you. It will be a battle between us, and I needn't point out to you I have more wit to fare better in my little finger than you in your entire frame. Do as I say.'

"Well, this startled him, though it shouldn't have; and he protested he had much to tell me, of things and types of people I might kill who would cause sudden death and places in the world I must never go and so forth and so on, nonsense that I could hardly endure. But I had no time for him. The overseer's lights were lit at Freniere; he was trying to quell the excitement of the runaway slaves and his own. And the fire of Pointe du Lac could be seen still against the sky. Babette was dressed and attending to business, having sent carriages to Pointe du Lac and slaves to help fight the blaze. The frightened runaways were kept away from the others, and at that point no one regarded their stories as any more than slave foolishness. Babette knew something dreadful had happened and suspected murder, never the supernatural. She was in the study making a note of the fire in the plantation diary when I found her. It was almost morning. I had only a few minutes to convince her she must help. I spoke to her at first, refusing to let her turn around, and calmly she listened. I told her I must have a room for the night, to rest. 'I've never brought you harm. I ask you now for a key, and your promise that no one will try to enter that room until tonight. Then I'll tell you all.' I was nearly desperate now. The sky was paling. Lestat was yards off in the orchard with the coffins. 'But why have you come to me tonight?' she asked. 'And why not to you?' I replied. 'Did I not help you at the very moment when you most needed guidance, when you alone stood strong among those who are dependent and weak? Did I not twice offer you good counsel? And haven't I watched over your happiness ever since?' I could see the figure of Lestat at the window. He was in a panic. 'Give me the key to a room. Let no one come near it till nightfall. I swear to you I would never bring you harm.' 'And if I don't . . . if I believe you come from the devil' she said now, and meant to turn her head. I reached for the candle and put it out. She saw me standing with my back to the graying windows. 'If you don't, and if you believe me to be the devil, I shall die.' I said. 'Give me the key. I could kill you now if I chose, do you see?' And now I moved close to her and showed myself to her more completely, so that she gasped and drew back, holding to the arm of her chair. 'But I would not. I would die rather than kill you. I will die if you don't give me such a key as I ask.'

"It was accomplished. What she thought, I don't know. But she gave me one of the ground-floor storage rooms where wine was aged, and I am sure she saw Lestat and me bringing the coffins. I not only locked the door but barricaded it.

"Lestat was up the next evening when I awoke."

"Then she kept her word."

"Yes. Only she had gone a step further. She had not only respected our locked door; she had locked it again from without."

"And the stories of the slaves . . . she'd heard them."

"Yes, she had. Lestat was the first to discover we were locked in, however. He became furious. He had planned to get to New Orleans as fast as possible. He was now completely suspicious of me. 'I only needed you as long as my father lived,' he said, desperately trying to find some opening somewhere. The place was a dungeon.

"'Now I won't put up with anything from you, I warn you.' He didn't even wish to turn his back on me. I sat there straining to hear voices in the rooms above, wishing that he would shut up, not wishing to confide for a moment my feeling for Babette or my hopes.

"I was also thinking something else. You ask me about feeling and detachment. One of its aspects—detachment with feeling, I should say—is that you can think of two things at the same time. You can think that you are not safe and may die, and you can think of something very abstract and remote. And this was definitely so with me. I was thinking at that moment, wordlessly and rather deeply, how sublime friendship between Lestat and me might have been; how few impediments to it there would have been, and how much to be shared. Perhaps it was the closeness of

Babette which caused me to feel it, for how could I truly ever come to know Babette, except, of course, through the one final way; to take her life, to become one with her in an embrace of death when my soul would become one with my heart and nourished with it. But my soul wanted to know Babette without my need to kill, without robbing her of every breath of life, every drop of blood. But Lestat, how we might have known each other, had he been a man of character, a man of even a little thought. The old man's words came back to me; Lestat a brilliant pupil, a lover of books that had been burned. I knew only the Lestat who sneered at my library, called it a pile of dust, ridiculed relentlessly my reading, my meditations.

"I became aware now that the house over our heads was quieting. Now and then feet moved and the boards creaked and the light in the cracks of the boards gave a faint, uneven illumination. I could see Lestat feeling along the brick walls, his hard enduring vampire face a twisted mask of human frustration. I was confident we must part ways at once, that I must if necessary put an ocean between us. And I realized that I'd tolerated him this long because of self-doubt. I'd fooled myself into believing I stayed for the old man, and for my sister and her husband. But I stayed with Lestat because I was afraid he did know essential secrets as a vampire which I could not discover alone and, more important, because he was the only one of my kind whom I knew. He had never told me how he had become a vampire or where I might find a single other member of our kind. This troubled me greatly then, as much as it had for four years. I hated him and wanted to leave him; yet could I leave him?

"Meantime, as all this passed through my thoughts, Lestat continued his diatribe: he didn't need me; he wasn't going to put up with anything, especially not any threat from the Frenieres. We had to be ready when that door opened. 'Remember!' he said to me finally. 'Speed and strength; they cannot match us in that. And fear. Remember always, to strike fear. Don't be sentimental now! You'll cost us everything.'

" 'You wish to be on your own after this?' I asked

him. I wanted him to say it. I did not have the courage. Or, rather, I did not know my own feelings.

" 'I want to get to New Orleans!' he said. 'I was simply warning you I don't need you. But to get out of here we need each other. You don't begin to know how to use your powers! You have no innate sense of what you are! Use your persuasive powers with this woman if she comes. But if she comes with others, then be prepared to act like what you are.'

" 'Which is what?' I asked him, because it had never seemed such a mystery to me as it did at that time. 'What am I?' He was openly disgusted. He threw up his hands.

" 'Be prepared . . .' he said, now baring his magnificent teeth, 'to kill!' He looked suddenly at the boards overhead. 'They're going to bed up there, do you hear them?' After a long silent time during which Lestat paced and I sat there musing, plumbing my mind for what I might do or say to Babette or, deeper still, for the answer to a harder question—what did I feel for Babette?—after a long time, a light flared beneath the door. Lestat was poised to jump whoever should open it. It was Babette alone and she entered with a lamp, not seeing Lestat, who stood behind her, but looking directly at me.

"I had never seen her as she looked then; her hair was down for bed, a mass of dark waves behind her white dressing gown; and her face was tight with worry and fear. This gave it a feverish radiance and made her large brown eyes all the more huge. As I have told you, I loved her strength and honesty, the greatness of her soul. And I did not feel passion for her as you would feel it. But I found her more alluring than any woman I'd known in mortal life. Even in the severe dressing gown, her arms and breasts were round and soft; and she seemed to me an intriguing soul clothed in rich, mysterious flesh. I who am hard and spare and dedicated to a purpose, felt drawn to her irresistibly; and, knowing it could only culminate in death, I turned away from her at once, wondering if when she gazed into my eyes she found them dead and soulless.

" 'You are the one who came to me before,' she said now, as if she hadn't been sure. 'And you are the owner of Pointe du Lac. You are!' I knew as she spoke that she must have heard the wildest stories of last night, and there would be no convincing her of any lie. I had used my unnatural appearance twice to reach her, to speak to her; I could not hide it or minimize it now.

" 'I mean you no harm,' I said to her. 'I need only a carriage and horses . . . the horses I left last night in the pasture.' She didn't seem to hear my words; she drew closer, determined to catch me in the circle of her light.

"And then I saw Lestat behind her, his shadow merging with her shadow on the brick wall; he was anxious and dangerous. 'You will give me the carriage?' I insisted. She was looking at me now, the lamp raised; and just when I meant to look away, I saw her face change. It went still, blank, as if her soul were losing its consciousness. She closed her eyes and shook her head. It occurred to me that I had somehow caused her to go into a trance without any effort on my part. 'What are you!' she whispered. 'You're from the devil. You were from the devil when you came to me!'

" 'The devil!' I answered her. This distressed me more than I thought I could be distressed. If she believed this, then she would think my counsel bad; she would question herself. Her life was rich and good, and I knew she mustn't do this. Like all strong people, she suffered always a measure of loneliness; she was a marginal outsider, a secret infidel of a certain sort. And the balance by which she lived might be upset if she were to question her own goodness. She stared at me with undisguised horror. It was as if in horror she forgot her own vulnerable position. And now Lestat, who was drawn to weakness like a parched man to water, grabbed her wrist, and she screamed and dropped the lamp. The flames leaped in the splattered oil, and Lestat pulled her backwards towards the open door. 'You get the carriage!' he said to her. 'Get it now, and the horses. You are in mortal danger; don't talk of devils!'

"I stomped on the flames and went for Lestat, shouting at him to leave her. He had her by both wrists, and she was furious. 'You'll rouse the house if you don't shut up!' he said to me. 'And I'll kill her! Get the carriage . . . lead us. Talk to the stable boy!' he said to her, pushing her into the open air.

"We moved slowly across the dark court, my distress almost unbearable, Lestat ahead of me; and before us both Babette, who moved backwards, her eyes peering at us in the dark. Suddenly she stopped. One dim light burned in the house above. 'I'll get you nothing!' she said. I reached for Lestat's arm and told him I must handle this. 'She'll reveal us to everyone unless you let me talk to her,' I whispered to him.

" 'Then get yourself in check,' he said disgustedly. 'Be strong. Don't quibble with her.'

" 'You go as I talk . . . go to the stables and get the carriage and the horses. But don't kill!' Whether he'd obey me or not I didn't know, but he darted away just as I stepped up to Babette. Her face was a mixture of fury and resolution. She said, *'Get thee behind me, Satan.'* And I stood there before her then, speechless, just holding her in my glance as surely as she held me. If she could hear Lestat in the night she gave no indication. Her hatred for me burned me like fire.

" 'Why do you say this to me?' I asked. 'Was the counsel I gave you bad? Did I do you harm? I came to help you, to give you strength. I thought only of you, when I had no need to think of you at all.'

"She shook her head. 'But why, why do you talk to me like this?' she asked. 'I know what you've done at Pointe du Lac; you've lived there like a devil! The slaves are wild with stories! All day men have been on the river road on the way to Pointe du Lac; my husband was there! He saw the house in ruins, the bodies of slaves throughout the orchards, the fields. *What are you!* Why do you speak to me gently! What do you want of *me?*' She clung now to the pillars of the porch and was backing slowly to the staircase. Something moved above in the lighted window.

" 'I cannot give you such answers now,' I said to her. 'Believe me when I tell you I came to you only to do you good. And would not have brought worry and care to you last night for anything, had I the choice!' "

The vampire stopped.

The boy sat forward, his eyes wide. The vampire was frozen, staring off, lost in his thoughts, his memory. And the boy looked down suddenly, as if this were the respectful thing to do. He glanced again at the vampire and then away, his own face as distressed as the vampire's; and then he started to say something, but he stopped.

The vampire turned towards him and studied him, so that the boy flushed and looked away again anxiously. But then he raised his eyes and looked into the vampire's eyes. He swallowed, but he held the vampire's gaze.

"Is this what you want?" the vampire whispered. "Is this what you wanted to hear?"

He moved the chair back soundlessly and walked to the window. The boy sat as if stunned looking at his broad shoulders and the long mass of the cape. The vampire turned his head slightly. "You don't answer me. I'm not giving you what you want, am I? You wanted an interview. Something to broadcast on the radio."

"That doesn't matter. I'll throw the tapes away if you want!" The boy rose. "I can't say I understand all you're telling me. You'd know I was lying if I said I did. So how can I ask you to go on, except to say what I do understand . . . what I do understand is like nothing I've ever understood before." He took a step towards the vampire. The vampire appeared to be looking down into Divisadero Street. Then he turned his head slowly and looked at the boy and smiled. His face was serene and almost affectionate. And the boy suddenly felt uncomfortable. He shoved his hands into his pockets and turned towards the table. Then he looked at the vampire tentatively and said. "Will you . . . please go on?"

The vampire turned with folded arms and leaned against the window. "Why?" he asked.

The boy was at a loss. "Because I want to hear it."

He shrugged. "Because I want to know what happened."

"All right," said the vampire, with the same smile playing on his lips. And he went back to the chair and sat opposite the boy and turned the recorder just a little and said, "Marvellous contraption, really . . . so let me go on.

"You must understand that what I felt for Babette now was a desire for communication, stronger than any other desire I then felt . . . except for the physical desire for . . . blood. It was so strong in me, this desire, that it made me feel the depth of my capacity for loneliness. When I'd spoken to her before, there had been a brief but direct communication which was as simple and as satisfying as taking a person's hand. Clasping it. Letting it go gently. All this in a moment of great need and distress. But now we were at odds. To Babette, I was a monster; and I found it horrible to myself and would have done anything to overcome her feeling. I told her the counsel I'd given her was right, that no instrument of the devil could do right even if he chose.

" 'I know!' she answered me. But by this she meant that she could no more trust me than the devil himself. I approached her and she moved back. I raised my hand and she shrank, clutching for the railing. 'All right, then,' I said, feeling a terrible exasperation. 'Why did you protect me last night! Why have you come to me alone!' What I saw in her face was cunning. She had a reason, but she would by no means reveal it to me. It was impossible for her to speak to me freely, openly, to give me the communication I desired. I felt weary looking at her. The night was already late, and I could see and hear that Lestat had stolen into the wine cellar and taken our caskets, and I had a need to get away; and other needs besides . . . the need to kill and drink. But it wasn't that which made me weary. It was something else, something far worse. It was as if this night were only one of thousands of nights, world without end, night curving into night to make a great arching line of which I couldn't see the end, a night in which I roamed alone under cold, mindless stars. I think I turned away from her and put my hand to my eyes. I felt oppressed and weak suddenly. I think I was making some sound without my will. And then on this vast and desolate landscape of night, where I was standing alone and where Babette was only an illusion, I saw suddenly a possibility that I'd never considered before, a possibility from which I'd fled, rapt as I was with the world, fallen into the senses of the vampire, in love with color and shape and sound and singing and softness and infinite variation. Babette was moving, but I took no note of it. She was taking something from her pocket; her great ring of household keys jingled there. She was moving up the steps. Let her go away, I was thinking. 'Creature of the devil!' I whispered. 'Get thee behind me, Satan,' I repeated. I turned to look at her now. She was frozen on the steps, with wide suspicious eyes. She'd reached the lantern which hung on the wall, and she held it in her hands just staring at me, holding it tight, like a valuable purse. 'You think I come from the devil?' I asked her.

"She quickly moved her left fingers around the hook of the lantern and with her right hand made the sign of the Cross, the Latin words barely audible to me; and her face blanched and her eyebrows rose when there was absolutely no change because of it. 'Did you expect me to go up in a puff of smoke?' I asked her. I drew closer now, for I had gained detachment from her by virtue of my thoughts. 'And where would I go?' I asked her. 'And where would I go, to hell, from whence I came? To the devil, from whom I came?' I stood at the foot of the steps. 'Suppose I told you I know nothing of the devil. Suppose I told you that I do not even know if he exists!' It was the devil I'd seen upon the landscape of my thoughts; it was the devil about whom I thought now. I turned away from her. She wasn't hearing me as you are now. She wasn't listening. I looked up at the stars. Lestat was ready, I knew it. It was as if he'd been ready there with the carriage for years; and she had stood upon the step for years. I had the sudden sensation my brother was there and had been there for ages also, and that he was talking to me low in an excited voice, and what he was saying was desperately important but it was going away from me as fast as he said it, like the rustle of rats in the rafters of an immense house. There was a scraping sound and a burst of light. 'I don't know whether I come from the devil or not! I don't know what I am!' I shouted at Babette, my voice deafening in my own sensitive ears. 'I am to live to the end of the world, and I do not even know what I am!' But the light flared before me; it was the lantern which she had lit with a match and held now so I couldn't see her face. For a moment I could see nothing but the light, and then the great weight of the lantern struck me full force in the chest and the glass shattered on the bricks and the flames roared on my legs, in my face. Lestat was shouting from the darkness, 'Put it out, put it out, idiot. It will consume you!' And I felt something thrashing me wildly in my blindness. It was Lestat's jacket. I'd fallen helpless back against the pillar, helpless as much from the fire and the blow as from the knowledge that Babette meant to destroy me, as from the knowledge that I did not know what I was.

"All this happened in a matter of seconds. The fire was out and I knelt in the dark with my hands on the bricks. Lestat at the top of the stairs had Babette again, and I flew up after him, grabbing him about the neck and pulling him backwards. He turned on me, enraged, and kicked me; but I clung to him and pulled him down on top of me to the bottom. Babette was petrified. I saw her dark outline against the sky and the glint of light in her eyes. 'Come on then!' Lestat said, scrambling to his feet. Babette was putting her hand to her throat. My injured eyes strained to gather the light to see her. Her throat bled. 'Remember!' I said to her. 'I might have killed you! Or let him kill you! I did not. You called me devil. You are wrong.' "

"Then you'd stopped Lestat just in time," said the boy.

"Yes. Lestat could kill and drink like a bolt of lightning. But I had saved only Babette's physical life. I was not to know that until later."

"In an hour and a half Lestat and I were in New Orleans, the horses nearly dead from exhaustion, the carriage parked on a side street a block from a new Spanish hotel. Lestat had an old man by the arm and was putting fifty dollars into his hand. 'Get us a suite,' he directed him, 'and order some champagne. Say it is for two gentlemen, and pay in advance. And when you come back I'll have another fifty for you. And I'll be watching for you, I wager.' His gleaming eyes held the man in thrall. I knew he'd kill him as soon as he returned with the hotel room keys, and he did. I sat in the carriage watching wearily as the man grew weaker and weaker and finally died, his body collapsing like a sack of rocks in a doorway as Lestat let him go. 'Good night, sweet prince,' said Lestat 'and here's your fifty dollars.' And he shoved the money into his pocket as if it were a capital joke.

"Now we slipped in the courtyard doors of the hotel and went up to the lavish parlor of our suite. Champagne glistened in a frosted bucket. Two glasses stood on the silver tray. I knew Lestat would fill one glass and sit there staring at the pale yellow color. And I, a man in a trance, lay on the settee staring at him as if nothing he could do mattered. I have to leave him or die, I thought. It would be sweet to die, I thought. Yes, die. I wanted to die before. Now I wish to die. I saw it with such sweet clarity, such dead calm.

" 'You're being morbid!' Lestat said suddenly. 'It's almost dawn.' He pulled the lace curtains back, and I could see the rooftops under the dark blue sky, and above, the great constellation Orion. 'Go kill!' said Lestat, sliding up the glass. He stepped out of the sill, and I heard his feet land softly on the rooftop beside the hotel. He was going for the coffins, or at least one. My thirst rose in me like fever, and I followed him. My desire to die was constant, like a pure thought in the mind, devoid of emotion. Yet I needed to feed. I've indicated to you I would not then kill people. I moved along the rooftop in search of rats."

"But why . . . you've said Lestat shouldn't have made you *start* with people. Did you mean . . . do you mean for you it was an aesthetic choice, not a moral one?"

"Had you asked me then, I would have told you it was aesthetic, that I wished to understand death in stages. That the death of an animal yielded such pleasure and experience to me that I had only begun to understand it, and wished to save the experience of human death for my mature understanding. But it was moral. Because all aesthetic decisions are moral, really."

"I don't understand," said the boy. "I thought aesthetic decisions could be completely immoral. What about the cliché of the artist who leaves his wife and children so he can paint? Or Nero playing the harp while Rome burned?"

"Both were moral decisions. Both served a higher good, in the mind of the artist. The conflict lies between the morals of the artist and the morals of society, not between aesthetics and morality. But often this isn't understood; and here comes the waste, the tragedy. An artist, stealing paints from a store, for example, imagines himself to have made an inevitable but immoral decision, and then he sees himself as fallen from grace; what follows is despair and petty irresponsibility, as if morality were a great glass world which can be utterly shattered by one act. But this was not my great concern then. I did not know these things then. I believed I killed animals for aesthetic reasons only, and I hedged against the great moral question of whether or not by my very nature I was damned.

"Because, you see, though Lestat had never said anything about devils or hell to me, I believed I was damned when I went over to him, just as Judas must have believed it when he put the noose around his neck. You understand?"

The boy said nothing. He started to speak but didn't. The color burned for a moment in blotches on his cheeks. "Were you?" he whispered.

The vampire only sat there, smiling, a small smile that played on his lips like the light. The boy was staring at him now as if he were just seeing him for the first time.

"Perhaps . . ." said the vampire drawing himself up and crossing his legs ". . . we should take things one at a time. Perhaps I should go on with my story."

"Yes, please . . ." said the boy.

"I was agitated that night, as I told you. I had hedged against this question as a vampire and now it completely overwhelmed me, and in that state I had no desire to live. Well, this produced in me, as it can in humans, a craving for that which will satisfy at least physical desire. I think I used it as an excuse. I have told you what the kill means to vampires; you can imagine from what I've said the difference between a rat and a man.

"I went down into the street after Lestat and walked for blocks. The streets were muddy then, the actual blocks islands above the gutters, and the entire city so dark compared to the cities of today. The lights were as beacons in a black sea. Even with morning rising slowly, only the dormers and high porches of the houses were emerging from the dark, and to a mortal man the narrow streets I found were like pitch. Am I damned? Am I from the devil? Is my very nature that of a devil? I was asking myself over and over. And if it is, why then do I revolt against it, tremble when Babette hurls a flaming lantern at me, turn away in disgust when Lestat kills? What have I become in becoming a vampire? Where am I to go? And all the while, as the death wish caused me to neglect my thirst, my thirst grew hotter; my veins were veritable threads of pain in my flesh; my temples throbbed; and finally I could stand it no longer. Torn apart by the wish to take no action—to starve, to wither in thought on the one hand; and driven to kill on the other—I stood in an empty, desolate street and heard the sound of a child crying.

"She was within. I drew close to the walls, trying in my habitual detachment only to understand the nature of her cry. She was weary and aching and utterly alone. She had been crying for so long now, that soon she would stop from sheer exhaustion. I slipped my hand up under the heavy wooden shutter and pulled it so the bolt slipped. There she sat in the dark room beside a dead woman, a woman who'd been dead for some days. The room itself was cluttered with trunks and packages as though a number of people had been packing to leave; but the mother lay half clothed, her body already in decay, and no one else was there but the child. It was moments before she saw me, but when she did she began to tell me that I must do something to help her mother. She was only five at most, and very thin, and her face was stained with dirt and tears. She begged me to help. They had to take a ship, she said, before the plague came; their father was waiting. She began to shake her mother now and to cry in the most pathetic and desperate way; and then she looked at me again and burst into the greatest flow of tears.

"You must understand that by now I was burning with physical need to drink. I could not have made it through another day without feeding. But there were alternatives: rats abounded in the streets, and somewhere very near a dog was howling hopelessly. I might have fled the room had I chosen and fed and gotten back easily. But the question pounded in me: Am I damned? If so, why do I feel such pity for her, for her gaunt face? Why do I wish to touch her tiny, soft arms, hold her now on my knee as I am doing, feel her bend her head to my chest as I gently touch the satin hair? Why do I do this? If I am damned I must want to kill her, I must want to make her nothing but food for a cursed existence, because being damned I must hate her.

"And when I thought of this, I saw Babette's face contorted with hatred when she had held the lantern waiting to light it, and I saw Lestat in my mind and hated him, and I felt, yes, damned and this is hell, and in that instant I had bent down and driven hard into her soft, small neck and, hearing her tiny cry, whispered even as I felt the hot blood on my lips, 'It's only for a moment and there'll be no more pain.' But she was locked to me, and I was soon incapable of saying anything. For four years I had not savored a human; for four years I hadn't really known; and now I heard her heart in that terrible rhythm, and such a heart—

not the heart of a man or an animal, but the rapid, tenacious heart of the child, beating harder and harder, refusing to die, beating like a tiny fist beating on a door, crying, 'I will not die, I will not die, I cannot die, I cannot die. . . .' I think I rose to my feet still locked to her, the heart pulling my heart faster with no hope of cease, the rich blood rushing too fast for me, the room reeling, and then, despite myself, I was staring over her bent head, her open mouth, down through the gloom at the mother's face; and through the half-mast lids her eyes gleamed at me as if they were alive! I threw the child down. She lay like a jointless doll. And turning in blind horror of the mother to flee, I saw the window filled with a familiar shape. It was Lestat, who backed away from it now laughing, his body bent as he danced in the mud street. 'Louis, Louis,' he taunted me, and pointed a long, bone-thin finger at me, as if to say he'd caught me in the act. And now he bounded over the sill, brushing me aside, and grabbed the mother's stinking body from the bed and made to dance with her."

"Good God!" whispered the boy.

"Yes, I might have said the same," said the vampire. "He stumbled over the child as he pulled the mother along in widening circles, singing as he danced, her matted hair falling in her face, as her head snapped back and a black fluid poured out of her mouth. He threw her down. I was out of the window and running down the street, and he was running after me. 'Are you afraid of me, Louis?' he shouted. 'Are you afraid? The child's alive, Louis, you left her breathing. Shall I go back and make her a vampire? We could use her, Louis, and think of all the pretty dresses we could buy for her. Louis, wait, Louis! I'll go back for her if you say!' And so he ran after me all the way back to the hotel, all the way across the rooftops, where I hoped to lose him, until I leaped in the window of the parlor and turned in rage and slammed the window shut. He hit it, arms outstretched, like a bird who seeks to fly through glass, and shook the frame. I was utterly out of my mind. I went round and round the room looking for some way to kill him. I pictured his body burned to a crisp on the roof below. Reason had altogether left me, so that I was consummate rage, and when he came through the broken glass, we fought as we'd never fought before. It was hell that stopped me, the thought of hell, of us being two souls in hell that grappled in hatred. I lost my confidence, my purpose, my grip. I was down on the floor then, and he was standing over me, his eyes cold, though his chest heaved. 'You're a fool, Louis,' he said. His voice was calm. It was so calm it brought me around. 'The sun's coming up,' he said, his chest heaving slightly from the struggle, his eyes narrow as he looked at the window. I'd never seen him quite like this. The fight had got the better of him in some way; or something had. 'Get in your coffin,' he said to me, without even the slightest anger. 'But tomorrow night . . . we talk.'

"Well, I was more than slightly amazed. Lestat talk! I couldn't imagine this. Never had Lestat and I really talked. I think I have described to you with accuracy our sparring matches, our angry go-rounds."

"He was desperate for the money, for your houses," said the boy. "Or was it that he was as afraid to be alone as you were?"

"These questions occurred to me. It even occurred to me that Lestat meant to kill me, some way that I didn't know. You see, I wasn't sure then why I awoke each evening when I did, whether it was automatic when the deathlike sleep left me, and why it happened sometimes earlier than at other times. It was one of the things Lestat would not explain. And he was often up before me. He was my superior in all the mechanics, as I've indicated. And I shut the coffin that morning with a kind of despair.

"I should explain now, though, that the shutting of the coffin is always disturbing. It is rather like going under a modern anesthetic on an operating table. Even a casual mistake on the part of an intruder might mean death."

"But how could he have killed you? He couldn't have exposed you to the light; he couldn't have stood it himself."

"This is true, but rising before me he might have

nailed my coffin shut. Or set it afire. The principal thing was, I didn't know what he might do, what he might know that I still did not know.

"But there was nothing to be done about it then, and with thoughts of the dead woman and child still in my brain, and the sun rising, I had no energy left to argue with him, and lay down to miserable dreams."

"You do dream!" said the boy.

"Often," said the vampire. "I wish sometimes that I did not. For such dreams, such long and clear dreams I never had as a mortal; and such twisted nightmares I never had either. In my early days, these dreams so absorbed me that often it seemed I fought waking as long as I could and lay sometimes for hours thinking of these dreams until the night was half gone; and dazed by them I often wandered about seeking to understand their meaning. They were in many ways as elusive as the dreams of mortals. I dreamed of my brother, for instance, that he was near me in some state between life and death, calling to me for help. And often I dreamed of Babette; and often—almost always—there was a great wasteland backdrop to my dreams, that wasteland of night I'd seen when cursed by Babette as I've told you. It was as if all figures walked and talked on the desolate home of my damned soul. I don't remember what I dreamed that day, perhaps because I remember too well what Lestat and I discussed the following evening. I see you're anxious for that, too.

"Well, as I've said, Lestat amazed me in his new calm, his thoughtfulness. But that evening I didn't wake to find him the same way, not at first. There were women in the parlor. The candles were a few, scattered on the small table and the carved buffet, and Lestat had his arm around one woman and was kissing her. She was very drunk and very beautiful, a great drugged doll of a woman with her careful coif falling slowly down on her bare shoulders and over her partially bared breasts. The other woman sat over a ruined supper table drinking a glass of wine. I could see that the three of them had dined (Lestat pretending to dine . . . you would be surprised how people do not notice that a vampire is only pretending to eat), and the woman at the table was bored. All this put me in a fit of agitation. I did not know what Lestat was up to. If I went into the room, the woman would turn her attentions to me. And what was to happen, I couldn't imagine, except that Lestat meant for us to kill them both. The woman on the settee with him was already teasing about his kisses, his coldness, his lack of desire for her. And the woman at the table watched with black almond eyes that seemed to be filled with satisfaction; when Lestat rose and came to her, putting his hands on her bare white arms, she brightened. Bending now to kiss her, he saw me through the crack in the door. And his eyes just stared at me for a moment, and then he went on talking with the ladies. He bent down and blew out the candles on the table. 'It's too dark in here,' said the woman on the couch. 'Leave us alone,' said the other woman. Lestat sat down and beckoned her to sit in his lap. And she did, putting her left arm around his neck, her right hand smoothing back his yellow hair. 'Your skin's icy,' she said, recoiling slightly. 'Not always,' said Lestat; and then he buried his face in the flesh of her neck. I was watching all this with fascination. Lestat was masterfully clever and utterly vicious, but I didn't know how clever he was until he sank his teeth into her now, his thumb pressing down on her throat, his other arm locking her tight, so that he drank his fill without the other woman even knowing. 'Your friend has no head for wine,' he said slipping out of the chair and seating the unconscious woman there, her arms folded under her face on the table. 'She's stupid,' said the other woman, who had gone to the window and had been looking out at the lights. New Orleans was then a city of many low buildings, as you probably know. And on such clear nights as this, the lamplit streets were beautiful from the high windows of this new Spanish hotel; and the stars of those days hung low over such dim light as they do at sea. 'I can warm that cold skin of yours better than she can.' She turned to Lestat, and I must confess I was feeling some relief that he would now take care of her as well. But he planned nothing so simple. 'Do you think so?' he said to her. He took her hand, and she said, 'Why, you're warm.' "

"You mean the blood had warmed him," said the boy.

"Oh, yes," said the vampire. "After killing, a vampire is as warm as you are now." And he started to resume; then, glancing at the boy, he smiled. "As I was saying . . . Lestat now held the woman's hand in his and said that the other had warmed him. His face, of course, was flushed; much altered. He drew her close now, and she kissed him, remarking through her laughter that he was a veritable furnace of passion.

" 'Ah, but the price is high,' he said to her, affecting sadness. 'Your pretty friend . . .' He shrugged his shoulders. 'I exhausted her.' And he stood back as if inviting the woman to walk to the table. And she did, a look of superiority on her small features. She bent down to see her friend, but then lost interest—until she saw something. It was a napkin. It had caught the last drops of blood from the wound in the throat. She picked it up, straining to see it in the darkness. 'Take down your hair,' said Lestat softly. And she dropped it, indifferent, and took down the last tresses, so that her hair fell blond and wavy down her back. 'Soft,' he said, 'so soft. I picture you that way, lying on a bed of satin.'

" 'Such things you say!' she scoffed and turned her back on him playfully.

" 'Do you know what manner of bed?' he asked. And she laughed and said *his* bed, she could imagine. She looked back at him as he advanced; and, never once looking away from her, he gently tipped the body of her friend, so that it fell backwards from the chair and lay with staring eyes upon the floor. The woman gasped. She scrambled away from the corpse, nearly upsetting a small end table. The candle went over and went out. ' "Put out the light . . . and then put out the light," ' Lestat said softly. And then he took her into his arms like a struggling moth and sank his teeth into her."

"But what were you thinking as you watched?"

asked the boy. "Did you want to stop him the way you wanted to stop him from killing Freniere?"

"No," said the vampire. "I could not have stopped him. And you must understand I knew that he killed humans every night. Animals gave him no satisfaction whatsoever. Animals were to be banked on when all else failed, but never to be chosen. If I felt any sympathy for the women, it was buried deep in my own turmoil. I still felt in my chest the little hammer heart of that starving child; I still burned with the questions of my own divided nature. I was angry that Lestat had staged this show for me, waiting till I woke to kill the women; and I wondered again if I might somehow break loose from him and felt both hatred and my own weakness more than ever.

"Meantime, he propped their lovely corpses at the table and went about the room lighting all the candles until it blazed as if for a wedding. 'Come in, Louis,' he said. 'I would have arranged an escort for you, but I know what a man you are about choosing your own. Pity Mademoiselle Freniere likes to hurl flaming lanterns. It makes a party unwieldy, don't you think? Especially for a hotel?' He seated the blond-haired girl so that her head lay to one side against the damask back of the chair, and the darker woman lay with her chin resting just above her breasts; this one had blanched, and her features had a rigid look to them already, as though she was one of those women in whom the fire of personality makes beauty. But the other looked only as if she slept; and I was not sure that she was even dead. Lestat had made two gashes, one in her throat and one above her left breast, and both still bled freely. He lifted her wrist now, and slitting it with a knife, filled two wine glasses and bade me to sit down.

" 'I'm leaving you,' I said to him at once. 'I wish to tell you that now.'

" 'I thought as much,' he answered, sitting back in the chair, 'and I thought as well that you would make a flowery announcement. Tell me what a monster I am; what a vulgar fiend.'

" 'I make no judgments upon you. I'm not interested

in you. I am interested in my own nature now, and I've come to believe I can't trust you to tell me the truth about it. You use knowledge for personal power,' I told him. And I suppose, in the manner of many people making such an announcement, I was not looking to him at all. I was mainly listening to my own words. But now I saw that his face was once again the way it had been when he'd said we would talk. He was *listening* to me. I was suddenly at a loss. I felt that gulf between us as painfully as ever.

" 'Why did you become a vampire?' I blurted out. 'And why such a vampire as you are! Vengeful and delighting in taking human life even when you have no need. This girl . . . why did you kill her when one would have done? And way did you frighten her so before you killed her? And why have you propped her here in some grotesque manner, as if tempting the gods to strike you down for your blasphemy?'

"All this he listened to without speaking, and in the pause that followed I again felt at a loss. Lestat's eyes were large and thoughtful; I'd seen them that way before, but I couldn't remember when, certainly not when talking to me.

" 'What do you think a vampire is?' he asked me sincerely.

" 'I don't pretend to know. You pretend to know. What is it?' I asked. And to this he answered nothing. It was as if he sensed the insincerity of it, the spite. He just sat there looking at me with the same still expression. Then I said, 'I know that after leaving you, I shall try to find out. I'll travel the world, if I have to, to find other vampires. I know they must exist; I don't know of any reasons why they shouldn't exist in great numbers. And I'm confident I shall find vampires who have more in common with me than I with you. Vampires who understand knowledge as I do and have used their superior vampire nature to learn secrets of which you don't even dream. If you haven't told me everything, I shall find things out for myself or from them, when I find them.'

"He shook his head. 'Louis!' he said. 'You are in love with your mortal nature! You chase after the phantoms of your former self. Freniere, his sister . . . these are images for you of what you were and what you still long to be. And in your romance with mortal life, you're dead to your vampire nature!'

"I objected to this at once. 'My vampire nature has been for me the greatest adventure of my life; all that went before it was confused, clouded; I went through mortal life like a blind man groping from solid object to solid object. It was only when I became a vampire that I respected for the first time all of life. I never saw a living, pulsing human being until I was a vampire; I never knew what life was until it ran out in a red gush over my lips, my hands!' I found myself staring at the two women, the darker one now turning a terrible shade of blue. The blonde was breathing. 'She's not dead!' I said to him suddenly.

" 'I know. Let her alone,' he said. He lifted her wrist and made a new gash by the scab of the other and filled his glass. 'All that you say makes sense,' he said to me, taking a drink. 'You are an intellect. I've never been. What I've learned I've learned from listening to men talk, not from books. I never went to school long enough. But I'm not stupid, and you must listen to me because you are in danger. You do not know your vampire nature. You are like an adult who, looking back on his childhood, realizes that he never appreciated it. You cannot, as a man, go back to the nursery and play with your toys, asking for the love and care to be showered on you again simply because now you know their worth. So it is with you and mortal nature. You've given it up. You no longer look "through a glass darkly." But you cannot pass back to the world of human warmth with your new eyes.'

" 'I know that well enough!' I said. 'But what is it that is our nature! If I can live from the blood of animals, why should I not live from the blood of animals rather than go through the world bringing misery and death to human creatures!'

" 'Does it bring you happiness?' he asked. 'You wander through the night, feeding on rats like a pauper and then moon at Babette's window, filled with care, yet helpless as the goddess who came by night to watch

Endymion sleep and could not have him. And suppose you could hold her in your arms and she would look on you without horror or disgust, what then? A few short years to watch her suffer every prick of mortality and then die before your eyes? Does this give happiness? This is insanity, Louis. This is vain. And what truly lies before you is vampire nature, which is killing. For I guarantee you that if you walk the streets tonight and strike down a woman as rich and beautiful as Babbette and suck her blood until she drops at your feet you will have no hunger left for Babbette's profile in the candlelight or for listening by the window for the sound of her voice. You will be filled, Louis, as you were meant to be, with all the life that you can hold; and you will have hunger when that's gone for the same, and the same, and the same. The red in this glass will be just as red; the roses on the wallpaper just as delicately drawn. And you'll see the moon the same way, and the same the flicker of a candle. And with that same sensibility that you cherish you will see death in all its beauty, life as it is only known on the very point of death. Don't you understand that, Louis? You alone of all creatures can see death that way with impunity. You . . . alone . . . under the rising moon . . . can strike like the hand of God!'

"He sat back now and drained the glass, and his eyes moved over the unconscious woman. Her breasts heaved and her eyebrows knit as if she were coming around. A moan escaped her lips. He'd never spoken such words to me before, and I had not thought him capable of it. 'Vampires are killers,' he said now. 'Predators. Whose all-seeing eyes were meant to give them detachment. The ability to see a human life in its entirety, not with any mawkish sorrow but with a thrilling satisfaction in being the end of that life, in having a hand in the divine plan.'

" 'That is how *you* see it!' I protested. The girl moaned again; her face was very white. Her head rolled against the back of the chair.

" 'That is the way it is,' he answered. 'You talk of finding other vampires! Vampires are killers! They don't want you or your sensibility! They'll see you coming long before you see them, and they'll see your flaw; and, distrusting you, they'll seek to kill you. They'd seek to kill you even if you were like me. Because they are lone predators and seek for companionship no more than cats in the jungle. They're jealous of their secret and of their territory; and if you find one or more of them together it will be for safety only, and one will be the slave of the other, the way you are of me.'

" 'I'm not your slave,' I said to him. But even as he spoke I realized I'd been his slave all along.

" 'That's how vampires increase . . . through slavery. How else?' he asked. He took the girl's wrist again, and she cried out as the knife cut. She opened her eyes slowly as he held her wrist over the glass. She blinked and strained to keep them open. It was as if a veil covered her eyes. 'You're tired, aren't you?' he asked her. She gazed at him as if she couldn't really see him. 'Tired!' he said, now leaning close and staring into her eyes. 'You want to sleep.' 'Yes . . .' she moaned softly. And he picked her up and took her into the bedroom. Our coffins rested on the carpet and against the wall; there was a velvet-draped bed. Lestat did not put her on the bed; he lowered her slowly into his coffin. 'What are you doing?' I asked him, coming to the door sill. The girl was looking around like a terrified child. 'No . . .' she was moaning. And then, as he closed the lid, she screamed. She continued to scream within the coffin.

" 'Why do you *do this*, Lestat?' I asked.

" 'I like to do it,' he said. 'I enjoy it.' He looked at me. 'I don't say that you have to enjoy it. Take your aesthete's tastes to purer things. Kill them swiftly if you will, but do it! Learn that you're a killer! Ah!' He threw up his hands in disgust. The girl had stopped screaming. Now he drew up a little curved-legged chair beside the coffin and, crossing his legs, he looked at the coffin lid. His was a black varnished coffin, not a pure rectangular box as they are now, but tapered at both ends and widest where the corpse might lay his hands upon his chest. It suggested the human form. It opened, and the girl sat up astonished, wild-eyed, her lips blue and trembling. 'Lie down, love,' he said to her, and pushed her back; and she lay, near-hysterical, staring up at him. 'You're dead, love,' he said to her; and she screamed and turned desperately in the coffin like a fish, as if her body could escape through the sides, through the bottom. 'It's a coffin, a coffin!' she cried. 'Let me out.'

" 'But we all must lie in coffins, eventually,' he said to her. 'Lie still, love. This is your coffin. Most of us never get to know what it feels like. You know what it feels like!' he said to her. I couldn't tell whether she was listening or not, or just going wild. But she saw me in the doorway, and then she lay still, looking at Lestat and then at me. 'Help me!' she said to me.

"Lestat looked at me. 'I expected you to feel these things instinctually, as I did,' he said. 'When I gave you that first kill, I thought you would hunger for the next and the next, that you would go to each human life as if to a full cup, the way I had. But you didn't. And all this time I suppose I kept from straightening you out because you were best weaker. I'd watch you playing shadow in the night, staring at the falling rain, and I'd think, He's easy to manage, he's simple. But you're weak, Louis. You're a mark. For vampires and now for humans alike. This thing with Babette has exposed us both. It's as if you want us both to be destroyed.'

" 'I can't stand to watch what you're doing,' I said, turning my back. The girl's eyes were burning into my flesh. She lay, all the time he spoke, staring at me.

"You can stand it!' he said. 'I saw you last night with that child. You're a vampire, the same as I am!'

"He stood up and came towards me, but the girl rose again and he turned to shove her down. 'Do you think we should make her a vampire? Share our lives with her?' he asked. Instantly I said, 'No!'

" 'Why, because she's nothing but a whore?' he asked. 'A damned expensive whore at that,' he said.

" 'Can she live now? Or has she lost too much?' I asked him.

" 'Touching!" he said. 'She can't live.'

" 'Then kill her.' She began to scream. He just sat there. I turned around. He was smiling, and the girl had turned her face to the satin and was sobbing. Her reason had almost entirely left her; she was crying and praying. She was praying to the Virgin to save her, her hands over her face now, now over her head, the wrist smearing blood in her hair and on the satin. I bent over the coffin. She was dying, it was true; her eyes were burning, but the tissue around them was already bluish and now she smiled. 'You won't let me die, will you?' she whispered. 'You'll save me.' Lestat reached over and took her wrist. 'But it's too late, love,' he said. 'Look at your wrist, your breast.' And then he touched the wound in her throat. She put her hands to her throat and gasped, her mouth open, the scream strangled. I stared at Lestat. I could not understand why he did this. His face was as smooth as mine is now, more animated for the blood, but cold and without emotion.

"He did not leer like a stage villain, nor hunger for her suffering as if the cruelty fed him. He simply watched her. 'I never meant to be bad,' she was crying. 'I only did what I had to do. You won't let this happen to me. You'll let me go. I can't die like this, I can't!' She was sobbing, the sobs dry and thin. 'You'll let me go. I have to go to the priest. You'll let me go.'

" 'But my friend is a priest,' said Lestat, smiling. As if he'd just thought of it as a joke. 'This is your funeral, dear. You see, you were at a dinner party and you died. But God has given you another chance to be absolved. Don't you see? Tell him your sins.'

"She shook her head at first, and then she looked at me again with those pleading eyes. 'Is it true?' she whispered. 'Well,' said Lestat, 'I suppose you're not contrite, dear. I shall have to shut the lid!'

" 'Stop this, Lestat!' I shouted at him. The girl was screaming again, and I could not stand the sight of it any longer. I bent down to her and took her hand. 'I can't remember my sins,' she said, just as I was looking at her wrist, resolved to kill her. 'You mustn't try. Tell God only that you are sorry,' I said, 'and then you'll die and it will be over.' She lay back, and her eyes shut. I sank my teeth into her wrist and began to suck her dry. She stirred once as if dreaming and said a name; and then, when I felt her heartbeat reach that hypnotic slowness, I drew back from her, dizzy, confused for the moment, my hands reaching for the door frame. I saw her as if in a dream. The candles glared in the corner of my eye. I saw her lying utterly still. And Lestat sat composed beside her, like a mourner. His face was still. 'Louis,' he said to me. 'Don't you understand? Peace will only come to you when you can do this every night of your life. There is nothing else. But this is everything!' His voice was almost tender as he spoke, and he rose and put both his hands on my shoulders. I walked into the parlor, shying away from his touch but not resolute enough to push him off. 'Come with me, out into the streets. It's late. You haven't drunk enough. Let me show you what you are. Really! Forgive me if I bungled it, left too much to nature. Come!'

" 'I can't bear it, Lestat,' I said to him. 'You chose your companion badly.'

" 'But Louis,' he said, 'you haven't tried!'

The vampire stopped. He was studying the boy. And the boy, astonished, said nothing.

"It was true what he'd said. I had not drunk enough; and shaken by the girl's fear, I let him lead me out of the hotel, down the back stairs. People were coming now from the Condé Street ballroom, and the narrow street was jammed. There were supper parties in the hotels, and the planter families were lodged in town in great numbers and we passed through them like a nightmare. My agony was unbearable. Never since I was a human being had I felt such mental pain. It was because all of Lestat's words had made sense to me. I knew peace only when I killed, only for that minute; and there was no question in my mind that the killing of anything less than a human being brought nothing but a vague longing, the discontent which had brought me close to humans, to watch their lives through glass. I was no vampire. And in my pain, I asked irrationally, like a child, Could I not return? Could I not be human again? Even as the blood of that girl was warm in me and I felt that physical thrill and strength, I asked that question. The faces of humans passed me like candle flames in the night dancing on dark waves. I was sinking into the darkness. I was weary of longing. I was turning around and around in the street, looking at the stars and thinking, Yes, it's true. I know what he is saying is true, that when I kill there is no longing; and I can't bear this truth, I can't bear it.

"Suddenly there was one of those arresting moments. The street was utterly quiet. We had strayed far from the main part of the old town and were near the ramparts. There were no lights, only the fire in a window and the far-off sound of people laughing. But no one here. No one near us. I could feel the breeze suddenly from the river and the hot air of the night rising and Lestat near me, so still he might have been made of stone. Over the long, low row of pointed roofs were the massive shapes of oak trees in the dark, great swaying forms of myriad sounds under the low-hung stars. The pain for the moment was gone; the confusion was gone. I closed my eyes and heard the wind and the sound of water flowing softly, swiftly in the river. It was enough, for one moment. And I knew that it would not endure, that it would fly away from me like something torn out of my arms, and I would fly after it, more desperately lonely than any creature under God, to get it back. And then a voice beside me rumbled deep in the sound of the night, a drumbeat as the moment ended, saying, 'Do what it is your nature to do. This is but a taste of it. Do what it is your nature to do.' And the moment was gone. I stood like the girl in the parlor in the hotel, dazed and ready for the slightest suggestion. I was nodding at Lestat as he nodded at me. 'Pain is terrible for you,' he said. 'You feel it like no other creature because you are a vampire. You don't want it to go on.'

" 'No,' I answered him. 'I'll feel as I felt with her, wed to her and weightless, caught as if by a dance.'

" 'That and more.' His hand tightened on mine. 'Don't turn away from it, come with me.'

"He led me quickly through the street, turning every time I hesitated, his hand out for mine, a smile on his lips, his presence as marvellous to me as the night he'd come in my mortal life and told me we would be vampires. 'Evil is a point of view,' he whispered now. 'We are immortal. And what we have before us are the rich feasts that conscience cannot appreciate and mortal men cannot know without regret. God kills, and so shall we; indiscriminately He takes the richest and the poorest, and so shall we; for no creatures under God are as we are, none so like Him as ourselves, dark angels not confined to the stinking limits of hell but wandering His earth and all its kingdoms. I want a child tonight. I am like a mother . . . I want a child!'

"I should have known what he meant. I did not. He had me mesmerized, enchanted. He was playing to me as he had when I was mortal; he was leading me. He was saying, 'Your pain will end.'

"We'd come to a street of lighted windows. It was a place of rooming houses, sailors, flatboat men. We entered a narrow door; and then, in a hollow stone passage in which I could hear my own breath like the wind, he crept along the wall until his shadow leapt out in the light of a doorway beside the shadow of another man, their heads bent together, their whispers like the rustling of dry leaves. 'What is it?' I drew near him as he came back, afraid suddenly this exhilaration in me would die. I saw again that nightmare landscape I'd seen when I spoke with Babette; I felt the chill of loneliness, the chill of guilt. 'She's there!' he said. 'Your wounded one. Your daughter.'

" 'What do you say, what are you talking about!'

" 'You've saved her,' he whispered. 'I knew it. You left the window wide on her and her dead mother, and people passing in the street brought her here.'

" 'The child. The little girl!' I gasped. But he was already leading me through the door to stand at the end of the long ward of wooden beds, each with a child beneath a narrow white blanket, one candle at the end of the ward, where a nurse bent over a small desk. We walked down the aisle between the rows. 'Starving children, orphans,' he said. 'Children of plague and fever.' He stopped. I saw the little girl

lying in the bed. And then the man was coming, and
he was whispering with Lestat; such care for the sleeping little ones. Someone in another room was crying.
The nurse rose and hurried away.

"And now the doctor bent and wrapped the child
in the blanket. Lestat had taken money from his
pocket and set it on the foot of the bed. The doctor
was saying how glad he was we'd come for her, how
most of them were orphans; they came in on the ships,
sometimes orphans too young even to tell which body
was that of their mother. He thought Lestat was the
father.

"And in moments, Lestat was running through the
streets with her, the white of the blanket gleaming
against his dark coat and cape; and even to my ex-
pert vision, as I ran after him it seemed sometimes as
if the blanket flew through the night with no one holding it, a shifting shape travelling on the wind like a
leaf stood upright and sent scurrying along a passage,
trying to gain the wind all the while and truly take
flight. I caught him finally as we approached the lamps
near the Place d'Armes. The child lay pale on his
shoulder, her cheeks still full like plums, though she
was drained and near death. She opened her eyes, or
rather the lids slid back; and beneath the long curling
lashes I saw a streak of white. 'Lestat, what are you
doing? Where are you taking her?' I demanded. But
I knew too well. He was heading for the hotel and
meant to take her into our room.

"The corpses were as we left them, one neatly set
in the coffin as if an undertaker had already attended
her, the other in her chair at the table. Lestat brushed
past them as if he didn't see them, while I watched
him in fascination. The candles had all burned down,
and the only light was that of the moon and the street.
I could see his iced and gleaming profile as he set
the child down on the pillow. 'Come here, Louis, you
haven't fed enough, I know you haven't,' he said with
the same calm, convincing voice he had used skillfully
all evening. He held my hand in his, his own warm
and tight. 'See her, Louis, how plump and sweet she
looks, as if even death can't take her freshness; the

will to live is too strong! He might make a sculpture of her tiny lips and rounded hands, but he cannot make her fade! You remember, the way you wanted her when you saw her in that room.' I resisted him. I didn't want to kill her. I hadn't wanted to last night. And then suddenly I remembered two conflicting things and was torn in agony: I remembered the powerful beating of her heart against mine and I hungered for it, hungered for it so badly I turned my back on her in the bed and would have rushed out of the room had not Lestat held me fast; and I remembered her mother's face and that moment of horror when I'd dropped the child and he'd come into the room. But he wasn't mocking me now; he was confusing me. 'You want her, Louis. Don't you see, once you've taken her, then you can take whomever you wish. You wanted her last night but you weakened, and that's why she's not dead.' I could feel it was true, what he said. I could feel again that ecstasy of being pressed to her, her little heart going and going. 'She's too strong for me . . . her heart, it wouldn't give up,' I said to him. 'Is she so strong?' he smiled. He drew me close to him. 'Take her, Louis, I know you want her.' And I did. I drew close to the bed now and just watched her. Her chest barely moved with her breath, and one small hand was tangled in her long, gold hair. I couldn't bear it, looking at her, wanting her not to die and wanting her; and the more I looked at her, the more I could taste her skin, feel my arm sliding under her back and pulling her up to me, feeling her soft neck. Soft, soft, that's what she was, so soft. I tried to tell myself it was best for her to die—what was to become of her?—but these were lying thoughts. I wanted her! And so I took her in my arms and held her, her burning cheek on mine, her hair falling down over my wrists and brushing my eyelids, the sweet perfume of a child strong and pulsing in spite of sickness and death. She moaned now, stirred in her sleep, and that was more than I could bear. I'd kill her before I'd let her wake and know it. I went into her throat and heard Lestat saying to me strangely, 'Just a little tear. It's just a little throat.' And I obeyed him.

"I won't tell you again what it was like, except that it caught me up just as it had done before, and as killing always does, only more; so that my knees bent and I half lay on the bed, sucking her dry, that heart pounding again that would not slow, would not give up. And suddenly, as I went on and on, the instinctual part of me waiting, waiting for the slowing of the heart which would mean death, Lestat wrenched me from her. 'But she's not dead,' I whispered. But it was over. The furniture of the room emerged from the darkness. I sat stunned, staring at her, too weak to move, my head rolling back against the headboard of the bed, my hands pressing down on the velvet spread. Lestat was snatching her up, talking to her, saying a name. 'Claudia, Claudia, listen to me, come round, Claudia.' He was carrying her now out of the bedroom into the parlor, and his voice was so soft I barely heard him. 'You're ill, do you hear me? You must do as I tell you to get well.' And then, in the pause that followed, I came to my senses. I realized what he was doing, that he had cut his wrist and given it to her and she was drinking. 'That's it dear; more,' he was saying to her. 'You must drink it to get well.'

" 'Damn you!' I shouted, and he hissed at me with blazing eyes. He sat on the settee with her locked to his wrist. I saw her white hand clutching at his sleeve, and I could see his chest heaving for breath and his face contorted the way I'd never seen it. He let out a moan and whispered again to her to go on; and when I moved from the threshold, he glared at me again, as if to say, 'I'll kill you!'

" 'But why, Lestat?' I whispered to him. He was trying now to push her off, and she wouldn't let go. With her fingers locked around his fingers and arm she held the wrist to her mouth, a growl coming out of her. 'Stop, stop!' he said to her. He was clearly in pain. He pulled back from her and held her shoulders with both hands. She tried desperately to reach his wrist with her teeth, but she couldn't; and then she looked at him with the most innocent astonishment. He stood back, his hand out lest she move. Then he clapped a handkerchief on his wrist and backed away from her, toward the bell rope. He pulled it sharply, his eyes still fixed on her.

" 'What have you done, Lestat?' I asked him. *'What have you done?'* I stared at her. She sat composed, revived, filled with life, no sign of pallor or weakness in her, her legs stretched out straight on the damask, her white gown soft and thin like an angel's gown around her small form. She was looking at Lestat. 'Not me,' he said to her, 'ever again. Do you understand? But I'll show you what to do!' When I tried to make him look at me and answer me as to what he was doing, he shook me off. He gave me such a blow with his arm that I hit the wall. Someone was knocking now. I knew what he meant to do. Once more I tried to reach out for him, but he spun so fast I didn't even see him hit me. When I did see him, I was sprawled in the chair and he was opening the door. 'Yes, come in, please, there's been an accident,' he said to the young slave boy. And then, shutting the door, he took him from behind, so that the boy never knew what happened. And even as he knelt over the body drinking, he beckoned for the child, who slid from the couch and went down on her knees and took the wrist offered her, quickly pushing back the cuff of the shirt. She gnawed first, as if she meant to devour his flesh, and then Lestat showed her what to do. He sat back and let her have the rest, his eye on the boy's chest, so that when the time came, he bent forward and said, 'No more, he's dying. . . . You must never drink after the heart stops or you'll be sick again, sick to death. Do you understand?' But she'd had enough and she sat next to him, their backs against the legs of the settee, their legs stretched out on the floor. The boy died in seconds. I felt weary and sickened, as if the night had lasted a thousand years. I sat there watching them, the child drawing close to Lestat now, snuggling near him as he slipped his arm around her, though his indifferent eyes remained fixed on the corpse. Then he looked up at me.

" 'Where is Mamma?' asked the child softly. She had a voice equal to her physical beauty, clear like a little silver bell. It was sensual. She was sensual. Her eyes were as wide and clear as Babette's. You understand that I was barely aware of what all this meant. I knew what it might mean, but I was aghast. Now Lestat stood up and scooped her from the floor and came towards me. 'She's our daughter,' he said. 'You're going to live with us now.' He beamed at her, but his eyes were cold, as if it were all a horrible joke; then he looked at me, and his face had conviction. He pushed her towards me. I found her on my lap, my arms around her, feeling again how soft she was, how plump her skin was, like the skin of warm fruit, plums warmed by sunlight; her huge luminescent eyes were fixed on me with trusting curiosity. 'This is Louis, and I am Lestat,' he said to her, dropping down beside her. She looked about and said that it was a pretty room, very pretty, but she wanted her mamma. He had his comb out and was running it through her hair, holding the locks so as not to pull with the comb; her hair was untangling and becoming like satin. She was the most beautiful child I'd ever seen, and now she glowed with the cold fire of a vampire. Her eyes were a woman's eyes, I could see it already. She would become white and spare like us but not lose her shape. I understood now what Lestat had said about death, what he meant. I touched her neck where the two red puncture wounds were bleeding just a little. I took Lestat's handkerchief from the floor and touched it to her neck. 'Your mamma's left you with us. She wants you to be happy,' he was saying with that same immeasurable confidence. 'She knows we can make you very happy.'

"'I want some more,' she said, turning to the corpse on the floor.

"'No, not tonight; tomorrow night,' said Lestat. And he went to take the lady out of his coffin. The child slid off my lap, and I followed her. She stood watching as Lestat put the two ladies and the slave boy into the bed. He brought the covers up to their chin. 'Are they sick?' asked the child.

"'Yes, Claudia,' he said. 'They're sick and they're dead. You see, they die when we drink from them.' He came towards her and swung her up into his arms again. We stood there with her between us. I was mesmerized by her, by her *transformed,* by her every gesture. She was not a child any longer, she was a vampire child. 'Now, Louis was going to leave us,' said Lestat, his eyes moving from my face to hers. 'He was going to go away. But now he's not. Because he wants to stay and take care of you and make you happy.' He looked at me. 'You're not going, are you, Louis?'

" 'You bastard!' I whispered to him. 'You fiend!'

" 'Such language in front of your daughter,' he said.

" 'I'm not your daughter,' she said with the silvery voice. 'I'm my mamma's daughter.'

" 'No, dear, not anymore,' he said to her. He glanced at the window, and then he shut the bedroom door behind us and turned the key in the lock. 'You're our daughter, Louis's daughter and my daughter, do you see? Now, whom should you sleep with? Louis or me?' And then looking at me, he said, 'Perhaps you should sleep with Louis. After all, when I'm tired . . . I'm not so kind.' "

THE VAMPIRE STOPPED. The boy said nothing. "A child vampire!" he whispered finally. The vampire glanced up suddenly as though startled, though his body made no movement. He glared at the tape recorder as if it were something monstrous.

The boy saw that the tape was almost out. Quickly, he opened his brief case and drew out a new cassette, clumsily fitting it into place. He looked at the vampire as he pressed the record button. The vampire's face looked weary, drawn, his cheekbones more prominent

and his brilliant green eyes enormous. They had begun
at dark, which had come early on this San Francisco
winter night, and now it was just before ten P.M.
The vampire straightened and smiled and said calmly,
"We are ready to go on?"

"He'd done this to the little girl just to keep you
with him?" asked the boy.

"That is difficult to say. It was a statement. I'm convinced that Lestat was a person who preferred not to
think or talk about his motives or beliefs, even to himself. One of those people who must act. Such a person
must be pushed considerably before he will open up
and confess that there is method and thought to the
way he lives. That is what had happened that night
with Lestat. He'd been pushed to where he had to
discover even for himself why he lived as he did.
Keeping me with him, that was undoubtedly part of
what pushed him. But I think, in retrospect, that he
himself wanted to know his own reasons for killing,
wanted to examine his own life. He was discovering
when he spoke what he did believe. But he did indeed
want me to remain. He lived with me in a way he
could never have lived alone. And, as I've told you,
I was careful never to sign any property over to him,
which maddened him. That, he could not persuade
me to do." The vampire laughed suddenly. "Look at
all the other things he persuaded me to do! How
strange. He could persuade me to kill a child, but not
to part with my money." He shook his head. "But,"
he said, "it wasn't greed, really, as you can see. It was
fear of him that made me tight with him."

"You speak of him as if he were dead. You say
Lestat *was* this or *was* that. Is he dead?" asked the
boy.

"I don't know," said the vampire. "I think perhaps
he is. But I'll come to that. We were talking of
Claudia, weren't we? There was something else I
wanted to say about Lestat's motives that night. Lestat
trusted no one, as you see. He was like a cat, by his
own admission, a lone predator. Yet he had com-
municated with me that night; he had to some extent
exposed himself simply by telling the truth. He had

dropped his mockery, his condescension. He had forgotten his perpetual anger for just a little while. And this for Lestat was exposure. When we stood alone in that dark street, I felt in him a communion with another I hadn't felt since I died. I rather think that he ushered Claudia into vampirism for revenge."

"Revenge, not only on you but on the world," suggested the boy.

"Yes. As I said, Lestat's motives for everything revolved around revenge."

"Was it all started with the father? With the school?"

"I don't know. I doubt it," said the vampire. "But I want to go on."

"Oh, please go on. You have to go on! I mean, it's only ten o'clock." The boy showed his watch.

The vampire looked at it, and then he smiled at the boy. The boy's face changed. It was blank as if from some sort of shock. "Are you still afraid of me?" asked the vampire.

The boy said nothing, but he shrank slightly from the edge of the table. His body elongated, his feet moved out over the bare boards and then contracted.

"I should think you'd be very foolish if you weren't," said the vampire. *"But don't be.* Shall we go on?"

"Please," said the boy. He gestured towards the machine.

"Well," the vampire began, "our life was much changed with Mademoiselle Claudia, as you can imagine. Her body died, yet her senses awakened much as mine had. And I treasured in her the signs of this. But I was not aware for quite a few days how much I wanted her, wanted to talk with her and be with her. At first, I thought only of protecting her from Lestat. I gathered her into my coffin every morning and would not let her out of my sight with him if possible. This was what Lestat wanted, and he gave little suggestions that he might do her harm. 'A starving child is a frightful sight,' he said to me, 'a starving vampire even worse.' They'd hear her screams in Paris, he said, were he to lock her away to die. But all this was meant for me, to draw me close and keep me there. Afraid of

fleeing alone, I would not conceive of risking it with
Claudia. She was a child. She needed care.

"And there was much pleasure in caring for her.
She forgot her five years of mortal life at once, or so
it seemed, for she was mysteriously quiet. And from
time to time I even feared that she had lost all sense,
that the illness of her mortal life, combined with the
great vampire shock, might have robbed her of reason;
but this proved hardly the case. She was simply unlike Lestat and me to such an extent I couldn't comprehend her; for little child she was, but also fierce
killer now capable of the ruthless pursuit of blood with
all a child's demanding. And though Lestat still threatened me with danger to her, he did not threaten her at
all but was loving to her, proud of her beauty, anxious
to teach her that we must kill to live and that we ourselves could never die.

"The plague raged in the city then, as I've indicated,
and he took her to the stinking cemeteries where the
yellow fever and plague victims lay in heaps while
the sounds of shovels never ceased all through the day
and night. 'This is death,' he told her, pointing to the
decaying corpse of a woman, 'which we cannot suffer.
Our bodies will stay always as they are, fresh and
alive; but we must never hesitate to bring death, because it is how we live.' And Claudia gazed on this
with inscrutable liquid eyes.

"If there was not understanding in the early years,
there was no smattering of fear. Mute and beautiful,
she played with dolls, dressing, undressing them by
the hour. Mute and beautiful, she killed. And I, transformed by Lestat's instruction, was now to seek out
humans in much greater numbers. But it was not only
the killing of them that soothed some pain in me
which had been constant in the dark, still nights on
Pointe du Lac, when I sat with only the company of
Lestat and the old man; it was their great, shifting
numbers everywhere in streets which never grew quiet,
cabarets which never shut their doors, balls which
lasted till dawn, the music and laughter streaming out
of the open windows; people all around me now, my
pulsing victims, not seen with that great love I'd felt

for my sister and Babette, but with some new detachment and need. And I did kill them, kills infinitely varied and great distances apart, as I walked with the vampire's sight and light movement through this teeming, burgeoning city, my victims surrounding me, seducing me, inviting me to their supper tables, their carriages, their brothels. I lingered only a short while, long enough to take what I must have, soothed in my great melancholy that the town gave me an endless train of magnificent strangers.

"For that was it. I fed on strangers. I drew only close enough to see the pulsing beauty, the unique expression, the new and passionate voice, then killed before those feelings of revulsion could be aroused in me, that fear, that sorrow.

"Claudia and Lestat might hunt and seduce, stay long in the company of the doomed victim, enjoying the splendid humor in his unwitting friendship with death. But I still could not bear it. And so to me, the swelling population was a mercy, a forest in which I was lost, unable to stop myself, whirling too fast for thought or pain, accepting again and again the invitation to death rather than extending it.

"We lived meantime in one of my new Spanish town houses in the Rue Royale, a long, lavish upstairs flat above a shop I rented to a tailor, a hidden garden court behind us, a well secure against the street, with fitted wooden shutters and a barred carriage door—a place of far greater luxury and security than Pointe du Lac. Our servants were free people of color who left us to solitude before dawn for their own homes, and Lestat bought the very latest imports from France and Spain: crystal chandeliers and Oriental carpets, silk screens with painted birds of paradise, canaries singing in great domed, golden cages, and delicate marble Grecian gods and beautifully painted Chinese vases. I did not need the luxury anymore than I had needed it before, but I found myself enthralled with the new flood of art and craft and design, could stare at the intricate pattern of the carpets for hours, or watch the gleam of the lamplight change the somber colors of a Dutch painting.

"All this Claudia found wondrous, with the quiet awe of an unspoiled child, and marvelled when Lestat hired a painter to make the walls of her room a magical forest of unicorns and golden birds and laden fruit trees over sparkling streams.

"An endless train of dressmakers and shoemakers and tailors came to our flat to outfit Claudia in the best of children's fashions, so that she was always a vision, not just of child beauty, with her curling lashes and her glorious yellow hair, but of the taste of finely trimmed bonnets and tiny lace gloves, flaring velvet coats and capes, and sheer white puffed-sleeve gowns with gleaming blue sashes. Lestat played with her as if she were a magnificent doll, and I played with her as if she were a magnificent doll; and it was her pleading that forced me to give up my rusty black for dandy jackets and silk ties and soft gray coats and gloves and black capes. Lestat thought the best color at all times for vampires was black, possibly the only aesthetic principle he steadfastly maintained, but he wasn't opposed to anything which smacked of style and excess. He loved the great figure we cut, the three of us in our box at the new French Opera House or the Théâtre d'Orléans, to which we went as often as possible, Lestat having a passion for Shakespeare which surprised me, though he often dozed through the operas and woke just in time to invite some lovely lady to midnight supper, where he would use all his skill to make her love him totally, then dispatch her violently to heaven or hell and come home with her diamond ring to give to Claudia.

"And all this time I was educating Claudia, whispering in her tiny seashell ear that our eternal life was useless to us if we did not see the beauty around us, the creation of mortals everywhere; I was constantly sounding the depth of her still gaze as she took the books I gave her, whispered the poetry I taught her, and played with a light but confident touch her own strange, coherent songs on the piano. She could fall for hours into the pictures in a book and listen to me read until she sat so still the sight of her jarred me, made me put the book down, and just stare back at her across the lighted room; then she'd move, a doll coming to life, and say in the softest voice that I must read some more.

"And then strange things began to happen, for though she said little and was the chubby, round-fingered child still, I'd find her tucked in the arm of my chair reading the work of Aristotle or Boethius or a new novel just come over the Atlantic. Or pecking out the music of Mozart we'd only heard the night before with an infallible ear and a concentration that made her ghostly as she sat there hour after hour discovering the music—the melody, then the bass, and finally bringing it together. Claudia was mystery. It was not possible to know what she knew or did not know. And to watch her kill was chilling. She would sit alone in the dark square waiting for the kindly gentleman or woman to find her, her eyes more mind-less than I had ever seen Lestat's. Like a child numbed with fright she would whisper her plea for help to her gentle, admiring patrons, and as they carried her out of the square, her arms would fix about their necks, her tongue between her teeth, her vision glazed with consuming hunger. They found death fast in those first years, before she learned to play with them, to lead them to the doll shop or the café where they gave her steaming cups of chocolate or tea to ruddy her pale cheeks, cups she pushed away, waiting, waiting, as if feasting silently on their terrible kindness.

"But when that was done, she was my companion, my pupil, her long hours spent with me consuming faster and faster the knowledge I gave her, sharing with me some quiet understanding which could not include Lestat. At dawn she lay with me, her heart beating against my heart, and many times when I looked at her—when she was at her music or painting and didn't know I stood in the room—I thought of that singular experience I'd had with her and no other, that I had killed her, taken her life from her, had drunk all of her life's blood in that fatal embrace I'd lavished on so many others, others who lay now moldering in the damp earth. But she lived, she lived to put her arms around my neck and press her tiny cupid's bow to my lips and put her gleaming eye to my eye until our lashes touched and, laughing, we reeled about the room as if to the wildest waltz. Father and Daughter. Lover and Lover. You can imagine how well it was Lestat did not envy us this, but only smiled on it from afar, waiting until she came to him. Then he would take her out into the street and they would wave to me beneath the window, off to share what they shared: the hunt, the seduction, the kill.

"Years passed in this way. Years and years and years. Yet it wasn't until some time had passed that an obvious fact occurred to me about Claudia. I suppose from the expression on your face you've already guessed, and you wonder why I didn't guess. I can only tell you, time is not the same for me, nor was it for us then. Day did not link to day making a taut and jerking chain; rather, the moon rose over lapping waves."

"Her body!" the boy said. "She was never to grow up."

The vampire nodded. "She was to be the demon child forever," he said, his voice soft as if he wondered at it. "Just as I am the young man I was when I died. And Lestat? The same. But her mind. It was a vampire's mind. And I strained to know how she moved towards womanhood. She came to talk more, though she was never other than a reflective person and could listen to me patiently by the hour without interruption. Yet more and more her doll-like face seemed to possess two totally aware adult eyes, and innocence seemed lost somewhere with neglected toys and the loss of a certain patience. There was something dreadfully sensual about her lounging on the settee in a tiny nightgown of lace and stitched pearls; she became an eerie and powerful seductress, her voice as clear and sweet as ever, though it had a resonance which was womanish, a sharpness sometimes that proved shocking. After days of her usual quiet, she would scoff suddenly at Lestat's predictions about the war; or drinking blood from a crystal glass say that there were no books in the house, we must get more even if we had to steal them, and then coldly tell me of a library

she'd heard of, in a palatial mansion in the Faubourg
St.-Marie, a woman who collected books as if they
were rocks or pressed butterflies. She asked if I might
get her into the woman's bedroom.

"I was aghast at such moments; her mind was unpredictable, unknowable. But then she would sit on
my lap and put her fingers in my hair and doze there
against my heart, whispering to me softly I should
never be as grown up as she until I knew that killing
was the more serious thing, not the books, the music.
'Always the music . . .' she whispered. 'Doll, doll,' I
called her. That's what she was. A magic doll. Laughter
and infinite intellect and then the round-cheeked face,
the bud mouth. 'Let me dress you, let me brush your
hair,' I would say to her out of old habit, aware of her
smiling and watching me with the thin veil of boredom
over her expression. 'Do as you like,' she breathed into
my ear as I bent down to fasten her pearl buttons.
'Only kill with me tonight. You never let me see you
kill, Louis!'

"She wanted a coffin of her own now, which left me
more wounded than I would let her see. I walked out
after giving my gentlemanly consent; for how many
years had I slept with her as if she were part of me I
couldn't know. But then I found her near the Ursuline
Convent, an orphan lost in the darkness, and she ran
suddenly towards me and clutched at me with a human
desperation. 'I don't want it if it hurts you,' she confided
so softly that a human embracing us both could not
have heard her or felt her breath. 'I'll stay with you
always. But I must see it, don't you understand? A
coffin for a child.'

"We were to go to the coffinmaker's. A play, a
tragedy in one act: I to leave her in his little parlor
and confide to him in the anteroom that she was to
die. Talk of love, she must have the best, but she
must not know; and the coffinmaker, shaken with the
tragedy of it, must make it for her, picturing her laid
there on the white satin, dabbing a tear from his eye
despite all the years. . . .

"'But, why, Claudia . . .' I pleaded with her. I
loathed to do it, loathed cat and mouse with the help-

less human. But hopelessly her lover, I took her there and set her on the sofa, where she sat with folded hands in her lap, her tiny bonnet bent down, as if she didn't know what we whispered about her in the foyer. The undertaker was an old and greatly refined man of color who drew me swiftly aside lest 'the baby' should hear. 'But why must she die?' he begged me, as if I were God who ordained it. 'Her heart, she cannot live,' I said, the words taking on for me a peculiar power, a disturbing resonance. The emotion in his narrow, heavily lined face disturbed me; something came to my mind, a quality of light, a gesture, the sound of something . . . a child crying in a stench-filled room. Now he unlocked one after another of his long rooms and showed me the coffins, black lacquer and silver, she wanted that. And suddenly I found myself backing away from him out of the coffin-house, hurriedly taking her hand. 'The order's been taken,' I said to her. 'It's driving me mad!' I breathed the fresh air of the street as though I'd been suffocated and then I saw her compassionless face studying mine. She slipped her small gloved hand back into my own. 'I want it, Louis,' she explained patiently.

"And then one night she climbed the undertaker's stairs, Lestat beside her, for the coffin, and left the coffinmaker, unawares, dead across the dusty piles of papers on his desk. And there the coffin lay in our bedroom, where she watched it often by the hour when it was new, as if the thing were moving or alive or unfolded some mystery to her little by little, as things do which change. But she did not sleep in it. She slept with me.

"There were other changes in her. I cannot date them or put them in order. She did not kill indiscriminately. She fell into demanding patterns. Poverty began to fascinate her; she begged Lestat or me to take a carriage out through the Faubourg St.-Marie to the riverfront places where the immigrants lived. She seemed obsessed with the women and children. These things Lestat told me with great amusement, for I was loath to go and would sometimes not be persuaded under any circumstance. But Claudia had a family there which she took one by one. And she had asked to enter the cemetery of the suburb city of Lafayette and there roam the high marble tombs in search of those desperate men who, having no place else to sleep, spend what little they have on a bottle of wine, and crawl into a rotting vault. Lestat was impressed, overcome. What a picture he made of her, the infant death, he called her. Sister death, and sweet death; and for me, mockingly, he had the term with a sweeping bow, Merciful Death! which he said like a woman clapping her hands and shouting out a word of exciting gossip: oh, merciful heavens! so that I wanted to strangle him.

"But there was no quarrelling. We kept to ourselves. We had our adjustments. Books filled our long flat from floor to ceiling in row after row of gleaming leather volumes, as Claudia and I pursued our natural tastes and Lestat went about his lavish acquisitions. Until she began to ask questions."

The vampire stopped. And the boy looked as anxious as before, as if patience took the greatest effort. But the vampire had brought his long, white fingers together as if to make a church steeple and then folded them and pressed his palms tight. It was as if he'd forgotten the boy altogether. "I should have known," he said, "that it was inevitable, and I should have seen the signs of it coming. For I was so attuned to her; I loved her so completely; she was so much the companion of my every waking hour, the only companion that I had, other than death. I should have known. But something in me was conscious of an enormous gulf of darkness very close to us, as though we walked always near a sheer cliff and might see it suddenly but too late if we made the wrong turn or became too lost in our thoughts. Sometimes the physical world about me seemed insubstantial except for that darkness. As if a fault in the earth were about to open and I could see the great crack breaking down the Rue Royale, and all the buildings were falling to dust in the rumble. But worst of all, they were transparent, gossamer, like stage drops made of silk. Ah . . . I'm distracted. What do I say? That I ignored the signs in her, that I clung desperately to the happiness she'd given me. And still gave me; and ignored all else.

"But these were the signs. She grew cold to Lestat. She fell to staring at him for hours. When he spoke, often she didn't answer him, and one could hardly tell if it was contempt or that she didn't hear. And our fragile domestic tranquillity erupted with his outrage. He did not have to be loved, but he would not be ignored; and once he even flew at her, shouting that he would slap her, and I found myself in the wretched position of fighting him as I'd done years before she'd come to us. 'She's not a child any longer,' I whispered to him. 'I don't know what it is. She's a woman.' I urged him to take it lightly, and he affected disdain and ignored her in turn. But one evening he came in flustered and told me she'd followed him—though she'd refused to go with him to kill, she'd followed him afterwards. 'What's the matter with her!' he flared at me, as though I'd given birth to her and must know.

"And then one night our servants vanished. Two of the best maids we'd ever retained, a mother and daughter. The coachman was sent to their house only to report they'd disappeared, and then the father was at our door, pounding the knocker. He stood back on the brick sidewalk regarding me with that grave suspicion that sooner or later crept into the faces of all mortals who knew us for any length of time, the forerunner of death, as pallor might be to a fatal fever; and I tried to explain to him they had not been here, mother or daughter, and we must begin some search.

" 'It's she!' Lestat hissed from the shadows when I shut the gate. 'She's done something to them and brought risk for us all. I'll make her tell me!' And he pounded up the spiral stairs from the courtyard. I knew that she'd gone, slipped out while I was at the gate, and I knew something else also: that a vague stench came across the courtyard from the shut, unused kitchen, a stench that mingled uneasily with the honeysuckle—the stench of graveyards. I heard Lestat com-

ing down as I approached the warped shutters, locked
with rust to the small brick building. No food was
ever prepared there, no work ever done, so that it lay
like an old brick vault under the tangles of honeysuckle. The shutters came loose, the nails having turned
to dust, and I heard Lestat's gasp as we stepped into
the reeking dark. There they lay on the bricks, mother
and daughter together, the arm of the mother fastened
around the waist of the daughter, the daughter's head
bent against the mother's breast, both foul with feces
and swarming with insects. A great cloud of gnats rose
as the shutter fell back, and I waved them away from
me in a convulsive disgust. Ants crawled undisturbed
over the eyelids, the mouths of the dead pair, and in
the moonlight I could see the endless map of silvery
paths of snails. 'Damn her!' Lestat burst out, and I
grabbed his arm and held him fast, pitting all my
strength against him. 'What do you mean to do with
her!' I insisted. 'What can you do? She's not a child
anymore that will do what we say simply because we
say it. We must teach her.'

    " 'She knows!' He stood back from me brushing his
coat. 'She knows! She's known for years what to do!
What can be risked and what cannot. I won't have her
do this without my permission! I won't tolerate it.'

    " 'Then, are you master of us all? You didn't teach
her that. Was she supposed to imbibe it from my
quiet subservience? I don't think so. She sees herself as
equal to us now, and us as equal to each other. I tell
you we must reason with her, instruct her to respect
what is ours. As all of us should respect it.'

    "He stalked off, obviously absorbed in what I'd said,
though he would give no admission of it to me. And
he took his vengeance to the city. Yet when he came
home, fatigued and satiated, she was still not there.
He sat against the velvet arm of the couch and stretched
his long legs out on the length of it. 'Did you bury
them?' he asked me.

    " 'They're gone,' I said. I did not care to say even
to myself that I had burned their remains in the old
unused kitchen stove. 'But there is the father to deal
with, and the brother,' I said to him. I feared his

temper. I wished at once to plan some way to quickly dispose of the whole problem. But he said now that the father and the brother were no more, that death had come to dinner in their small house near the ramparts and stayed to say grace when everyone was done. 'Wine,' he whispered now, running his finger on his lip. 'Both of them had drunk too much wine. I found myself tapping the fence posts with a stick to make a tune,' he laughed. 'But I don't like it, the dizziness. Do you like it?' And when he looked at me I had to smile at him because the wine was working in him and he was mellow; and in that moment when his face looked warm and reasonable, I leaned over and said, 'I hear Claudia's tap on the stairs. Be gentle with her. It's all done.'

"She came in then, with her bonnet ribbons undone and her little boots caked with dirt. I watched them tensely, Lestat with a sneer on his lips, she as unconscious of him as if he weren't there. She had a bouquet of white chrysanthemums in her arms, such a large bouquet it made her all the more a small child. Her bonnet fell back now, hung on her shoulder for an instant, and then fell to the carpet. And all through her golden hair I saw the narrow petals of the chrysanthemums. 'Tomorrow is the Feast of All Saints,' she said. 'Do you know?'

" 'Yes,' I said to her. It is the day in New Orleans when all the faithful go to the cemeteries to care for the graves of their loved ones. They whitewash the plaster walls of the vaults, clean the names cut into the marble slabs. And finally they deck the tombs with flowers. In the St. Louis Cemetery, which was very near our house, in which all the great Louisiana families were buried, in which my own brother was buried, there were even little iron benches set before the graves where the families might sit to receive the other families who had come to the cemetery for the same purpose. It was a festival in New Orleans; a celebration of death, it might have seemed to tourists who didn't understand it, but it was a celebration of the life after. 'I bought this from one of the vendors,' Claudia said. Her voice was soft and inscrutable. Her eyes opaque and without emotion.

" 'For the two you left in the kitchen!' Lestat said fiercely. She turned to him for the first time, but she said nothing. She stood there staring at him as if she'd never seen him before. And then she took several steps towards him and looked at him, still as if she were positively examining him. I moved forward. I could feel his anger. Her coldness. And now she turned to me. And then, looking from one to the other of us, she asked:

" 'Which of you did it? *Which of you made me what I am?'*

"I could not have been more astonished at anything she might have said or done. And yet it was inevitable that her long silence would thus be broken. She seemed very little concerned with me, though. Her eyes fixed on Lestat. 'You speak of us as if we always existed as we are now,' she said, her voice soft, measured, the child's tone rounded with the woman's seriousness. 'You speak of them out there as mortals, us as vampires. But it was not always so. Louis had a mortal sister, I remember her. And there is a picture of her in his trunk. I've seen him look at it! He was mortal the same as she; and so was I. Why else this size, this shape?' She opened her arms now and let the chrysanthemums fall to the floor. I whispered her name. I think I meant to distract her. It was impossible. The tide had turned. Lestat's eyes burned with a keen fascination, a malignant pleasure.

" 'You made us what we are, didn't you?' she accused him.

"He raised his eyebrows now in mock amazement. 'What you are?' he asked. 'And would you be something other than what you are!' He drew up his knees and leaned forward, his eyes narrow. 'Do you know how long it's been? Can you picture yourself? Must I find a hag to show you your mortal countenance now if I had let you alone?'

"She turned away from him, stood for a moment as if she had no idea what she would do, and then she moved towards the chair beside the fireplace and, climbing on it, curled up like the most helpless child. She brought her knees up close to her, her velvet coat open, her silk dress tight around her knees, and she stared at the ashes in the hearth. But there was nothing helpless about her stare. Her eyes had independent life, as if the body were possessed.

" 'You could be dead by now if you were mortal!' Lestat insisted to her, pricked by her silence. He drew his legs around and set his boots on the floor. 'Do you hear me? Why do you ask me this now? Why do you make such a thing of it? You've known all your life you're a vampire.' And so he went on in a tirade, saying much the same things he'd said to me many times over: know your nature, kill, be what you are. But all of this seemed strangely beside the point. For Claudia had no qualms about killing. She sat back now and let her head roll slowly to where she could see him across from her. She was studying him again, as if he were a puppet on strings. 'Did you do it to me? And how?' she asked, her eyes narrowing. 'How did you do it?'

" 'And why should I tell you? It's my power.'

" 'Why yours alone?' she asked, her voice icy, her eyes heartless. *'How was it done?'* she demanded suddenly in rage.

"It was electric. He rose from the couch, and I was on my feet immediately, facing him. 'Stop her!' he said to me. He wrung his hands. 'Do something about her! I can't endure her!' And then he started for the door, but turned and, coming back, drew very close so that he towered over Claudia, putting her in a deep shadow. She glared up at him fearlessly, her eyes moving back and forth over his face with total detachment. 'I can undo what I did. Both to you and to him,' he said to her, his finger pointing at me across the room. 'Be glad I made you what you are,' he sneered. 'Or I'll break you in a thousand pieces!' "

"Well, the peace of the house was destroyed, though there was quiet. Days passed and she asked no questions, though now she was deep into books of the occult, of witches and witchcraft, and of vampires. This was mostly fancy, you understand. Myth, tales, sometimes mere romantic horror tales. But she read it all. Till dawn she read, so that I had to go and collect her and bring her to bed.

"Lestat, meantime, hired a butler and maid and had a team of workers in to make a great fountain in the courtyard with a stone nymph pouring water eternal from a widemouthed shell. He had goldfish brought and boxes of rooted water lilies set into the fountain so their blossoms rested upon the surface and shivered in the ever-moving water.

"A woman had seen him kill on the Nyades Road, which ran to the town of Carrolton, and there were stories of it in the papers, associating him with a haunted house near Nyades and Melpomene, all of which delighted him. He was the Nyades Road ghost for some time, though it finally fell to the back pages; and then he performed another grisly murder in another public place and set the imagination of New Orleans to working. But all this had about it some quality of fear. He was pensive, suspicious, drew close to me constantly to ask where Claudia was, where she'd gone, and what she was doing.

" 'She'll be all right,' I assured him, though I was estranged from her and in agony, as if she'd been my bride. She hardly saw me now, as she'd not seen Lestat before, and she might walk away while I spoke to her.

" 'She had better be all right!" he said nastily.

" 'And what will you do if she's not?' I asked, more in fear than accusation.

"He looked up at me, with his cold gray eyes. 'You take care of her, Louis. You talk to her!' he said. 'Everything was perfect, and now this. There's no need for it.'

"But it was my choice to let her come to me, and she did. It was early one evening when I'd just awakened. The house was dark. I saw her standing by the French windows; she wore puffed sleeves and a pink sash, and was watching with lowered lashes the evening rush in the Rue Royale. I could hear Lestat in his room, the sound of water splashing from his pitcher. The faint smell of his cologne came and went like the sound of music from the café two doors down from us. 'He'll tell me nothing,' she said softly. I hadn't realized she knew that I had opened my eyes. I came towards her and knelt beside her. 'You'll tell me, won't you? How it was done.'

" 'Is this what you truly want to know?' I asked, searching her face. 'Or is it why it was done to you . . . and what you were before? I don't understand what you mean by "how," for if you mean how was it done so that you in turn may do it. . . .'

" 'I don't even know what it is. What you're saying,' she said with a touch of coldness. Then she turned full around and put her hands on my face. 'Kill with me tonight,' she whispered as sensuously as a lover. 'And tell me all that you know. What are we? Why are we not like them?' She looked down into the street.

" 'I don't know the answers to your questions,' I said to her. Her face contorted suddenly, as if she were straining to hear me over a sudden noise. And then she shook her head. But I went on. 'I wonder the same things you wonder. I do not know. How I was made, I'll tell you that . . . that Lestat did it to me. But the real "how" of it, I don't know!' Her face had that same look of strain. I was seeing in it the first traces of fear, or something worse and deeper than fear. 'Claudia,' I said to her, putting my hands over her hands and pressing them gently against my skin. 'Lestat has one wise thing to tell you. Don't ask these questions. You've been my companion for countless years in my search for all that I could learn of mortal life and mortal creation. Don't be my companion now in this anxiety. He can't give us the answers. And I have none.'

"I could see she could not accept this, but I hadn't expected the convulsive turning away, the violence with which she tore at her own hair for an instant and then stopped as if the gesture were useless, stupid. It filled me with apprehension. She was looking at the sky. It was smoky, starless, the clouds blowing fast from the direction of the river. She made a sudden movement of her lips as if she'd bitten into them, then she turned to me and, still whispering, she said, 'Then he made me . . . he did it . . . you did not!' There was something so dreadful about her expression, I'd left her before I meant to do it. I was standing before the fireplace lighting a single candle in front of the tall mirror. And there suddenly, I saw something which startled me, gathering out of the gloom first as a hideous mask, then becoming its three-dimensional reality: a weathered skull. I stared at it. It smelled faintly of the earth still, but had been scrubbed. 'Why don't you answer me?' she was asking. I heard Lestat's door open. He would go out to kill at once, at least to find the kill. I would not.

"I would let the first hours of the evening accumulate in quiet, as hunger accumulated in me, till the drive grew almost too strong, so that I might give myself to it all the more completely, blindly. I heard her question again clearly, as though it had been floating in the air like the reverberation of a bell . . . and felt my heart pounding. 'He did make me, of course! He said so himself. But you hide something from me. Something he hints at when I question him. He says that it could not have been done without you!'

"I found myself staring at the skull, yet hearing her as if the words were lashing me, lashing me to make me turn around and face the lash. The thought went through me more like a flash of cold than a thought, that nothing should remain of me now but such a skull. I turned around and saw in the light from the street her eyes, like two dark flames in her white face. A doll from whom someone had cruelly ripped the eyes and replaced them with a demonic fire. I found myself moving towards her, whispering her name, some thought forming on my lips, then dying, coming towards her, then away from her, fussing for her coat and her hat. I saw a tiny glove on the floor which was phosphorescent in the shadows, and for just a moment I thought it a tiny, severed hand.

" 'What's the matter with you . . .?' She drew nearer, looking up into my face. 'What has *always* been the matter? Why do you stare at the skull like that, at the glove?' She asked this gently, but . . . not gently enough.

"There was a slight calculation in her voice, an unreachable detachment.

" 'I need you,' I said to her, without wanting to say it. 'I cannot bear to lose you. You're the only companion I have in immortality.'

" 'But surely there must be others! Surely we are not the only vampires on earth!' I heard her saying it as I had said it, heard my own words coming back to me now on the tide of her self-awareness, her searching. But there's no pain, I thought suddenly. There's urgency, heartless urgency. I looked down at her. 'Aren't you the same as I?' She looked at me. 'You've taught me all I know!'

" 'Lestat taught you to kill.' I fetched the glove. 'Here, come . . . let's go out. I want to go out. . . .' I was stammering, trying to force the gloves on her. I lifted the great curly mass of her hair and placed it gently over her coat. 'But you taught me to see!' she said. 'You taught me the words vampire eyes,' she said. 'You taught me to drink the world, to hunger for more than . . .'

" 'I never meant those words that way, vampire eyes,' I said to to her. 'It has a different ring when you say it. . . .' She was tugging at me, trying to make me look at her. 'Come,' I said to her, 'I've something to show you. . . .' And quickly I led her down the passage and down the spiral stairs through the dark courtyard. But I no more knew what I had to show her, really, than I knew where I was going. Only that I had to move toward it with a sublime and doomed instinct.

"We rushed through the early evening city, the sky overhead a pale violet now that the clouds were gone, the stars small and faint, the air around us sultry and fragrant even as we moved away from the spacious gardens, towards those mean and narrow streets where the flowers erupt in the cracks of the stones, and the huge oleander shoots out thick, waxen stems of white and pink blooms, like a monstrous weed in the empty lots. I heard the staccato of Claudia's steps as she rushed beside me, never once asking me to slacken my pace; and she stood finally, her face infinitely patient, looking up at me in a dark and narrow street where a few old slope-roofed French houses remained among the Spanish façades, ancient little houses, the plaster blistered from the moldering brick beneath. I had found the house now by a blind effort, aware that I had always known where it was and avoided it, always turned before this dark lampless corner, not wishing to pass the low window where I'd first heard Claudia cry. The house was standing still. Sunk lower than it was in those days, the alley way crisscrossed with sagging cords of laundry, the weeds high along the low foundation, the two dormer windows broken and patched with cloth. I touched the shutters. 'It was here I first saw you,' I said to her, thinking to tell it to her so she would understand, yet feeling now the chill of her gaze, the distance of her stare. 'I heard you crying. You were there in a room with your mother. And your mother was dead. Dead for days, and you didn't know. You clung to her, whining . . . crying pitifully, your body white and feverish and hungry. You were trying to wake her from the dead, you were hugging her for warmth, for fear. It was almost morning and . . .'

"I put my hand to my temples. 'I opened the shutters . . . I came into the room. I felt pity for you. Pity. But . . . something else.'

"I saw her lips slack, her eyes wide. 'You . . . fed on me?' she whispered. 'I was your victim!'

" 'Yes!' I said to her. 'I did it.'

"There was a moment so elastic and painful as to be unbearable. She stood stark-still in the shadows, her huge eyes gathering the light, the warm air rising suddenly with a soft noise. And then she turned. I heard the clicking of her slippers as she ran. And ran. And ran. I stood frozen, hearing the sound grow smaller and smaller; and then I turned, the fear in me unravelling, growing huge and insurmountable, and I ran after her. It was unthinkable that I not catch her, that I not overtake her at once and tell her that I loved her, must have her, must keep her, and every second that I ran headlong down the dark street after her was like her slipping away from me drop by drop; my heart was pounding, unfed, pounding and rebelling against the strain. Until I came suddenly to a dead stop. She stood beneath a lamppost, staring mutely, as if she didn't know me. I took her small waist in both hands and lifted her into the light. She studied me, her face contorted, her head turning as if she wouldn't give me her direct glance, as if she must deflect an overpowering feeling of revulsion. 'You killed me,' she whispered. 'You took my life!'

" 'Yes,' I said to her, holding her so that I could feel her heart pounding. 'Rather, I tried to take it. To drink it away. But you had a heart like no other heart I've ever felt, a heart that beat and beat until I had to let you go, had to cast you away from me lest you quickened my pulse till I would die. And it was Lestat who found me out; Louis the sentimentalist, the fool, feasting on a golden-haired child, a Holy Innocent, *a little girl*. He brought you back from the hospital where they'd put you, and I never knew what he meant to do except teach me my nature. "Take her, finish it," he said. And I felt that passion for you again. Oh, I know I've lost you now forever. I can see it in your eyes! You look at me as you look at mortals, from aloft, from some region of cold self-sufficiency I can't understand. But I did it. I felt it for you again, a vile unsupportable hunger for your hammering heart, this cheek, this skin. You were pink and fragrant as mortal children are, sweet with the bite of salt and dust. I held you again, I took you again. And when I thought your heart would kill me and I didn't care, he parted us and, gashing his own wrist, gave it to you to drink. And drink you did. And drink and drink until you nearly drained him and he was reeling. But you were a vampire then. And that very night you drank a human's blood and have every night thereafter.'

"Her face had not changed. The flesh was like the wax of ivory candles; only the eyes showed life. There was nothing more to say to her. I set her down. 'I took your life,' I said. 'He gave it back to you.'

" 'And here it is,' she said under her breath. 'And I hate you both!' "

The vampire stopped.

"But why did you tell her?" asked the boy after a respectful pause.

"How could I not tell her?" The vampire looked up in mild astonishment. "She had to know it. She had to weigh one thing against the other. It was not as if Lestat had taken her full from life as he had taken me; I had stricken her. She would have died! There would have been no mortal life for her. But what's the difference? For all of us it's a matter of years, dying! So what she saw more graphically then was what all men knew: that death will come inevitably, unless one chooses . . . this!" He opened his white hands now and looked at the palms.

"And did you lose her? Did she go?"

"Go! Where would she have gone? She was a child no bigger than that. Who would have sheltered her? Would she have found some vault, like a mythical vampire, lying down with worms and ants by day and rising to haunt some small cemetery and its surroundings? But that's not why she didn't go. Something in her was as akin to me as anything in her could have been. That thing in Lestat was the same. We could not bear to live alone! We needed our little company! A wilderness of mortals surrounded us, groping, blind, preoccupied, and the brides and bridegrooms of death.

" 'Locked together in hatred,' she said to me calmly afterwards. I found her by the empty hearth, picking the small blossoms from a long stem of lavender. I was so relieved to see her there that I would have done anything, said anything. And when I heard her ask me in a low voice if I would tell her all I knew, I did this gladly. For all the rest was nothing compared to that old secret, that I had claimed her life. I told her of myself as I've told you, of how Lestat came to me and what went on the night he carried her from the little hospital. She asked no questions and only occasionally looked up from her flowers. And then, when it was finished and I was sitting there, staring again at that wretched skull and listening to the soft slithering of the petals of the flowers on her dress and feeling a dull misery in my limbs and mind, she said to me, 'I don't despise you!' I wakened. She slipped off the high, rounded damask cushion and came towards me, covered with the scent of flowers, the petals in her hand. 'Is this the aroma of mortal child?' she whispered. 'Louis. Lover.' I remember holding her and burying my head in her small chest, crushing her bird-shoulders, her small hands working into my hair, soothing me, holding me. 'I was mortal to you,' she said, and when I lifted my eyes I saw her smiling; but the softness on her lips was evanescent, and in a moment she was looking past me like someone listening for faint, important music. 'You gave me your immortal kiss,' she said, though not to me, but to herself. 'You loved me with your vampire nature.'

" 'I love you now with my human nature, if ever I had it,' I said to her.

" 'Ah yes . . .' she answered, still musing. 'Yes, and that's your flaw, and why your face was miserable when I said as humans say, "I hate you," and why you look at me as you do now. Human nature. I have no human nature. And no short story of a mother's corpse and hotel rooms where children learn monstrosity can give me one. I have none. Your eyes grow cold with fear when I say this to you. Yet I have your tongue. Your passion for the truth. Your need to drive the needle of the mind right to the heart of it all, like the beak of the hummingbird, who beats so wild and fast that mortals might think he had no tiny feet, could never set, just go from quest to quest, going again and again for the heart of it. I am your vampire self more than you are. And now the sleep of sixty-five years has ended.'

"The sleep of sixty-five years has ended! I heard her say it, disbelieving, not wanting to believe she knew and meant precisely what she'd said. For it had been exactly that since the night I tried to leave Lestat and failed and, falling in love with her, forgot my teeming

brain, my awful questions. And now she had the awful questions on her lips and must know. She'd strolled slowly to the center of the room and strewn the crumpled lavender all around her. She broke the brittle stem and touched it to her lips. And having heard the whole story said, 'He made me then . . . to be your companion. No chains could have held you in your loneliness, and he could give you nothing. He gives me nothing. . . . I used to think him charming. I liked the way he walked, the way he tapped the flagstones with his walking stick and swung me in his arms. And the abandon with which he killed, which was as I felt. But I no longer find him charming. And you never have. And we've been his puppets, you and I; you remaining to take care of him, and I your saving companion. Now's time to end it, Louis. Now's time to leave him.'

"Time to leave him.

"I hadn't thought of it, dreamed of it in so long; I'd grown accustomed to him, as if he were a condition of life itself. I could hear a vague mingling of sounds now, which meant he had entered the carriage way, that he would soon be on the back stairs. And I thought of what I always felt when I heard him coming, a vague anxiety, a vague need. And then the thought of being free of him forever rushed over me like water I'd forgotten, waves and waves of cool water. I was standing now, whispering to her that he was coming.

" 'I know,' she smiled. 'I heard him when he turned the far corner.'

" 'But he'll never let us leave,' I whispered, though I'd caught the implication of her words; her vampire sense was keen. She stood *en garde* magnificently. 'But you don't know him if you think he'll let us leave,' I said to her, alarmed at her self-confidence. 'He will not let us go.'

"And she, still smiling, said, 'Oh . . . *really?*' "

"It was agreed then to make plans. At once. The following night my agent came with his usual complaints about doing business by the light of one wretched candle and took my explicit orders for an ocean crossing. Claudia and I would go to Europe, on the first available ship, regardless of what port we had to settle for. And paramount was that an important chest be shipped with us, a chest which might have to be fetched carefully from our house during the day and put on board, not in the freight but in our cabin. And then there were arrangements for Lestat. I had planned to leave him the rents for several shops and town houses and a small construction company operating in the Faubourg Marigny. I put my signature to these things readily. I wanted to buy our freedom: to convince Lestat we wanted only to take a trip together and that he could remain in the style to which he was accustomed; he would have his own money and need come to me for nothing. For all these years, I'd kept him dependent on me. Of course, he demanded his funds from me as if I were merely his banker, and thanked me with the most acrimonious words at his command; but he loathed his dependence. I hoped to deflect his suspicion by playing to his greed. And, convinced that he could read any emotion in my face, I was more than fearful. I did not believe it would be possible to escape him. Do you understand what that means? I acted as though I believed it, but I did not.

"Claudia, meantime, was flirting with disaster, her equanimity overwhelming to me as she read her vampire books and asked Lestat questions. She remained undisturbed by his caustic outbursts, sometimes asking the same question over and over again in different ways and carefully considering what little information he might let escape in spite of himself. 'What vampire made you what you are?' she asked, without looking up from her book and keeping her lids lowered under his onslaught. 'Why do you never talk about him?' she went on, as if his fierce objections were thin air. She seemed immune to his irritation.

" 'You're greedy, both of you!' he said the next night as he paced back and forth in the dark of the center of the room, turning a vengeful eye on Claudia, who was fitted into her corner, in the circle of her candle flame, her books in stacks about her. 'Immortality is not enough for you! No, you would look the Gift Horse of God in the mouth! I could offer it to any man out there in the street and he would jump for it . . .'

" 'Did you jump for it?' she asked softly, her lips barely moving.

" '. . . but you, you would know the *reason* for it. Do you want to end it? I can give you death more easily than I gave you life!' He turned to me, her fragile flame throwing his shadow across me. It made a halo around his blond hair and left his face, except for the gleaming cheekbone, dark. 'Do you want death?'

" 'Consciousness is not death,' she whispered.

" 'Answer me! Do you want death!'

" 'And you give all these things. They proceed from you. Life and death,' she whispered, mocking him.

" 'I have,' he said. 'I do.'

" 'You know nothing,' she said to him gravely, her voice so low that the slightest noise from the street interrupted it, might carry her words away, so that I found myself straining to hear her against myself as I lay with my head back against the chair. 'And suppose the vampire who made you knew nothing, and the vampire who made that vampire knew nothing, and the vampire before him knew nothing, and so it goes back and back, nothing proceeding from nothing, until there is nothing! And we must live with the knowledge that there is no knowledge.'

" 'Yes!' he cried out suddenly, his hands out, his voice tinged with something other than anger.

"He was silent. She was silent. He turned, slowly, as if I'd made some movement which alerted him, as if I were rising behind him. It reminded me of the way humans turn when they feel my breath against them and know suddenly that where they thought themselves to be utterly alone . . . that moment of awful suspicion before they see my face and gasp. He was looking at me now, and I could barely see his lips moving. And then I sensed it. He was afraid. Lestat afraid.

"And she was staring at him with the same level gaze, evincing no emotion, no thought.

" 'You infected her with this . . .' he whispered.

"He struck a match now with a sharp crackle and lit the mantel candles, lifted the smoky shades of the lamps, went around the room making light, until Claudia's small flame took on a solidity and he stood with his back to the marble mantel looking from light to light as if they restored some peace. 'I'm going out,' he said.

"She rose the instant he had reached the street, and suddenly she stopped in the center of the room and stretched, her tiny back arched, her arms straight up into small fists, her eyes squeezed shut for a moment and then wide open as if she were waking to the room from a dream. There was something obscene about her gesture; the room seemed to shimmer with Lestat's fear, echo with his last response. It *demanded* her attention. I must have made some involuntary movement to turn away from her, because she was standing at the arm of my chair now and pressing her hand flat upon my book, a book I hadn't been reading for hours. 'Come out with me.'

" 'You were right. He knows nothing. There is nothing he can tell us,' I said to her.

" 'Did you ever really think that he did?' she asked me in the same small voice. 'We'll find others of our kind,' she said. 'We'll find them in central Europe. That is where they live in such numbers that the stories, both fiction and fact, fill volumes. I'm convinced it was from there that all vampires came, if they came from any place at all. We've tarried too long with him. Come out. Let the flesh instruct the mind.'

"I think I felt a tremor of delight when she said these words, *Let the flesh instruct the mind.* 'Put books aside and kill,' she was whispering to me. I followed her down the stairs, across the courtyard and down a narrow alley to another street. Then she turned with outstretched arms for me to pick her up and carry her, though, of course, she was not tired; she wanted only to be near my ear, to clutch my neck. 'I haven't told him my plan, about the voyage, the money,' I was saying to her, conscious of something about her that was beyond me as she rode my measured steps, weightless in my arms.

" 'He killed the other vampire,' she said.

" 'No, why do you say this?' I asked her. But it wasn't the saying of it that disturbed me, stirred my soul as if it were a pool of water longing to be still. I felt as if she were moving me slowly towards something, as if she were the pilot of our slow walk through the dark street. 'Because I know it now,' she said with authority. 'The vampire made a slave of him, and he would no more be a slave than I would be a slave, and so he killed him. Killed him before he knew what he might know, and then in panic made a slave of you. And you've been his slave.'

" 'Never really . . .' I whispered to her. I felt the press of her cheek against my temple. She was cold and needed the kill. 'Not a slave. Just some sort of mindless accomplice,' I confessed to her, confessed to myself. I could feel the fever for the kill rising in me, a knot of hunger in my insides, a throbbing in the temples, as if the veins were contracting and my body might become a map of tortured vessels.

" 'No, slave,' she persisted in her grave monotone, as though thinking aloud, the words revelations, pieces of a puzzle. 'And I shall free us both.'

"I stopped. Her hand pressed me, urged me on. We were walking down the long wide alley beside the cathedral, towards the lights of Jackson Square, the water rushing fast in the gutter down the center of the alley, silver in the moonlight. She said, *I will kill him.*

"I stood still at the end of the alley. I felt her shift in my arm, move down as if she could accomplish being free of me without the awkward aid of my hands. I set her on the stone sidewalk. I said no to her, I shook my head. I had that feeling then which I described before, that the building around me—the Cabildo, the cathedral, the apartments along the square—all this was silk and illusion and would ripple suddenly in a horrific wind, and a chasm would open in the earth that was the reality. 'Claudia,' I gasped, turning away from her.

" 'And why not kill him!' she said now, her voice rising, silvery and finally shrill. 'I have no use for him! I can get nothing from him! And he causes me pain, which I will not abide!'

" 'And if he had so little use for us!' I said to her. But the vehemence was false. Hopeless. She was at a distance from me now, small shoulders straight and determined, her pace rapid, like a little girl who, walking out on Sundays with her parents, wants to walk ahead and pretend she is all alone. 'Claudia!' I called after her, catching up with her in a stride. I reached for the small waist and felt her stiffen as if she had become iron. 'Claudia, you cannot kill him!' I whispered. She moved backwards, skipping, clicking on the stones, and moved out into the open street. A cabriolet rolled past us with a sudden surge of laughter and the clatter of horses and wooden wheels. The street was suddenly silent. I reached out for her and moved forward over an immense space and found her standing at the gate of Jackson Square, hands gripping the wrought-iron bars. I drew down close to her. 'I don't care what you feel, what you say, you cannot mean to kill him,' I said to her.

" 'And why not? Do you think him so strong!' she said, her eyes on the statue in the square, two immense pools of light.

" 'He is stronger than you know! Stronger than you dream! How do you mean to kill him? You can't measure his skill. You don't know!' I pleaded with her but could see her utterly unmoved, like a child staring in fascination through the window of a toy shop. Her tongue moved suddenly between her teeth and touched her lower lip in a strange flicker that sent a mild shock through my body. I tasted blood. I felt something palpable and helpless in my hands. I wanted to kill. I could smell and hear humans on the paths of the square, moving about the market, along the levee. I was about to take her, making her look at me, shake her if I had to, to make her listen, when she turned to me with her great liquid eyes. 'I love you, Louis,' she said.

" 'Then listen to me, Claudia, I beg you,' I whispered, holding her, pricked suddenly by a nearby collection of whispers, the slow, rising articulation of human speech over the mingled sounds of the night. 'He'll destroy you if you try to kill him. There is no way you can do such a thing for sure. You don't know how. And pitting yourself against him you'll lose everything. Claudia, I can't bear this.'

"There was a barely perceptible smile on her lips. 'No, Louis,' she whispered. 'I can kill him. And I want to tell you something else now, a secret between you and me.'

"I shook my head but she pressed even closer to me, lowering her lids so that her rich lashes almost brushed the roundness of her cheeks. 'The secret is, Louis, that I want to kill him. I will enjoy it!'

"I knelt beside her, speechless, her eyes studying me as they'd done so often in the past; and then she said, 'I kill humans every night. I seduce them, draw them close to me, with an insatiable hunger, a constant never-ending search for something . . . something, I don't know what it is . . .' She brought her fingers to her lips now and pressed her lips, her mouth partly open so I could see the gleam of her teeth. 'And I care nothing about them—where they came from, where they would go—if I did not meet them on the way. But I dislike him! I *want* him dead and will have him dead. I shall enjoy it.'

" 'But Claudia, he is not mortal. He's immortal. No illness can touch him. Age has no power over him. You threaten a life which might endure to the end of the world!'

" 'Ah, yes, that's it, precisely!' she said with reverential awe. 'A lifetime that might have endured for centuries. Such blood, such power. Do you think I'll possess his power and my own power when I take him?'

"I was enraged now. I rose suddenly and turned away from her. I could hear the whispering of humans near me. They were whispering of the father and the daughter, of some frequent sight of loving devotion. I realized they were talking of us.

" 'It's not necessary,' I said to her. 'It goes beyond all need, all common sense, all . . .'

" 'What! Humanity? He's a killer!' she hissed. 'Lone predator!' She repeated his own term, mocking it. 'Don't interfere with me or seek to know the time I choose to do it, nor try to come between us. . . .' She raised her hand now to hush me and caught mine in an iron grasp, her tiny fingers biting into my tight, tortured flesh. 'If you do, you will bring me destruction by your interference. I can't be discouraged.'

"She was gone then in a flurry of bonnet ribbons and clicking slippers. I turned, paying no attention to where I went, wishing the city would swallow me, conscious now of the hunger rising to overtake reason. I was almost loath to put an end to it. I needed to let the lust, the excitement blot out all consciousness, and I thought of the kill over and over and over, walking slowly up this street and down the next, moving inexorably towards it, saying, It's a string which is pulling me through the labyrinth. I am not pulling the string. The string is pulling me. . . . And then I stood in the Rue Conti listening to a dull thundering, a familiar sound. It was the fencers above in the salon, advancing on the hollow wooden floor, forward, back again, scuttling, and the silver zinging of the foils. I stood back against the wall, where I could see them through the high naked windows, the young men duelling late into the night, left arm poised like the arm of a dancer, grace advancing towards death, grace thrusting for the heart, images of the young Freniere now driving the silver blade forward, now being pulled by it towards hell. Someone had come down the narrow wooden steps to the street—a young boy, a boy so young he had the smooth, plump cheeks of a child; his face was pink and flushed from the fencing, and beneath his smart gray coat and ruffled shirt there was the sweet smell of cologne and salt. I could feel his heat as he emerged from the dim light of the stairwell. He was laughing to himself, talking almost inaudibly to himself, his brown hair falling down over his eyes as he went along, shaking his head, the whispers rising, then falling off. And then he stopped short, his eyes on me. He stared, and his eyelids quivered and he laughed quickly, nervously. 'Excuse me!' he said now in French. 'You gave me a start!' And then, just as he moved to make a ceremonial bow and perhaps go around me, he stood still, and the shock spread over his flushed face. I could see the heart beating in the pink flesh of his cheeks, smell the sudden sweat of his young, taut body.

" 'You saw me in the lamplight,' I said to him. 'And my face looked to you like the mask of death.'

"His lips parted and his teeth touched and involuntarily he nodded, his eyes dazed.

" 'Pass by!' I said to him. 'Fast!' "

The vampire paused, then moved as if he meant to go on. But he stretched his long legs under the table and, leaning back, pressed his hands to his head as if exerting a great pressure on his temples.

The boy, who had drawn himself up into a crouched position, his hands hugging his arms, unwound slowly. He glanced at the tapes and then back at the vampire. "But you killed someone that night," he said.

"Every night," said the vampire.

"Why did you let him go then?" asked the boy.

"I don't know," said the vampire, but it did not have the tone of truly I don't know, but rather, let it be. "You look tired," said the vampire. "You look cold."

"It doesn't matter," said the boy quickly. "The room's a little cold; I don't care about that. You're not cold, are you?"

"No." The vampire smiled and then his shoulders moved with silent laughter.

A moment passed in which the vampire seemed to be thinking and the boy to be studying the vampire's face. The vampire's eyes moved to the boy's watch.

"She didn't succeed, did she?" the boy asked softly.

"What do you honestly think?" asked the vampire. He had settled back in his chair. He looked at the boy intently.

"That she was . . . as you said, destroyed," said the boy; and he seemed to feel the words, so that he swallowed after he'd said the word *destroyed*. "Was she?" he asked.

"Don't you think that she could do it?" asked the vampire.

"But he was so powerful. You said yourself you never knew what powers he had, what secrets he knew. How could she even be sure how to kill him? How did she try?"

The vampire looked at the boy for a long time, his expression unreadable to the boy, who found himself looking away, as though the vampire's eyes were burning lights. "Why don't you drink from that bottle in your pocket?" asked the vampire. "It will make you warm."

"Oh, that . . ." said the boy. "I was going to. I just. . . ."

The vampire laughed. "You didn't think it was polite!" he said, and he suddenly slapped his thigh.

"That's true," the boy shrugged, smiling now; and he took the small flask out of his jacket pocket, unscrewed the gold cap, and took a sip. He held the bottle, now looking at the vampire.

"No," the vampire smiled and raised his hand to wave away the offer.

Then his face became serious again and, sitting back, he went on.

"Lestat had a musician friend in the Rue Dumaine. We had seen him at a recital in the home of a Madame LeClair, who lived there also, which was at that time an extremely fashionable street; and this Madame LeClair, with whom Lestat was also occasionally amusing himself, had found the musician a room in another mansion nearby, where Lestat visited him often. I told you he played with his victims, made friends with them, seduced them into trusting and liking him, even loving him, before he killed. So he apparently played with this young boy, though it had gone on longer than any other such friendship I had ever observed. The young boy wrote good music, and often Lestat brought fresh sheets of it home and played the songs on the square grand in our parlor. The boy had a great talent, but you could tell that this music would not sell, because it was too disturbing. Lestat gave him money and spent evening after evening with him, often taking him to restaurants the boy could have never afforded, and he bought him all the paper and pens which he needed for the writing of his music.

"As I said, it had gone on far longer than any such friendship Lestat had ever had. And I could not tell whether he had actually become fond of a mortal in spite of himself or was simply moving towards a particularly grand betrayal and cruelty. Several times he'd indicated to Claudia and me that he was headed out to kill the boy directly, but he had not. And, of course, I never asked him what he felt because it wasn't worth the great uproar my question would have produced. Lestat entranced with a mortal! He probably would have destroyed the parlor furniture in a rage.

"The next night—after that which I just described to you—he jarred me miserably by asking me to go with him to the boy's flat. He was positively friendly, in one of those moods when he wanted my companionship. Enjoyment could bring that out of him. Wanting to see a good play, the regular opera, the ballet. He always wanted me along. I think I must have seen *Macbeth* with him fifteen times. We went to every performance, even those by amateurs, and Lestat would stride home afterwards, repeating the lines to me and and even shouting out to passers-by with an outstretched finger, 'Tomorrow and tomorrow and tomorrow!' until they skirted him as if he were drunk. But this effervescence was frenetic and likely to vanish in an instant; just a word or two of amiable feeling on my part, some suggestion that I found his companionship pleasant, could banish all such affairs for months. Even years. But now he came to me in such a mood and asked me to go to the boy's room. He was not above pressing my arm as he urged me. And I, dull, catatonic, gave him some miserable excuse—thinking only of Claudia, of the agent, of imminent disaster. I could feel it and wondered that he did not feel it. And finally he picked up a book from the floor and threw it at me, shouting, 'Read your damn poems, then! Rot!' And he bounded out.

"This disturbed me. I cannot tell you how it disturbed me. I wished him cold, impassive, gone. I resolved to plead with Claudia to drop this. I felt powerless, and hopelessly fatigued. But her door had been locked until she left, and I had glimpsed her only for a second while Lestat was chattering, a vision of lace and loveliness as she slipped on her coat; puffed sleeves again and a violet ribbon on her breast, her white lace stockings showing beneath the hem of the little gown, and her white slippers immaculate. She cast a cold look at me as she went out.

"When I returned later, satiated and for a while too sluggish for my own thoughts to bother me, I gradually began to sense that this was the night. She would try tonight.

"I cannot tell you how I knew this. Things about the flat disturbed me, alerted me. Claudia moved in the back parlor behind closed doors. And I fancied I heard another voice there, a whisper. Claudia never brought anyone to our flat; no one did except Lestat, who brought his women of the streets. But I knew there was someone there, yet I got no strong scent, no proper sounds. And then there were aromas in the air of food and drink. And chrysanthemums stood in the silver vase on the square grand—flowers which, to Claudia, meant death.

"Then Lestat came, singing something soft under his breath, his walking stick making a rat-tat-tat on the rails of the spiral stairs. He came down the long hall, his face flushed from the kill, his lips pink; and he set his music on the piano. 'Did I kill him or did I not kill him!' He flashed the question at me now with a pointing finger. 'What's your guess?'

" 'You did not,' I said numbly. 'Because you invited me to go with you, and would never have invited me to share that kill.'

" 'Ah, but! Did I kill him in a rage because you would not go with me!' he said and threw back the cover from the keys. I could see that he would be able to go on like this until dawn. He was exhilarated.

I watched him flip through the music, thinking, Can he die? Can he actually die? And does she mean to do this? At one point, I wanted to go to her and tell her we must abandon everything, even the proposed trip, and live as we had before. But I had the feeling now that there was no retreat. Since the day she'd begun to question him, this—whatever it was to be—was inevitable. And I felt a weight on me, holding me in the chair.

"He pressed two chords with his hands. He had an immense reach and even in life could have been a fine pianist. But he played without feeling; he was always outside the music, drawing it out of the piano as if by magic, by the virtuosity of his vampire senses and control; the music did not come through him, was not drawn through him by himself. 'Well, did I kill him?' he asked me again.

" 'No, you did not,' I said again, though I could just as easily have said the opposite. I was concentrating on keeping my face a mask.

" 'You're right. I did not,' he said. 'It excites me to be close to him, to think over and over, I can kill him and I will kill him but not now. And then to leave him and find someone who looks as nearly like him as possible. If he had brothers . . . why, I'd kill them one by one. The family would succumb to a mysterious fever which dried up the very blood in their bodies!' he said, now mocking a barker's tone. 'Claudia has a taste for families. Speaking of families, I suppose you heard. The Freniere place is supposed to be haunted; they can't keep an overseer and the slaves run away.'

"This was something I did not wish to hear in particular. Babette had died young, insane, restrained finally from wandering towards the ruins of Pointe du Lac, insisting she had seen the devil there and must find him; I'd heard of it in wisps of gossip. And then came the funeral notices. I'd thought occasionally of going to her, of trying some way to rectify what I had done; and other times I thought it would all heal itself; and in my new life of nightly killing, I had grown far from the attachment I'd felt for her or for my sister or any mortal. And I watched the tragedy finally as one might from a theater balcony, moved from time to time, but never sufficiently to jump the railing and join the players on the stage.

" 'Don't talk of her,' I said.

" 'Very well. I was talking of the plantation. Not her. Her! Your lady love, your fancy.' He smiled at me. 'You know, I had it all my way finally in the end, didn't I? But I was telling you about my young friend and how . . .'

" 'I wish you would play the music,' I said softly, un-obtrusively, but as persuasively as possible. Sometimes this worked with Lestat. If I said something just right he found himself doing what I'd said. And now he did just that: with a little snarl, as if to say, 'You fool,' he began playing the music. I heard the doors of the back parlor open and Claudia's steps move down the hall. Don't come, Claudia, I was thinking, feeling; go away from it before we're all destroyed. But she came on steadily until she reached the hall mirror. I could hear her opening the small table drawer, and then the zinging of her hairbrush. She was wearing a floral perfume. I turned slowly to face her as she appeared in the door, still all in white, and moved across the carpet silently toward the piano. She stood at the end of the keyboard, her hands folded on the wood, her chin resting on her hands, her eyes fixed on Lestat.

"I could see his profile and her small face beyond, looking up at him. 'What is it now!' he said, turning the page and letting his hand drop to his thigh. 'You irritate me. Your very presence irritates me!' His eyes moved over the page.

" 'Does it?' she said in her sweetest voice.

" 'Yes, it does. And I'll tell you something else. I've met someone who would make a better vampire than you do.'

"This stunned me. But I didn't have to urge him to go on. 'Do you get my meaning?' he said to her.

" 'Is it supposed to frighten me?' she asked.

" 'You're spoiled because you're an only child,' he said. 'You need a brother. Or rather, I need a brother. I get weary of you both. Greedy, brooding vampires that haunt our own lives. I dislike it.'

" 'I suppose we could people the world with vampires, the three of us,' she said.

" 'You think so!' he said, smiling, his voice with a note of triumph. 'Do you think you could do it? I suppose Louis has told you how it was done or how he thinks it was done. You don't have the power. *Either* of you,' he said.

"This seemed to disturb her. Something she had not accounted for. She was studying him. I could see she did not entirely believe him.

" 'And what gave you the power?' she asked softly, but with a touch of sarcasm.

" 'That, my dear, is one of those things which you may never know. For even the Erebus in which we live must have its aristocracy.'

" 'You're a liar,' she said with a short laugh. And just as he touched his fingers to the keys again, she said, 'But you upset my plans.'

" 'Your plans?' he asked.

" 'I came to make peace with you, even if you are the father of lies. You're my father,' she said. 'I want to make peace with you. I want things to be as they were.'

"Now he was the one who did not believe. He threw a glance at me, then looked at her. 'That can be. Just stop asking me questions. Stop following me. Stop searching in every alleyway for other vampires. There are no other vampires! And this is where you live and this is where you stay!' He looked confused for the moment, as if raising his own voice had confused him. 'I take care of you. You don't need anything.'

" 'And you don't know anything, and that is why you detest my questions. All that's clear. So now let's have peace, because there's nothing else to be had. I have a present for you.'

" 'And I hope it's a beautiful woman with endowments you'll never possess,' he said, looking her up and down. Her face changed when he did this. It was as if she almost lost some control I'd never seen her lose. But then she just shook her head and reached out one small, rounded arm and tugged at his sleeve.

" 'I meant what I said. I'm weary of arguing with you. Hell is hatred, people living together in eternal hatred. We're not in hell. You can take the present or not, I don't care. It doesn't matter. Only let's have an end to all this. Before Louis, in disgust, leaves us both.' She was urging him now to leave the piano, bringing down the wooden cover again over the keys, turning him on the piano stool until his eyes followed her to the door.

" 'You're serious. Present, what do you mean, present?'

" 'You haven't fed enough, I can tell by your color, by your eyes. You've never fed enough at this hour. Let's say that I can give you a precious moment. *Suffer the little children to come unto me,'* she whispered, and was gone. He looked at me. I said nothing. I might as well have been drugged. I could see the curiosity in his face, the suspicion. He followed her down the hall. And then I heard him let out a long, conscious moan, a perfect mingling of hunger and lust.

"When I reached the door, and I took my time, he was bending over the settee. Two small boys lay there, nestled among the soft velvet pillows, totally abandoned to sleep as children can be, their pink mouths open, their small round faces utterly smooth. Their skin was moist, radiant, the curls of the darker of the two damp and pressed to the forehead. I saw at once by their pitiful and identical clothes that they were orphans. And they had ravaged a meal set before them on our best china. The tablecloth was stained with wine, and a small bottle stood half full among the greasy plates and forks. But there was an aroma in the room I did not like. I moved closer, better to see the sleeping ones, and I could see their throats were bare but untouched. Lestat had sunk down beside the darker one; he was by far the more beautiful. He might have been lifted to the painted dome of a cathedral. No more than seven years old, he had that perfect beauty that is of neither sex, but angelic. Lestat brought his hand down gently on the pale throat, and then he touched the silken lips. He let out a sigh which had again that longing, that sweet, painful anticipation. 'Oh . . . Claudia . . .' he sighed. 'You've outdone yourself. Where did you find them?'

"She said nothing. She had receded to a dark armchair and sat back against two large pillows, her legs out straight on the rounded cushion, her ankles drooping so that you did not see the bottom of her white slippers but the curved insteps and the tight, delicate little straps. She was staring at Lestat. 'Drunk on brandy wine,' she said. 'A thimbleful!' and gestured to the table. 'I thought of you when I saw them . . . I thought if I share this with him, even he will forgive.'

"He was warmed by her flattery. He looked at her now and reached out and clutched her white lace ankle. 'Ducky!' he whispered to her and laughed, but then he hushed, as if he didn't wish to wake the doomed children. He gestured to her, intimately, seductively, 'Come sit beside him. You take him, and I'll take this one. Come.' He embraced her as she passed and nestled beside the other boy. He stroked the boy's moist hair, he ran his fingers over the rounded lids and along the fringe of lashes. And then he put his whole softened hand across the boy's face and felt at the temples, cheeks, and jaw, massaging the unblemished flesh. He had forgotten I was there or she was there, but he withdrew his hand and sat still for a moment, as though his desire was making him dizzy. He glanced at the ceiling and then down at the perfect feast. He turned the boy's head slowly against the back of the couch, and the boy's eyebrows tensed for an instant and a moan escaped his lips.

"Claudia's eyes were steady on Lestat, though now she raised her left hand and slowly undid the buttons of the child who lay beside her and reached inside the shabby little shirt and felt the bare flesh. Lestat did the same, but suddenly it was as if his hand had life itself and drew his arm into the shirt and around the boy's small chest in a tight embrace; and Lestat slid down off the cushions of the couch to his knees on the floor, his arm locked to the boy's body, pulling it up close to him so that his face was buried in the boy's neck. His lips moved over the neck and over the chest and over the tiny nipple of the chest and then, putting his other arm into the open shirt, so that the boy lay hopelessly wound in both arms, he drew the boy up tight and sank his teeth into his throat. The boy's head fell back, the curls loose as he was lifted, and again he let out a small moan and his eyelids fluttered—but never opened. And Lestat knelt, the boy pressed against him, sucking hard, his own back arched and rigid, his body rocking back and forth carrying the boy, his long moans rising and falling in time with the slow rocking, until suddenly his whole body tensed, and his hands seemed to grope for some way to push the boy away, as if the boy himself in his helpless slumber were clinging to Lestat; and finally he embraced the boy again and moved slowly forward over him, letting him down among the pillows, the sucking softer, now almost inaudible.

"He withdrew. His hands pressed the boy down. He knelt there, his head thrown back, so the wavy blond hair hung loose and dishevelled. And then he slowly sank to the floor, turning, his back against the leg of the couch. 'Ah . . . God . . .' he whispered, his head back, his lids half-mast. I could see the color rushing to his cheeks, rushing into his hands. One hand lay on his bent knee, fluttering, and then it lay still.

"Claudia had not moved. She lay like a Botticelli angel beside the unharmed boy. The other's body already withered, the neck like a fractured stem, the heavy head falling now at an odd angle, the angle of death, into the pillow.

"But something was wrong. Lestat was staring at the ceiling. I could see his tongue between his teeth. He lay too still, the tongue, as it were, trying to get out of the mouth, trying to move past the barrier of the teeth and touch the lip. He appeared to shiver, his shoulders convulsing . . . then relaxing heavily; yet he did not move. A veil had fallen over his clear gray eyes. He was peering at the ceiling. Then a sound came out of him. I stepped forward from the shadows of the hallway, but Claudia said in a sharp hiss, 'Go back!'

" 'Louis . . .' he was saying. I could hear it now . . . 'Louis . . . Louis. . . .'

" 'Don't you like it, Lestat?' she asked him.

" 'Something's wrong with it,' he gasped, and his eyes widened as if the mere speaking were a colossal effort. He could not move. I saw it. He could not move at all. 'Claudia!' He gasped again, and his eyes rolled towards her.

" 'Don't you like the taste of children's blood . . . ?' she asked softly.

" 'Louis . . .' he whispered, finally lifting his head just for an instant. It fell back on the couch. 'Louis, it's . . . it's absinthe! Too much absinthe!' he gasped. 'She's poisoned them with it. She's poisoned me. Louis. . . .' He tried to raise his hand. I drew nearer, the table between us.

" 'Stay back!' she said again. And now she slid off the couch and approached him, peering down into his face as he had peered at the child. 'Absinthe, Father,' she said, 'and laudanum!'

" 'Demon!' he said to her. 'Louis . . . put me in my coffin.' He struggled to rise. 'Put me in my coffin!' His voice was hoarse, barely audible. The hand fluttered, lifted, and fell back.

" 'I'll put you in your coffin, Father,' she said, as though she were soothing him. 'I'll put you in it forever.' And then, from beneath the pillows of the couch, she drew a kitchen knife.

" 'Claudia! Don't do this thing!' I said to her. But she flashed at me a virulency I'd never seen in her face, and as I stood there paralyzed, she gashed his throat, and he let out a sharp, choking cry. 'God!' he shouted out. 'God!'

"The blood poured out of him, down his shirt front, down his coat. It poured as it might never pour from a human being, all the blood with which he had filled himself before the child and from the child; and he kept turning his head, twisting, making the bubbling gash gape. She sank the knife into his chest now and he pitched forward, his mouth wide, his fangs exposed, both hands convulsively flying towards the knife, fluttering around its handle, slipping off its handle. He looked up at me, the hair falling down into his eyes. 'Louis! Louis!' He let out one more gasp and fell sideways on the carpet. She stood looking down at him. The blood flowed everywhere like water. He was groaning, trying to raise himself, one arm pinned beneath his chest, the other shoving at the floor. And now, suddenly, she flew at him and clamping both arms about his neck, bit deep into him as he struggled. 'Louis, Louis!' he gasped over and over, struggling, trying desperately to throw her off; but she rode him, her body lifted by his shoulder, hoisted and dropped, hoisted and dropped, until she pulled away; and, finding the floor quickly, she backed away from him, her hands to her lips, her eyes for the moment clouded, then clear. I turned away from her, my body convulsed by what I'd seen, unable to look any longer. 'Louis!' she said; but I only shook my head. For a moment, the whole house seemed to sway. But she said, 'Look what's happening to him!'

"He had ceased to move. He lay now on his back. And his entire body was shrivelling, drying up, the skin thick and wrinkled, and so white that all the tiny veins showed through it. I gasped, but I could not take my eyes off it, even as the shape of the bones began to show through, his lips drawing back from his teeth, the flesh of his nose drying to two gaping holes. But his eyes, they remained the same, staring wildly at the ceiling, the irises dancing from side to side, even as the flesh cleaved to the bones, became nothing but a parchment wrapping for the bones, the clothes hollow and limp over the skeleton that remained. Finally the irises rolled to the top of his head, and the whites of his eyes went dim. The thing lay still. A great mass of wavy blond hair, a coat, a pair of gleaming boots; and this horror that had been Lestat, and I staring helplessly at it."

"For a long time, Claudia merely stood there. Blood

had soaked the carpet, darkening the woven wreaths of flowers. It gleamed sticky and black on the floor-boards. It stained her dress, her white shoes, her cheek. She wiped at it with a crumpled napkin, took a swipe at the impossible stains of the dress, and then she said, 'Louis, you must help me get him out of here!'

"I said, 'No!' I'd turned my back on her, on the corpse at her feet.

" 'Are you mad, Louis? It can't remain here!' she said to me. 'And the boys. You must help me! The other one's dead from the absinthe! Louis!'

"I knew that this was true, necessary; and yet it seemed impossible.

"She had to prod me then, almost lead me every step of the way. We found the kitchen stove still heaped with the bones of the mother and daughter she'd killed—a dangerous blunder, a stupidity. So she scraped them out now into a sack and dragged the sack across the courtyard stones to the carriage. I hitched the horse myself, shushing the groggy coach-man, and drove the hearse out of the city, fast in the direction of the Bayou St. Jean, towards the dark swamp that stretched to Lake Pontchartrain. She sat beside me, silent, as we rode on and on until we'd passed the gas-lit gates of the few country houses, and the shell road narrowed and became rutted, the swamp rising on either side of us, a great wall of seem-ingly impenetrable cypress and vine. I could smell the stench of the muck, hear the rustling of the animals.

"Claudia had wrapped Lestat's body in a sheet be-fore I would even touch it, and then, to my horror, she had sprinkled it over with the long-stemmed chrysan-themums. So it had a sweet, funereal smell as I lifted it last of all from the carriage. It was almost weightless, as limp as something made of knots and cords, as I put it over my shoulder and moved down into the dark water, the water rising and filling my boots, my feet seeking some path in the ooze beneath, away from where I'd laid the two boys. I went deeper and deeper in with Lestat's remains, though why, I did not know. And finally, when I could barely see the pale space of the road and the sky which was coming dangerously close to dawn, I let his body slip down out of my arms into the water. I stood there shaken, looking at the amorphous form of the white sheet beneath the slimy surface. The numbness which had protected me since the carriage left the Rue Royale threatened to lift and leave me flayed suddenly, staring, thinking: This is Lestat. This is all of transformation and mystery, dead, gone into eternal darkness. I felt a pull suddenly, as if some force were urging me to go down with him, to descend into the dark water and never come back. It was so distinct and so strong that it made the articulation of voices seem only a murmur by comparison. It spoke without language, saying, 'You know what you must do. Come down into the darkness. Let it all go away.'

"But at that moment I heard Claudia's voice. She was calling my name. I turned, and, through the tangled vines, I saw her distant and tiny, like a white flame on the faint luminescent shell road.

"That morning, she wound her arms around me, pressed her head against my chest in the closeness of the coffin, whispering she loved me, that we were free now of Lestat forever. 'I love you, Louis,' she said over and over as the darkness finally came down with the lid and mercifully blotted out all consciousness.

"When I awoke, she was going through his things. It was a tirade, silent, controlled, but filled with a fierce anger. She pulled the contents from cabinets, emptied drawers onto the carpets, pulled one jacket after another from his armoires, turning the pockets inside out, throwing the coins and theater tickets and bits and pieces of paper away. I stood in the door of his room, astonished, watching her. His coffin lay there, heaped with scarves and pieces of tapestry. I had the compulsion to open it. I had the wish to see him there. 'Nothing!' she finally said in disgust. She wadded the clothes into the grate. 'Not a hint of where he came from, who made him!' she said. 'Not a scrap.' She looked to me as if for sympathy. I turned away from her. I was unable to look at her. I moved back into that bedroom which I kept for myself, that room filled with my own books and what things I'd saved from my mother and sister, and I sat on the bed. I could hear her at the door, but I would not look at her. 'He deserved to die!' she said to me.

" 'Then we deserve to die. The same way. Every night of our lives,' I said back to her. 'Go away from me.' It was as if my words were my thoughts, my mind alone only formless confusion. 'I'll care for you because you can't care for yourself. But I don't want you near me. Sleep in that box you bought for yourself. Don't come near me.'

" 'I told you I was going to do it. I told you . . .' she said. Never had her voice sounded so fragile, so like a little silvery bell. I looked up at her, startled but unshaken. Her face seemed not her face. Never had anyone shaped such agitation into the features of a doll. 'Louis, I told you!' she said, her lips quivering. 'I did it for us. So we could be free.' I couldn't stand the sight of her. Her beauty, her seeming innocence, and this terrible agitation. I went past her, perhaps knocking her backwards, I don't know. And I was almost to the railing of the steps when I heard a strange sound.

"Never in all the years of our life together had I heard this sound. Never since the night long ago when I had first found her, a mortal child, clinging to her mother. She was crying!

"It drew me back now against my will. Yet it sounded so unconscious, so hopeless, as though she meant no one to hear it, or didn't care if it were heard by the whole world. I found her lying on my bed in the place where I often sat to read, her knees drawn up, her whole frame shaking with her sobs. The sound of it was terrible. It was more heartfelt, more awful than her mortal crying had ever been. I sat down slowly, gently, beside her and put my hand on her shoulder. She lifted her head, startled, her eyes wide, her mouth trembling. Her face was stained with tears, tears that were tinted with blood. Her eyes brimmed with them, and the faint touch of red stained her tiny hand. She didn't seem to be conscious of this, to see it. She pushed her hair back from her forehead. Her body quivered then with a long, low, pleading sob.

'Louis . . . if I lose you, I have nothing,' she whispered.
'I would undo it to have you back. I can't undo what
I've done.' She put her arms around me, climbing up
against me, sobbing against my heart. My hands were
reluctant to touch her; and then they moved as if I
couldn't stop them, to enfold her and hold her and
stroke her hair. 'I can't live without you . . .' she
whispered. 'I would die rather than live without you.
I would die the same way he died. I can't bear you
to look at me the way you did. I cannot bear it if you
do not love me!' Her sobs grew worse, more bitter,
until finally I bent and kissed her soft neck and cheeks.
Winter plums. Plums from an enchanted wood where
the fruit never falls from the boughs. Where the
flowers never wither and die. 'All right, my dear . . .'
I said to her. 'All right, my love . . .' And I rocked her
slowly, gently in my arms, until she dozed, murmuring
something about our being eternally happy, free of
Lestat forever, beginning the great adventure of our
lives."

"The great adventure of our lives. What does it
mean to die when you can live until the end of the
world? And what is 'the end of the world' except a
phrase, because who knows even what is the world
itself? I had now lived in two centuries, seen the
illusions of one utterly shattered by the other, been
eternally young and eternally ancient, possessing no
illusions, living moment to moment in a way that made
me picture a silver clock ticking in a void: the painted
face, the delicately carved hands looked upon by no
one, looking out at no one, illuminated by a light
which was not a light, like the light by which God
made the world before He had made light. Ticking,
ticking, ticking, the precision of the clock, in a room
as vast as the universe.

"I was walking the streets again, Claudia gone her
way to kill, the perfume of her hair and dress lingering
on my fingertips, on my coat, my eyes moving far
ahead of me like the pale beam of a lantern. I found

myself at the cathedral. What does it mean to die when you can live until the end of the world? I was thinking of my brother's death, of the incense and the rosary. I had the desire suddenly to be in that funeral room, listening to the sound of the women's voices rising and falling with the *Aves*, the clicking of the beads, the smell of the wax. I could remember the crying. It was palpable, as if it were just yesterday, just behind a door. I saw myself walking fast down a corridor and gently giving the door a shove.

"The great façade of the cathedral rose in a dark mass opposite the square, but the doors were open and I could see a soft, flickering light within. It was Saturday evening early, and the people were going to confession for Sunday Mass and Communion. Candles burned dim in the chandeliers. At the far end of the nave the altar loomed out of the shadows, laden with white flowers. It was to the old church on this spot that they had brought my brother for the final service before the cemetery. And I realized suddenly that I hadn't been in this place since, never once come up the stone steps, crossed the porch, and passed through the open doors.

"I had no fear. If anything, perhaps, I longed for something to happen, for the stones to tremble as I entered the shadowy foyer and saw the distant tabernacle on the altar. I remembered now that I had passed here once when the windows were ablaze and the sound of singing poured out into Jackson Square. I had hesitated then, wondering if there were some secret Lestat had never told me, something which might destroy me were I to enter. I'd felt compelled to enter, but I had pushed this out of my mind, breaking loose from the fascination of the open doors, the throng of people making one voice. I had had something for Claudia, a doll I was taking to her, a bridal doll I'd lifted from a darkened toy shop window and placed in a great box with ribbons and tissue paper. A doll for Claudia. I remembered pressing on with it, hearing the heavy vibrations of the organ behind me, my eyes narrow from the great blaze of the candles.

"Now I thought of that moment; that fear in me at

the very sight of the altar, the sound of the *Pange Lingua*. And I thought again, persistently, of my brother. I could see the coffin rolling along up the center aisle, the procession of mourners behind it. I felt no fear now. As I said, I think if anything I felt a longing for some fear, for some reason for fear as I moved slowly along the dark, stone walls. The air was chill and damp in spite of summer. The thought of Claudia's doll came back to me. Where was that doll? For years Claudia had played with that doll. Suddenly I saw myself searching for the doll, in the relentless and meaningless manner one searches for something in a nightmare, coming on doors that won't open or drawers that won't shut, struggling over and over against the same meaningless thing, not knowing why the effort seems so desperate, why the sudden sight of a chair with a shawl thrown over it inspires the mind with horror.

"I was in the cathedral. A woman stepped out of the confessional and passed the long line of those who waited. A man who should have stepped up next did not move; and my eye, sensitive even in my vulnerable condition, noted this, and I turned to see him. He was staring at me. Quickly I turned my back on him. I heard him enter the confessional and shut the door. I walked up the aisle of the church and then, more from exhaustion than from any conviction, went into an empty pew and sat down. I had almost genuflected from old habit. My mind seemed as muddled and tortured as that of any human. I closed my eyes for a moment and tried to banish all thoughts. Hear and see, I said to myself. And with this act of will, my senses emerged from the torment. All around me in the gloom I heard the whisper of prayers, the tiny click of the rosary beads; soft the sighing of the woman who knelt now at the Twelfth Station. Rising from the sea of wooden pews came the scent of rats. A rat moving somewhere near the altar, a rat in the great woodcarved side altar of the Virgin Mary. The gold candlesticks shimmered on the altar; a rich white chrysanthemum bent suddenly on its stem, droplets glistening on the crowded petals, a sour fragrance rising from a score of vases, from altars and side altars, from statues of Virgins and Christs and saints. I stared at the statues; I became obsessed suddenly and completely with the lifeless profiles, the staring eyes, the empty hands, the frozen folds. Then my body convulsed with such violence that I found myself pitched forward, my hand on the pew before me. It was a cemetery of dead forms, of funereal effigy and stone angels. I looked up and saw myself in a most palpable vision ascending the altar steps, opening the tiny sacrosanct tabernacle, reaching with monstrous hands for the consecrated ciborium, and taking the Body of Christ and strewing Its white wafers all over the carpet; and walking then on the sacred wafers, walking up and down before the altar, giving Holy Communion to the dust. I rose up now in the pew and stood there staring at this vision. I knew full well the meaning of it.

"God did not live in this church; these statues gave an image to nothingness. *I* was the supernatural in this cathedral. I was the only supermortal thing that stood conscious under this roof! Loneliness. Loneliness to the point of madness. The cathedral crumbled in my vision; the saints listed and fell. Rats ate the Holy Eucharist and nested on the sills. A solitary rat with an enormous tail stood tugging and gnawing at the rotted altar cloth until the candlesticks fell and rolled on the slime-covered stones. And I remained standing. Untouched. Undead—reaching out suddenly for the plaster hand of the Virgin and seeing it break in my hand, so that I held the hand crumbling in my palm, the pressure of my thumb turning it to powder.

"And then suddenly through the ruins, up through the open door through which I could see a wasteland in all directions, even the great river frozen over and stuck with the encrusted ruins of ships, up through these ruins now came a funeral procession, a band of pale, white men and women, monsters with gleaming eyes and flowing black clothes, the coffin rumbling on the wooden wheels, the rats scurrying across the broken and buckling marble, the procession advancing, so that I could see then Claudia in the procession, her eyes staring from behind a thin black veil, one gloved hand locked upon a black prayer book, the other on the coffin as it moved beside her. And there now in the coffin, beneath a glass cover, I saw to my horror the skeleton of Lestat, the wrinkled skin now pressed into the very texture of his bones, his eyes but sockets, his blond hair billowed on the white satin.

"The procession stopped. The mourners moved out, filling the dusty pews without a sound, and Claudia, turning with her book, opened it and lifted the veil back from her face, her eyes fixed on me as her finger touched the page. 'And now art thou cursed from the earth,' she whispered, her whisper rising in echo in the ruins. 'And now art thou cursed from the earth, which hath opened her mouth to receive thy brother's blood from thy hand. When thou tillest the ground, it shall not henceforth yield unto thee her strength. A fugitive and a vagabond shalt thou be in the earth . . . and whoever slayeth thee, vengeance shall be taken on him seven-fold.'

"I shouted at her, I screamed, the scream rising up out of the depths of my being like some great rolling black force that broke from my lips and sent my body reeling against my will. A terrible sighing rose from the mourners, a chorus growing louder and louder, as I turned to see them all about me, pushing me into the aisle against the very sides of the coffin, so that I turned to get my balance and found both my hands upon it. And I stood there staring down not at the remains of Lestat, but at the body of my mortal brother. A quiet descended, as if a veil had fallen over all and made their forms dissolve beneath its soundless folds. There was my brother, blond and young and sweet as he had been in life, as real and warm to me now as he'd been years and years beyond which I could never have remembered him thus, so perfectly was he re-created, so perfectly in every detail. His blond hair brushed back from his forehead, his eyes closed as if he slept, his smooth fingers around the crucifix on his breast, his lips so pink and silken I could hardly bear to see them and not touch them.

And as I reached out just to touch the softness of his skin, *the vision ended.*

"I was sitting still in the Saturday night cathedral, the smell of the tapers thick in the motionless air, the woman of the stations gone and darkness gathering—behind me, across from me, and now above me. A boy appeared in the black cassock of a lay brother, with a long extinguisher on a golden pole, putting its little funnel down upon one candle and then another and then another. I was stupefied. He glanced at me and then away, as if not to disturb a man deep in prayer. And then, as he moved on up to the next chandelier, I felt a hand on my shoulder.

"That two humans should pass this close to me without my hearing, without my even caring, registered somewhere within me that I was in danger, but I did not care. I looked up now and saw a gray-haired priest. 'You wish to go to confession?' he asked. 'I was about to lock up the church.' He narrowed his eyes behind his thick glasses. The only light now came from the racks of little red-glass candles which burned before the saints; and shadows leaped upon the towering walls. 'You *are* troubled, aren't you? Can I help you?'

" 'It's too late, too late,' I whispered to him, and rose to go. He backed away from me, still apparently unaware of anything about my appearance that should alarm him, and said kindly, to reassure me, 'No, it's still early. Do you want to come into the confessional?'

"For a moment I just stared at him. I was tempted to smile. And then it occurred to me to do it. But even as I followed him down the aisle, in the shadows of the vestibule, I knew this would be nothing, that it was madness. Nevertheless, I knelt down in the small wooden booth, my hands folded on the priedieu as he sat in the booth beside it and slid back the panel to show me the dim outline of his profile. I stared at him for a moment. And then I said it, lifting my hand to make the Sign of the Cross. 'Bless me, father, for I have sinned, sinned so often and so long I do not know how to change, nor how to confess before God what I've done.'

" ' Son, God is infinite in His capacity to forgive,'

he whispered to me. 'Tell Him in the best way you know how and from your heart.'

" 'Murders, father, death after death. The woman who died two nights ago in Jackson Square, I killed her, and thousands of others before her, one and two a night, father, for seventy years. I have walked the streets of New Orleans like the Grim Reaper and fed on human life for my own existence. I am not mortal, father, but immortal and damned, like angels put in hell by God. I am a vampire.'

"The priest turned. 'What is this, some sort of sport for you? Some joke? You take advantage of an old man!' he said. He slid the wooden panel back with a *splat*. Quickly I opened the door and stepped out to see him standing there. 'Young man, do you fear God at all? Do you know the meaning of sacrilege?' He glared at me. Now I moved closer to him, slowly, very slowly, and at first he merely stared at me, outraged. Then, confused, he took a step back. The church was hollow, empty, black, the sacristan gone and the candles throwing ghastly light only on the distant altars. They made a wreath of soft, gold fibers about his gray head and face. 'Then there is no mercy!' I said to him and suddenly clamping my hands on his shoulders, I held him in a preternatural lock from which he couldn't hope to move and held him close beneath my face. His mouth fell open in horror. 'Do you see what I am! Why, if God exists, does He suffer me to exist!' I said to him. 'You talk of sacrilege!' He dug his nails into my hands, trying to free himself, his missal dropping to the floor, his rosary clattering in the folds of his cassock. He might as well have fought the animated statues of the saints. I drew my lips back and showed him my virulent teeth. 'Why does He suffer me to live?' I said. His face infuriated me, his fear, his contempt, his rage. I saw in it all the hatred I'd seen in Babette, and he hissed at me, 'Let me go! Devil!' in sheer mortal panic.

"I released him, watching with a sinister fascination as he floundered, moving up the center aisle as if he plowed through snow. And then I was after him, so swift that I surrounded him in an instant with my outstretched arms, my cape throwing him into darkness, his legs scrambling still. He was cursing me, calling on God at the altar. And then I grabbed him on the very steps to the Communion rail and pulled him down to face me there and sank my teeth into his neck."

* * *

The vampire stopped.

Sometime before, the boy had been about to light a cigarette. And he sat now with the match in one hand, the cigarette in the other, still as a store dummy, staring at the vampire. The vampire was looking at the floor. He turned suddenly, took the book of matches from the boy's hand, struck the match, and held it out. The boy bent the cigarette to receive it. He inhaled and let the smoke out quickly. He uncapped the bottle and took a deep drink, his eyes always on the vampire.

He was patient again, waiting until the vampire was ready to resume.

"I didn't remember Europe from my childhood. Not even the voyage to America, really. That I had been born there was an abstract idea. Yet it had a hold over me which was as powerful as the hold France can have on a colonial. I spoke French, read French, remembered waiting for the reports of the Revolution and reading the Paris newspaper accounts of Napoleon's victories. I remember the anger I felt when he sold the colony of Louisiana to the United States. How long the mortal Frenchman lived in me I don't know. He was gone by this time, really, but there was in me that great desire to see Europe and to know it, which comes not only from the reading of all the literature and the philosophy, but from the feeling of having been shaped by Europe more deeply and keenly than the rest of Americans. I was a Creole who wanted to see where it had all begun.

"And so I turned my mind to this now. To divesting my closets and trunks of everything that was not essential to me. And very little was essential to me, really. And much of that might remain in the town house, to which I was certain I would return sooner or later, if only to move my possessions to another similar one and start a new life in New Orleans. I couldn't conceive of leaving it forever. Wouldn't. But I fixed my mind and heart on Europe.

"It began to penetrate for the first time that I might see the world if I wanted. That I was, as Claudia said, free.

"Meantime, she made a plan. It was her idea most definitely that we must go first to central Europe, where the vampire seemed most prevalent. She was certain we could find something there that would instruct us, explain our origins. But she seemed anxious for more than answers: a communion with her own kind. She mentioned this over and over, 'My own kind,' and she said it with a different intonation than I might have used. She made me feel the gulf that separated us. In the first years of our life together, I had thought her like Lestat, imbibing his instinct to kill, though she shared my tastes in everything else. Now I knew her to be less human than either of us, less human than either of us might have dreamed. Not the faintest conception bound her to the sympathies of human existence. Perhaps this explained why—despite everything I had done or failed to do—she clung to me. I was not her *own kind*. Merely the closest thing to it."

"But wouldn't it have been possible," asked the boy suddenly, "to instruct her in the ways of the human heart the way you'd instructed her in everything else?"

"To what avail?" asked the vampire frankly. "So she might suffer as I did? Oh, I'll grant you I should have taught her something to prevail against her desire to kill Lestat. For my own sake, I should have done that. But you see, I had no *confidence* in anything else. Once fallen from grace, I had confidence in nothing."

The boy nodded. "I didn't mean to interrupt you. You were coming to something," he said.

"Only to the point that it was possible to forget what had happened to Lestat by turning my mind to Europe. And the thought of the other vampires inspired me also. I had not been cynical for one moment about the existence of God. Only lost from it. Drifting, preternatural, through the natural world.

"But we had another matter before we left for Europe. Oh, a great deal happened indeed. It began with the musician. He had called while I was gone that evening to the cathedral, and the next night he was to come again. I had dismissed the servants and went down to him myself. And his appearance startled me at once.

"He was much thinner than I'd remembered him and very pale, with a moist gleam about his face that suggested fever. And he was perfectly miserable. When I told him Lestat had gone away, he refused at first to believe me and began insisting Lestat would have left him some message, something. And then he went off up the Rue Royale, talking to himself about it, as if he had little awareness of anyone around him. I caught up with him under a gas lamp. 'He did leave you something,' I said, quickly feeling for my wallet. I didn't know how much I had in it, but I planned to give it to him. It was several hundred dollars. I put it into his hands. They were so thin I could see the blue veins pulsing beneath the watery skin. Now he became exultant, and I sensed at once that the matter went beyond the money. 'Then he spoke of me, he told you to give this to me!' he said, holding onto it as though it were a relic. 'He must have said something else to you!' He stared at me with bulging, tortured eyes. I didn't answer him at once, because during these moments I had seen the puncture wounds in his neck. Two red scratch-like marks to the right, just above his soiled collar. The money flapped in his hand; he was oblivious to the evening traffic of the street, the people who pushed close around us. 'Put it away,' I whispered. 'He did speak of you, that it was important you go on with your music.'

"He stared at me as if anticipating something else. 'Yes? Did he say anything else?' he asked me. I didn't know what to tell him. I would have made up anything if it would have given him comfort, and also kept him away. It was painful for me to speak of Lestat; the words evaporated on my lips. And the puncture wounds amazed me. I couldn't fathom this. I was saying nonsense to the boy finally—that Lestat wished him well, that he had to take a steamboat up to St. Louis, that he would be back, that war was imminent and he had business there . . . the boy hungering after every word, as if he couldn't possibly get enough and was pushing on with it for the thing he wanted. He was trembling; the sweat broke out fresh on his forehead as he stood there pressing me, and suddenly he bit his lip hard and said, 'But why did he go!' as if nothing had sufficed.

" 'What is it?' I asked him. 'What did you need from him? I'm sure he would want me to . . .'

" 'He was my friend!' He turned on me suddenly, his voice dropping with repressed outrage.

" 'You're not well,' I said to him. 'You need rest. There's something . . .' and now I pointed to it, attentive to his every move '. . . on your throat.' He didn't even know what I meant. His fingers searched for the place, found it, rubbed it.

" 'What does it matter? I don't know. The insects, they're everywhere,' he said, turning away from me. 'Did he say anything else?'

"For a long while I watched him move up the Rue Royale, a frantic, lanky figure in rusty black, for whom the bulk of the traffic made way.

"I told Claudia at once about the wound on his throat.

"It was our last night in New Orleans. We'd board the ship just before midnight tomorrow for an early-morning departure. We had agreed to walk out together. She was being solicitous, and there was something remarkably sad in her face, something which had not left after she had cried. 'What could the marks mean?' she asked me now. 'That he fed on the boy when the boy slept, that the boy allowed it? I can't imagine . . .' she said.

" 'Yes, that must be what it is.' But I was uncertain. I remembered now Lestat's remark to Claudia that he knew a boy who would make a better vampire than she. Had he planned to do that? Planned to make another one of us?

" 'It doesn't matter now, Louis,' she reminded me. We had to say our farewell to New Orleans. We were walking away from the crowds of the Rue Royale. My senses were keen to all around me, holding it close, reluctant to say this was the last night.

"The old French city had been for the most part burned a long time ago, and the architecture of these days was as it is now, Spanish, which meant that, as we walked slowly through the very narrow street where one cabriolet had to stop for another, we passed white-washed walls and great courtyard gates that revealed distant lamplit courtyard paradises like our own, only each seemed to hold such promise, such sensual mystery. Great banana trees stroked the galleries of the inner courts, and masses of fern and flower crowded the mouth of the passage. Above, in the dark, figures sat on the balconies, their backs to the open doors, their hushed voices and the flapping of their fans barely audible above the soft river breeze; and over the walls grew wisteria and passiflora so thick that we could brush against it as we passed and stop occasionally at this place or that to pluck a luminescent rose or tendrils of honeysuckle. Through the high windows we saw again and again the play of candlelight on richly embossed plaster ceilings and often the bright iridescent wreath of a crystal chandelier. Occasionally a figure dressed for evening appeared at the railings, the glitter of jewels at her throat, her perfume adding a lush evanescent spice to the flowers in the air.

"We had our favorite streets, gardens, corners, but inevitably we reached the outskirts of the old city and saw the rise of swamp. Carriage after carriage passed us coming in from the Bayou Road bound for the theater or the opera. But now the lights of the city lay behind us, and its mingled scents were drowned in the thick odor of swamp decay. The very sight of the tall, wavering trees, their limbs hung with moss, had sickened me, made me think of Lestat. I was thinking of him as I'd thought of my brother's body. I was seeing him sunk deep among the roots of cypress and oak, that hideous withered form folded in the white sheet. I wondered if the creatures of the dark shunned him, knowing instinctively the parched, crackling thing there was virulent, or whether they swarmed about him in the reeking water, picking his ancient dried flesh from the bones.

"I turned away from the swamps, back to the heart of the old city, and felt the gentle press of Claudia's hand comforting. She had gathered a natural bouquet from all the garden walls, and she held it crushed to the bosom of her yellow dress, her face buried in its perfume. Now she said to me in such a whisper that I bent my ear to her, 'Louis, it troubles you. You know the remedy. Let the flesh . . . let the flesh instruct the mind.' She let my hand go, and I watched her move away from me, turning once to whisper the same command. 'Forget him. Let the flesh instruct the mind. . . .' It brought back to me that book of poems I'd held in my hand when she first spoke these words to me, and I saw the verse upon the page:

> *Her* lips were red, *her* looks were free,
> Her locks were yellow as gold:
> Her skin was as white as leprosy,
> The Night-mare LIFE-IN-DEATH was she,
> Who thicks man's blood with cold.

"She was smiling from the far corner, a bit of yellow silk visible for a moment in the narrowing dark, then gone. My companion, my companion forever.

"I was turning into the Rue Dumaine, moving past darkened windows. A lamp died very slowly behind a broad scrim of heavy lace, the shadow of the pattern on the brick expanding, growing fainter, then vanishing into blackness. I moved on, nearing the house of Madame LeClair, hearing faint but shrill the violins from the upstairs parlor and then the thin metallic laughter of the guests. I stood across from the house in the shadows, seeing a small handful of them moving in the lighted room; from window to window to window moved one guest, a pale lemon-colored wine in his stem glass, his face turned towards the moon as if he sought something from a better vantage and found it finally at the last window, his hand on the dark drape.

"Across from me a door stood open in the brick wall, and a light fell on the passage at the far end. I moved silently over the narrow street and met the thick aromas of the kitchen rising on the air past the gate. The slightly nauseating smell of cooking meat. I stepped into the passage. Someone had just walked fast across the courtyard and shut a rear door. But then I saw another figure. She stood by the kitchen fire, a lean black woman with a brilliant tignon around her head, her features delicately chiselled and gleaming in the light like a figure in diorite. She stirred the mixture in the kettle. I caught the sweet smell of the spices and the fresh green of marjoram and bay; and then in a wave came the horrid smell of the cooking meat, the blood and flesh decaying in the boiling fluids. I drew near and saw her set down her long iron spoon and stand with her hands on her generous, tapered hips, the white of her apron sash outlining her small, fine waist. The juices of the pot foamed on the lip and spit in the glowing coals below. Her dark odor came to me, her dusky spiced perfume, stronger than the curious mixture from the pot, tantalizing as I drew nearer and rested back against a wall of matted vine. Upstairs the thin violins began a waltz, and the floorboards groaned with the dancing couples. The jasmine of the wall enclosed me and then receded like water leaving the clean-swept beach; and again I sensed her salt perfume. She had moved to the kitchen door, her long black neck gracefully bent as she peered into the shadows beneath the lighted window. 'Monsieur!' she said, and stepped out now into the shaft of yellow light. It fell on her great round breasts and long sleek silken arms and now on the long cold beauty of her face. 'You're looking for the party, Monsieur?' she asked. 'The party's upstairs. . . .'

" 'No, my dear, I wasn't looking for the party,' I said to her, moving forward out of the shadows. 'I was looking for you.' "

"Everything was ready when I woke the next evening: the wardrobe trunk on its way to the ship as well as a chest which contained a coffin; the servants gone; the furnishings draped in white. The sight of the tickets and a collection of notes of credit and some other papers all placed together in a flat black wallet made the trip emerge into the bright light of reality. I would have forgone killing had that been possible, and so I took care of this early, and perfunctorily, as did Claudia; and as it neared time for us to leave, I was alone in the flat, waiting for her. She had been gone too long for my nervous frame of mind. I feared for her—though she could bewitch almost anyone into assisting her if she found herself too far away from home, and had many times persuaded strangers to bring her to her very door, to her father, who thanked them profusely for returning his lost daughter.

"When she came now she was running, and I fancied as I put my book down that she had forgotten the time. She thought it later than it was. By my pocket watch we had an hour. But the instant she reached the door, I knew that this was wrong. 'Louis, the doors!' she gasped, her chest heaving, her hand at her heart. She ran back down the passage with me behind her and, as she desperately signalled me, I shut up the doors to the gallery. 'What is it?' I asked her. 'What's come over you?' But she was moving to the front windows now, the long French windows which opened onto the narrow balconies over the street. She lifted the shade of the lamp and quickly blew out the flame. The room went dark, and then lightened gradually with the illumination of the street. She stood panting, her hand on her breast, and then she reached out for me and drew me close to her beside the window.

" 'Someone followed me,' she whispered now. 'I could hear him block after block behind me. At first, I thought it was nothing!' She stopped for breath, her face blanched in the bluish light that came from the windows across the way. 'Louis, it was the musician,' she whispered.

" 'But what does that matter? He must have seen you with Lestat.'

" 'Louis, he's down there. Look out the window. Try to see him.' She seemed so shaken, almost afraid.

As if she would not stand exposed on the threshold.
I stepped out on the balcony, though I held her hand
as she hovered by the drape; and she held me so
tightly that it seemed she feared for me. It was eleven
o'clock and the Rue Royale for the moment was quiet:
shops shut, the traffic of the theater just gone away.
A door slammed somewhere to my right, and I saw
a woman and a man emerge and hurry towards the
corner, the woman's face hidden beneath an enormous
white hat. Their steps died away. I could see no one,
sense no one. I could hear Claudia's labored breathing.
Something stirred in the house; I started, then recognized it as the jingling and rustling of the birds. We'd
forgotten the birds. But Claudia had started worse
than I, and she pulled near to me. 'There is no one,
Claudia . . .' I started to whisper to her.

"Then I saw the musician.

"He had been standing so still in the doorway of
the furniture shop that I had been totally unaware of
him, and he must have wanted this to be so. For now
he turned his face upwards, towards me, and it shone
from the dark like a white light. The frustration and
care were utterly erased from his stark features; his
great dark eyes peered at me from the white flesh. He
had become a vampire.

" 'I see him,' I murmured to her, my lips as still as
possible, my eyes holding his eyes. I felt her move
closer, her hand trembling, a heart beating in the palm
of her hand. She let out a gasp when she saw him now.
But at that same moment, something chilled me even
as I stared at him and he did not move. Because I
heard a step in the lower passage. I heard the gate-
hinge groan. And then that step again, deliberate,
loud, echoing under the arched ceiling of the carriage
way, deliberate, familiar. That step advancing now up
the spiral stairs. A thin scream rose from Claudia, and
then she caught it at once with her hand. The vampire
in the furniture shop door had not moved. And I
knew the step on the stairs. I knew the step on the
porch. It was Lestat. Lestat pulling on the door, now
pounding on it, now ripping at it, as if to tear it loose
from the very wall. Claudia moved back into the

corner of the room, her body bent, as if someone had struck her a sharp blow, her eyes moving frantically from the figure in the street to me. The pounding on the door grew louder. And then I heard his voice. 'Louis!' he called to me. 'Louis!' he roared against the door. And then came the smash of the back parlor window. And I could hear the latch turning from within. Quickly, I grabbed the lamp, struck a match hard and broke it in my frenzy, then got the flame as I wanted it and held the small vessel of kerosene poised in my hand. 'Get away from the window. Shut it,' I told her. And she obeyed as if the sudden clear, spoken command released her from a paroxysm of fear. 'And light the other lamps, now, at once.' I heard her crying as she struck the match. Lestat was coming down the hallway.

"And then he stood at the door. I let out a gasp, and, not meaning to, I must have taken several steps backwards when I saw him. I could hear Claudia's cry. It was Lestat beyond question, restored and intact as he hung in the doorway, his head thrust forward, his eyes bulging, as if he were drunk and needed the door jamb to keep him from plunging headlong into the room. His skin was a mass of scars, a hideous covering of injured flesh, as though every wrinkle of his 'death' had left its mark upon him. He was seared and marked as if by the random strokes of a hot poker, and his once clear gray eyes were shot with hemorrhaged vessels.

" 'Stay back . . . for the love of God . . .' I whispered. 'I'll throw it at you. I'll burn you alive,' I said to him. And at the same moment I could hear a sound to my left, something scraping, scratching against the façade of the town house. It was the other one. I saw his hands now on the wrought-iron balcony. Claudia let out a piercing scream as he threw his weight against the glass doors.

"I cannot tell you all that happened then. I cannot possibly recount it as it was. I remember heaving the lamp at Lestat; it smashed at his feet and the flames rose at once from the carpet. I had a torch then in my hands, a great tangle of sheet I'd pulled from the couch and ignited in the flames. But I was struggling with him before that, kicking and driving savagely at his great strength. And somewhere in the background were Claudia's panicked screams. And the other lamp was broken. And the drapes of the windows blazed. I remember that his clothes reeked of kerosene and that he was at one point smacking wildly at the flames. He was clumsy, sick, unable to keep his balance; but when he had me in his grip, I even tore at his fingers with my teeth to get him off. There was noise rising in the street, shouts, the sound of a bell. The room itself had fast become an inferno, and I did see in one clear blast of light Claudia battling the fledgling vampire. He seemed unable to close his hands on her, like a clumsy human after a bird. I remember rolling over and over with Lestat in the flames, feeling the suffocating heat in my face, seeing the flames above his back when I rolled under him. And then Claudia rose up out of the confusion and was striking at him over and over with the poker until his grip broke and I scrambled loose from him. I saw the poker coming down again and again on him and could hear the snarls rising from Claudia in time with the poker, like the stress of an unconscious animal. Lestat was holding his hand, his face a grimace of pain. And there, sprawled on the smoldering carpet, lay the other one, blood flowing from his head.

"What happened then is not clear to me. I think I grabbed the poker from her and gave him one fine blow with it to the side of the head. I remember that he seemed unstoppable, invulnerable to the blows. The heat, by this time, was singeing my clothes, had caught Claudia's gossamer gown, so that I grabbed her up and ran down the passage trying to stifle the flames with my body. I remember taking off my coat and beating at the flames in the open air, and men rushing up the stairs and past me. A great crowd swelled from the passage into the courtyard, and someone stood on the sloped roof of the brick kitchen. I had Claudia in my arms now and was rushing past them all, oblivious to the questions, thrusting a shoulder through them, making them divide. And then I was free with her, hearing her pant and sob in my ear, running blindly down the Rue Royale, down the first narrow street, running and running until there was no sound but the sound of my running. And her breath. And we stood there, the man and the child, scorched and aching, and breathing deep in the quiet of night."

PART II

ALL NIGHT LONG I stood on the deck of the French ship *Mariana,* watching the gangplanks. The long levee was crowded, and parties lasted late in the lavish staterooms, the decks rumbling with passengers and guests. But finally, as the hours moved toward dawn, the parties were over one by one, and carriages left the narrow riverfront streets. A few late passengers came aboard, a couple lingered for hours at the rail nearby. But Lestat and his apprentice, if they survived the fire (and I was convinced that they had) did not find their way to the ship. Our luggage had left the flat that day; and if anything had remained to let them know our destination, I was sure it had been destroyed. Yet still I watched. Claudia sat securely locked in our stateroom, her eyes fixed on the porthole. But Lestat did not come.

"Finally, as I'd hoped, the commotion of putting out commenced before daylight. A few people waved from the pier and the grassy hump of the levee as the great ship began first to shiver, then to jerk violently to one side, and then to slide out in one great majestic motion into the current of the Mississippi.

"The lights of New Orleans grew small and dim until there appeared behind us only a pale phosphorescence against the lightening clouds. I was fatigued beyond my worst memory, yet I stood on the deck for as long as I could see that light, knowing that I might never see it again. In moments we were carried downstream past the piers of Freniere and Pointe du Lac and then, as I could see the great wall of cottonwood and cypress growing green out of the darkness along the shore, I knew it was almost morning. Too perilously close.

"And as I put the key into the lock of the cabin

I felt the greatest exhaustion perhaps that I'd ever known. Never in all the years I'd lived in our select family had I know the fear I'd experienced tonight, the vulnerability, the sheer terror. And there was to be no sudden relief from it. No sudden sense of safety. Only that relief which weariness at last imposes, when neither mind nor body can endure the terror any longer. For though Lestat was now miles away from us, he had in his resurrection awakened in me a tangle of complex fears which I could not escape. Even as Claudia said to me, 'We're safe, Louis, safe,' and I whispered the word *yes* to her, I could see Lestat hanging in that doorway, see those bulbous eyes, that scarred flesh. How had he come back, how had he triumphed over death? How could any creature have survived that shrivelled ruin he'd become? Whatever the answer, what did it mean—not only for him, but for Claudia, for me? Safe from him we were, but safe from ourselves?

"The ship was struck by a strange 'fever.' It was amazingly clean of vermin, however, though occasionally their bodies might be found, weightless and dry, as if the creatures had been dead for days. Yet there was this fever. It struck a passenger first in the form of weakness and a soreness about the throat; occasionally there were marks there, and occasionally the marks were someplace else; or sometimes there were no recognizable marks at all, though an old wound was reopened and painful again. And sometimes the passenger who fell to sleeping more and more as the voyage progressed and the fever progressed died in his sleep. So there were burials at sea on several occasions as we crossed the Atlantic. Naturally afraid of fever, I shunned the passengers, did not wish to join them in the smoking room, get to know their stories, hear their dreams and expectations. I took my 'meals' alone. But Claudia liked to watch the passengers, to stand on deck and see them come and go in the early evening, to say softly to me later as I sat at the porthole, 'I think she'll fall prey. . . .'

"I would put the book down and look out the port-hole, feeling the gentle rocking of the sea, seeing the stars, more clear and brilliant than they had ever been on land, dipping down to touch the waves. It seemed at moments, when I sat alone in the dark stateroom, that the sky had come down to meet the sea and that some great secret was to be revealed in that meeting, some great gulf miraculously closed forever. But who was to make this revelation when the sky and sea became indistinguishable and neither any longer was chaos? God? Or Satan? It struck me suddenly what consolation it would be to know Satan, to look upon his face, no matter how terrible that countenance was, to know that I belonged to him totally, and thus put to rest forever the torment of this ignorance. To step through some veil that would forever separate me from all that I called human nature.

"I felt the ship moving closer and closer to this secret. There was no visible end to the firmament; it closed about us with breathtaking beauty and silence. But then the words *put to rest* became horrible. Because there would be no rest in damnation, could be no rest; and what was this torment compared to the restless fires of hell? The sea rocking beneath those constant stars—those stars themselves—what had this to do with Satan? And those images which sound so static to us in childhood when we are all so taken up with mortal frenzy that we can scarce imagine them desirable: seraphim gazing forever upon the face of God—and the face of God itself—this was rest eternal, of which this gentle, cradling sea was only the faintest promise.

"But even in these moments, when the ship slept and all the world slept, neither heaven nor hell seemed more than a tormenting fancy. To know, to believe, in one or the other . . . that was perhaps the only salvation for which I could dream.

"Claudia, with Lestat's liking for light, lit the lamps when she rose. She had a marvellous pack of playing cards, acquired from a lady on board; the picture cards were in the fashion of Marie Antoinette, and the backs of the cards bore gold fleurs-de-lis on gleaming violet. She played a game of solitaire in which the cards made the numbers of a clock. And she asked me until I finally began to answer her, how Lestat had accomplished it. She was no longer shaken. If she remembered her screams in the fire she did not care to dwell on them. If she remembered that, before the fire, she had wept real tears in my arms, it made no change in her; she was, as always in the past, a person of little indecision, a person for whom habitual quiet did not mean anxiety or regret.

" 'We should have burned him,' she said. 'We were fools to think from his appearance that he was dead.'

" 'But how could he have survived?' I asked her. 'You saw him, you know what became of him.' I had no taste for it, really. I would have gladly pushed it to the back of my mind, but my mind would not allow me to. And it was she who gave me the answers now, for the dialogue was really with herself. 'Suppose, though, he had ceased to fight us,' she explained, 'that he was still living, locked in that helpless dried corpse, conscious and calculating. . . .'

" 'Conscious in that state!' I whispered.

" 'And suppose, when he reached the swamp waters and heard the sounds of our carriage going away, that he had strength enough to propel those limbs to move. There were creatures all around him in the dark. I saw him once rip the head of a small garden lizard and watch the blood run down into a glass. Can you imagine the tenacity of the will to live in him, his hands groping in that water for anything that moved?'

" 'The will to live? Tenacity?' I murmured. 'Suppose it was something else. . . .'

" 'And then, when he'd felt the resuscitation of his strength, just enough perhaps to have sustained him to the road, somewhere along that road he found someone. Perhaps he crouched, waiting for a passing carriage; perhaps he crept, gathering still what blood he could until he came to the shacks of those immigrants or those scattered country houses. And what a spectacle he must have been!' She gazed at the hanging lamp, her eyes narrow, her voice muted, without emotion. 'And then what did he do? It's clear to me. If he could not have gotten back to New Orleans in

time, he could most definitely have reached the Old
Bayou cemetery. The charity hospital feeds it fresh
coffins every day. And I can see him clawing his way
through the moist earth for such a coffin, dumping the
fresh contents out in the swamps, and securing himself
until the next nightfall in that shallow grave where no
manner of man would be wont to disturb him. Yes . . .
that is what he did, I'm certain.'

"I thought of this for a long time, picturing it, seeing that it must have happened. And then I heard her
add thoughtfully, as she laid down her card and looked
at the oval face of a white-coiffed king, 'I could have
done it.

" 'And why do you look that way at me?' she asked,
gathering up her cards, her small fingers struggling to
make a neat pack of them and then to shuffle them.

" 'But you do believe . . . that had we burned his
remains he would have died?' I asked.

" 'Of course I believe it. If there is nothing to rise,
there is nothing to rise. What are you driving at?' She
was dealing out the cards now, dealing a hand for me
on the small oak table. I looked at the cards, but I
did not touch them.

" 'I don't know . . .' I whispered to her. 'Only that
perhaps there was no will to live, no tenacity . . .
because very simply there was no need of either.'

"Her eyes gazed at me steadily, giving no hint of
her thoughts or that she understood mine.

" 'Because perhaps he was incapable of dying . . .
perhaps he is, and we are . . . truly immortal?'

"For a long time she sat there looking at me.

" 'Consciousness in that state . . .' I finally added,
as I looked away from her. 'If it were so, then mightn't
there be consciousness in any other? Fire, sunlight . . .
what does it matter?'

" 'Louis,' she said, her voice soft. 'You're afraid.
You don't stand *en garde* against fear. You don't
understand the danger of fear itself. We'll know these
answers when we find those who can tell us, those
who've possessed knowledge for centuries, for however long creatures such as ourselves have walked the

earth. That knowledge was our birthright, and he deprived us. He earned his death.'

" 'But he didn't die . . .' I said.

" 'He's dead,' she said. 'No one could have escaped that house unless they'd run with us, at our very side. No. He's dead, and so is that trembling aesthete, his friend. Consciousness, what does it matter?'

"She gathered up the cards and put them aside, gesturing for me to hand her the books from the table beside the bunk, those books which she'd unpacked immediately on board, the few select records of vampire lore which she'd taken to be her guides. They included no wild romances from England, no stories of Edgar Allan Poe, no fancy. Only those few accounts of the vampires of eastern Europe, which had become for her a sort of Bible. In those countries indeed they did burn the remains of the vampire when they found him, and the heart was staked and the head severed. She would read these now for hours, these ancient books which had been read and reread before they ever found their way across the Atlantic; they were travellers' tales, the accounts of priests and scholars. And she would plan our trip, not with the need of any pen or paper, only in her mind. A trip that would take us at once away from the glittering capitals of Europe towards the Black Sea, where we would dock at Varna and begin that search in the rural countryside of the Carpathians.

"For me it was a grim prospect, bound as I was to it, for there were longings in me for other places and other knowledge which Claudia did not begin to comprehend. Seeds of these longings had been planted in me years ago, seeds which came to bitter flower as our ship passed through the Straits of Gibraltar and into the waters of the Mediterranean Sea.

"I wanted those waters to be blue. And they were not. They were the nighttime waters, and how I suffered then, straining to remember the seas that a young man's untutored senses had taken for granted, that an undisciplined memory had let slip away for eternity. The Mediterranean was black, black off the coast of Italy, black off the coast of Greece, black always, black when in the small cold hours before dawn, as even Claudia slept, weary of her books and the meager fare that caution allowed her vampire hunger, I lowered a lantern down, down through the rising vapor until the fire blazed right over the lapping waters; and nothing came to light on that heaving surface but the light itself, the reflection of that beam travelling constant with me, a steady eye which seemed to fix on me from the depths and say, 'Louis, your quest is for darkness only. This sea is not your sea. The myths of men are not your myths. Men's treasures are not yours.'

"But oh, how the quest for the Old World vampires filled me with bitterness in those moments, a bitterness I could all but taste, as if the very air had lost its freshness. For what secrets, what truths had those monstrous creatures of night to give us? What, of necessity, must be their terrible limits, if indeed we were to find them at all? What can the damned really say to the damned?

"I never stepped ashore at Piraeus. Yet in my mind I roamed the Acropolis at Athens, watching the moon rise through the open roof of the Parthenon, measuring my height by the grandeur of those columns, walking the streets of those Greeks who died at Marathon, listening to the sound of wind in the ancient olives. These were the monuments of men who could not die, not the stones of the living dead; here the secrets that had endured the passage of time, which I had only dimly begun to understand. And yet nothing turned me from our quest and nothing could turn me, but over and over, committed as I was, I pondered the great risk of our questions, the risk of any question that is truthfully asked; for the answer must carry an incalculable price, a tragic danger. Who knew that better than I, who had presided over the death of my own body, seeing all I called human wither and die only to form an unbreakable chain which held me fast to this world yet made me forever its exile, a specter with a beating heart?

"The sea lulled me to bad dreams, to sharp remembrances. A winter night in New Orleans when I wandered through the St. Louis cemetery and saw my sister, old and bent, a bouquet of white roses in her arms, the thorns carefully bound in an old parchment, her gray head bowed, her steps carrying her steadily along through the perilous dark to the grave where the stone of her brother Louis was set, side by side with that of his younger brother. . . . Louis, who had died in the fire of Pointe du Lac leaving a generous legacy to a godchild and namesake she never knew. Those flowers were for Louis, as if it had not been half a century since his death, as if her memory, like Louis's memory, left her no peace. Sorrow sharpened her ashen beauty, sorrow bent her narrow back. And what I would not have given, as I watched her, to touch her silver hair, to whisper love to her, if love would not have loosed on her remaining years a horror worse than grief. I left her with grief. Over and over and over.

"And I dreamed now too much. I dreamed too long, in the prison of this ship, in the prison of my body, attuned as it was to the rise of every sun as no mortal body had ever been. And my heart beat faster for the mountains of eastern Europe, finally, beat faster for the one hope that somewhere we might find in that primitive countryside the answer to why under God this suffering was allowed to exist—why under God it was allowed to begin, and how under God it might be ended. I had not the courage to end it, I knew, without that answer. And in time the waters of the Mediterranean became, in fact, the waters of the Black Sea."

THE VAMPIRE SIGHED. The boy was resting on his elbow, his face cradled in his right palm; and his avid expression was incongruous with the redness of his eyes.

"Do you think I'm playing with you?" the vampire asked, his fine dark eyebrows knitted for an instant.

"No," the boy said quickly. "I know better than to ask you any more questions. You'll tell me everything in your own time." And his mouth settled, and he looked at the vampire as though he were ready for him to begin again.

There was a sound then from far off. It came from somewhere in the old Victorian building around them, the first such sound they'd heard. The boy looked up towards the hallway door. It was as if he'd forgotten the building existed. Someone walked heavily on the old boards. But the vampire was undisturbed. He looked away as if he were again disengaging himself from the present.

"That village. I can't tell you the name of it; the name's gone. I remember it was miles from the coast, however, and we'd been travelling alone by carriage. And such a carriage! It was Claudia's doing, that carriage, and I should have expected it; but then, things are always taking me unawares. From the first moment we arrived in Varna, I had perceived certain changes in her which made me at once aware she was Lestat's daughter as well as my own. From me she had learned the value of money, but from Lestat she had inherited a passion for spending it; and she wasn't to leave without the most luxurious black coach we could manage, outfitted with leather seats that might have accommodated a band of travellers, let alone a man and a child who used the magnificent compartment only for the transportation of an ornately carved oak chest. To the back were strapped two trunks of the finest clothes the shops there could provide, and we went speeding along, those light enormous wheels and fine springs carrying that bulk with a frightening ease over the mountain roads. There was a thrill to that when there was nothing else in this strange country, those horses at a gallop and the gentle listing of that carriage.

"And it was strange country. Lonely, dark, as rural country is always dark, its castles and ruins often obscured when the moon passed behind the clouds, so that I felt an anxiety during those hours I'd never quite experienced in New Orleans. And the people themselves were no relief. We were naked and lost in their tiny hamlets, and conscious always that amongst them we were in grave danger.

"Never in New Orleans had the kill to be disguised. The ravages of fever, plague, crime—these things competed with us always there, and outdid us. But here we had to go to great lengths to make the kill unnoticed. Because these simple country people, who might have found the crowded streets of New Orleans terrifying, believed completely that the dead did walk and did drink the blood of the living. They knew our names: vampire, devil. And we, who were on the lookout for the slightest rumor, wanted under no circumstances to create rumor ourselves.

"We travelled alone and fast and lavishly amongst them, struggling to be safe within our ostentation, finding talk of vampires all too cheap by the inn fires, where, my daughter sleeping peacefully against my chest, I invariably found someone amongst the peasants or guests who spoke enough German or, at times, even French to discuss with me the familiar legends.

"But finally we came to that village which was to be the turning point in our travels. I savor nothing about that journey, not the freshness of the air, the coolness of the nights. I don't talk of it without a vague tremor even now.

"We had been at a farmhouse the night before, and so no news prepared us—only the desolate appearance of the place: because it wasn't late when we reached it, not late enough for all the shutters of the little street to be bolted or for a darkened lantern to be swinging from the broad archway of the inn.

"Refuse was collected in the doorways. And there were other signs that something was wrong. A small box of withered flowers beneath a shuttered shop window. A barrel rolling back and forth in the center of the inn yard. The place had the aspect of a town under siege by the plague.

"But even as I was setting Claudia down on the packed earth beside the carriage, I saw the crack of light beneath the inn door. 'Put the hood of your cape up,' she said quickly. 'They're coming.' Someone inside was pulling back the latch.

"At first all I saw was the light behind the figure in the very narrow margin she allowed. Then the light from the carriage lanterns glinted in her eye.

" 'A room for the night!' I said in German. 'And my horses need tending, badly!'

" 'The night's no time for travelling . . .' she said to me in a peculiar, flat voice. 'And with a child.' As she said this, I noticed others in the room behind her. I could hear their murmurings and see the flickering of a fire. From what I could see there were mostly peasants gathered around it, except for one man who was dressed much like myself in a tailored coat, with an overcoat over his shoulders; but his clothes were neglected and shabby. His red hair gleamed in the firelight. He was a foreigner, like ourselves, and he was the only one not looking at us. His head wagged slightly as if he were drunk.

" 'My daughter's tired,' I said to the woman. 'We've no place to stay but here.' And now I took Claudia into my arms. She turned her face towards me, and I heard her whisper, 'Louis, the garlic, the crucifix above the door!'

"I had not seen these things. It was a small crucifix, with the body of Christ in bronze fixed to the wood, and the garlic was wreathed around it, a fresh garland entwined with an old one, in which the buds were withered and dried. The woman's eye followed my eyes, and then she looked at me sharply and I could see how exhausted she was, how red were her pupils, and how the hand which clutched at the shawl at her breast trembled. Her black hair was completely dishevelled. I pressed nearer until I was almost at the threshold, and she opened the door wide suddenly as if she'd only just decided to let us in. She said a prayer as I passed her, I was sure of it, though I couldn't understand the Slavic words.

"The small, low-beamed room was filled with people, men and women along the rough, panelled walls, on benches and even on the floor. It was as if the entire village were gathered there. A child slept in a woman's lap and another slept on the staircase, bundled in blankets, his knees tucked in against one step, his arms making a pillow for his head on the next. And everywhere there was the garlic hanging from nails and hooks, along with the cooking pots and flagons. The fire was the only light, and it threw distorting shadows on the still faces as they watched us.

"No one motioned for us to sit or offered us anything, and finally the woman told me in German I might take the horses into the stable if I liked. She was staring at me with those slightly wild, red-rimmed eyes, and then her face softened. She told me she'd stand at the inn door for me with a lantern, but I must hurry and leave the child here.

"But something else had distracted me, a scent I detected beneath the heavy fragrance of burning wood and the wine. It was the scent of death. I could feel Claudia's hand press my chest, and I saw her tiny finger pointing to a door at the foot of the stairs. The scent came from there.

"The woman had a cup of wine waiting when I returned, and a bowl of broth. I sat down, Claudia on my knee, her head turned away from the fire towards that mysterious door. All eyes were fixed on us as before, except for the foreigner. I could see his profile now clearly. He was much younger than I'd thought, his haggard appearance stemming from emotion. He had a lean but very pleasant face actually, his light, freckled skin making him seem like a boy. His wide, blue eyes were fixed on the fire as though he were talking to it, and his eyelashes and eyebrows were golden in the light, which gave him a very innocent, open expression. But he was miserable, disturbed, drunk. Suddenly he turned to me, and I saw he'd been crying. 'Do you speak English?' he said, his voice booming in the silence.

" 'Yes, I do,' I said to him. And he glanced at the others, triumphantly. They stared at him stonily.

" 'You speak English!' he cried, his lips stretching into a bitter smile, his eyes moving around the ceiling and then fixing on mine. 'Get out of this country,' he said. 'Get out of it now. Take your carriage, your horses, drive them till they drop, but get out of it!' Then his shoulders convulsed as if he were sick. He put his hand to his mouth. The woman who stood against the wall now, her arms folded over her soiled apron, said calmly in German, 'At dawn you can go. At dawn.'

" 'But what is it?' I whispered to her; and then I looked to him. He was watching me, his eyes glassy and red. No one spoke. A log fell heavily in the fire.

" 'Won't you tell me?' I asked the Englishman gently. He stood up. For a moment I thought he was going to fall. He loomed over me, a much taller man than myself, his head pitching forward, then backward, before he righted himself and put his hands on the edge of the table. His black coat was stained with wine, and so was his shirt cuff. 'You want to see?' he gasped as he peered into my eyes. 'Do you want to see for yourself?' There was a soft, pathetic tone to his voice as he spoke these words.

" 'Leave the child!' said the woman abruptly, with a quick, imperious gesture.

" 'She's sleeping,' I said. And, rising, I followed the Englishman to the door at the foot of the stairs.

"There was a slight commotion as those nearest the door moved away from it. And we entered a small parlor together.

"Only one candle burned on the sideboard, and the first thing I saw was a row of delicately painted plates on a shelf. There were curtains on the small window, and a gleaming picture of the Virgin Mary and Christ child on the wall. But the walls and chairs barely enclosed a great oak table, and on that table lay the body of a young woman, her white hands folded on her breast, her auburn hair mussed and tucked about her thin, white throat and under her shoulders. Her pretty face was already hard with death. Amber rosary beads gleamed around her wrist and down the side of her dark wool skirt. And beside her lay a very pretty red felt hat with a wide, soft brim and a veil, and a pair of dark gloves. It was all laid there as if she would very soon rise and put these things on. And the Englishman patted the hat carefully now as he drew close to her. He was on the verge of breaking down altogether. He'd drawn a large handkerchief out of his coat, and he had put it to his face. 'Do you know what they want to do with her?' he whispered as he looked at me. 'Do you have any idea?'

"The woman came in behind us and reached for his arm, but he roughly shook her off. 'Do you know?' he demanded of me with his eyes fierce. 'Savages!'

" 'You stop now!' she said under her breath.

"He clenched his teeth and shook his head, so that a shock of his red hair loosened in his eyes. 'You get away from me,' he said to the woman in German. 'Get away from me.' Someone was whispering in the other room. The Englishman looked again at the young woman, and his eyes filled with tears. 'So innocent,' he said softly; and then he glanced at the ceiling and, making a fist with his right hand, he gasped, 'Damn you . . . God! Damn you!'

" 'Lord,' the woman whispered, and quickly she made the Sign of the Cross.

" 'Do you see this?' he asked me. And he pried very carefully at the lace of the dead woman's throat, as though he could not, did not wish to actually touch the hardening flesh. There on her throat, unmistakable, were the two puncture wounds, as I'd seen them a thousand times upon a thousand, engraved in the yellowing skin. The man drew his hands up to his face, his tall. lean body rocking on the balls of his feet. 'I think I'm going mad!' he said.

" 'Come now,' said the woman, holding onto him as he struggled, her face suddenly flushed.

" 'Let him be,' I said to her. 'Just let him be. I'll take care of him.'

"Her mouth contorted. 'I'll throw you all out of here, out into that dark, if you don't stop.' She was too weary for this, too close to some breaking point herself. But then she turned her back on us, drawing her shawl tight around her, and padded softly out, the men who'd gathered at the door making way for her.

"The Englishman was crying.

"I could see what I must do, but it wasn't only that I wanted so much to learn from him, my heart pounding with silent excitement. It was heartrending to see him this way. Fate brought me too mercilessly close to him.

" 'I'll stay with you,' I offered. And I brought two chairs up beside the table. He sat down heavily, his eyes on the flickering candle at his side. I shut the door, and the walls seemed to recede and the circle of the candle to grow brighter around his bowed head. He leaned back against the sideboard and wiped his face with his handkerchief. Then he drew a leather-bound flask from his pocket and offered it to me, and I said no.

" 'Do you want to tell me what happened?'

"He nodded. " 'Perhaps you can bring some sanity to this place,' he said. 'You're a Frenchman, aren't you? You know, I'm English.'

" 'Yes,' I nodded.

"And then, pressing my hand fervently, the liquor so dulling his senses that he never felt the coldness of it, he told me his name was Morgan and he needed me desperately, more than he'd ever needed anyone in his life. And at that moment, holding that hand, feeling the fever of it, I did a strange thing. I told him my name, which I confided to almost no one. But he was looking at the dead woman as if he hadn't heard me, his lips forming what appeared to be the faintest smile, the tears standing in his eyes. His expression would have moved any human being; it might have been more than some could bear.

" 'I did this,' he said, nodding. 'I brought her here.' And he raised his eyebrows as if wondering at it.

" 'No,' I said quickly. 'You didn't do it. Tell me who did.'

"But then he seemed confused, lost in thought. 'I'd never been out of England,' he started. 'I was painting, you see . . . as if it mattered now . . . the paintings, the book! I thought it all so quaint! So picturesque!' His eyes moved over the room, his voice trailing off. For a long time he looked at her again, and then softly he said to her, 'Emily,' and I felt I'd glimpsed something precious he held to his heart.

"Gradually, then, the story began to come. A honeymoon journey, through Germany, into this country, wherever the regular coaches would carry them, wherever Morgan found scenes to paint. And they'd come to this remote place finally because there was a ruined monastery nearby which was said to be a very well-preserved place.

"But Morgan and Emily had never reached that monastery. Tragedy had been waiting for them here.

"It turned out the regular coaches did not come this way, and Morgan had paid a farmer to bring them by cart. But the afternoon they arrived, there was a great commotion in the cemetery outside of town. The farmer, taking one look, refused to leave his cart to see further.

" 'It was some kind of procession, it seemed,' Morgan said, 'with all the people outfitted in their best, and some with flowers; and the truth was I thought it quite fascinating. I wanted to see it. I was so eager I had the fellow leave us, bags and all. We could see the village just up ahead. Actually it was I more than Emily, of course, but she was so agreeable, you see. I left her, finally, seated on our suitcases, and I went on up the hill without her. Did you see it when you were coming, the cemetery? No, of course you didn't. Thank God that carriage of yours brought you here safe and sound. Though, if you'd driven on, no matter how bad off your horses were . . .' He stopped.

" 'What's the danger?' I urged him, gently.

" 'Ah . . . danger! Barbarians!' he murmured. And he glanced at the door. Then he took another drink from his flask and capped it.

" 'Well, it was no procession. I saw that right off,' he said. 'The people wouldn't even speak to me when I came up—you know what they are; but they had no objection to letting me watch. The truth was, you wouldn't have thought I was standing there at all. You won't believe me when I tell you what I saw, but you must believe me; because if you don't, I'm mad, I know it.'

" 'I will believe you, go on,' I said.

" 'Well, the cemetery was full of fresh graves, I saw that at once, some of them with new wooden crosses and some of them just mounds of earth with flowers still fresh; and the peasants there, they were holding flowers, a few of them, as though they meant to be trimming these graves; but all of them were standing stock-still, their eyes on these two fellows who had a white horse by the bridle—and what an animal that was! It was pawing and stomping and shying to one side, as if it wanted no part of the place; a beautiful thing it was, though, a splendid animal—a stallion, and pure white. Well, at some point—and I couldn't tell you how they agreed upon it, because not a one of them said a word—one fellow, the leader, I think, gave the horse a tremendous whack with the handle of a shovel, and it took off up the hill, just wild. You can imagine, I thought that was the last we'd see of that horse for a while for sure. But I was wrong. In a minute it had slowed to a gallop, and it was turning around amongst the old graves and coming back down the hill towards the newer ones. And the people all stood there watching it. No one made a sound. And here it came trotting right over the mounds, right through the flowers, and no one made a move to get hold of the bridle. And then suddenly it came to a stop, right on one of the graves.'

"He wiped at his eyes, but the tears were almost gone. He seemed fascinated with his tale, as I was.

" 'Well, here's what happened,' he continued. 'The animal just stood there. And suddenly a cry went up from the crowd. No, it wasn't a cry, it was as though they were all gasping and moaning, and then everything went quiet. And the horse was just standing there, tossing its head; and finally this fellow who was the leader burst forward and shouted to several of the others; and one of the women—she screamed, and threw herself on the grave almost under the horse's hooves. I came up then as close as I could. I could see the stone with the deceased's name on it; it was a young woman, dead only six months, the dates carved right there, and there was this miserable woman on her knees in the dirt, with her arms around the stone now, as if she meant to pull it right up out of the earth. And these fellows trying to pick her up and get her away.

" 'Now I almost turned back, but I couldn't, not until I saw what they meant to do. And, of course, Emily was quite safe, and none of these people took the slightest notice of either of us. Well, two of them finally did have that woman up, and then the other had come with shovels and had begun to dig right into the grave. Pretty soon one of them was down in the grave, and everyone was so still you could hear the slightest sound, that shovel digging in there and the earth thrown up in a heap. I can't tell you what it was like. Here was the sun high above us and not a cloud in the sky, and all of them standing around, holding onto one another now, and even that pathetic woman . . .' He stopped now, because his eyes had fallen on Emily. I just sat there waiting for him. I could hear the whiskey when he lifted the flask again, and I felt glad for him that there was so much there, that he could drink it and deaden this pain. 'It might as well have been midnight on that hill,' he said, looking at me, his voice very low. 'That's how it felt. And then I could hear this fellow in the grave. He was cracking the coffin lid with his shovel! Then out came the broken boards. He was just tossing them out, right and left. And suddenly he let out an awful cry. The other fellows drew up close, and all at once there was a rush to the grave; and then they all fell back like a wave, all of them crying out, and some of them turning and trying to push away. And the poor woman, she was wild, bending her knees, and trying to get free of those men that were holding onto her. Well,

I couldn't help but go up. I don't suppose anything could have kept me away; and I'll tell you that's the first time I've ever done such a thing, and, God help me, it's to be the last. Now, you must believe me, you must! But there, right there in that coffin, with that fellow standing on the broken boards over her feet, was the dead woman, and I tell you . . . I tell you she was as fresh, as pink'—his voice cracked, and he sat there, his eyes wide, his hand poised as if he held something invisible in his fingers, pleading with me to believe him—'as pink as if she were alive! Buried six months! And there she lay! The shroud was thrown back off her, and her hands lay on her breast just as if she were asleep.'

"He sighed. His hand dropped to his leg and he shook his head, and for a moment he just sat staring. 'I swear to you!' he said. 'And then this fellow who was in the grave, he bent down and lifted the dead woman's hand. I tell you that arm moved as freely as my arm! And he held her hand out as if he were looking at her nails. Then he shouted; and that woman beside the grave, she was kicking at those fellows and shoving at the earth with her foot, so it fell right down in the corpse's face and hair. And oh, she was so pretty, that dead woman; oh, if you could have seen her, and what they did then!'

" 'Tell me what they did,' I said to him softly. But I knew before he said it.

" 'I tell you . . .' he said. 'We don't know the meaning of something like that until we see it!' And he looked at me, his eyebrow arched as if he were confiding a terrible secret. 'We just don't know.'

" 'No, we don't,' I said.

" 'I'll tell you. They took a stake, a wooden stake, mind you; and this one in the grave, he took the stake with a hammer and he put it right to her breast. I didn't believe it! And then with one great blow he drove it right into her. I tell you, I couldn't have moved even if I'd wanted to; I was rooted there. And then that fellow, that beastly fellow, he reached up for his shovel and with both his arms he drove it sharp, right into the dead woman's throat. The head was off like that.' He shut his eyes, his face contorted, and put his head to the side.

"I looked at him, but I wasn't seeing him at all. I was seeing this woman in her grave with the head severed, and I was feeling the most keen revulsion inside myself, as if a hand were pressing on my throat and my insides were coming up inside me and I couldn't breathe. Then I felt Claudia's lip against my wrist. She was staring at Morgan, and apparently she had been for some time.

"Slowly Morgan looked up at me, his eyes wild. 'It's what they want to do with *her*,' he said. 'With Emily! Well I won't let them.' He shook his head adamantly. 'I won't let them. You've got to help me, Louis.' His lips were trembling, and his face so distorted now by his sudden desperation that I might have recoiled from it despite myself. 'The same blood flows in our veins, you and I. I mean, French, English, we're civilized men, Louis. They're savages!'

" 'Try to be calm now, Morgan,' I said, reaching out for him. 'I want you to tell me what happened then. You and Emily . . .'

"He was struggling for his bottle. I drew it out of his pocket, and he took off the cap. 'That's a fellow, Louis; that's a friend,' he said emphatically. 'You see, I took her away fast. They were going to burn that corpse right there in the cemetery; and Emily was not to see that, not while I . . .' He shook his head. 'There wasn't a carriage to be found that would take us out of here; not a single one of them would leave now for the two days' drive to get us to a decent place!'

" 'But how did they explain it to you, Morgan?' I insisted. I could see he did not have much time left.

" 'Vampires!' he burst out, the whiskey sloshing on his hand. 'Vampires, Louis. Can you believe that!' And he gestured to the door with the bottle. 'A plague of vampires! All this in whispers, as if the devil himself were listening at the door! Of course, God have mercy, they put a stop to it. That unfortunate woman in the cemetery, they'd stopped her from clawing her way up nightly to feed on the rest of us!' He put the bottle to his lips. 'Oh . . . God . . .' he moaned.

"I watched him drink, patiently waiting.

" 'And Emily . . .' he continued. 'She thought it fascinating. What with the fire out there and a decent dinner and a proper glass of wine. She hadn't seen that woman! She hadn't seen what they'd done,' he said desperately. 'Oh, I wanted to get out of here; I offered them money. "If it's over," I kept saying to them, "one of you ought to want this money, a small fortune just to drive us out of here." '

" 'But it wasn't over . . .' I whispered.

"And I could see the tears gathering in his eyes, his mouth twisting with pain.

" 'How did it happen to her?' I asked him.

" 'I don't know,' he gasped, shaking his head, the flask pressed to his forehead as if it were something cool, refreshing, when it was not.

" 'It came into the inn?'

" 'They said she went out to it,' he confessed, the tears coursing down his cheeks. 'Everything was locked! They saw to that. Doors, windows! Then it was morning and they were all shouting, and she was gone. The window stood wide open, and she wasn't there. I didn't even take time for my robe. I was running. I came to a dead halt over her, out there, behind the inn. My foot all but came down on her . . . she was just lying there under the peach trees. She held an empty cup. Clinging to it, an empty cup! They said it lured her . . . she was trying to give it water. . . .'

"The flask slipped from his hands. He clapped his hands over his ears, his body bent, his head bowed.

"For a long time I sat there watching him; I had no words to say to him. And when he cried softly that they wanted to desecrate her, that they said she, Emily, was now a vampire, I assured him softly, though I don't think he ever heard me, that she was not.

"He moved forward finally, as if he might fall. He appeared to be reaching for the candle, and before his arm rested on the buffet, his finger touched it so the hot wax extinguished the tiny bit that was left of the wick. We were in darkness then, and his head had fallen on his arm.

"All of the light of the room seemed gathered now

in Claudia's eyes. But as the silence lengthened and I sat there, wondering, hoping Morgan wouldn't lift his head again, the woman came to the door. Her candle illuminated him, drunk, asleep.

" 'You go now,' she said to me. Dark figures crowded around her, and the old wooden inn was alive with the shuffling of men and women. 'Go by the fire!'

" 'What are you going to do!' I demanded of her, rising and holding Claudia. 'I want to know what you propose to do!'

" 'Go by the fire,' she commanded.

" 'No, don't do this,' I said. But she narrowed her eyes and bared her teeth. 'You go!' she growled.

" 'Morgan,' I said to him; but he didn't hear me, he couldn't hear me.

" 'Leave him be,' said the woman fiercely.

" 'But it's stupid, what you're doing; don't you understand? This woman's dead!' I pleaded with her.

" 'Louis,' Claudia whispered, so that they couldn't hear her, her arm tightening around my neck beneath the fur of my hood. 'Let these people alone.'

"The others were moving into the room now, encircling the table, their faces grim as they looked at us.

" 'But where do these vampires come from!' I whispered. 'You've searched your cemetery! If it's vampires, where do they hide from you? This woman can't do you harm. Hunt your vampires if you must.'

" 'By day,' she said gravely, winking her eye and slowly nodding her head. 'By day. We get them, by day.'

" 'Where, out there in the graveyard, digging up the graves of your own villagers?'

"She shook her head. 'The ruins,' she said. 'It was always the ruins. We were wrong. In my grandfather's time it was the ruins, and it is the ruins again. We'll take them down stone by stone if we have to. But you . . . you go now. Because if you don't go, we'll drive you out there into that dark now!'

"And then out from behind her apron she drew her clenched fist with the stake in it and held it up in the flickering light of the candle. 'You hear me, you go!' she said; and the men pressed in close behind her, their mouths set, their eyes blazing in the light.

" 'Yes . . .' I said to her. 'Out there. I would prefer that. Out there.' And I swept past her, almost throwing her aside, seeing them scuttle back to make way. I had my hand on the latch of the inn door and slid it back with one quick gesture.

" 'No!' cried the woman in her guttural German. 'You're mad!' And she rushed up to me and then stared at the latch, dumbfounded. She threw her hands up against the rough boards of the door. 'Do you know what you do!'

" 'Where are the ruins?' I asked her calmly. 'How far? Do they lie to the left of the road, or to the right?'

" 'No, no.' She shook her head violently. I pried the door back and felt the cold blast of air on my face. One of the women said something sharp and angry from the wall, and one of the children moaned in its sleep. 'I'm going. I want one thing from you. Tell me where the ruins lie, so I may stay clear of them. Tell me.'

" 'You don't know, you don't know,' she said; and then I laid my hand on her warm wrist and drew her slowly through the door, her feet scraping on the boards, her eyes wild. The men moved nearer but, as she stepped out against her will into the night, they stopped. She tossed her head, her hair falling down into her eyes, her eyes glaring at my hand and at my face. 'Tell me . . .' I said.

"I could see she was staring not at me but at Claudia. Claudia had turned towards her, and the light from the fire was on her face. The woman did not see the rounded cheeks nor the pursed lips, I knew, but Claudia's eyes, which were gazing at her with a dark, demonic intelligence. The woman's teeth bit down into the flesh of her lip.

" 'To the north or south?'

" 'To the north . . .' she whispered.

" 'To the left or the right?'

" 'The left.'

" 'And how far?'

"Her hand struggled desperately. 'Three miles,' she gasped. And I released her, so that she fell back against the door, her eyes wide with fear and confusion. I had turned to go, but suddenly behind me she cried out for me to wait. I turned to see she'd ripped the crucifix from the beam over her head, and she had it thrust out towards me now. And out of the dark nightmare landscape of my memory I saw Babette gazing at me as she had so many years ago, saying those words, *'Get thee behind me, Satan.'* But the woman's face was desperate. 'Take it, please, in the name of God,' she said. 'And ride fast.' And the door shut, leaving Claudia and me in total darkness."

"In minutes the tunnel of the night closed upon the weak lanterns of our carriage, as if the village had never existed. We lurched forward, around a bend, the springs creaking, the dim moon revealing for an instant the pale outline of the mountains beyond the pines. I could not stop thinking of Morgan, stop hearing his voice. It was all tangled with my own horrified anticipation of meeting the thing which had killed Emily, the thing which was unquestionably one of our own. But Claudia was in a frenzy. If she could have driven the horses herself, she would have taken the reins. Again and again she urged me to use the whip. She struck savagely at the few low branches that dipped suddenly into the lamps before our faces; and the arm that clung to my waist on the rocking bench was as firm as iron.

"I remember the road turning sharply, the lanterns clattering, and Claudia calling out over the wind: 'There, Louis, do you see it?' And I jerked hard on the reins.

"She was on her knees, pressed against me, and the carriage was swaying like a ship at sea.

"A great fleecy cloud had released the moon, and high above us loomed the dark outline of the tower. One long window showed the pale sky beyond it. I sat there, clutching the bench, trying to steady a motion

that continued in my head as the carriage settled on
its springs. One of the horses whinnied. Then everything
was still.

"Claudia was saying, 'Louis, come. . . .'

"I whispered something, a swift irrational negation.
I had the distinct and terrifying impression that Morgan was near to me, talking to me in that low, im-
passioned way he'd pleaded with me in the inn. Not
a living creature stirred in the night around us. There
was only the wind and the soft rustling of the leaves.

" 'Do you think he knows we're coming?' I asked,
my voice unfamiliar to me over this wind. I was in
that little parlor, as if there were no escape from it,
as if this dense forest were not real. I think I shuddered. And then I felt Claudia's hand very gently touch
the hand I lifted to my eyes. The thin pines were
billowing behind her and the rustle of the leaves grew
louder, as if a great mouth sucked the breeze and
began a whirlwind. 'They'll bury her at the cross-
roads? Is that what they'll do? An Englishwoman!' I
whispered.

" 'Would that I had your size . . .' Claudia was saying. 'And would that you had my heart. Oh, Louis. . . .'
And her head inclined to me now, so like the attitude
of the vampire bending to kiss that I shrank back from
her; but her lips only gently pressed my own, finding a
part there to suck the breath and let it flow back into
me as my arms enclosed her. 'Let me lead you . . .'
she pleaded. 'There's no turning back now. Take me
in your arms,' she said, 'and let me down, on the
road.'

"But it seemed an eternity that I just sat there feeling her lips on my face and on my eyelids. Then she
moved, the softness of her small body suddenly
snatched from me, in a movement so graceful and
swift that she seemed now poised in the air beside
the carriage, her hand clutching mine for an instant,
then letting it go. And then I looked down to see
her looking up at me, standing on the road in the
shuddering pool of light beneath the lantern. She
beckoned to me, as she stepped backwards, one small
boot behind the other. 'Louis, come down . . .' until

she threatened to vanish into the darkness. And in a second I'd unfastened the lamp from its hook, and I stood beside her in the tall grass.

" 'Don't you sense the danger?' I whispered to her. 'Can't you breathe it like the air?' One of those quick, elusive smiles played on her lips, as she turned towards the slope. The lantern pitched a pathway through the rising forest. One small, white hand drew the wool of her cape close, and she moved forward.

" 'Wait only for a moment. . . .'

" 'Fear's your enemy . . .' she answered, but she did not stop.

"She proceeded ahead of the light, feet sure, even as the tall grass gave way gradually to low heaps of rubble, and the forest thickened, and the distant tower vanished with the fading of the moon and the great weaving of the branches overhead. Soon the sound and scent of the horses died on the low wind. 'Be *en garde*,' Claudia whispered, as she moved, relentlessly, pausing only now and again where the tangled vines and rock made it seem for moments there was a shelter. But the ruins were ancient. Whether plague or fire or a foreign enemy had ravaged the town, we couldn't know. Only the monastery truly remained.

"Now something whispered in the dark that was like the wind and the leaves, but it was neither. I saw Claudia's back straighten, saw the flash of her white palm as she slowed her step. Then I knew it was water, winding its way slowly down the mountain, and I saw it far ahead through the black trunks, a straight, moonlit waterfall descending to a boiling pool below. Claudia emerged silhouetted against the fall, her hand clutching a bare root in the moist earth beside it; and now I saw her climbing hand over hand up the overgrown cliff, her arm trembling ever so slightly, her small boots dangling, then digging in to hold, then swinging free again. The water was cold, and it made the air fragrant and light all around it, so that for a moment I rested. Nothing stirred around me in the forest. I listened, senses quietly separating the tune of the leaves, but nothing else stirred. And then it struck me gradually, like a chill coming over my arms and my throat and finally my face, that the night was too desolate, too lifeless. It was as if even the birds had shunned this place, as well as all the myriad creatures that should have been moving about the banks of this stream. But Claudia, above me on the ledge, was reaching for the lantern, her cape brushing my face. I lifted it, so that suddenly she sprang into light, like an eerie cherub. She put her hand out for me as if, despite her small size, she could help me up the embankment. In a moment we were moving on again, over the stream, up the mountain. 'Do you sense it?' I whispered. 'It's too still.'

"But her hand tightened on mine, as if to say, 'Quiet.' The hill was growing steeper, and the quiet was unnerving. I tried to stare at the limits of the light, to see each new bark as it loomed before us. Something did move, and I reached for Claudia, almost pulling her sharply near to me. But it was only a reptile, shooting through the leaves with a whip of his tail. The leaves settled. But Claudia moved back against me, under the folds of my cape, a hand firmly clasping the cloth of my coat; and she seemed to propel me forward, my cape falling over the loose fabric of her own.

"Soon the scent of the water was gone, and when the moon shone clear for an instant I could see right ahead of us what appeared to be a break in the woods. Claudia firmly clasped the lantern and shut its metal door. I moved to stop this, my hand struggling with hers; but then she said to me quietly, 'Close your eyes for an instant, and then open them slowly. And when you do, you will see it.'

"A chill rose over me as I did this, during which I held fast to her shoulder. But then I opened my eyes and saw beyond the distant bark of the trees the long, low walls of the monastery and the high square top of the massive tower. Far beyond it, above an immense black valley, gleamed the snow-capped peaks of the mountains. 'Come,' she said to me, 'quiet, as if your body has no weight.' And she started without hesitation right towards those walls, right towards whatever might have been waiting in their shelter.

"In moments we had found the gap that would admit us, the great opening that was blacker still than the walls around it, the vines encrusting its edges as if to hold the stones in place. High above, through the open room, the damp smell of the stones strong in my nostrils, I saw, beyond the streaks of clouds, a faint sprinkling of stars. A great staircase moved upward, from corner to corner, all the way to the narrow windows that looked out upon the valley. And beneath the first rise of the stair, out of the gloom emerged the vast, dark opening to the monastery's remaining rooms.

"Claudia was still now, as if she had become the stones. In the damp enclosure not even the soft tendrils of her hair moved. She was listening. And then I was listening with her. There was only the low backdrop of the wind. She moved, slowly, deliberately, and with one pointed foot gradually cleared a space in the moist earth in front of her. I could see a flat stone there, and it sounded hollow as she gently tapped it with her heel. Then I could see the broad size of it and how it rose at one distant corner; and an image came to mind, dreadful in its sharpness, of that band of men and women from the village surrounding the stone, raising it with a giant lever. Claudia's eyes moved over the staircase and then fixed on the crumbling doorway beneath it. The moon shone for an instant through a lofty window. Then Claudia moved, so suddenly that she stood beside me without having made a sound. 'Do you hear it?' she whispered. 'Listen.'

"It was so low no mortal could have heard it. And it did not come from the ruins. It came from far off, not the long, meandering way that we had come up the slope, but another way, up the spine of the hill, directly from the village. Just a rustling now, a scraping, but it was steady; and then slowly the round tramping of a foot began to distinguish itself. Claudia's hand tightened on mine, and with a gentle pressure she moved me silently beneath the slope of the stairway. I could see the folds of her dress heave slightly beneath the edge of her cape. The tramp of the feet grew louder, and I began to sense that one step preceded the other very sharply, the second dragging slowly across the earth. It was a limping step, drawing nearer and nearer over the low whistling of the wind. My own heart beat hard against my chest, and I felt the veins in my temples tighten, a tremor passing through my limbs, so that I could feel the fabric of my shirt against me, the stiff cut of the collar, the very scraping of the buttons against my cape.

"Then a faint scent came with the wind. It was the scent of blood, at once arousing me, against my will, the warm, sweet scent of human blood, blood that was spilling, flowing and then I sensed the smell of living flesh and I heard in time with the feet a dry, hoarse breathing. But with it came another sound, faint and intermingled with the first, as the feet tramped closer and closer to the walls, the sound of yet another creature's halting, strained breath. And I could hear the heart of that creature, beating irregularly, a fearful throbbing; but beneath that was another heart, a steady, pulsing heart growing louder and louder, a heart as strong as my own! Then, in the jagged gap through which we'd come, I saw him.

'His great, huge shoulder emerged first and one long, loose arm and hand, the fingers curved; then I saw his head. Over his other shoulder he was carrying a body. In the broken doorway he straightened and shifted the weight and stared directly into the darkness towards us. Every muscle in me became iron as I looked at him, saw the outline of his head looming there against the sky. But nothing of his face was visible except the barest glint of the moon on his eye as if it were a fragment of glass. Then I saw it glint on his buttons and heard them rustle as his arm swung free again and one long leg bent as he moved forward and proceeded into the tower right towards us.

"I held fast to Claudia, ready in an instant to shove her behind me, to step forward to meet him. But then I saw with astonishment that his eyes did not see me as I saw him, and he was trudging under the weight of the body he carried towards the monastery door. The moon fell now on his bowed head, on a mass of wavy black hair that touched his bent shoulder, and on the full black sleeve of his coat. I saw something about his coat; the flap of it was badly torn and the sleeve appeared to be ripped from the seam. I almost fancied I could see his flesh through the shoulder. The human in his arms stirred now, and moaned miserably. And the figure stopped for a moment and appeared to stroke the human with his hand. And at that moment I stepped forward from the wall and went towards him.

"No words passed my lips: I knew none to say. I only knew that I moved into the light of the moon before him and that his dark, wavy head rose with a jerk, and that I saw his eyes.

"For one full instant he looked at me, and I saw the light shining in those eyes and then glinting on two sharp canine teeth; and then a low strangled cry seemed to rise from the depths of his throat which, for a second, I thought to be my own. The human crashed to the stones, a shuddering moan escaping his lips. And the vampire lunged at me, that strangled cry rising again as the stench of fetid breath rose in my nostrils and the clawlike fingers cut into the very fur of my cape. I fell backwards, my head cracking against the wall, my hands grabbing at his head, clutching a mass of tangled filth that was his hair. At once the wet, rotting fabric of his coat ripped in my grasp, but the arm that held me was like iron; and, as I struggled to pull the head backwards, the fangs touched the flesh of my throat. Claudia screamed behind him. Something hit his head hard, which stopped him suddenly; and then he was hit again. He turned as if to strike her a blow, and I sent my fist against his face as powerfully as I could. Again a stone struck him as she darted away, and I threw my full weight against him and felt his crippled leg buckling. I remember pounding his head over and over, my fingers all but pulling that filthy hair out by the roots, his fangs projected towards me, his hands scratching, clawing at me. We rolled over and over, until I pinned him down again and the moon shone full on his face. And I realized, through my frantic sobbing breaths, what it was I held in my arms. The two huge eyes bulged from naked sockets and two small, hideous holes made up his nose; only a putrid, leathery flesh enclosed his skull, and the rank, rotting rags that covered his frame were thick with earth and slime and blood. I was battling a mindless, animated corpse. But no more.

"From above him, a sharp stone fell full on his forehead, and a fount of blood gushed from between his eyes. He struggled, but another stone crashed with such force I heard the bones shatter. Blood seeped out beneath the matted hair, soaking into the stones and grass. The chest throbbed beneath me, but the arms shuddered and grew still. I drew up, my throat knotted, my heart burning, every fiber of my body aching from the struggle. For a moment the great tower seemed to tilt, but then it righted itself. I lay against the wall, staring at the thing, the blood rushing in my ears. Gradually I realized that Claudia knelt on his chest, that she was probing the mass of hair and bone that had been his head. She was scattering the fragments of his skull. We had met the European vampire, the creature of the Old World. He was dead."

"For a long time I lay on the broad stairway, oblivious to the thick earth that covered it, my head feeling very cool against the earth, just looking at him. Claudia stood at his feet, hands hanging limply at her sides. I saw her eyes close for an instant, two tiny lids that made her face like a small, moonlit white statue as she stood there. And then her body began to rock very slowly. 'Claudia,' I called to her. She awakened. She was gaunt such as I had seldom seen her. She pointed to the human who lay far across the floor of the tower near the wall. He was still motionless, but I knew that he was not dead. I'd forgotten him completely, my body aching as it was, my senses still clouded with the stench of the bleeding corpse. But now I saw the man. And in some part of my mind I knew what his fate would be, and I cared nothing for it. I knew it was only an hour at most before dawn.

" 'He's moving,' she said to me. And I tried to rise off the steps. Better that he not wake, better that he never wake at all, I wanted to say; she was walking towards him, passing indifferently the dead thing that had nearly killed us both. I saw her back and the man stirring in front of her, his foot twisting in the grass. I don't know what I expected to see as I drew nearer, what terrified peasant or farmer, what miserable wretch that had already seen the face of that thing that had brought it here. And for a moment I did not realize who it was that lay there, that it was Morgan, whose pale face showed now in the moon, the marks of the vampire on his throat, his blue eyes staring mute and expressionless before him.

"Suddenly they widened as I drew close to him. 'Louis!' he whispered in astonishment, his lips moving as if he were trying to frame words but could not. 'Louis . . .' he said again; and then I saw he was smiling. A dry, rasping sound came from him as he struggled to his knees, and he reached out for me. His blanched, contorted face strained as the sound died in his throat, and he nodded desperately, his red hair loose and dishevelled, falling into his eyes. I turned and ran from him. Claudia shot past me, gripping me by the arm. 'Do you see the color of the sky!' she hissed at me. Morgan fell forward on his hands behind her. 'Louis,' he called out again, the light gleaming in his eyes. He seemed blind to the ruins, blind to the night, blind to everything but a face he recognized, that one word again issuing from his lips. I put my hands to my ears, backing away from him. His hand was bloody now as he lifted it. I could smell the blood as well as see it. And Claudia could smell it, too.

"Swiftly she descended on him, pushing him down against the stones, her white fingers moving through his red hair. He tried to raise his head. His outstretched hands made a frame about her face, and then suddenly he began to stroke her yellow curls. She sank her teeth, and the hands dropped helpless at his side.

"I was at the edge of the forest when she caught up with me. 'You must go to him, take him,' she commanded. I could smell the blood on her lips, see the warmth in her cheeks. Her wrist burned against me, yet I did not move. 'Listen to me, Louis,' she said, her voice at once desperate and angry. 'I left him for you, but he's dying . . . there's no time.'

"I swung her up into my arms and started the long descent. No need for caution, no need for stealth, no preternatural host waiting. The door to the secrets of eastern Europe was shut against us. I was plowing through the dark to the road. 'Will you listen to me,' she cried out. But I went on in spite of her, her hands clutching at my coat, my hair. 'Do you see the sky, do you see it!' she railed.

"She was all but sobbing against my breast as I splashed through the icy stream and ran headlong in search of the lantern at the road.

"The sky was a dark blue when I found the carriage. 'Give me the crucifix,' I shouted to Claudia as I cracked the whip. 'There's only one place to go.' She was thrown against me as the carriage rocked into its turn and headed for the village.

"I had the eeriest feeling then as I could see the mist rising amongst the dark brown trees. The air was cold and fresh and the birds had begun. It was as if the sun were rising. Yet I did not care. And yet I knew that it was not rising, that there was still time. It was a marvellous, quieting feeling. The scrapes and cuts burned my flesh and my heart ached with hunger, but my head felt marvellously light. Until I saw the gray shapes of the inn and the steeple of the church; they were too clear. And the stars above were fading fast.

"In a moment I was hammering on the door of the inn. As it opened, I put my hood up around my face tightly and held Claudia beneath my cape in a bundle. 'Your village is rid of the vampire!' I said to the woman, who stared at me in astonishment. I was clutching the crucifix which she'd given me. 'Thanks be to God he's dead. You'll find the remains in the tower. Tell this to your people at once.' I pushed past her into the inn.

"The gathering was roused into commotion instantly, but I insisted that I was tired beyond endurance. I must pray and rest. They were to get my chest from the carriage and bring it to a decent room where I might sleep. But a message was to come for me from the bishop at Varna and for this, and this only, was I to be awakened. 'Tell the good father when he arrives that the vampire is dead, and then give him food and drink and have him wait for me,' I said. The woman was crossing herself. 'You understand,' I said to her, as I hurried towards the stairs, 'I couldn't reveal my mission to you until after the vampire had been. . . .' 'Yes, yes,' she said to me. 'But you are not a priest . . . the child!' 'No, only too well-versed in these matters. The Unholy One is no match for me,' I said to her. I stopped. The door of the little parlor stood open, with nothing but a white square of cloth on the oak table. 'Your friend,' she said to me, and she looked at the floor. 'He rushed out into the night . . . he was mad.' I only nodded.

"I could hear them shouting when I shut the door of the room. They seemed to be running in all directions; and then came the sharp sound of the church bell in the rapid peal of alarm. Claudia had slipped down from my arms, and she was staring at me gravely as I bolted the door. Very slowly I unlatched the shutter of the window. An icy light seeped into the room. Still she watched me. Then I felt her at my side. I looked down to see she was holding out her hand to me. 'Here,' she said. She must have seen I was confused. I felt so weak that her face was shimmering as I looked at it, the blue of her eyes dancing on her white cheeks.

" 'Drink,' she whispered, drawing nearer. 'Drink.' And she held the soft, tender flesh of the wrist towards me. 'No, I know what to do; haven't I done it in the past?' I said to her. It was she who bolted the window tight, latched the heavy door. I remember kneeling by the small grate and feeling the ancient panelling. It was rotten behind the varnished surface, and it gave under my fingers. Suddenly I saw my fist go through it and felt the sharp jab of splinter in my wrist. And then I remember feeling in the dark and catching hold of something warm and pulsing. A rush of cold, damp air hit my face and I saw a darkness rising about me, cool and damp as if this air were a silent water that seeped through the broken wall and filled the room. The room was gone. I was drinking from a never-ending stream of warm blood that flowed down my throat and through my pulsing heart and through my veins, so that my skin warmed against this cool, dark water. And now the pulse of the blood I drank slackened, and all my body cried out for it not to slacken, my heart pounding, trying to make that heart pound with it. I felt myself rising, as if I were floating in the darkness, and then the darkness, like the heartbeat, began to fade. Something glimmered in my swoon; it shivered ever so slightly with the pounding of feet on the stairs, on the floorboards, the rolling of wheels and horses' hooves on the earth, and it gave off a tinkling sound as it shivered. It had a small wooden frame around it, and in that frame there emerged, through the glimmer, the figure of a man. He was familiar. I knew his long, slender build, his black, wavy hair. Then I saw that his green eyes were gazing at me. And in his teeth, in his teeth, he was clutching something huge and soft and brown, which he pressed tightly with both his hands. It was a rat. A great loathsome brown rat he held, its feet poised, its mouth agape, its great curved tail frozen in the air. Crying out, he threw it down and stared aghast, blood flowing from his open mouth.

"A searing light hit my eyes. I struggled to open them against it, and the entire room was glowing. Claudia was right in front of me. She was not a tiny child, but someone much larger who drew me forward towards her with both hands. She was on her knees, and my arms encircled her waist. Then darkness descended, and I had her folded against me. The lock slid into place. Numbness came over my limbs, and then the paralysis of oblivion."

A ND THAT WAS HOW it was throughout
Transylvania and Hungary and Bulgaria, and through
all those countries where the peasants know that the
living dead walk, and the legends of the vampires
abound. In every village where we did encounter the
vampire, it was the same."

"A mindless corpse?" the boy asked.

"Always," said the vampire. "When we found these
creatures at all. I remember a handful at most. Sometimes we only watched them from a distance, all too
familiar with their wagging, bovine heads, their haggard shoulders, their rotted, ragged clothing. In one
hamlet it was a woman, only dead for perhaps a few
months; the villagers had glimpsed her and knew her
by name. It was she who gave us the only hope we
were to experience after the monster in Transylvania,
and that hope came to nothing. She fled from us
through the forest and we ran after her, reaching out
for her long, black hair. Her white burial gown was
soaked with dried blood, her fingers caked with the
dirt of the grave. And her eyes . . . they were mindless, two pools that reflected the moon. No secrets, no
truths, only despair."

"But what were these creatures? Why were they like
this?" asked the boy, his lips grimacing with disgust.
"I don't understand. How could they be so different
from you and Claudia, yet exist?"

"I had my theories. So did Claudia. But the main
thing which I had then was despair. And in despair
the recurring fear that we had killed the only other
vampire like us, Lestat. Yet it seemed unthinkable.
Had he possessed the wisdom of a sorcerer, the powers
of a witch . . . I might have come to understand that
he had somehow managed to wrest a conscious life

197

from the same forces that governed these monsters. But he was only Lestat, as I've described him to you: devoid of mystery, finally, his limits as familiar to me in those months in eastern Europe as his charms. I wanted to forget him, and yet it seemed I thought of him always. It was as if the empty nights were made for thinking of him. And sometimes I found myself so vividly aware of him it was as if he had only just left the room and the ring of his voice were still there. And somehow there was a disturbing comfort in that, and, despite myself, I'd envision his face—not as it had been the last night in the fire, but on other nights, that last evening he spent with us at home, his hand playing idly with the keys of the spinet, his head tilted to one side. A sickness rose in me more wretched than anguish when I saw what my dreams were doing. I wanted him alive! In the dark nights of eastern Europe, Lestat was the only vampire I'd found.

"But Claudia's waking thoughts were of a far more practical nature. Over and over, she had me recount that night in the hotel in New Orleans when she'd become a vampire, and over and over she searched the process for some clue to why these things we met in the country graveyards had no mind. What if, after Lestat's infusion of blood, she'd been put in a grave, closed up in it until the preternatural drive for blood caused her to break the stone door of the vault that held her, what then would her mind have been, starved, as it were, to the breaking point? Her body might have saved itself when no mind remained. And through the world she would have blundered, ravaging where she could, as we saw these creatures do. That was how she explained them. But what had fathered them, how had they begun? That was what she couldn't explain and what gave her hope of discovery when I, from sheer exhaustion, had none. 'They spawn their own kind, it's obvious, but where does it begin?' she asked. And then, somewhere near the outskirts of Vienna, she put the question to me which had never before passed her lips. Why could I not do what Lestat had done with both of us? Why could I not make another vampire? I don't know why at first I didn't even understand her, except that in loathing what I was with every impulse in me I had a particular fear of that question, which was almost worse than any other. You see, I didn't understand something strong in myself. Loneliness had caused me to think on that very possibility years before, when I had fallen under the spell of Babette Freniere. But I held it locked inside of me like an unclean passion. I shunned mortal life after her. I killed strangers. And the Englishman Morgan, because I knew him, was as safe from my fatal embrace as Babette had been. They both caused me too much pain. Death I couldn't think of giving them. Life in death—it was monstrous. I turned away from Claudia. I wouldn't answer her. But angry as she was, wretched as was her impatience, she could not stand this turning away. And she drew near to me, comforting me with her hands and her eyes as if she were my loving daughter.

" 'Don't think on it, Louis,' she said later, when we were comfortably situated in a small suburban hotel. I was standing at the window, looking at the distant glow of Vienna, so eager for that city, its civilization, its sheer size. The night was clear and the haze of the city was on the sky. 'Let me put your conscience at ease, though I'll never know precisely what it is,' she said into my ear, her hand stroking my hair.

" 'Do that, Claudia,' I answered her. 'Put it at ease. Tell me that you'll never speak to me of making vampires again.'

" 'I want no orphans such as ourselves!' she said, all too quickly. My words annoyed her. My feeling annoyed her. 'I want answers, knowledge, she said. 'But tell me, Louis, what makes you so certain that you've never done this without your knowing it?'

"Again there was that deliberate obtuseness in me. I must look at her as if I didn't know the meaning of her words. I wanted her to be silent and to be near me, and for us to be in Vienna. I drew her hair back and let my fingertips touch her long lashes and looked away at the light.

" 'After all, what does it take to make those creatures?' she went on. 'Those vagabond monsters? How many drops of your blood intermingled with a man's blood . . . and what kind of heart to survive that first attack?'

"I could feel her watching my face, and I stood there, my arms folded, my back to the side of the window, looking out.

" 'That pale-faced Emily, that miserable Englishman . . .' she said, oblivious to the flicker of pain in my face. 'Their hearts were nothing, and it was the fear of death as much as the drawing of blood that killed them. The idea killed them. But what of the hearts that survive? Are you sure you haven't fathered a league of monsters who, from time to time, struggled vainly and instinctively to follow in your footsteps? What was their life span, these orphans you left behind you—a day there, a week here, before the sun burnt them to ashes or some mortal victim cut them down?'

" 'Stop it,' I begged her. 'If you knew how completely I envision everything you describe, you would not describe it. I tell you it's never happened! Lestat drained me to the point of death to make me a vampire. And gave back all that blood mingled with his own. That is how it was done!'

"She looked away from me, and then it seemed she was looking down at her hands. I think I heard her sigh, but I wasn't certain. And then her eyes moved over me, slowly, up and down, before they finally met mine. Then it seemed she smiled. 'Don't be frightened of my fancy,' she said softly. 'After all, the final decision will always rest with you. Is that not so?'

" 'I don't understand,' I said. And a cold laughter erupted from her as she turned away.

" 'Can you picture it?' she said, so softly I scarcely heard. 'A coven of children? That is all I could provide. . . .'

" 'Claudia,' I murmured.

" 'Rest easy,' she said abruptly, her voice still low. 'I tell you that as much as I hated Lestat . . .' She stopped.

" 'Yes . . .' I whispered. 'Yes. . . .'

" 'As much as I hated him, with him we were . . .

complete.' She looked at me, her eyelids quivering, as if the slight rise in her voice had disturbed her even as it had disturbed me.

" 'No, only you were complete . . .' I said to her. 'Because there were two of us, one on either side of you, from the beginning.'

"I thought I saw her smile then, but I was not certain. She bowed her head, but I could see her eyes moving beneath the lashes, back and forth, back and forth. Then she said, 'The two of you at my side. Do you picture that as you say it, as you picture everything else?'

"One night, long gone by, was as material to me as if I were in it still, but I didn't tell her. She was desperate in that night, running away from Lestat, who had urged her to kill a woman in the street from whom she'd backed off, clearly alarmed. I was sure the woman had resembled her mother. Finally she'd escaped us entirely, but I'd found her in the armoire, beneath the jackets and coats, clinging to her doll. And, carrying her to her crib, I sat beside her and sang to her, and she stared at me as she clung to that doll, as if trying blindly and mysteriously to calm a pain she herself did not begin to understand. Can you picture it, this splendid domesticity, dim lamps, the vampire father singing to the vampire daughter? Only the doll had a human face, only the doll.

" 'But we must get away from here!' said the present Claudia suddenly, as though the thought had just taken shape in her mind with a special urgency. She had her hand to her ear, as if clutching it against some awful sound. 'From the roads behind us, from what I see in your eyes now, because I give voice to thoughts which are nothing more to me than plain considerations . . .'

" 'Forgive me,' I said as gently as I could, withdrawing slowly from that long-ago room, that ruffled crib, that frightened monster child and monster voice. And Lestat, where was Lestat? A match striking in the other room, a shadow leaping suddenly into life, as light and dark come alive where there was only darkness.

" 'No, you forgive me . . .' she was saying to me

now, in this little hotel room near the first capital of western Europe. 'No, we forgive each other. But we don't forgive him; and, without him, you see what things are between us.'

" 'Only now because we are tired, and things are dreary . . .' I said to her and to myself, because there was no one else in the world to whom I could speak.

" 'Ah, yes; and that is what must end. I tell you, I begin to understand that we have done it all wrong from the start. We must bypass Vienna. We need our language, our people. I want to go directly now to Paris.' "

PART III

I THINK the very name of Paris brought a rush of pleasure to me that was extraordinary, a relief so near to well-being that I was amazed, not only that I could feel it, but that I'd so nearly forgotten it.

"I wonder if you can understand what it meant. My expression can't convey it now, for what Paris means to me is very different from what it meant then, in those days, at that hour; but still, even now, to think of it, I feel something akin to that happiness. And I've more reason now than ever to say that happiness is not what I will ever know, or will ever deserve to know. I am not so much in love with happiness. Yet the name Paris makes me feel it.

"Mortal beauty often makes me ache, and mortal grandeur can fill me with that longing I felt so hopelessly in the Mediterranean Sea. But Paris, Paris drew me close to her heart, so I forgot myself entirely. Forgot the damned and questing preternatural thing that doted on mortal skin and mortal clothing. Paris overwhelmed, and lightened and rewarded more richly than any promise.

"It was the mother of New Orleans, understand that first; it had given New Orleans its life, its first populace; and it was what New Orleans had for so long tried to be. But New Orleans, though beautiful and desperately alive, was desperately fragile. There was something forever savage and primitive there, something that threatened the exotic and sophisticated life both from within and without. Not an inch of those wooden streets nor a brick of the crowded Spanish houses had not been bought from the fierce wilderness that forever surrounded the city, ready to engulf it. Hurricanes, floods, fevers, the plague—and the damp of the Louisiana climate itself worked tirelessly on every hewn plank or stone façade, so that New Orleans seemed at all times like a dream in the imagination of her striving populace, a dream held intact at every second by a tenacious, though unconscious, collective will.

"But Paris, Paris was a universe whole and entire unto herself, hollowed and fashioned by history; so she seemed in this age of Napoleon III with her towering buildings, her massive cathedrals, her grand boulevards and ancient winding medieval streets—as vast and indestructible as nature itself. All was embraced by her, by her volatile and enchanted populace thronging the galleries, the theaters, the cafés, giving birth over and over to genius and sanctity, philosophy and war, frivolity and the finest art; so it seemed that if all the world outside her were to sink into darkness, what was fine, what was beautiful, what was essential might there still come to its finest flower. Even the majestic trees that graced and sheltered her streets were attuned to her—and the waters of the Seine, contained and beautiful as they wound through her heart; so that the earth on that spot, so shaped by blood and consciousness, had ceased to be the earth and had become Paris.

"We were alive again. We were in love, and so euphoric was I after those hopeless nights of wandering in eastern Europe that I yielded completely when Claudia moved us into the Hôtel Saint-Gabriel on the Boulevard des Capucines. It was rumored to be one of the largest hotels in Europe, its immense rooms dwarfing the memory of our old town house, while at the same time recalling it with a comfortable splendor. We were to have one of the finest suites. Our windows looked out over the gas-lit boulevard itself where, in the early evening, the asphalt sidewalks teemed with strollers and an endless stream of carriages flowed past, taking lavishly dressed ladies and their gentlemen to the Opéra or the Opéra Comique, the ballet, the theaters, the balls and receptions without end at the Tuileries.

"Claudia put her reasons for expense to me gently and logically, but I could see that she became impatient ordering everything through me; it was wearing for her.

The hotel, she said, quietly afforded us complete freedom, our nocturnal habits going unnoticed in the continual press of European tourists, our rooms immaculately maintained by an anonymous staff, while the immense price we paid guaranteed our privacy and our security. But there was more to it than that. There was a feverish purpose to her buying.

" 'This is my world,' she explained to me as she sat in a small velvet chair before the open balcony, watching the long row of broughams stopping one by one before the hotel doors. 'I must have it as I like,' she said, as if speaking to herself. And so it was as she liked, stunning wallpaper of rose and gold, an abundance of damask and velvet furniture, embroidered pillows and silk trappings for the fourposter bed. Dozens of roses appeared daily for the marble mantels and the inlaid tables, crowding the curtained alcove of her dressing room, reflected endlessly in tilted mirrors. And finally she crowded the high French windows with a veritable garden of camellia and fern. 'I miss the flowers; more than anything else I miss the flowers,' she mused. And sought after them even in the paintings which we brought from the shops and the galleries, magnificent canvases such as I'd never seen in New Orleans—from the classically executed lifelike bouquets, tempting you to reach for the petals that fell on a three-dimensional tablecloth, to a new and disturbing style in which the colors seemed to blaze with such intensity they destroyed the old lines, the old solidity, to make a vision like to those states when I'm nearest my delirium and flowers grow before my eyes and crackle like the flames of lamps. Paris flowed into these rooms.

"I found myself at home there, again forsaking dreams of ethereal simplicity for what another's gentle insistence had given me, because the air was sweet like the air of our courtyard in the Rue Royale, and all was alive with a shocking profusion of gas light that rendered even the ornate lofty ceilings devoid of shadows. The light raced on the gilt curlicues, flickered in the baubles of the chandeliers. Darkness did not exist. Vampires did not exist.

"And even bent as I was on my quest, it was sweet

to think that, for an hour, father and daughter climbed into the cabriolet from such civilized luxury only to ride along the banks of the Seine, over the bridge into the Latin Quarter to roam those darker, narrower streets in search of history, not victims. And then to return to the ticking clock and the brass andirons and the playing cards laid out upon the table. Books of poets, the program from a play, and all around the soft humming of the vast hotel, distant violins, a woman talking in a rapid, animated voice above the zinging of a hairbrush, and a man high above on the top floor repeating over and over to the night air, 'I understand, I am just beginning, I am just beginning to understand. . . .'

" 'Is it as you would have it?' Claudia asked, perhaps just to let me know she hadn't forgotten me, for she was quiet now for hours; no talk of vampires. But something was wrong. It was not the old serenity, the pensiveness that was recollection. There was a brooding there, a smoldering dissatisfaction. And though it would vanish from her eyes when I would call to her or answer her, anger seemed to settle very near the surface.

" 'Oh, you know how I would have it,' I answered, persisting in the myth of my own will. 'Some garret near the Sorbonne, near enough to the noise of the Rue St. Michel, far enough away. But I would mainly have it as you would have it.' And I could see her warmed, but looking past me, as if to say, 'You have no remedy; don't draw too near; don't ask of me what I ask of you: are you content?'

"My memory is too clear; too sharp; things should wear at the edges, and what is unresolved should soften. So, scenes are near my heart like pictures in lockets, yet monstrous pictures no artist or camera would ever catch; and over and over I would see Claudia at the piano's edge that last night when Lestat was playing, preparing to die, her face when he was taunting her, that contortion that at once became a mask; attention might have saved his life, if, in fact, he were dead at all.

"Something was collecting in Claudia, revealing itself

slowly to the most unwilling witness in the world. She had a new passion for rings and bracelets children did not wear. Her jaunty, straight-backed walk was not a child's, and often she entered small boutiques ahead of me and pointed a commanding finger at the perfume or the gloves she would then pay for herself. I was never far away, and always uncomfortable—not because I feared anything in this vast city, but because I feared her. She'd always been the 'lost child' to her victims, the 'orphan,' and now it seemed she would be something else, something wicked and shocking to the passers-by who succumbed to her. But this was often private; I was left for an hour haunting the carved edifices of Notre-Dame, or sitting at the edge of a park in the carriage.

"And then one night, when I awoke on the lavish bed in the suite of the hotel, my book crunched uncomfortably under me, I found her gone altogether. I didn't dare ask the attendants if they'd seen her. It was our practice to spirit past them; we had no name. I searched the corridors for her, the side streets, even the ballroom, where some almost inexplicable dread came over me at the thought of her there alone. But then I finally saw her coming through the side doors of the lobby, her hair beneath her bonnet brim sparkling from the light rain, the child rushing as if on a mischievous escapade, lighting the faces of doting men and women as she mounted the grand staircase and passed me, as if she hadn't seen me at all. An impossibility, a strange graceful slight.

"I shut the door behind me just as she was taking off her cape, and, in a flurry of golden raindrops, she shook it, shook her hair. The ribbons crushed from the bonnet fell loose and I felt a palpable relief to see the childish dress, those ribbons, and something wonderfully comforting in her arms, a small china doll. Still she said nothing to me; she was fussing with the doll. Jointed somehow with hooks or wire beneath its flouncing dress, its tiny feet tinkled like a bell. 'It's a lady doll,' she said, looking up at me. 'See? A lady doll.' She put it on the dresser.

" 'So it is,' I whispered.

" 'A woman made it,' she said. 'She makes baby dolls, all the same, baby dolls, a shop of baby dolls, until I said to her, "I want a lady doll." '

"It was taunting, mysterious. She sat there now with the wet strands of hair streaking her high forehead, intent on that doll. 'Do you know why she made it for me?' she asked. I was wishing now the room had shadows, that I could retreat from the warm circle of the superfluous fire into some darkness, that I wasn't sitting on the bed as if on a lighted stage, seeing her before me and in her mirrors, puffed sleeves and puffed sleeves.

" 'Because you are a beautiful child and she wanted to make you happy,' I said, my voice small and foreign to myself.

"She was laughing soundlessly. 'A beautiful child,' she said glancing up at me. 'Is that what you still think I am?' And her face went dark as again she played with the doll, her fingers pushing the tiny crocheted neckline down toward the china breasts. 'Yes, I resemble her baby dolls, I am her baby dolls. You should see her working in that shop; bent on her dolls, each with the same face, lips.' Her finger touched her own lip. Something seemed to shift suddenly, something within the very walls of the room itself, and the mirrors trembled with her image as if the earth had sighed beneath the foundations. Carriages rumbled in the streets; but they were too far away. And then I saw what her still childish figure was doing: in one hand she held the doll, the other to her lips; and the hand that held the doll was crushing it, crushing it and popping it so it bobbed and broke in a heap of glass that fell now from her open, bloody hand onto the carpet. She wrung the tiny dress to make a shower of littering particles as I averted my eyes, only to see her in the tilted mirror over the fire, see her eyes scanning me from my feet to the top of my head. She moved through that mirror towards me and drew close on the bed.

" 'Why do you look away, why don't you look at me?' she asked, her voice very smooth, very like a silver bell. But then she laughed softly, a woman's laugh, and said, 'Did you think I'd be your daughter forever? Are you the father of fools, the fool of fathers?'

" 'Your tone is unkind with me,' I answered.

" 'Hmmm . . . unkind.' I think she nodded. She was a blaze in the corner of my eye, blue flames, golden flames.

" 'And what do they think of you,' I asked as gently as I could, 'out there?' I gestured to the open window.

" 'Many things.' She smiled. 'Many things. Men are marvellous at explanations. Have you see the "little people" in the parks, the circuses, the freaks that men pay money to laugh at?'

" 'I was a sorcerer's apprentice only!' I burst out suddenly, despite myself. 'Apprentice!' I said. I wanted to touch her, to stroke her hair, but I sat there afraid of her, her anger like a match about to kindle.

"Again she smiled, and then she drew my hand into her lap and covered it as best she could with her own. 'Apprentice, yes,' she laughed. 'But tell me one thing, one thing from that lofty height. What was it like . . . making love?'

"I was walking away from her before I meant to, I was searching like a dim-witted mortal man for cape and gloves. 'You don't remember?' she asked with perfect calm, as I put my hand on the brass door handle.

"I stopped, feeling her eyes on my back, ashamed, and then I turned around and made as if to think, Where am I going, what shall I do, why do I stand here?

" 'It was something hurried,' I said, trying now to meet her eyes. How perfectly, coldly blue they were. How earnest. 'And . . . it was seldom savored . . . something acute that was quickly lost. I think that it was the pale shadow of killing.'

" 'Ahhh . . .' she said. 'Like hurting you as I do now . . . that is also the pale shadow of killing.'

" 'Yes, madam,' I said to her. 'I am inclined to believe that is correct.' And bowing swiftly, I bade her good-night."

"It was a long time after I'd left her that I slowed my pace. I'd crossed the Seine. I wanted darkness. To hide from her and the feelings that welled up in me, and the great consuming fear that I was utterly inadequate to make her happy, or to make myself happy by pleasing her.

"I would have given the world to please her, the world we now possessed, which seemed at once empty and eternal. Yet I was injured by her words and by her eyes, and no amount of explanations to her— which passed through and through my mind now, even forming on my lips in desperate whispers as I left the Rue St. Michel and went deeper and deeper into the older, darker streets of the Latin Quarter—no amount of explanations seemed to soothe what I imagined to be her grave dissatisfaction, or my own pain.

"Finally I left off words except for a strange chant. I was in the black silence of a medieval street, and blindly I followed its sharp turns, comforted by the height of its narrow tenements, which seemed at any moment capable of falling together, closing this alley-way under the indifferent stars like a seam. 'I cannot make her happy, I do not make her happy; and her unhappiness increases every day.' This was my chant, which I repeated like a rosary, a charm to change the facts, her inevitable disillusionment with our quest, which left us in this limbo where I felt her drawing away from me, dwarfing me with her enormous need. I even conceived a savage jealousy of the dollmaker to whom she'd confided her request for that tinkling diminutive lady, because that dollmaker had for a moment given her something which she held close to herself in my presence as if I were not there at all.

"What did it amount to, where could it lead?

"Never since I'd come to Paris months before did I so completely feel the city's immense size, how I might pass from this twisting, blind street of my choice into a world of delights, and never had I so keenly felt its uselessness. Uselessness to her if she could not abide this anger, if she could not somehow grasp the limits of which she seemed so angrily, bitterly aware. I was helpless. She was helpless. But she was stronger

than I. And I knew, had known even at the moment
when I turned away from her in the hotel, that behind
her eyes there was for me her continuing love.

"And dizzy and weary and now comfortably lost, I
became aware with a vampire's inextinguishable senses
that I was being followed.

"My first thought was irrational. She'd come out
after me. And, cleverer than I, had tracked me at a
great distance. But as surely as this came to mind,
another thought presented itself, a rather cruel thought
in light of all that had passed between us. The steps
were too heavy for hers. It was just some mortal walking in this same alley, walking unwarily towards death.

"So I continued on, almost ready to fall into my
pain again because I deserved it, when my mind said,
You are a fool; listen. And it dawned on me that these
steps, echoing as they were at a great distance behind
me, were in perfect time with my own. An accident.
Because if mortal they were, they were too far off for
mortal hearing. But as I stopped now to consider that,
they stopped. And as I turned saying, Louis, you deceive yourself, and started up, they started up. Footfall with my footfall, gaining speed now as I gained
speed. And then something remarkable, undeniable occurred. *En garde* as I was for the steps that were behind
me, I tripped on a fallen roof tile and was pitched
against the wall. And behind me, those steps echoed to
perfection the sharp shuffling rhythm of my fall.

"I was astonished. And in a state of alarm well
beyond fear. To the right and left of me the street was
dark. Not even a tarnished light shone in a garret
window. And the only safety afforded me, the great
distance between myself and these steps, was as I said
the guarantee that they were not human. I was at a
complete loss as to what I might do. I had the near-
irresistible desire to call out to this being and welcome
it, to let it know as quickly and as completely as
possible that I awaited it, had been searching for it,
would confront it. Yet I was afraid. What seemed
sensible was to resume walking, waiting for it to gain
on me; and as I did so I was again mocked by my
own pace, and the distance between us remained the

same. The tension mounted in me, the dark around me becoming more and more menacing; and I said over and over, measuring these steps, Why do you track me, why do you let me know you are there?

"Then I rounded a sharp turn in the street, and a gleam of light showed ahead of me at the next corner. The street sloped up towards it, and I moved on very slowly, my heart deafening in my ears, reluctant to eventually reveal myself in that light.

"And as I hesitated—stopped, in fact—right before the turn, something rumbled and clattered above, as if the roof of the house beside me had all but collapsed. I jumped back just in time, before a load of tiles crashed into the street, one of them brushing my shoulder. All was quiet now. I stared at the tiles, listening, waiting. And then slowly I edged around the turn into the light, only to see there looming over me at the top of the street beneath the gas lamp the unmistakable figure of another vampire.

"He was enormous in height though gaunt as myself, his long, white face very bright under the lamp, his large, black eyes staring at me in what seemed undisguised wonder. His right leg was slightly bent as though he'd just come to a halt in mid-step. And then suddenly I realized that not only was his black hair long and full and combed precisely like my own, and not only was he dressed in identical coat and cape to my own, but he stood imitating my stance and facial expression to perfection. I swallowed and let my eyes pass over him slowly, while I struggled to hide from him the rapid pace of my pulse as his eyes in like manner passed over me. And when I saw him blink I realized I had just blinked, and as I drew my arms up and folded them across my chest he slowly did the same. It was maddening. Worse than maddening. Because, as I barely moved my lips, he barely moved his lips, and I found the words dead and I couldn't make other words to confront this, to stop it. And all the while, there was that height and those sharp black eyes and that powerful attention which was, of course, perfect mockery, but nevertheless riveted to myself. *He* was the vampire; *I* seemed the mirror.

" 'Clever,' I said to him shortly and desperately, and, of course, he echoed that word as fast as I said it. And maddened as I was more by that than anything else, I found myself yielding to a slow smile, defying the sweat which had broken from every pore and the violent tremor in my legs. He also smiled, but his eyes had a ferocity that was animal, unlike my own, and the smile was sinister in its sheer mechanical quality.

"Now I took a step forward and so did he; and when I stopped short, staring, so did he. But then he slowly, very slowly, lifted his right arm, though mine remained poised and gathering his fingers into a fist, he now struck at his chest in quickening time to mock my heartbeat. Laughter erupted from him. He threw back his head, showing his canine teeth, and the laughter seemed to fill the alleyway. I loathed him. Completely.

" 'You mean me harm?' I asked, only to hear the words mockingly obliterated.

" 'Trickster!' I said sharply. 'Buffoon!'

"That word stopped him. Died on his lips even as he was saying it, and his face went hard.

"What I did then was impulse. I turned my back on him and started away, perhaps to make him come after me and demand to know who I was. But in a movement so swift I couldn't possibly have seen it, he stood before me again, as if he had materialized there. Again I turned my back on him—only to face him under the lamp again, the settling of his dark, wavy hair the only indication that he had in fact moved.

" 'I've been looking for you! I've come to Paris looking for you!' I forced myself to say the words, seeing that he didn't echo them or move, only stood staring at me.

"Now he moved forward slowly, gracefully, and I saw his own body and his own manner had regained possession of him and, extending his hand as if he meant to ask for mine, he very suddenly pushed me backwards, off-balance. I could feel my shirt drenched and sticking to my flesh as I righted myself, my hand grimed from the damp wall.

"And as I turned to confront him, he threw me completely down.

"I wish I could describe to you his power. You would know, if I were to attack you, to deal you a sharp blow with an arm you never saw move towards you.

"But something in me said, Show him your own power; and I rose up fast, going right for him with both arms out. And I hit the night, the empty night swirling beneath that lamppost, and stood there looking about me, alone and a complete fool. This was a test of some sort, I knew it then, though consciously I fixed my attention on the dark street, the recesses of the doorways, anyplace he might have hidden. I wanted no part of this test, but saw no way out of it. And I was contemplating some way to disdainfully make that clear when suddenly he appeared again, jerking me around and flinging me down the sloping cobblestones where I'd fallen before. I felt his boot against my ribs. And, enraged, I grabbed hold of his leg, scarcely believing it when I felt the cloth and the bone. He'd fallen against the stone wall opposite and let out a snarl of unrepressed anger.

"What happened then was pure confusion. I held tight to that leg, though the boot strained to get at me. And at some point, after he'd toppled over me and pulled loose from me, I was lifted into the air by strong hands. What might have happened I can well imagine. He could have flung me several yards from himself, he was easily that strong. And battered, severely injured, I might have lost consciousness. It was violently disturbing to me even in that melee that I didn't know whether I could lose consciousness. But it was never put to a test. For, confused as I was, I was certain someone else had come between us, someone who was battling him decisively, forcing him to relinquish his hold.

"When I looked up, I was in the street, and I saw two figures only for an instant, like the flicker of an image after the eye is shut. Then there was only a swirling of black garments, a boot striking the stones, and the night was empty. I sat, panting, the sweat pouring down my face, staring around me and then up at the narrow ribbon of faint sky. Slowly, only because my eye was totally concentrated upon it now, a figure emerged from the darkness of the wall above me. Crouched on the jutting stones of the lintel, it turned so that I saw the barest gleam of light on the hair and then the stark, white face. A strange face, broader and not so gaunt as the other, a large dark eye that was holding me steadily. A whisper came from the lips, though they never appeared to move. 'You are all right.'

"I was more than all right. I was on my feet, ready to attack. But the figure remained crouched, as if it were part of the wall. I could see a white hand working in what appeared to be a waistcoat pocket. A card appeared, white as the fingers that extended it to me. I didn't move to take it. 'Come to us, tomorrow night,' said that same whisper from the smooth, expressionless face, which still showed only one eye to the light. 'I won't harm you,' he said, 'And neither will that other. I won't allow it.' And his hand did that thing which vampires can make happen; that is, it seemed to leave his body in the dark to deposit the card in my hand, the purple script immediately shining in the light. And the figure, moving upwards like a cat on the wall, vanished fast between the garret gables overhead.

"I knew I was alone now, could feel it. And the pounding of my heart seemed to fill the empty little street as I stood under the lamp reading that card. The address I knew well enough, because I had been to theaters along that street more than once. But the name was astonishing: 'Théâtre des Vampires,' and the time noted, nine P.M.

"I turned it over and discovered written there the note, 'Bring the petite beauty with you. You are most welcome. Armand.'

"There was no doubt that the figure who'd given it to me had written this message. And I had only a very short time to get to the hotel and to tell Claudia of these things before dawn. I was running fast, so that even the people I passed on the boulevards did not actually see the shadow that brushed them."

The Théâtre des Vampires was by invitation only, and the next night the doorman inspected my card for a moment while the rain fell softly all around us: on the man and the woman stopped at the shut-up box office; on the crinkling posters of penny-dreadful vampires with their outstretched arms and cloaks resembling bat wings ready to close on the naked shoulders of a mortal victim; on the couple that pressed past us into the packed lobby, where I could easily perceive that the crowd was all human, no vampires among them, not even this boy who admitted us finally into the press of conversation and damp wool and ladies' gloved fingers fumbling with felt-brimmed hats and wet curls. I pressed for the shadows in a feverish excitement. We had fed earlier only so that in the bustling street of this theater our skin would not be too white, our eyes too unclouded. And that taste of blood which I had not enjoyed had left me all the more uneasy; but I had no time for it. This was no night for killing. This was to be a night of revelations, no matter how it ended. I was certain.

"Yet here we stood with this all too human crowd, the doors opening now on the auditorium, and a young boy pushing towards us, beckoning, pointing above the shoulders of the crowd to the stairs. Ours was a box, one of the best in the house, and if the blood had not dimmed my skin completely nor made Claudia into a human child as she rode in my arms, this usher did not seem at all to notice it nor to care. In fact, he smiled all too readily as he drew back the curtain for us on two chairs before the brass rail.

" 'Would you put it past them to have human slaves?' Claudia whispered.

" 'But Lestat never trusted human slaves,' I answered. I watched the seats fill, watched the marvellously flowered hats navigating below me through the rows of silk chairs. White shoulders gleamed in the deep curve of the balcony spreading out from us; diamonds glittered in the gas light. 'Remember, be sly for once,' came Claudia's whisper from beneath her bowed blond head. 'You're too much of a gentleman.'

"The lights were going out, first in the balcony, and then along the walls of the main floor. A knot of musicians had gathered in the pit below the stage, and at the foot of the long, green velvet curtain the gas flickered, then brightened, and the audience receded as if enveloped by a gray cloud through which only the diamonds sparkled, on wrists, on throats, on fingers. And a hush descended like that gray cloud until all the sound was collected in one echoing persistent cough. Then silence. And the slow, rhythmical beating of a tambourine. Added to that was the thin melody of a wooden flute, which seemed to pick up the sharp metallic tink of the bells of the tambourine, winding them into a haunting melody that was medieval in sound. Then the strumming of strings that emphasized the tambourine. And the flute rose, in that melody singing of something melancholy, sad. It had a charm to it, this music, and the whole audience seemed stilled and united by it, as if the music of that flute were a luminous ribbon unfurling slowly in the dark. Not even the rising curtain broke the silence with the slightest sound. The lights brightened, and it seemed the stage was not the stage but a thickly wooded place, the light glittering on the roughened tree trunks and the thick clusters of leaves beneath the arch of darkness above; and through the trees could be seen what appeared the low, stone bank of a river and above that, beyond that, the glittering waters of the river itself, this whole three-dimensional world produced in painting upon a fine silk scrim that shivered only slightly in a faint draft.

"A sprinkling of applause greeted the illusion, gathering adherents from all parts of the auditorium until it reached its short crescendo and died away. A dark, draped figure was moving on the stage from tree trunk to tree trunk, so fast that as he stepped into the lights he seemed to appear magically in the center, one arm flashing out from his cloak to show a silver scythe and the other to hold a mask on a slender stick before the invisible face, a mask which showed the gleaming countenance of Death, a painted skull.

"There were gasps from the crowd. It was Death standing before the audience, the scythe poised, Death at the edge of a dark wood. And something in me was responding now as the audience responded, not in fear, but in some human way, to the magic of that fragile painted set, the mystery of the lighted world there, the world in which this figure moved in his billowing black cloak, back and forth before the audience with the grace of a great panther, drawing forth, as it were, those gasps, those sighs, those reverent murmurs.

"And now, behind this figure, whose very gestures seemed to have a captivating power like the rhythm of the music to which it moved, came other figures from the wings. First an old woman, very stooped and bent, her gray hair like moss, her arm hanging down with the weight of a great basket of flowers. Her shuttling steps scraped on the stage, and her head bobbed with the rhythm of the music and the darting steps of the Grim Reaper. And then she started back as she laid eyes on him and, slowly setting down her basket, made her hands into the attitude of prayer. She was tired; her head leaned now on her hands as if in sleep, and she reached out for him, supplicating. But as he came towards her, he bent to look directly into her face, which was all shadows to us beneath her hair, and started back then, waving his hand as if to freshen the air. Laughter erupted uncertainly from the audience. But as the old woman rose and took after Death, the laughter took over.

"The music broke into a jig with their running, as round and round the stage the old woman pursued Death, until he finally flattened himself into the dark of a tree trunk, bowing his masked face under his wing like a bird. And the old woman, lost, defeated, gathered up her basket as the music softened and slowed to her pace, and made her way off the stage. I did not like it. I did not like the laughter. I could see the other figures moving in now, the music orchestrating their gestures, cripples on crutches and beggars with rags the color of ash, all reaching out for Death, who whirled, escaping this one with a sudden arching of the back, fleeing from that one with an effeminate gesture of disgust, waving them all away finally in a foppish display of weariness and boredom.

"It was then I realized that the languid, white hand that made these comic arcs was not painted white. It was a vampire hand which wrung laughter from the crowd. A vampire hand lifted now to the grinning skull, as the stage was finally clear, as if stifling a yawn. And then this vampire, still holding the mask before his face, adopted marvellously the attitude of resting his weight against a painted silken tree, as if he were falling gently to sleep. The music twittered like birds, rippled like the flowing of the water; and the spotlight, which encircled him in a yellow pool, grew dim, all but fading away as he slept.

"And another spot pierced the scrim, seeming to melt it altogether, to reveal a young woman standing alone far upstage. She was majestically tall and all but enshrined by a voluminous mane of golden blond hair. I could feel the awe of the audience as she seemed to flounder in the spotlight, the dark forest rising on the perimeter, so that she seemed to be lost in the trees. And she was lost; and not a vampire. The soil on her mean blouse and skirt was not stage paint, and nothing had touched her perfect face, which gazed into the light now, as beautiful and finely chiselled as the face of a marble Virgin, that hair her haloed veil. She could not see in the light, though all could see her. And the moan which escaped her lips as she floundered seemed to echo over the thin, romantic singing of the flute, which was a tribute to that beauty. The figure of Death woke with a start in his pale spotlight and turned to see her as the audience had seen her, and to throw up his free hand in tribute, in awe.

"The twitter of laughter died before it became real. She was too beautiful, her gray eyes too distressed. The performance too perfect. And then the skull mask was thrown suddenly into the wings and Death showed a beaming white face to the audience, his hurried hands stroking his handsome black hair, straightening a waistcoat, brushing imaginary dust from his lapels. Death in love. And clapping rose for the luminous countenance, the gleaming cheekbones, the winking black eye, as if it were all masterful illusion when in fact it was merely and certainly the face of a vampire, the vampire who had accosted me in the Latin Quarter, that leering, grinning vampire, harshly illuminated by the yellow spot.

"My hand reached for Claudia's in the dark and pressed it tightly. But she sat still, as if enrapt. The forest of the stage, through which that helpless mortal girl stared blindly towards the laughter, divided in two phantom halves, moving away from the center, freeing the vampire to close in on her.

"And she who had been advancing towards the footlights, saw him suddenly and came to a halt, making a moan like a child. Indeed, she was very like a child, though clearly a full-grown woman. Only a slight wrinkling of the tender flesh around her eyes betrayed her age. Her breasts though small were beautifully shaped beneath her blouse, and her hips though narrow gave her long, dusty skirt a sharp, sensual angularity. As she moved back from the vampire, I saw the tears standing in her eyes like glass in the flicker of the lights, and I felt my spirit contract in fear for her, and in longing. Her beauty was heartbreaking.

"Behind her, a number of painted skulls suddenly moved against the blackness, the figures that carried the masks invisible in their black clothes, except for free white hands that clasped the edge of a cape, the folds of a skirt. Vampire women were there, moving in with the men towards the victim, and now they all, one by one, thrust the masks away so they fell in an artful pile, the sticks like bones, the skulls grinning into the darkness above. And there they stood, seven vampires, the women vampires three in number, their molded white breasts shining over the tight black bodices of their gowns, their hard luminescent faces staring with dark eyes beneath curls of black hair. Starkly beautiful, as they seemed to float close around that florid human figure, yet pale and cold compared to that sparkling golden hair, that petal-pink skin. I could hear the breath of the audience, the halting, the soft sighs. It was a spectacle, that circle of white faces pressing closer and closer, and that leading figure, that Gentleman Death, turning to the audience now with his hands crossed over his heart, his head bent in longing to elicit their sympathy: was she not irresistible! A murmur of accenting laughter, of sighs.

"But it was she who broke the magic silence.

" 'I don't want to die . . .' she whispered. Her voice was like a bell.

" 'We *are* death,' he answered her; and from around her came the whisper, 'Death.' She turned, tossing her hair so it became a veritable shower of gold, a rich and living thing over the dust of her poor clothing. 'Help me!' she cried out softly, as if afraid even to raise her voice. 'Someone . . .' she said to the crowd she knew must be there. A soft laughter came from Claudia. The girl on stage only vaguely understood where she was, what was happening, but knew infinitely more than this house of people that gaped at her.

" 'I don't want to die! I don't want to!' Her delicate voice broke, her eyes fixed on the tall, malevolent leader vampire, that demon trickster who now stepped out of the circle of the others towards her.

" 'We all die,' he answered her. 'The one thing you share with every mortal is death.' His hand took in the orchestra, the distant faces of the balcony, the boxes.

" 'No,' she protested in disbelief. 'I have so many years, so many. . . .' Her voice was light, lilting in her pain. It made her irresistible, just as did the movement of her naked throat and the hand that fluttered there.

" 'Years!' said the master vampire. 'How do you know you have so many years? Death is no respecter of age! There could be a sickness in your body now, already devouring you from within. Or, outside, a man might be waiting to kill you simply for your yellow hair!' And his fingers reached for it, the sound of his deep, preternatural voice sonorous. 'Need I tell what fate may have in store for you?'

" 'I don't care . . . I'm not afraid,' she protested, her clarion voice so fragile after him. 'I would take my chance. . . .'

" 'And if you do take that chance and live, live for years, what would be your heritage? The humpbacked, toothless visage of old age?' And now he lifted her hair behind her back, exposing her pale throat. And slowly he drew the string from the loose gathers of her blouse. The cheap fabric opened, the sleeves slipping off her narrow, pink shoulders; and she clasped it, only to have him take her wrists and thrust them sharply away. The audience seemed to sigh in a body, the women behind their opera glasses, the men leaning forward in their chairs. I could see the cloth falling, see the pale, flawless skin pulsing with her heart and the tiny nipples letting the cloth slip precariously, the vampire holding her right wrist tightly at her side, the tears coarsing down her blushing cheeks, her teeth biting into the flesh of her lip. 'Just as sure as this flesh is pink, it will turn gray, wrinkled with age,' he said.

" 'Let me live, please,' she begged, her face turning away from him. 'I don't care . . . I don't care.'

" 'But then, why should you care if you die now? If these things don't frighten you . . . these horrors?'

"She shook her head, baffled, outsmarted, helpless. I felt the anger in my veins, as sure as the passion. With a bowed head she bore the whole responsibility for defending life, and it was unfair, monstrously unfair that she should have to pit logic against his for what was obvious and sacred and so beautifully embodied in her. But he made her speechless, made her overwhelming instinct seem petty, confused. I could feel her dying inside, weakening, and I hated him.

"The blouse slipped to her waist. A murmur moved through the titillated crowd as her small, round breasts stood exposed. She struggled to free her wrist, but he held it fast.

" 'And suppose we were to let you go . . . suppose the Grim Reaper had a heart that could resist your beauty . . . to whom would he turn his passion? Someone must die in your place. Would you pick the person for us? The person to stand here and suffer as you suffer now?' He gestured to the audience. Her confusion was terrible. 'Have you a sister . . . a mother . . . a child?'

" 'No,' she gasped. 'No . . .' shaking the mane of hair.

" 'Surely someone could take your place, a friend? Choose!'

" 'I can't. I wouldn't. . . .' She writhed in his tight grasp. The vampires around her looked on, still, their faces evincing no emotion, as if the preternatural flesh were masks. 'Can't you do it?' he taunted her. And I knew, if she said she could, how he would only condemn her, say she was as evil as he for marking someone for death, say that she deserved her fate.

" 'Death waits for you everywhere,' he sighed now as if he were suddenly frustrated. The audience could not perceive it, I could. I could see the muscles of his smooth face tightening. He was trying to keep her gray eyes on his eyes, but she looked desperately, hopefully away from him. On the warm, rising air I could smell the dust and perfume of her skin, hear the soft beating of her heart. 'Unconscious death . . . the fate of all mortals.' He bent closer to her, musing, infatuated with her, but struggling. 'Hmmm. . . . but we are *conscious* death! That would make you a bride. Do you know what it means to be loved by Death?' He all but kissed her face, the brilliant stain of her tears. 'Do you know what it means to have Death know your name?'

"She looked at him, overcome with fear. And then her eyes seemed to mist over, her lips to go slack. She was staring past him at the figure of another vampire who had emerged slowly from the shadows. For a long time he had stood on the periphery of the gathering, his hands clasped, his large, dark eyes very still. His attitude was not the attitude of hunger. He did not appear rapt. But she was looking into his eyes now, and her pain bathed her in a beauteous light, a light which made her irresistibly alluring. It was this that held the jaded audience, this terrible pain. I could feel her skin, feel the small, pointed breasts, feel my

arms caressing her. I shut my eyes against it and saw her
starkly against that private darkness. It was what they
felt all around her, this community of vampires. She
had no chance.

"And, looking up again, I saw her shimmering in
the smoky light of the footlamps, saw her tears like
gold as soft from that other vampire who stood at a
distance came the words . . . 'No pain.'

"I could see the trickster stiffen, but no one else
would see it. They would see only the girl's smooth,
childlike face, those parted lips, slack with innocent
wonder as she gazed at that distant vampire, hear her
soft voice repeat after him, 'No pain?'

" 'Your beauty is a gift to us.' His rich voice effortlessly filled the house, seemed to fix and subdue the
mounting wave of excitement. And slightly, almost imperceptibly, his hand moved. The trickster was receding, becoming one of those patient, white faces, whose
hunger and equanimity were strangely one. And slowly,
gracefully, the other moved towards her. She was
languid, her nakedness forgotten, those lids fluttering,
a sigh escaping her moist lips. 'No pain,' she accented.
I could hardly bear it, the sight of her yearning towards
him, seeing her dying now, under this vampire's power.
I wanted to cry out to her, to break her swoon. And
I wanted her. Wanted her, as he was moving in on her,
his hand out now for the drawstring of her skirt as
she inclined towards him, her head back, the black
cloth slipping over her hips, over the golden gleam
of the hair between her legs—a child's down, that
delicate curl—the skirt dropping to her feet. And this
vampire opened his arms, his back to the flickering
footlights, his auburn hair seeming to tremble as the
gold of her hair fell around his black coat. 'No pain . . .
no pain . . .' he was whispering to her, and she was
giving herself over.

"And now, turning her slowly to the side so that
they could all see her serene face, he was lifting her,
her back arching as her naked breasts touched his
buttons, her pale arms enfolded his neck. She stiffened,
cried out as he sank his teeth, and her face was still
as the dark theater reverberated with shared passion.

His white hand shone on her florid buttocks, her hair
dusting it, stroking it. He lifted her off the boards as
he drank, her throat gleaming against his white cheek.
I felt weak, dazed, hunger rising in me, knotting my
heart, my veins. I felt my hand gripping the brass bar
of the box, tighter, until I could feel the metal creaking in its joints. And that soft, wrenching sound which
none of those mortals might hear seemed somehow to
hook me to the solid place where I was.

"I bowed my head; I wanted to shut my eyes. The
air seemed fragrant with her salted skin, and close
and hot and sweet. Around her the other vampires
drew in, the white hand that held her tight quivered,
and the auburn-haired vampire let her go, turning
her, displaying her, her head fallen back as he gave her
over, one of those starkly beautiful vampire women
rising behind her, cradling her, stroking her as she
bent to drink. They were all about her now, as she
was passed from one to another and to another, before
the enthralled crowd, her head thrown forward over
the shoulder of a vampire man, the nape of her neck
as enticing as the small buttocks or the flawless skin
of her long thighs, the tender creases behind her limply
bent knees.

"I was sitting back in the chair, my mouth full of
the taste of her, my veins in torment. And in the
corner of my eyes was that auburn-haired vampire
who had conquered her, standing apart as he had been
before, his dark eyes seeming to pick me from the
darkness, seeming to fix on me over the currents of
warm air.

"One by one the vampires were withdrawing. The
painted forest came back, sliding soundlessly into
place. Until the mortal girl, frail and very white, lay
naked in that mysterious wood, nestled in the silk
of a black bier as if on the floor of the forest itself;
and the music had begun again, eerie and alarming,
growing louder as the lights grew dimmer. All the
vampires were gone, except the trickster, who had
gathered his scythe from the shadows and also his
hand-held mask. And he crouched near the sleeping
girl as the lights slowly faded, and the music alone

had power and force in the enclosing dark. And then that died also.

"For a moment, the entire crowd was utterly still.

"Then applause began here and there and suddenly united everyone around us. The lights rose in the sconces on the walls and heads turned to one another, conversation erupting all round. A woman rising in the middle of a row to pull her fox fur sharply from the chair, though no one had yet made way for her; someone else pushing out quickly to the carpeted aisle; and the whole body was on its feet as if driven to the exits.

"But then the hum became the comfortable, jaded hum of the sophisticated and perfumed crowd that had filled the lobby and the vault of the theater before. The spell was broken. The doors were flung open on the fragrant rain, the clop of horses' hooves, and voices calling for taxis. Down in the sea of slightly askew chairs, a white glove gleamed on a green silk cushion.

"I sat watching, listening, one hand shielding my lowered face from anyone and no one, my elbow resting on the rail, the passion in me subsiding, the taste of the girl on my lips. It was as though on the smell of the rain came her perfume still, and in the empty theater I could hear the throb of her beating heart. I sucked in my breath, tasted the rain, and glimpsed Claudia sitting infinitely still, her gloved hands in her lap.

"There was a bitter taste in my mouth, and confusion. And then I saw a lone usher moving on the aisle below, righting the chairs, reaching for the scattered programs that littered the carpet. I was aware that this ache in me, this confusion, this blinding passion which only let me go with a stubborn slowness would be obliterated if I were to drop down to one of those curtained archways beside him and draw him up fast in the darkness and take him as that girl was taken. I wanted to do it, and I wanted nothing. Claudia said near my bowed ear, 'Patience, Louis. Patience.'

"I opened my eyes. Someone was near, on the periphery of my vision; someone who had outsmarted my hearing, my keen anticipation, which penetrated like a sharp antenna even this distraction, or so I thought. But there he was, soundless, beyond the curtained entrance of the box, that vampire with the auburn hair, that detached one, standing on the carpeted stairway looking at us. I knew him now to be, as I'd suspected, the vampire who had given me the card admitting us to the theater. Armand.

"He would have startled me, except for his stillness, the remote dreamy quality of his expression. It seemed he'd been standing against that wall for the longest time, and betrayed no sign of change as we looked at him, then came towards him. Had he not so completely absorbed me, I would have been relieved he was not the tall, black-haired one; but I didn't think of this. Now his eyes moved languidly over Claudia with no tribute whatsoever to the human habit of disguising the stare. I placed my hand on Claudia's shoulder. 'We've been searching for you a very long time,' I said to him, my heart growing calmer, as if his calm were drawing off my trepidation, my care, like the sea drawing something into itself from the land. I cannot exaggerate this quality in him. Yet I can't describe it and couldn't then; and the fact that my mind sought to describe it even to myself unsettled me. He gave me the very feeling that he knew what I was doing, and his still posture and his deep, brown eyes seemed to say there was no use in what I was thinking, or particularly the words I was struggling to form now. Claudia said nothing.

"He moved away from the wall and began to walk down the stairs, while at the same time he made a gesture that welcomed us and bade us follow; but all this was fluid and fast. My gestures were the caricature of human gestures compared to his. He opened a door in the lower wall and admitted us to the rooms below the theater, his feet only brushing the stone stairway as we descended, his back to us with complete trust.

"And now we entered what appeared to be a vast subterranean ballroom, carved, as it were, out of a cellar more ancient than the building overhead. Above

us, the door that he had opened fell shut, and the light
died away before I could get a fair impression of the
room. I heard the rustle of his garments in the dark
and then the sharp explosion of a match. His face
appeared like a great flame over the match. And then
a figure moved into the light beside him, a young
boy, who brought him a candle. The sight of the
boy brought back to me in a shock the teasing pleasure of the naked woman on the stage, her prone
body, the pulsing blood. And he turned and gazed at
me now, much in the manner of the auburn-haired
vampire, who had lit the candle and whispered to him,
'Go.' The light expanded to the distant walls, and
the vampire held the light up and moved along the
wall, beckoning us both to follow.

"I could see a world of frescoes and murals surrounded us, their colors deep and vibrant above the
dancing flame, and gradually the theme and content
beside us came clear. It was the terrible 'Triumph of
Death' by Breughel, painted on such a massive scale
that all the multitude of ghastly figures towered over
us in the gloom, those ruthless skeletons ferrying the
helpless dead in a fetid moat or pulling a cart of
human skulls, beheading an outstretched corpse or
hanging humans from the gallows. A bell tolled over
the endless hell of scorched and smoking land, towards
which great armies of men came with the hideous,
mindless march of soldiers to a massacre. I turned
away, but the auburn-haired one touched my hand
and led me further along the wall to see 'The Fall
of the Angels' slowly materializing with the damned
being driven from the celestial heights into a lurid
chaos of feasting monsters. So vivid, so perfect was
it, I shuddered. The hand that had touched me did
the same again, and I stood still despite it, deliberately
looking above to the very height of the mural, where
I could make out of the shadows two beautiful angels
with trumpets to their lips. And for a second the spell
was broken. I had the strong sense of the first evening I had entered Notre-Dame; but then that was
gone, like something gossamer and precious snatched
away from me.

"The candle rose. And horrors rose all around me: the dumbly passive and degraded damned of Bosch, the bloated coffined corpses of Traini, the monstrous horsemen of Dürer, and blown out of all endurable scale a promenade of medieval woodcut, emblem, and engraving. The very ceiling writhed with skeletons and moldering dead, with demons and the instruments of pain, as if this were the cathedral of death itself.

"Where we stood finally in the center of the room, the candle seemed to pull the images to life everywhere around us. Delirium threatened, that awful shifting of the room began, that sense of falling. I reached out for Claudia's hand. She stood musing, her face passive, her eyes distant when I looked to her, as if she'd have me let her alone; and then her feet shot off from me with a rapid tapping on the stone floor that echoed all along the walls, like fingers tapping on my temples, on my skull. I held my temples, staring dumbly at the floor in search of shelter, as if to lift my eyes would force me to look on some wretched suffering I would not, could not endure. Then again I saw the vampire's face floating in his flame, his ageless eyes circled in dark lashes. His lips were very still, but as I stared at him he seemed to smile without making even the slightest movement. I watched him all the harder, convinced it was some powerful illusion I could penetrate with keen attention; and the more I watched, the more he seemed to smile and finally to be animated with a soundless whispering, musing, singing. I could hear it like something curling in the dark, as wallpaper curls in the blast of a fire or paint peels from the face of a burning doll. I had the urge to reach for him, to shake him violently so that his still face would move, admit to this soft singing; and suddenly I found him pressed against me, his arm around my chest, his lashes so close I could see them matted and gleaming above the incandescent orb of his eye, his soft, tasteless breath against my skin. It *was* delirium.

"I moved to get away from him, and yet I was drawn to him and I didn't move at all, his arm exerting its firm pressure, his candle blazing now against my eye, so that I felt the warmth of it; all my cold flesh yearned for that warmth, but suddenly I waved to snuff it but couldn't find it, and all I saw was his radiant face, as I had never seen Lestat's face, white and poreless and sinewy and male. The other vampire. All other vampires. An infinite procession of my own kind.

"The moment ended.

"I found myself with my hand outstretched, touching his face; but he was a distance away from me, as if he'd never moved near me, making no attempt to brush my hand away. I drew back, flushed, stunned.

"Far away in the Paris night a bell chimed, the dull, golden circles of sound seeming to penetrate the walls, the timbers that carried that sound down into the earth like great organ pipes. Again came that whispering, that inarticulate singing. And through the gloom I saw that mortal boy watching me, and I smelled the hot aroma of his flesh. The vampire's facile hand beckoned him, and he came towards me, his eyes fearless and exciting, and he drew up to me in the candlelight and put his arms around my shoulders.

"Never had I felt this, never had I experienced it, this yielding of a conscious mortal. But before I could push him away for his own sake, I saw the bluish bruise on his tender neck. He was offering it to me. He was pressing the length of his body against me now, and I felt the hard strength of his sex beneath his clothes pressing against my leg. A wretched gasp escaped my lips, but he bent close, his lips on what must have been so cold, so lifeless for him; and I sank my teeth into his skin, my body rigid, that hard sex driving against me, and I lifted him in passion off the floor. Wave after wave of his beating heart passed into me as, weightless, I rocked with him, devouring him, his ecstasy, his conscious pleasure.

"Then, weak and gasping, I saw him at a distance from me, my arms empty, my mouth still flooded with the taste of his blood. He lay against that auburn-haired vampire, his arm about the vampire's waist, and he gazed at me in that same pacific manner of the vampire, his eyes misted over and weak from the loss of life. I remember moving mutely forward, drawn to him and seemingly unable to control it, that gaze taunting me, that conscious life defying me; he should die and would not die; he would live on, comprehending, surviving that intimacy! I turned. The host of vampires moved in the shadows, their candles whipped and fleeting on the cool air; and above them loomed a great broadcast of ink-drawn figures: the sleeping corpse of a woman ravaged by a vulture with a human face; a naked man bound hand and foot to a tree, beside him hanging the torso of another, his severed arms tied still to another branch, and on a spike this dead man's staring head.

"The singing came again, that thin, ethereal singing. Slowly the hunger in me subsided, obeyed, but my head throbbed and the flames of the candles seemed to merge in burnished circles of light. Someone touched me suddenly, pushed me roughly, so that I almost lost my balance, and when I straightened I saw the thin, angular face of the trickster vampire I despised. He reached out for me with his white hands. But the other one, the distant one, moved forward suddenly and stood between us. It seemed he struck the other vampire, that I saw him move, and then again I did not see him move; both stood still like statues, eyes fixed on one another, and time passed like wave after wave of water rolling back from a still beach. I cannot say how long we stood there, the three of us in those shadows, and how utterly still they seemed to me, only the shimmering flames seeming to have life behind them. Then I remember floundering along the wall and finding a large oak chair into which I all but collapsed. It seemed Claudia was near and speaking to someone in a hushed but sweet voice. My forehead teemed with blood, with heat.

" 'Come with me,' said the auburn-haired vampire. I was searching his face for the movement of his lips that must have preceded the sound, yet it was so hopelessly long after the sound. And then we were walking, the three of us, down a long stone stairway deeper beneath the city, Claudia ahead of us, her shadow long against the wall. The air grew cool and refreshing with the fragrance of water, and I could see the droplets bleeding through the stones like beads of gold in the light of the vampire's candle.

"It was a small chamber we entered, a fire burning in a deep fireplace cut into the stone wall. A bed lay at the other end, fitted into the rock and enclosed with two brass gates. At first I saw these things clearly, and saw the long wall of books opposite the fireplace and the wooden desk that was against it, and the coffin to the other side. But then the room began to waver, and the auburn-haired vampire put his hands on my shoulders and guided me down into a leather chair. The fire was intensely hot against my legs, but this felt good to me, sharp and clear, something to draw me out of this confusion. I sat back, my eyes only half open, and tried to see again what was about me. It was as if that distant bed were a stage and on the linen pillows of the little stage lay that boy, his black hair parted in the middle and curling about his ears, so that he looked now in his dreamy, fevered state like one of those lithe androgynous creatures of a Botticelli painting; and beside him, nestled against him, her tiny white hand stark against his ruddy flesh, lay Claudia, her face buried in his neck. The masterful auburn-haired vampire looked on, his hands clasped in front of him; and when Claudia rose now, the boy shuddered. The vampire picked her up, gently, as I might pick her up, her hands finding a hold on his neck, her eyes half shut with the swoon, her lips rouged with blood. He set her gently on the desk, and she lay back against the leatherbound books, her hands falling gracefully into the lap of her lavender dress. The gates closed on the boy and, burying his face in the pillows, he slept.

"There was something disturbing to me in the room, and I didn't know what it was. I didn't in truth know what was wrong with me, only that I'd been drawn forcefully either by myself or someone else from two fierce, consuming states: an absorption with those grim paintings, and the kill to which I'd abandoned myself, obscenely, in the eyes of others.

"I didn't know what it was that threatened me now, what it was that my mind sought escape from. I kept looking at Claudia, the way she lay against the books, the way she sat amongst the objects of the desk, the polished white skull, the candle-holder, the open parchment book whose hand-painted script gleamed in the light; and then above her there emerged into focus the lacquered and shimmering painting of a medieval devil, horned and hoofed, his bestial figure looming over a coven of worshipping witches. Her head was just beneath it, the loose curling strands of her hair just stroking it; and she watched the brown-eyed vampire with wide, wondering eyes. I wanted to pick her up suddenly, and frightfully, horribly, I saw her in my kindled imagination flopping like a doll. I was gazing at the devil, that monstrous face preferable to the sight of her in her eerie stillness.

" 'You won't awaken the boy if you speak,' said the brown-eyed vampire. 'You've come from so far, you've travelled so long.' And gradually my confusion subsided, as if smoke were rising and moving away on a current of fresh air. And I lay awake and very calm, looking at him as he sat in the opposite chair. Claudia, too, looked at him. And he looked from one to the other of us, his smooth face and pacific eyes very like they'd been all along, as though there had never been any change in him at all.

" 'My name is Armand,' he said. 'I sent Santiago to give you the invitation. I know your names. I welcome you to my house.'

"I gathered my strength to speak, my voice sounding strange to me when I told him that we had feared we were alone.

" 'But how did you come into existence?' he asked. Claudia's hand rose ever so slightly from her lap, her eyes moving mechanically from his face to mine. I saw this and knew that he must have seen it, and yet he gave no sign. I knew at once what she meant to tell me. 'You don't want to answer,' said Armand, his voice low and even more measured than Claudia's voice, far less human than my own. I sensed myself slipping away again into contemplation of that voice and those eyes, from which I had to draw myself up with great effort.

" 'Are you the leader of this group?' I asked him.

" 'Not in the way you mean *leader*,' he answered. 'But if there were a leader here, I would be that one.'

" 'I haven't come . . . you'll forgive me . . . to talk of how I came into being. Because that's no mystery to me, it presents no question. So if you have no power to which I might be required to render respect, I don't wish to talk of those things.'

" 'If I told you I did have such power, would you respect it?' he asked.

"I wish I could describe his manner of speaking, how each time he spoke he seemed to arise out of a state of contemplation very like that state into which I felt I was drifting, from which it took so much to wrench myself; and yet he never moved, and seemed at all times alert. This distracted me while at the same time I was powerfully attracted by it, as I was by this room, its simplicity, its rich, warm combination of essentials: the books, the desk, the two chairs by the fire, the coffin, the pictures. The luxury of those rooms in the hotel seemed vulgar, but more than that, meaningless, beside this room. I understood all of it except for the mortal boy, the sleeping boy, whom I didn't understand at all.

" 'I'm not certain,' I said, unable to keep my eyes off that awful medieval Satan. 'I would have to know from what . . . from whom it comes. Whether it came from other vampires . . . or elsewhere.'

" 'Elsewhere . . .' he said. 'What is elsewhere?'

" 'That!' I pointed to the medieval picture.

" 'That is a picture,' he said.

" 'Nothing more?'

" 'Nothing more.'

" 'Then Satan . . . some satanic power doesn't give you your power here, either as leader or as vampire?'

" 'No,' he said calmly, so calmly it was impossible for me to know what he thought of my questions, if he thought of them at all in the manner which I knew to be thinking.

" 'And the other vampires?'

" 'No,' he said.

" 'Then we are not . . .' I sat forward. '. . . the children of Satan?'

" 'How could we be the children of Satan?' he asked. 'Do you believe that Satan made this world around you?'

" 'No, I believe that God made it, if anyone made it. But He also must have made Satan, and I want to know if we are his children!'

" 'Exactly, and consequently if you believe God made Satan, you must realize that all Satan's power comes from God and that Satan is simply God's child, and that we are God's children also. There are no children of Satan, really.'

"I couldn't disguise my feelings at this. I sat back against the leather, looking at that small woodcut of the devil, released for the moment from any sense of obligation to Armand's presence, lost in my thoughts, in the undeniable implications of his simple logic.

" 'But why does this concern you? Surely what I say doesn't surprise you,' he said. 'Why do you let it affect you?'

" 'Let me explain,' I began. 'I know that you're a master vampire. I respect you. But I'm incapable of your detachment. I know what it is, and I do not possess it and I doubt that I ever will. I accept this.'

" 'I understand,' he nodded. 'I saw you in the theater, your suffering, your sympathy with that girl. I saw your sympathy for Denis when I offered him to you; you die when you kill, as if you feel that you deserve to die, and you stint on nothing. But why, with this passion and this sense of justice, do you wish to call yourself the child of Satan!'

" 'I'm evil, evil as any vampire who ever lived! I've killed over and over and will do it again. I took that boy, Denis, when you gave him to me, though I was incapable of knowing whether he would survive or not.'

" 'Why does that make you as evil as any vampire? Aren't there gradations of evil? Is evil a great perilous gulf into which one falls with the first sin, plummeting to the depth?'

" 'Yes, I think it is,' I said to him. 'It's not logical, as you would make it sound. But it's that dark, that empty. And it is without consolation.'

" 'But you're not being fair,' he said with the first glimmer of expression in his voice. 'Surely you attribute great degrees and variations to goodness. There is the goodness of the child which is innocence, and then there is the goodness of the monk who has given up everything to others and lives a life of self-deprivation and service. The goodness of saints, the goodness of good housewives. Are all these the same?'

" 'No. But equally and infinitely different from evil.' I answered.

"I didn't know I thought these things. I spoke them now as my thoughts. And they were my most profound feelings taking a shape they could never have taken had I not spoken them, had I not thought them out this way in conversation with another. I thought myself then possessed of a passive mind, in a sense. I mean that my mind could only pull itself together, formulate thought out of the muddle of longing and pain, when it was touched by another mind; fertilized by it; deeply excited by that other mind and driven to form conclusions. I felt now the rarest, most acute alleviation of loneliness. I could easily visualize and suffer that moment years before in another century, when I had stood at the foot of Babette's stairway, and feel the perpetual metallic frustration of years with Lestat; and then that passionate and doomed affection for Claudia which made loneliness retreat behind the soft indulgence of the senses, the same senses that longed for the kill. And I saw the desolate mountaintop in eastern Europe where I had confronted that mindless vampire and killed him in the monastery ruins. And it was as if the great feminine longing of my mind were being awakened again to be satisfied. And this I felt despite my own words: 'But it's that dark, that empty. And it is without consolation.'

"I looked at Armand, at his large brown eyes in that taut, timeless face, watching me again like a painting; and I felt the slow shifting of the physical world I'd felt in the painted ballroom, the pull of my old delirium, the wakening of a need so terrible that the very promise of its fulfillment contained the unbearable possibility of disappointment. And yet there was the question, the awful, ancient, hounding question of evil.

"I think I put my hands to my head as mortals do when so deeply troubled that they instinctively cover the face, reach for the brain as if they could reach through the skull and massage the living organ out of its agony.

" 'And how is this evil achieved?' he asked. 'How does one fall from grace and become in one instant as evil as the mob tribunal of the Revolution or the most cruel of the Roman emperors? Does one merely have to miss Mass on Sunday, or bite down on the Communion Host? Or steal a loaf of bread . . . or sleep with a neighbor's wife?'

" 'No. . . .' I shook my head. 'No.'

" 'But if evil is without gradation, and it does exist, this state of evil, then only one sin is needed. Isn't that what you are saying? That God exists and. . . .'

" 'I don't know if God exists,' I said. 'And for all I do know . . . He doesn't exist.'

" 'Then no sin matters,' he said. 'No sin achieves evil.'

" 'That's not true. Because if God doesn't exist we are the creatures of highest consciousness in the universe. We alone understand the passage of time and the value of every minute of human life. And what constitutes evil, real evil, is the taking of a single human life. Whether a man would have died tomorrow or the day after or eventually . . . it doesn't matter. Because if God does not exist, this life . . . every second of it . . . is all we have.'

"He sat back, as if for the moment stopped, his large eyes narrowing, then fixing on the depths of the fire. This was the first time since he had come for me that he had looked away from me, and I found myself looking at him unwatched. For a long time he sat in this manner and I could all but feel his thoughts, as if they were palpable in the air like smoke. Not read them, you understand, but feel the power of them. It seemed he possessed an aura and even though his face was very young, which I knew meant nothing, he appeared infinitely old, wise. I could not define it, because I could not explain how the youthful lines of his face, how his eyes expressed innocence and this age and experience at the same time.

"He rose now and looked at Claudia, his hands loosely clasped behind his back. Her silence all this time had been understandable to me. These were not her questions, yet she was fascinated with him and was waiting for him and no doubt learning from him all the while that he spoke to me. But I understood something else now as they looked at each other. He had moved to his feet with a body totally at his command, devoid of the habit of human gesture, gesture rooted in necessity, ritual, fluctuation of mind; and his stillness now was unearthly. And she, as I'd never seen before, possessed the same stillness. And they were gazing at each other with a preternatural understanding from which I was simply excluded.

"I was something whirling and vibrating to them, as mortals were to me. And I knew when he turned towards me again that he'd come to understand she did not believe or share my concept of evil.

"His speech commenced without the slightest warning. 'This is the only real evil left,' he said to the flames.

" 'Yes,' I answered, feeling that all-consuming subject alive again, obliterating all concerns as it always had for me.

" 'It's true,' he said, shocking me, deepening my sadness, my despair.

" 'Then God does not exist . . . you have no knowledge of His existence?'

" 'None,' he said.

" 'No knowledge!' I said it again, unafraid of my simplicity, my miserable human pain.

" 'None.'

" 'And no vampire here has discourse with God or with the devil!'

" 'No vampire that I've ever known,' he said, musing, the fire dancing in his eyes. 'And as far as I know today, after four hundred years, I am the oldest living vampire in the world.'

"I stared at him, astonished.

"Then it began to sink in. It was as I'd always feared, and it was as lonely, it was as totally without hope. Things would go on as they had before, on and on. My search was over. I sat back listlessly watching those licking flames.

"It was futile to leave him to continue it, futile to travel the world only to hear again the same story. 'Four hundred years'—I think I repeated the words— 'four hundred years.' I remember staring at the fire. There was a log falling very slowly in the fire, drifting downwards in a process that would take it the night, and it was pitted with tiny holes where some substance that had larded it through and through had burned away fast, and in each of these tiny holes there danced a flame amid the larger flames: and all of these tiny flames with their black mouths seemed to me faces that made a chorus; and the chorus sang without singing. The chorus had no need of singing; in one breath in the fire, which was continuous, it made its soundless song.

"All at once Armand moved in a loud rustling of garments, a descent of crackling shadow and light that left him kneeling at my feet, his hands outstretched holding my head, his eyes burning.

" 'This evil, this concept, it comes from disappointment, from bitterness! Don't you see? Children of Satan! Children of God! Is this the only question you bring to me, is this the only power that obsesses you, so that you must make us gods and devils yourself when the only power that exists is inside ourselves? How could you believe in these old fantastical lies, these myths, these emblems of the supernatural?' He snatched the devil from above Claudia's still countenance so swiftly that I couldn't see the gesture, only the demon leering before me and then crackling in the flames.

"Something was broken inside me when he said this; something ripped aside, so that a torrent of feeling became one with my muscles in every limb. I was on my feet now, backing away from him.

"'Are you mad?' I asked, astonished at my own anger, my own despair. 'We stand here, the two of us, immortal, ageless, rising nightly to feed that immortality on human blood; and there on your desk against the knowledge of the ages sits a flawless child as demonic as ourselves; and you ask me how I could believe I would find a meaning in the supernatural! I tell you, after seeing what I have become, I could damn well believe anything! Couldn't you? And believing thus, being thus confounded, I can now accept the most fantastical truth of all: that there is no meaning to any of this!'

"I backed towards the door, away from his astonished face, his hand hovering before his lips, the finger curling to dig into his palm. 'Don't! Come back . . .' he whispered.

"'No, not now. Let me go. Just a while . . . let me go. . . . Nothing's changed; it's all the same. Let that sink into me . . . just let me go.'

"I looked back before I shut the door. Claudia's face was turned towards me, though she sat as before, her hands clasped on her knee. She made a gesture then, subtle as her smile, which was tinged with the faintest sadness, that I was to go on.

"It was my desire to escape the theater then entirely, to find the streets of Paris and wander, letting the vast accumulation of shocks gradually wear away. But, as I groped along the stone passage of the lower cellar, I became confused. I was perhaps incapable of exerting my own will. It seemed more than ever absurd to me that Lestat should have died, if in fact he had; and looking back on him, as it seemed I was always doing, I saw him more kindly than before. Lost like the rest of us. Not the jealous protector of any knowledge he was afraid to share. He knew nothing. There was nothing to know.

"Only, that was not quite the thought that was gradually coming clear to me. I had hated him for all the wrong reasons; yes, that was true. But I did not fully understand it yet. Confounded, I found myself sitting finally on those dark steps, the light from the ballroom throwing my own shadow on the rough floor, my hands holding my head, a weariness overcoming me. My mind said, Sleep. But more profoundly, my mind said, Dream. And yet I made no move to return to the Hôtel Saint-Gabriel, which seemed a very secure and airy place to me now, a place of subtle and luxurious mortal consolation where I might lie in a chair of puce velvet, put one foot on an ottoman and watch the fire lick the marble tile, looking for all the world to myself in the long mirrors like a thoughtful human. Flee to that, I thought, flee all that is pulling you. And again came that thought: I have wronged Lestat, I have hated him for all the wrong reasons. I whispered it now, trying to withdraw it from the dark, inarticulate pool of my mind, and the whispering made a scratching sound in the stone vault of the stairs.

"But then a voice came softly to me on the air, too faint for mortals: 'How is this so? How did you wrong him?'

"I turned round so sharp that my breath left me. A vampire sat near me, so near as to almost brush my shoulder with the tip of his boot, his legs drawn up close to him, his hands clasped around them. For a moment I thought my eyes deceived me. It was the trickster vampire, whom Armand had called Santiago.

"Yet nothing in his manner indicated his former self, that devilish, hateful self that I had seen, even only a few hours ago when he had reached out for me and Armand had struck him. He was staring at me over his drawn-up knees, his hair dishevelled, his mouth slack and without cunning.

" 'It makes no difference to anyone else,' I said to him, the fear in me subsiding.

" 'But you said a name; I heard you say a name,' he said.

" 'A name I don't want to say again,' I answered, looking away from him. I could see now how he'd fooled me, why his shadow had not fallen over mine; he crouched in my shadow. The vision of him slithering down those stone stairs to sit behind me was slightly disturbing. Everything about him was disturbing, and

I reminded myself that he could in no way be trusted. It seemed to me then that Armand, with his hypnotic power, aimed in some way for the maximum truth in presentation of himself: he had drawn out of me without words my state of mind. But this vampire was a liar. And I could feel his power, a crude, pounding power that was almost as strong as Armand's.

" 'You come to Paris in search of us, and then you sit alone on the stairs . . .' he said, in a conciliatory tone. 'Why don't you come up with us? Why don't you speak to us and talk to us of this person whose name you spoke; I know who it was, I know the name.'

" 'You don't know, couldn't know. It was a mortal,' I said now, more from instinct than conviction. The thought of Lestat disturbed me, the thought that this creature should know of Lestat's death.

" 'You came here to ponder mortals, justice done to mortals?' he asked; but there was no reproach or mockery in his tone.

" 'I came to be alone, let me not offend you. It's a fact,' I murmured.

" 'But alone in this frame of mind, when you don't even hear my steps. . . . I like you. I want you to come upstairs.' And as he said this, he slowly pulled me to my feet beside him.

"At that moment the door of Armand's cell threw a long light into the passage. I heard him coming, and Santiago let me go. I was standing there baffled. Armand appeared at the foot of the steps, with Claudia in his arms. She had that same dull expression on her face which she'd had all during my talk with Armand. It was as if she were deep in her own considerations and saw nothing around her; and I remember noting this, though not knowing what to think of it, that it persisted even now. I took her quickly from Armand, and felt her soft limbs against me as if we were both in the coffin, yielding to that paralytic sleep.

"And then, with a powerful thrust of his arm, Armand pushed Santiago away. It seemed he fell backwards, but was up again only to have Armand pull him towards the head of the steps, all of this happening so swiftly I could only see the blur of their garments and hear the scratching of their boots. Then Armand stood alone at the head of the steps, and I went upward towards him.

" 'You cannot safely leave the theater tonight,' he whispered to me. 'He is suspicious of you. And my having brought you here, he feels that it is his right to know you better. Our security depends on it.' He guided me slowly into the ballroom. But then he turned to me and pressed his lips almost to my ear: 'I must warn you. Answer no questions. Ask and you open one bud of truth for yourself after another. But give nothing, nothing, especially concerning your origin.'

"He moved away from us now, but beckoning for us to follow him into the gloom where the others were gathered, clustered like remote marble statues, their faces and hands all too like our own. I had the strong sense then of how we were all made from the same material, a thought which had only occurred to me occasionally in all the long years in New Orleans; and it disturbed me, particularly when I saw one or more of the others reflected in the long mirrors that broke the density of those awful murals.

"Claudia seemed to awaken as I found one of the carved oak chairs and settled into it. She leaned towards me and said something strangely incoherent, which seemed to mean that I must do as Armand said: say nothing of our origin. I wanted to talk with her now, but I could see that tall vampire, Santiago, watching us, his eyes moving slowly from us to Armand. Several women vampires had gathered around Armand, and I felt a tumult of feeling as I saw them put their arms around his waist. And what appalled me as I watched was not their exquisite form, their delicate features and graceful hands made hard as glass by vampire nature, or their bewitching eyes which fixed on me now in a sudden silence; what appalled me was my own fierce jealousy. I was afraid when I saw them so close to him, afraid when he turned and kissed them each. And, as he brought them near to me now, I was unsure and confused.

"Estelle and Celeste are the names I remember, por-

celain beauties, who fondled Claudia with the license
of the blind, running their hands over her radiant hair,
touching even her lips, while she, her eyes still misty
and distant, tolerated it all, knowing what I also knew
and what they seemed unable to grasp: that a woman's
mind as sharp and distinct as their own lived within
that small body. It made me wonder as I watched her
turning about for them, holding out her lavender skirts
and smiling coldly at their adoration, how many times
I must have forgotten, spoken to her as if she were the
child, fondled her too freely, brought her into my arms
with an adult's abandon. My mind went in three
directions: that last night in the Hôtel Saint-Gabriel,
which seemed a year ago, when she talked of love
with rancor; my reverberating shock at Armand's
revelations or lack of them; and a quiet absorption of
the vampires around me, who whispered in the dark
beneath the grotesque murals. For I could learn much
from the vampires without ever asking a question, and
vampire life in Paris was all that I'd feared it to be,
all that the little stage in the theater above had indicated
it was.

"The dim lights of the house were mandatory, and
the paintings appreciated in full, added to almost
nightly when some vampire brought a new engraving
or picture by a contemporary artist into the house.
Celeste, with her cold hand on my arm, spoke with
contempt of men as the originators of these pictures,
and Estelle, who now held Claudia on her lap, emphasized to me, the naïve colonial, that vampires had
not made such horrors themselves but merely collected
them, confirming over and over that men were capable
of far greater evil than vampires.

" 'There is evil in making such paintings?' Claudia
asked softly in her toneless voice.

"Celeste threw back her black curls and laughed.
'What can be imagined can be done,' she answered
quickly, but her eyes reflected a certain contained
hostility. 'Of course, we strive to rival men in kills of
all kinds, do we not!' She leaned forward and touched
Claudia's knee. But Claudia merely looked at her,
watching her laugh nervously and continue. Santiago

drew near, to bring up the subject of our rooms in the Hôtel Saint-Gabriel; frightfully unsafe, he said, with an exaggerated stage gesture of the hands. And he showed a knowledge of those rooms which was amazing. He knew the chest in which we slept; it struck him as vulgar. 'Come here!' he said to me, with that near childlike simplicity he had evinced on the steps. 'Live with us and such disguise is unnecessary. We have our guards. And tell me, where do you come from!' he said, dropping to his knees, his hand on the arm of my chair. 'Your voice, I know that accent; speak again.'

"I was vaguely horrified at the thought of having an accent to my French, but this wasn't my immediate concern. He was strong-willed and blatantly possessive, throwing back at me an image of that possessiveness which was flowering in me more fully every moment. And meanwhile, the vampires around us talked on, Estelle explaining that black was the color for a vampire's clothes, that Claudia's lovely pastel dress was beautiful but tasteless. 'We blend with the night,' she said. 'We have a funereal gleam.' And now, bending her cheek next to Claudia's cheek, she laughed to soften her criticism; and Celeste laughed, and Santiago laughed, and the whole room seemed alive with unearthly tinkling laughter, preternatural voices echoing against the painted walls, rippling the feeble candle flames. 'Ah, but to cover up such curls,' said Celeste, now playing with Claudia's golden hair. And I realized what must have been obvious: that all of them had dyed their hair black, but for Armand; and it was that, along with the black clothes, that added to the disturbing impression that we were statues from the same chisel and paint brush. I cannot emphasize too much how disturbed I was by that impression. It seemed to stir something in me deep inside, something I couldn't fully grasp.

"I found myself wandering away from them to one of the narrow mirrors and watching them all over my shoulder. Claudia gleamed like a jewel in their midst; so would that mortal boy who slept below. The realization was coming to me that I found them dull in some awful way: dull, dull everywhere that I looked, their sparkling vampire eyes repetitious, their wit like a dull, brass bell.

"Only the knowledge I needed distracted me from these thoughts. 'The vampires of eastern Europe . . .' Claudia was saying. 'Monstrous creatures, what have they to do with us?'

" 'Revenants,' Armand answered softly over the distance that separated them, playing on faultless preternatural ears to hear what was more muted than a whisper. The room fell silent. 'Their blood is different, vile. They increase as we do but without skill or care. In the old days—' Abruptly he stopped. I could see his face in the mirror. It was strangely rigid.

" 'Oh, but tell us about the old days,' said Celeste, her voice shrill, at human pitch. There was something vicious in her tone.

"And now Santiago took up the same baiting manner. 'Yes, tell us of the covens, and the herbs that would render us invisible.' He smiled. 'And the burnings at the stake!'

"Armand fixed his eyes on Claudia. 'Beware those monsters,' he said, and calculatedly his eyes passed over Santiago and then Celeste. 'Those revenants. They will attack you as if you were human.'

"Celeste shuddered, uttering something in contempt, an aristocrat speaking of vulgar cousins who bear the same name. But I was watching Claudia because it seemed her eyes were misted again as before. She looked away from Armand suddenly.

"The voices of the others rose again, affected party voices, as they conferred with one another on the night's kills, describing this or that encounter without a smattering of emotion, challenges to cruelty erupting from time to time like flashes of white lightning: a tall, thin vampire being accosted in one corner for a needless romanticizing of mortal life, a lack of spirit, a refusal to do the most entertaining thing at the moment it was available to him. He was simple, shrugging, slow at words, and would fall for long periods into a stupefied silence, as if, near-choked with blood, he would as soon have gone to his coffin as remained here.

And yet he remained, held by the pressure of this
unnatural group who had made of immortality a
conformist's club. How would Lestat have found it?
Had he been here? What had caused him to leave?
No one had dictated to Lestat—he was master of
his small circle; but how they would have praised
his inventiveness, his catlike toying with his victims.
And waste . . . that word, that value which had been
all-important to me as a fledgling vampire, was spoken
of often. You 'wasted' the opportunity to kill this
child. You 'wasted' the opportunity to frighten this
poor woman or drive that man to madness, which
only a little prestidigitation would have accomplished.
    "My head was spinning. A common mortal head-
ache. I longed to get away from these vampires, and
only the distant figure of Armand held me, despite
his warnings. He seemed remote from the others now,
though he nodded often enough and uttered a few
words here and there so that he seemed a part of
them, his hand only occasionally rising from the lion's
paw of his chair. And my heart expanded when I
saw him this way, saw that no one amongst the small
throng caught his glance as I caught his glance,
and no one held it from time to time as I held it.
Yet he remained aloof from me, his eyes alone returning to me. His warning echoed in my ears, yet I
disregarded it. I longed to get away from the theater
altogether and stood listlessly, garnering information
at last that was useless and infinitely dull.
    " 'But is there no crime amongst you, no cardinal
crime?' Claudia asked. Her violet eyes seemed fixed
on me, even in the mirror, as I stood with my back
to her.
    " 'Crime! Boredom!' cried out Estelle, and she
pointed a white finger at Armand. He laughed softly
with her from his distant position at the end of the
room. 'Boredom is death!' she cried and bared her
vampire fangs, so that Armand put a languid hand to
his forehead in a stage gesture of fear and falling.
    "But Santiago, who was watching with his hands
behind his back, intervened. 'Crime!' he said. 'Yes,
there is a crime. A crime for which we would hunt

another vampire down until we destroyed him. Can you guess what that is?' He glanced from Claudia to me and back again to her masklike face. 'You should know, who are so secretive about the vampire that made you.'

" 'And why is that?' she asked, her eyes widening ever so slightly, her hands resting still in her lap.

"A hush fell over the room, gradually then completely, all those white faces turned to face Santiago as he stood there, one foot forward, his hands clasped behind his back, towering over Claudia. His eyes gleamed as he saw he had the floor. And then he broke away and crept up behind me, putting his hand on my shoulder. 'Can you guess what that crime is? Didn't your vampire master tell you?'

"And drawing me slowly around with those invading familiar hands, he tapped my heart lightly in time with its quickening pace.

" 'It is the crime that means death to any vampire anywhere who commits it. It is to kill your own kind!'

" 'Aaaaah!' Claudia cried out, and lapsed into peals of laughter. She was walking across the floor now with swirling lavender silk and crisp resounding steps. Taking my hand, she said, 'I was so afraid it was to be born like Venus out of the foam, as we were! Master vampire! Come, Louis, let's go!' she beckoned, as she pulled me away.

"Armand was laughing. Santiago was still. And it was Armand who rose when we reached the door. 'You're welcome tomorrow night,' he said. 'And the night after.'

"I don't think I caught my breath until I'd reached the street. The rain was still falling, and all of the street seemed sodden and desolate in the rain, but beautiful. A few scattered bits of paper blowing in the wind, a gleaming carriage passing slowly with the thick, rhythmic clop of the horse. The sky was pale violet. I sped fast, with Claudia beside me leading the way, then finally frustrated with the length of my stride, riding in my arms.

" 'I don't like them,' she said to me with a steel

fury as we neared the Hôtel Saint-Gabriel. Even its immense, brightly lit lobby was still in the pre-dawn hour. I spirited past the sleepy clerks, the long faces at the desk. 'I've searched for them the world over, and I despise them!' She threw off her cape and walked into the center of the room. A volley of rain hit the French windows. I found myself turning up the lights one by one and lifting the candelabrum to the gas flames as if I were Lestat or Claudia. And then, seeking the puce velvet chair I'd envisioned in that cellar, I slipped down into it, exhausted. It seemed for the moment as if the room blazed about me; as my eyes fixed on a gilt-framed painting of pastel trees and serene waters, the vampire spell was broken. They couldn't touch us here, and yet I knew this to be a lie, a foolish lie.

" 'I am in danger, danger,' Claudia said with that smoldering wrath.

" 'But how can they know what we did to him? Besides, we are in danger! Do you think for a moment I don't acknowledge my own guilt! And if you were the only one . . .' I reached out for her now as she drew near, but her fierce eyes settled on me and I let my hands drop back limp. 'Do you think I would leave you in danger?'

"She was smiling. For a moment I didn't believe my eyes. 'No, you would not, Louis. You would not. Danger holds you to me. . . .'

" 'Love holds me to you,' I said softly.

" 'Love?' she mused. 'What do you mean by love?' And then, as if she could see the pain in my face, she came close and put her hands on my cheek. She was cold, unsatisfied, as I was cold and unsatisfied, teased by that mortal boy but unsatisfied.

" 'That you take my love for granted always,' I said to her. 'That we are wed. . . .' But even as I said these words I felt my old conviction waver; I felt that torment I'd felt last night when she had taunted me about mortal passion. I turned away from her.

" 'You would leave me for Armand if he beckoned to you. . . .'

" 'Never . . .' I said to her.

" 'You would leave me, and he wants you as you want him. He's been waiting for you. . . .'

" 'Never. . . .' I rose now and made my way to that chest. The doors were locked, but they would not keep those vampires out. Only we could keep them out by rising as early as the light would let us. I turned to her and told her to come. And she was at my side. I wanted to bury my face in her hair, I wanted to beg her forgiveness. Because, in truth, she was right; and yet I loved her, loved her as always. And now, as I drew her in close to me, she said: 'Do you know what it was that he told me over and over without ever speaking a word; do you know what was the kernel of the trance he put me in so my eyes could only look at him, so that he pulled me as if my heart were on a string?'

" 'So you felt it . . .' I whispered. 'So it was the same.'

" 'He rendered me powerless!' she said. I saw the image of her against those books above his desk, her limp neck, her dead hands.

" 'But what are you saying? That he spoke to you, that he . . .'

" 'Without words!' she repeated. I could see the gaslights going dim, the candle flames too solid in their stillness. The rain beat on the panes. 'Do you know what he said . . . that I should die!' she whispered. 'That I should let you go.'

"I shook my head, and yet in my monstrous heart I felt a surge of excitement. She spoke the truth as she believed it. There was a film in her eyes, glassy and silver. 'He draws life out of me into himself,' she said, her lovely lips trembling so, I couldn't bear it. I held her tight, but the tears stood in her eyes. 'Life out of the boy who is his slave, life out of me whom he would make his slave. He loves you. He loves you. He would have you, and he would not have me stand in the way.'

" 'You don't understand him!' I fought it, kissing her; I wanted to shower her with kisses, her cheek, her lips.

" 'No, I understand him only too well,' she whispered

to my lips, even as they kissed her. 'It is you who don't understand him. Love's blinded you, your fascination with his knowledge, his power. If you knew how he drinks death you'd hate him more than you ever hated Lestat. Louis, you must never return to him. I tell you, I'm in danger!' "

"Early the next night, I left her, convinced that Armand alone among the vampires of the theater could be trusted. She let me go reluctantly, and I was troubled, deeply, by the expression in her eyes. Weakness was unknown to her, and yet I saw fear and something beaten even now as she let me go. And I hurried on my mission, waiting outside the theater until the last of the patrons had gone and the doormen were tending to the locks.

"What they thought I was, I wasn't certain. An actor, like the others, who did not take off his paint? It didn't matter. What mattered was that they let me through, and I passed them and the few vampires in the ballroom, unaccosted, to stand at last at Armand's open door. He saw me immediately, no doubt had heard my step a long way off, and he welcomed me at once and asked me to sit down. He was busy with his human boy, who was dining at the desk on a silver plate of meats and fish. A decanter of white wine stood next to him, and though he was feverish and weak from last night, his skin was florid and his heat and fragrance were a torment to me. Not apparently to Armand, who sat in the leather chair by the fire opposite me, turned to the human, his arms folded on the leather arm. The boy filled his glass and held it up now in a salute. 'My master,' he said, his eyes flashing on me as he smiled; but the toast was to Armand.

" 'Your slave,' Armand whispered with a deep intake of breath that was passionate. And he watched, as the boy drank deeply. I could see him savoring the wet lips, the mobile flesh of the throat as the wine went down. And now the boy took a morsel of white meat, making that same salute, and consumed it slowly, his eyes fixed on Armand. It was as though Armand feasted upon the feast, drinking in that part of life which he could not share any longer except with his eyes. And lost though he seemed to it, it was calculated; not that torture I'd felt years ago when I stood outside Babette's window longing for her human life.

"When the boy had finished, he knelt with his arms around Admand's neck as if he actually savored the icy flesh. And I could remember the night Lestat first came to me, how his eyes seemed to burn, how his white face gleamed. You know what I am to you now.

"Finally, it was finished. He was to sleep, and Armand locked the brass gates against him. And in minutes, heavy with his meal, he was dozing, and Armand sat opposite me, his large, beautiful eyes tranquil and seemingly innocent. When I felt them pull me towards him, I dropped my eyes, wished for a fire in the grate, but there were only ashes.

" 'You told me to say nothing of my origin, why was this?' I asked, looking up at him. It was if he could sense my holding back, yet wasn't offended, only regarding me with a slight wonder. But I was weak, too weak for his wonder, and again I looked away from him.

" 'Did you kill this vampire who made you? Is that why you are here without him, why you won't say his name? Santiago thinks that you did.'

" 'And if this is true, or if we can't convince you otherwise, you would try to destroy us?' I asked.

" 'I would not try to do anything to you,' he said, calmly. 'But as I told you, I am not the leader here in the sense that you asked.'

" 'Yet they believe you to be the leader, don't they? And Santiago, you shoved him away from me twice.'

" 'I'm more powerful than Santiago, older. Santiago is younger than you are,' he said. His voice was simple, devoid of pride. These were facts.

" 'We want no quarrel with you.'

" 'It's begun,' he said. 'But not with me. With those above.'

" 'But what reason has he to suspect us?'

"He seemed to be thinking now, his eyes cast down, his chin resting on his closed fist. After a while which seemed interminable, he looked up. 'I could give you reasons,' he said. 'That you are too silent. That the vampires of the world are a small number and live in terror of strife amongst themselves and choose their fledglings with great care, making certain that they respect the other vampires mightily. There are fifteen vampires in this house, and the number is jealously guarded. And weak vampires are feared; I should say this also. That you are flawed is obvious to them: you feel too much, you think too much. As you said yourself, vampire detachment is not of great value to you. And then there is this mysterious child: a child who can never grow, never be self-sufficient. I would not make a vampire of that boy there now if his life, which is so precious to me, were in serious danger, because he is too young, his limbs not strong enough, his mortal cup barely tasted: yet you bring with you this child. What manner of vampire made her, they ask; did you make her? So, you see, you bring with you these flaws and this mystery and yet you are completely silent. And so you cannot be trusted. And Santiago looks for an excuse. But there is another reason closer to the truth than all those things which I've just said to you. And that is simply this: that when you first encountered Santiago in the Latin Quarter you . . . unfortunately . . . called him a buffoon.'

" 'Aaaaah.' I sat back.

" 'It would perhaps have been better all around if you had said nothing.' And he smiled to see that I understood with him the irony of this.

"I sat reflecting upon what he'd said, and what weighed as heavily upon me through all of it were Claudia's strange admonitions, that this gentle-eyed young man had said to her, 'Die,' and beyond that my slowly accumulating disgust with the vampires in the ballroom above.

"I felt an overwhelming desire to speak to him of these things. Of her fear, no, not yet, though I couldn't believe when I looked into his eyes that he'd tried to wield this power over her: his eyes said, Live. His eyes said, Learn. And oh, how much I wanted to confide to him the breadth of what I didn't understand; how, searching all these years, I'd been astonished to discover those vampires above had made of immortality a club of fads and cheap conformity. And yet through this sadness, this confusion, came the clear realization: Why should it be otherwise? What had I expected? What right had I to be so bitterly disappointed in Lestat that I would let him die! Because he wouldn't show me what I must find in myself? Armand's words, what had they been? *The only power that exists is inside ourselves. . . .*

" 'Listen to me,' he said now. 'You must stay away from them. Your face hides nothing. You would yield to me now were I to question you. Look into my eyes.'

"I didn't do this. I fixed my eyes firmly on one of those small paintings above his desk until it ceased to be the Madonna and Child and became a harmony of line and color. Because I knew what he was saying to me was true.

" 'Stop them if you will, advise them that we don't mean any harm. Why can't you do this? You say yourself we're not your enemies, no matter what we've done. . . .'

"I could hear him sigh, faintly. 'I have stopped them for the time being,' he said. 'But I don't want such power over them as would be necessary to stop them entirely. Because if I exercise such power, then I must protect it. I will make enemies. And I would have forever to deal with my enemies when all I want here is a certain space, a certain peace. Or not to be here at all. I accept the scepter of sorts they've given me, but not to rule over them, only to keep them at a distance.'

" 'I should have known,' I said, my eyes still fixed on that painting.

" 'Then, you must stay away. Celeste has a great deal of power, being one of the oldest, and she is jealous of the child's beauty. And Santiago, as you can see, is only waiting for a shred of proof that you're outlaws.'

"I turned slowly and looked at him again where he sat with that eerie vampire stillness, as if he were in fact not alive at all. The moment lengthened. I heard his words just as if he were speaking them again: 'All I want here is a certain space, a certain peace. Or not to be here at all.' And I felt a longing for him so strong that it took all my strength to contain it, merely to sit there gazing at him, fighting it. I wanted it to be this way: Claudia safe amongst these vampires somehow, guilty of no crime they might ever discover from her or anyone else, so that I might be free, free to remain forever in this cell as long as I could be welcome, even tolerated, allowed here on any condition whatsoever.

"I could see that mortal boy again as if he were not asleep on the bed but kneeling at Armand's side with his arms around Armand's neck. It was an icon for me of love. The love I felt. Not physical love, you must understand. I don't speak of that at all, though Armand was beautiful and simple, and no intimacy with him would ever have been repellent. For vampires, physical love culminates and is satisfied in one thing, the kill. I speak of another kind of love which drew me to him completely as the teacher which Lestat had never been. Knowledge would never be withheld by Armand, I knew it. I would pass through him as through a pane of glass so that I might bask in it and absorb it and grow. I shut my eyes. And I thought I heard him speak, so faintly I wasn't certain. It seemed he said, 'Do you know why I am here?'

"I looked up at him again, wondering if he knew my thoughts, could actually read them, if such could conceivably be the extent of that power. Now after all these years I could forgive Lestat for being nothing but an ordinary creature who could not show me the uses of my powers; and yet I still longed for this, could fall into it without resistance. A sadness pervaded it all, sadness for my own weakness and my own awful dilemma. Claudia waited for me. Claudia, who was my daughter and my love.

" 'What am I to do?' I whispered. 'Go away from them, go away from you? After all these years . . .'

" '*They* don't matter to you,' he said.

"I smiled and nodded.

" 'What is it you want to do?' he asked. And his voice assumed the most gentle, sympathetic tone.

" 'Don't you know, don't you have that power?' I asked. 'Can't you read my thoughts as if they were words?'

"He shook his head. 'Not the way you mean. I only know the danger to you and the child is real because it's real to you. And I know your loneliness even with her love is almost more terrible than you can bear.'

"I stood up then. It would seem a simple thing to do, to rise, to go to the door, to hurry quickly down that passage; and yet it took every ounce of strength, every smattering of that curious thing I've called my detachment.

" 'I ask you to keep them away from us,' I said at the door; but I couldn't look back at him, didn't even want the soft intrusion of his voice.

" 'Don't go,' he said.

" 'I have no choice.'

"I was in the passage when I heard him so close to me that I started. He stood beside me, eye level with my eye, and in his hand he held a key which he pressed into mine.

" 'There is a door there,' he said, gesturing to the dark end, which I'd thought to be merely a wall. 'And a stairs to the side street which no one uses but myself. Go this way now, so you can avoid the others. You are anxious and they will see it.' I turned around to go at once, though every part of my being wanted to remain there. 'But let me tell you this,' he said, and lightly he pressed the back of his hand against my heart. 'Use the power inside you. Don't abhor it anymore. Use that power! And when they see you in the streets above, use that power to make your face a mask and think as you gaze on them as on anyone: beware. Take that word as if it were an amulet I'd given you to wear about your neck. And when your eyes meet Santiago's eyes, or the eyes of any other vampire, speak to them politely what you will, but think of that word and that word only. Remember what I say. I speak to you simply because you respect what is simple. You understand this. That's your strength.'

"I took the key from him, and I don't remember actually putting it into the lock or going up the steps. Or where he was or what he'd done. Except that, as I was stepping into the dark side street behind the theater, I heard him say very softly to me from someplace close to me: 'Come here, to me, when you can.' I looked around for him but was not surprised that I couldn't see him. He had told me also sometime or other that I must not leave the Hôtel Saint-Gabriel, that I must not give the others the shred of evidence of guilt they wanted. 'You see,' he said, 'killing other vampires is very exciting; that is why it is forbidden under penalty of death.'

"And then I seemed to awake. To the Paris street shining with rain, to the tall, narrow buildings on either side of me, to the fact that the door had shut to make a solid dark wall behind me and that Armand was no longer there.

"And though I knew Claudia waited for me, though I passed her in the hotel window above the gas lamps, a tiny figure standing among waxen petaled flowers, I moved away from the boulevard, letting the darker streets swallow me, as so often the streets of New Orleans had done.

"It was not that I did not love her; rather, it was that I knew I loved her only too well, that the passion for her was as great as the passion for Armand. And I fled them both now, letting the desire for the kill rise in me like a welcome fever, threatening consciousness, threatening pain.

"Out of the mist which had followed the rain, a man was walking towards me. I can remember him as roaming on the landscape of a dream, because the night around me was dark and unreal. The hill might have been anywhere in the world, and the soft lights of Paris were an amorphous shimmering in the fog. And sharp-eyed and drunk, he was walking blindly into the arms of death itself, his pulsing fingers reaching out to touch the very bones of my face.

"I was not crazed yet, not desperate. I might have said to him, 'Pass by.' I believe my lips did form the word Armand had given me, 'Beware.' Yet I let him slip his bold, drunken arm around my waist; I yielded to his adoring eyes, to the voice that begged to paint me now and spoke of warmth, to the rich, sweet smell of the oils that streaked his loose shirt. I was following him, through Montmartre, and I whispered to him, 'You are not a member of the dead.' He was leading me through an overgrown garden, through the sweet, wet grasses, and he was laughing as I said, 'Alive, alive,' his hand touching my cheek, stroking my face, clasping finally my chin as he guided me into the light of the low doorway, his reddened face brilliantly illuminated by the oil lamps, the warmth seeping about us as the door closed.

"I saw the great sparkling orbs of his eyes, the tiny red veins that reached for the dark centers, that warm hand burning my cold hunger as he guided me to a chair. And then all around me I saw faces blazing, faces rising in the smoke of the lamps, in the shimmer of the burning stove, a wonderland of colors on canvases surrounding us beneath the small, sloped roof, a blaze of beauty that pulsed and throbbed. 'Sit down, sit down . . .' he said to me, those feverish hands against my chest, clasped by my hands, yet sliding away, my hunger rising in waves.

"And now I saw him at a distance, eyes intent, the palette in his hand, the huge canvas obscuring the arm that moved. And mindless and helpless, I sat there drifting with his paintings, drifting with those adoring eyes, letting it go on and on till Armand's eyes were gone and Claudia was running down that stone passage with clicking heels away from me, away from me.

"'You are alive . . .' I whispered. 'Bones,' he answered me. 'Bones . . .' And I saw them in heaps, taken from those shallow graves in New Orleans as they are and put in chambers behind the sepulcher so that another can be laid in that narrow plot. I felt my eyes close; I felt my hunger become agony, my heart crying out for a living heart; and then I felt him moving forward, hands out to right my face—that fatal step, that fatal lurch. A sigh escaped my lips. 'Save yourself,' I whispered to him. 'Beware.'

"And then something happened in the moist radiance of his face, something drained the broken vessels of his fragile skin. He backed away from me, the brush falling from his hands. And I rose over him, feeling my teeth against my lip, feeling my eyes fill with the colors of his face, my ears fill with his struggling cry, my hands fill with that strong, fighting flesh until I drew him up to me, helpless, and tore that flesh and had the blood that gave it life. 'Die,' I whispered when I held him loose now, his head bowed against my coat, 'die,' and felt him struggle to look up at me. And again I drank and again he fought, until at last he slipped, limp and shocked and near to death, on the floor. Yet his eyes did not close.

"I settled before his canvas, weak, at peace, gazing down at him, at his vague, graying eyes, my own hands florid, my skin so luxuriously warm. 'I am mortal again,' I whispered to him. 'I am alive. With your blood I am alive.' His eyes closed. I sank back against the wall and found myself gazing at my own face.

"A sketch was all he'd done, a series of bold black lines that nevertheless made up my face and shoulders perfectly, and the color was already begun in dabs and splashes: the green of my eyes, the white of my cheek. But the horror, the horror of seeing my expression! For he had captured it perfectly, and there was nothing of horror in it. Those green eyes gazed at me from out of that loosely drawn shape with a mindless innocence, the expressionless wonder of that overpowering craving which he had not understood. Louis of a hundred years ago lost in listening to the sermon of the priest at Mass, lips parted and slack, hair careless, a hand curved in the lap and limp. A mortal Louis. I believe I was laughing, putting my hands to my face and laughing so that the tears nearly rose in my eyes; and when I took my fingers down, there was the stain of the tears, tinged with mortal blood. And already there was begun in me the tingling of the monster that had killed, and would kill again, who was gathering up the painting now and starting to flee with it from the small house.

"When suddenly, up from the floor, the man rose with an animal groan and clutched at my boot, his hands sliding off the leather. With some colossal spirit that defied me, he reached up for the painting and held fast to it with his whitening hands. 'Give it back!' he growled at me. 'Give it back!' And we held fast, the two of us, I staring at him and at my own hands that held so easily what he sought so desperately to rescue, as if he would take it to heaven or hell; I the thing that his blood could not make human, he the man that my evil had not overcome. And then, as if I were not myself, I tore the painting loose from him and, wrenching him up to my lips with one arm, gashed his throat in rage."

"Entering the rooms of the Hôtel Saint-Gabriel, I set the picture on the mantel above the fire and looked at it a long time. Claudia was somewhere in the rooms, and some other presence intruded, as though on one of the balconies above a woman or a man stood near, giving off an unmistakable personal perfume. I didn't know why I had taken the picture, why I'd fought for it so that it shamed me now worse than the death, and why I still held onto it at the marble mantel, my head bowed, my hands visibly trembling. And then slowly I turned my head. I wanted the rooms to take shape around me; I wanted the flowers, the velvet, the candles in their sconces. To be mortal and trivial and safe. And then, as if in a mist, I saw a woman there.

"She was seated calmly at that lavish table where Claudia attended to her hair; and so still she sat, so utterly without fear, her green taffeta sleeves reflected in the tilted mirrors, her skirts reflected, that she was not one still woman but a gathering of women. Her dark-red hair was parted in the middle and drawn back to her ears, though a dozen little ringlets escaped to make a frame for her pale face. And she was looking at me with two calm, violet eyes and a child's mouth that seemed almost obdurately soft, obdurately the cupid's bow unsullied by paint or personality; and the mouth smiled now and said, as those eyes seemed to fire: 'Yes, he's as you said he would be, and I love him already. He's as you said.' She rose now, gently lifting that abundance of dark taffeta, and the three small mirrors emptied at once.

"And utterly baffled and almost incapable of speech, I turned to see Claudia far off on the immense bed, her small face rigidly calm, though she clung to the silk curtain with a tight fist. 'Madeleine,' she said under her breath, 'Louis is shy.' And she watched with cold eyes as Madeleine only smiled when she said this and, drawing closer to me, put both of her hands to the lace fringe around her throat, moving it back so I could see the two small marks there. Then the smile died on her lips, and they became at once sullen and sensual as her eyes narrowed and she breathed the word, 'Drink.'

"I turned away from her, my fist rising in a consternation for which I couldn't find words. But then Claudia had hold of that fist and was looking up at me with relentless eyes. 'Do it, Louis,' she commanded. 'Because I cannot do it.' Her voice was painfully calm, all the emotion under the hard, measured tone. 'I haven't the size, I haven't the strength! You saw to that when you made me! Do it!'

"I broke away from her, clutching my wrist as if she'd burned it. I could see the door, and it seemed to me the better part of wisdom to leave by it at once. I could feel Claudia's strength, her will, and the mortal woman's eyes seemed afire with that same will. But Claudia held me, not with a gentle pleading, a miserable coaxing that would have dissipated that power, making me feel pity for her as I gathered my own forces. She held me with the emotion her eyes had evinced even through her coldness and the way that she turned away from me now, almost as if she'd been instantly defeated. I did not understand the manner in which she sank back on the bed, her head bowed, her lips moving feverishly, her eyes rising only to scan the walls. I wanted to touch her and say to her that what she asked was impossible; I wanted to soothe that fire that seemed to be consuming her from within.

"And the soft, mortal woman had settled into one of the velvet chairs by the fire, with the rustling and iridescence of her taffeta dress surrounding her like part of the mystery of her, of her dispassionate eyes which watched us now, the fever of her pale face. I remember turning to her, spurred on by that childish, pouting mouth set against the fragile face. The vampire kiss had left no visible trace except the wound, no inalterable change on the pale pink flesh. 'How do we appear to you?' I asked, seeing her eyes on Claudia. She seemed excited by the diminutive beauty, the awful woman's-passion knotted in the small dimpled hands.

"She broke her gaze and looked up at me. 'I ask you . . . how do we appear? Do you think us beautiful, magical, our white skin, our fierce eyes? Oh, I remember perfectly what mortal vision was, the dimness of it, and how the vampire's beauty burned through that veil, so powerfully alluring, so utterly deceiving! Drink, you tell me. You haven't the vaguest conception under God of what you ask!'

"But Claudia rose from the bed and came towards me. 'How dare you!' she whispered. 'How dare you make this decision for both of us! Do you know how I despise you! Do you know that I despise you with a passion that eats at me like a canker!' Her small form trembled, her hands hovering over the pleated bodice of her yellow gown. 'Don't you look away from me! I am sick at heart with your looking away, with your suffering. You understand nothing. Your evil is that you cannot be evil, and I must suffer for it. I tell you, I will suffer no longer!' Her fingers bit into the flesh of my wrist; I twisted, stepping back from her, floundering in the face of the hatred, the rage rising like some dormant beast in her, looking out through her eyes. 'Snatching me from mortal hands like two grim monsters in a nightmare fairy tale, you idle, blind parents! Fathers!' She spat the word. 'Let tears gather in your eyes. You haven't tears enough for what

you've done to me. Six more mortal years, seven, eight
. . . I might have had that shape!' Her pointed finger
flew at Madeleine, whose hands had risen to her face,
whose eyes had clouded over. Her moan was almost
Claudia's name. But Claudia did not hear her. 'Yes,
that shape, I might have known what it was to walk
at your side. Monsters! To give me immortality in
this hopeless guise, this helpless form!' The tears stood
in her eyes. The words had died away, drawn in, as
it were, on her breast.

" 'Now, you give her to me!' she said, her head
bowing, her curls tumbling down to make a concealing
veil. 'You give her to me. You do this, or you finish
what you did to me that night in the hotel in New
Orleans. I will not live with this hatred any longer,
I will not live with this rage! I cannot. I will not abide
it!' And tossing her hair, she put her hands to her ears
as if to stop the sound of her own words, her breath
drawn in rapid gasps, the tears seeming to scald her
cheeks.

"I had sunk to my knees at her side, and my arms
were outstretched as if to enfold her. Yet I dared not
touch her, dared not even say her name, lest my
own pain break from me with the first syllable in a
monstrous outpouring of hopelessly inarticulate cries.
'Oooh.' She shook her head now, squeezing the tears
out onto her cheeks, her teeth clenched tight together.
'I love you still, that's the torment of it. Lestat I never
loved. But you! The measure of my hatred is that love.
They are the same! Do you know now how much I
hate you!' She flashed at me through the red film that
covered her eyes.

" 'Yes,' I whispered. I bowed my head. But she was
gone from me into the arms of Madeleine, who enfolded her desperately, as if she might protect Claudia
from me—the irony of it, the pathetic irony—protect
Claudia from herself. She was whispering to Claudia,
'Don't cry, don't cry!' her hands stroking Claudia's
face and hair with a fierceness that would have bruised
a human child.

"But Claudia seemed lost against her breast suddenly,
her eyes closed, her face smooth, as if all passion were

drained away from her, her arm sliding up around Madeleine's neck, her head falling against the taffeta and lace. She lay still, the tears staining her cheeks, as if all this that had risen to the surface had left her weak and desperate for oblivion, as if the room around her, as if I, were not there.

"And there they were together, a tender mortal crying unstintingly now, her warm arms holding what she could not possibly understand, this white and fierce and unnatural childthing she believed she loved. And if I had not felt for her, this mad and reckless woman flirting with the damned, if I had not felt all the sorrow for her I felt for my mortal self, I would have wrested the demon thing from her arms, held it tight to me, denying over and over the words I'd just heard. But I knelt there still, thinking only, The love is equal to the hatred; gathering that selfishly to my own breast, holding onto that as I sank back against the bed.

"A long time before Madeleine was to know it, Claudia had ceased crying and sat still as a statue on Madeleine's lap, her liquid eyes fixed on me, oblivious to the soft, red hair that fell around her or the woman's hand that still stroked her. And I sat slumped against the bedpost, staring back at those vampire eyes, unable and unwilling to speak in my defense. Madeleine was whispering into Claudia's ear, she was letting her tears fall into Claudia's tresses. And then gently, Claudia said to her, 'Leave us.'

" 'No.' She shook her head, holding tight to Claudia. And then she shut her eyes and trembled all over with some terrible vexation, some awful torment. But Claudia was leading her from the chair, and she was now pliant and shocked and white-faced, the green taffeta ballooning around the small yellow silk dress.

"In the archway of the parlor they stopped, and Madeleine stood as if confused, her hand at her throat, beating like a wing, then going still. She looked about her like that hapless victim on the stage of the Théâtre des Vampires who did not know where she was. But Claudia had gone for something. And I saw her emerge from the shadows with what appeared to be a large doll. I rose on my knees to look at it. It was a doll, the doll of a little girl with raven hair and green eyes, adorned with lace and ribbons, sweet-faced and wide-eyed, its porcelain feet tinkling as Claudia put it into Madeleine's arms. And Madeleine's eyes appeared to harden as she held the doll, and her lips drew back from her teeth in a grimace as she stroked its hair. She was laughing low under her breath. 'Lie down,' Claudia said to her; and together they appeared to sink into the cushions of the couch, the green taffeta rustling and giving way as Claudia lay with her and put her arms around her neck. I saw the doll sliding, dropping to the floor, yet Madeleine's hand groped for it and held it dangling, her own head thrown back, her eyes shut tight, and Claudia's curls stroking her face.

"I settled back on the floor and leaned against the soft siding of the bed. Claudia was speaking now in a low voice, barely above a whisper, telling Madeleine to be patient, to be still. I dreaded the sound of her step on the carpet; the sound of the doors sliding closed to shut Madeleine away from us, and the hatred that lay between us like a killing vapor.

"But when I looked up to her, Claudia was standing there as if transfixed and lost in thought, all rancor and bitterness gone from her face, so that she had the blank expression of that doll.

" 'All you've said to me is true,' I said to her. 'I deserve your hatred. I've deserved it from those first moments when Lestat put you in my arms.'

"She seemed unaware of me, and her eyes were infused with a soft light. Her beauty burned into my soul so that I could hardly stand it, and then she said, wondering, 'You could have killed me then, despite him. You could have done it.' Then her eyes rested on me calmly. 'Do you wish to do it now?'

" 'Do it now!' I put my arm around her, moved her close to me, warmed by her softened voice. 'Are you mad, to say such things to me? Do I want to do it now!'

" 'I want you to do it,' she said. 'Bend down now as you did then, draw the blood out of me drop by drop, all you have the strength for; push my heart to the brink. I am small, you can take me. I won't resist you, I am something frail you can crush like a flower.'

" 'You mean these things? You mean what you say to me?' I asked. 'Why don't you place the knife here, why don't you turn it?'

" 'Would you die with me?' she asked, with a sly, mocking smile. 'Would you in fact die with me?' she pressed. 'Don't you understand what is happening to me? That he's killing me, that master vampire who has you in thrall, that he won't share your love with me, not a drop of it? I see his power in your eyes. I see your misery, your distress, the love for him you can't hide. Turn around, I'll make you look at me with those eyes that want him, I'll make you listen.'

" 'Don't anymore, don't . . . I won't leave you. I've sworn to you, don't you see? I cannot give you that woman.'

" 'But I'm fighting for my life! Give her to me so she can care for me, complete the guise I must have to live! And he can have you then! I am fighting for my life!'

"I all but shoved her off. 'No, no, it's madness, it's witchery,' I said, trying to defy her. 'It's you who will not share me with him, it's you who want every drop of that love. If not from me, from her. He overpowers you, he disregards you, and it's you who wish him dead the way that you killed Lestat. Well, you won't make me a party to this death, I tell you, not this death! I will not make her one of us, I will not damn the legions of mortals who'll die at her hands if I do! Your power over me is broken. I will not!'

"Oh, if she could only have understood!

"Not for a moment could I truly believe her words against Armand, that out of that detachment which was beyond revenge he could selfishly wish for her death. But that was nothing to me now; something far more terrible than I could grasp was happening, something I was only beginning to understand, against which my anger was nothing but a mockery, a hollow attempt to oppose her tenacious will. She hated me, she loathed me, as she herself had confessed, and my heart shrivelled inside me, as if, in depriving me of that love which had sustained me a lifetime, she had dealt me a mortal blow. The knife was there. I was dying for her, dying for that love as I was that very first night when Lestat gave her to me, turned her eyes to me, and told her my name; that love which had warmed me in my self-hatred, allowed me to exist. Oh, how Lestat had understood it, and now at last his plan was undone.

"But it went beyond that, in some region from which I was shrinking as I strode back and forth, back and forth, my hands opening and closing at my sides, feeling not only that hatred in her liquid eyes: It was her pain. She had shown me her pain! *To give me immortality in this hopeless guise, this helpless form.* I put my hands to my ears, as if she spoke the words yet, and the tears flowed. For all these years I had depended utterly upon her cruelty, her absolute lack of pain! And pain was what she showed to me, undeniable pain. Oh, how Lestat would have laughed at us. That was why she had put the knife to him, because he would have laughed. To destroy me utterly she need only show me that pain. The child I made a vampire suffered. Her agony was as my own.

"There was a coffin in that other room, a bed for Madeleine, to which Claudia retreated to leave me alone with what I could not abide. I welcomed the silence. And sometime during the few hours that remained of the night I found myself at the open window, feeling the slow mist of the rain. It glistened on the fronds of the ferns, on sweet white flowers that listed, bowed, and finally broke from their stems. A carpet of flowers littering the little balcony, the petals pounded softly by the rain. I felt weak now, and utterly alone. What had passed between us tonight could never be undone, and what had been done to Claudia by me could never be undone.

"But I was somehow, to my own bewilderment, empty of all regret. Perhaps it was the night, the starless sky, the gas lamps frozen in the mist that gave some strange comfort for which I never asked and didn't know how, in this emptiness and aloneness, to receive. I am alone, I was thinking. I am alone. It seemed just, perfectly, and so to have a pleasing, inevitable form. And I pictured myself then forever alone, as if on gaining that vampire strength the night of my death I had left Lestat and never looked back for him, as if I had moved on away from him, beyond the need of him and anyone else. As if the night had said to me, 'You are the night and the night alone understands you and enfolds you in its arms.' One with the shadows. Without nightmare. An inexplicable peace.

"Yet I could feel the end of this peace as surely as I'd felt my brief surrender to it, and it was breaking like the dark clouds. The urgent pain of Claudia's loss pressed in on me, behind me, like a shape gathered from the corners of this cluttered and oddly alien room. But outside, even as the night seemed to dissolve in a fierce driving wind, I could feel something calling to me, something inanimate which I'd never known. And a power within me seemed to answer that power, not with resistance but with an inscrutable, chilling strength.

"I moved silently through the rooms, gently dividing the doors until I saw, in the dim light cast by the flickering gas flames behind me, that sleeping woman lying in my shadow on the couch, the doll limp against her breast. Sometime before I knelt at her side I saw her eyes open, and I could feel beyond her in the collected dark those other eyes watching me, that breathless tiny vampire face waiting.

" 'Will you care for her, Madeleine?' I saw her hands clutch at the doll, turning its face against her breast. And my own hand went out for it, though I did not know why, even as she was answering me.

" 'Yes!' She repeated it again desperately.

" 'Is this what you believe her to be, a doll?' I asked her, my hand closing on the doll's head, only to feel her snatch it away from me, see her teeth clenched as she glared at me.

" 'A child who can't die! That's what she is,' she said, as if she were pronouncing a curse.

" 'Aaaaah . . .' I whispered.

" 'I've done with dolls,' she said, shoving it away from her into the cushions of the couch. She was fumbling with something on her breast, something she wanted me to see and not to see, her fingers catching hold of it and closing over it. I knew what it was, had noticed it before. A locket fixed with a gold pin. I wish I could describe the passion that infected her round features, how her soft baby mouth was distorted.

" 'And the child who did die?' I guessed, watching her. I was picturing a doll shop, dolls with the same face. She shook her head, her hand pulling hard on the locket so the pin ripped the taffeta. It was fear I saw in her now, a consuming panic. And her hand bled as she opened it from the broken pin. I took the locket from her fingers. 'My daughter,' she whispered, her lip trembling.

"It was a doll's face on the small fragment of porcelain, Claudia's face, a baby face, a saccharine, sweet mockery of innocence an artist had painted there, a child with raven hair like the doll. And the mother, terrified, was staring at the darkness in front of her.

" 'Grief . . .' I said gently.

" 'I've done with grief,' she said, her eyes narrowing as she looked up at me. 'If you knew how I long to have your power; I'm ready for it, I hunger for it.' And she turned to me, breathing deeply, so that her breast seemed to swell under her dress.

"A violent frustration rent her face then. She turned away from me, shaking her head, her curls. 'If you were a mortal man; man *and* monster!' she said angrily. 'If I could only show you my power . . .' and she smiled malignantly, defiantly at me '. . . I could make you want me, desire me! But you're unnatural!' Her mouth went down at the corners. 'What can I give you! What can I do to make you give me what you have!' Her hand hovered over her breasts, seeming to caress them like a man's hand.

"It was strange, that moment; strange because I could never have predicted the feeling her words incited in me, the way that I saw her now with that small enticing waist, saw the round, plump curve of her breasts and those delicate, pouting lips. She never dreamed what the mortal man in me was, how tormented I was by the blood I'd only just drunk. Desire her I did, more than she knew; because she didn't understand the nature of the kill. And with a man's pride I wanted to prove that to her, to humiliate her for what she had said to me, for the cheap vanity of her provocation and the eyes that looked away from me now in disgust. But this was madness. These were not the reasons to grant eternal life.

"And cruelly, surely, I said to her, 'Did you love this child?'

"I will never forget her face then, the violence in her, the absolute hatred. 'Yes.' She all but hissed the words at me. 'How dare you!' She reached for the locket even as I clutched it. It was guilt that was consuming her, not love. It was guilt—that shop of dolls Claudia had described to me, shelves and shelves of the effigy of that dead child. But guilt that absolutely understood the finality of death. There was something as hard in her as the evil in myself, something as powerful. She had her hand out towards me. She touched my waistcoat and opened her fingers there, pressing them against my chest. And I was on my knees, drawing close to her, her hair brushing my face.

" 'Hold fast to me when I take you,' I said to her, seeing her eyes grow wide, her mouth open. 'And when the swoon is strongest, listen all the harder for the beating of my heart. Hold and say over and over, "I will live." '

" 'Yes, yes,' she was nodding, her heart pounding with her excitement.

"Her hands burned on my neck, fingers forcing their way into my collar. 'Look beyond me at that distant light; don't take your eyes off of it, not for a second, and say over and over, "I will live." '

"She gasped as I broke the flesh, the warm current coming into me, her breasts crushed against me, her body arching up, helpless, from the couch. And I could see her eyes, even as I shut my own, see that taunting, provocative mouth. I was drawing on her, hard, lifting her, and I could feel her weakening, her hands dropping limp at her sides. 'Tight, tight,' I whispered over the hot stream of her blood, her heart thundering in my ears, her blood swelling my satiated veins. 'The lamp,' I whispered, 'look at it!' Her heart was slowing, stopping, and her head dropped back from me on the velvet, her eyes dull to the point of death. It seemed for a moment I couldn't move, yet I knew I had to, that someone else was lifting my wrist to my mouth as the room turned round and round, that I was focusing on that light as I had told her to do, as I tasted my own blood from my own wrist, and then forced it into her mouth. 'Drink it. Drink,' I said to her. But she lay as if dead. I gathered her close to me, the blood pouring over her lips. Then she opened her eyes, and I felt the gentle pressure of her mouth, and then her hands closing tight on the arm as she began to suck. I was rocking her, whispering to her, trying desperately to break my swoon; and then I felt her powerful pull. Every blood vessel felt it. I was threaded through and through with her pulling, my hand holding fast to the couch now, her heart beating fierce against my heart, her fingers digging deep into my arm, my outstretched palm. It was cutting me, scoring me, so I all but cried out as it went on and on, and I was backing away from her, yet pulling her with me, my life passing through my arm, her moaning breath in time with her pulling. And those strings which were my veins, those searing wires pulled at my very heart harder and harder until, without will or direction, I had wrenched free of her and fallen away from her, clutching that bleeding wrist tight with my own hand.

"She was staring at me, the blood staining her open mouth. An eternity seemed to pass as she stared. She doubled and tripled in my blurred vision, then collapsed into one trembling shape. Her hand moved to her mouth, yet her eyes did not move but grew large in her face as she stared. And then she rose slowly, not as if by her own power but as if lifted from the couch bodily by some invisible force which held her now, staring as she turned round and round, her massive skirt moving stiff as if she were all of a piece, turning like some great carved ornament on a music box that dances helplessly round and round to the music. And suddenly she was staring down at the taffeta, grabbing hold of it, pressing it between her fingers so it zinged and rustled, and she let it fall, quickly covering her ears, her eyes shut tight, then opened wide again. And then it seemed she saw the lamp, the distant, low gas lamp of the other room that gave a fragile light through the double doors. And she ran to it and stood beside it, watching it as if it were alive. 'Don't touch it . . .' Claudia said to her, and gently guided her away. But Madeleine had seen the flowers on the balcony and she was drawing close to them now, her outstretched palms brushing the petals and then pressing the droplets of rain to her face.

"I was hovering on the fringes of the room, watching her every move, how she took the flowers and crushed them in her hands and let the petals fall all around her and how she pressed her fingertips to the mirror and stared into her own eyes. My own pain had ceased, a handkerchief bound the wound, and I was waiting, waiting, seeing now that Claudia had no knowledge from memory of what was to come next. They were dancing together, as Madeleine's skin grew paler and paler in the unsteady golden light. She scooped Claudia into her arms, and Claudia rode round in circles with her, her own small face alert and wary behind her smile.

"And then Madeleine weakened. She stepped backwards and seemed to lose her balance. But quickly she righted herself and let Claudia go gently down to the ground. On tiptoe, Claudia embraced her. 'Louis.' She signalled to me under her breath. 'Louis. . . .'

"I beckoned for her to come away. And Madeleine, not seeming even to see us, was staring at her own outstretched hands. Her face was blanched and drawn, and suddenly she was scratching at her lips and staring at the dark stains on her fingertips. 'No, no!' I cautioned her gently, taking Claudia's hand and holding her close to my side. A long moan escaped Madeleine's lips.

" 'Louis,' Claudia whispered in that preternatural voice which Madeleine could not yet hear.

" 'She is dying, which your child's mind can't remember. You were spared it, it left no mark on you,' I whispered to her, brushing the hair back from her ear, my eyes never leaving Madeleine, who was wandering from mirror to mirror, the tears flowing freely now, the body giving up its life.

" 'But, Louis, if she dies . . .' Claudia cried.

" 'No.' I knelt down, seeing the distress in her small face. 'The blood was strong enough, she will live. But she will be afraid, terribly afraid.' And gently, firmly, I pressed Claudia's hand and kissed her cheek. She looked at me then with mingled wonder and fear. And she watched me with that same expression as I wandered closer to Madeleine, drawn by her cries. She reeled now, her hands out, and I caught her and held her close. Her eyes already burned with unnatural light, a violet fire reflected in her tears.

" 'It's mortal death, only mortal death,' I said to her gently. 'Do you see the sky? We must leave it now and you must hold tight to me, lie by my side. A sleep as heavy as death will come over my limbs, and I won't be able to solace you. And you will lie there and you will struggle with it. But you hold tight to me in the darkness, do you hear? You hold tight to my hands, which will hold your hands as long as I have feeling.'

"She seemed lost for the moment in my gaze, and I sensed the wonder that surrounded her, how the radiance of my eyes was the radiance of all colors and how all those colors were all the more reflected for her in my eyes. I guided her gently to the coffin, telling her again not to be afraid. 'When you arise, you will be immortal,' I said. 'No natural cause of death can harm you. Come, lie down.' I could see her fear of it, see her shrink from the narrow box, its satin no comfort. Already her skin began to glisten, to have that brilliance that Claudia and I shared. I knew now she would not surrender until I lay with her.

"I held her and looked across the long vista of the room to where Claudia stood, with that strange coffin, watching me. Her eyes were still but dark with an undefined suspicion, a cool distrust. I set Madeleine down beside her bed and moved towards those eyes. And, kneeling calmly beside her, I gathered Claudia in my arms. 'Don't you recognize me?' I asked her. 'Don't you know who I am?'

"She looked at me. 'No.' she said.

"I smiled. I nodded. 'Bear me no ill will,' I said. 'We are even.'

"At that she moved her head to one side and studied me carefully, then seemed to smile despite herself and to nod in assent.

" 'For you see,' I said to her in that same calm voice, 'what died tonight in this room was not that woman. It will take her many nights to die, perhaps years. What has died in this room tonight is the last vestige in me of what was human.'

"A shadow fell over her face; clear, as if the composure were rent like a veil. And her lips parted, but only with a short intake of breath. Then she said, 'Well, then you are right. Indeed. We are even.' "

" 'I want to burn the doll shop!'

"Madeleine told us this. She was feeding to the fire in the grate the folded dresses of that dead daughter, white lace and beige linen, crinkled shoes, bonnets that smelled of camphor balls and sachet. 'It means nothing now, any of it.' She stood back watching the fire blaze. And she looked at Claudia with triumphant, fiercely devoted eyes.

"I did not believe her, so certain I was—even though night after night I had to lead her away from men and women she could no longer drain dry, so satiated was she with the blood of earlier kills, often lifting her victims off their feet in her passion, crushing their throats with her ivory fingers as surely as she drank their blood—so certain I was that sooner or later this mad intensity must abate, and she would take hold of the trappings of this nightmare, her own luminescent flesh, these lavish rooms of the Hôtel Saint-Gabriel, and cry out to be awakened; to be free. She did not understand it was no experiment; showing her fledgling teeth to the gilt-edged mirrors, she was mad.

"But I still did not realize how mad she was, and how accustomed to dreaming; and that she would not cry out for reality, rather would feed reality to her dreams, a demon elf feeding her spinning wheel with the reeds of the world so she might make her own web-like universe.

"I was just beginning to understand her avarice, her magic.

"She had a dollmaker's craft from making with her old lover over and over the replica of her dead child, which I was to understand crowded the shelves of this shop we were soon to visit. Added to that was a vampire's skill and a vampire's intensity, so that in the space of one night when I had turned her away from killing, she, with that same insatiable need, created out of a few sticks of wood, with her chisel and knife, a perfect rocking chair, so shaped and proportioned for Claudia that seated in it by the fire, she appeared a woman. To that must be added, as the nights passed, a table of the same scale; and from a toy shop a tiny oil lamp, a china cup and saucer; and from a lady's purse a little leather-bound book for notes which in Claudia's hands became a large volume. The world crumbled and ceased to exist at the boundary of the small space which soon became the length and breadth of Claudia's dressing room: a bed whose posters reached only to my breast buttons, and small mirrors that reflected only the legs of an unwieldy giant when I found myself lost among them; paintings hung low for Claudia's eye; and finally, upon her little vanity table, black evening gloves for tiny fingers, a woman's low-cut gown of midnight velvet, a tiara from a child's masked ball. And Claudia, the crowning jewel, a fairy queen with bare white shoulders wandering with her sleek tresses among the rich items of her tiny world while I watched from the doorway, spellbound, ungainly, stretched out on the carpet so I could lean my head on my elbow and gaze up into my paramour's eyes, seeing them mysteriously softened for the time being by the perfection of this sanctuary. How beautiful she was in black lace, a cold, flaxen-haired woman with a kewpie doll's face and liquid eyes which gazed at me so serenely and so long that, surely, I must have been forgotten; the eyes must be seeing something other than me as I lay there on the floor dreaming; something other than the clumsy universe surrounding me, which was now marked off and nullified by someone who had suffered in it, someone who had suffered always, but who was not seeming to suffer now, listening as it were to the tinkling of a toy music box, putting a hand on the toy clock. I saw a vision of shortened hours and little golden minutes. I felt I was mad.

"I put my hands under my head and gazed at the chandelier; it was hard to disengage myself from one world and enter the other. And Madeleine, on the couch, was working with that regular passion, as if immortality could not conceivably mean rest, sewing cream lace to lavender satin for the small bed, only stopping occasionally to blot the moisture tinged with blood from her white forehead.

"I wondered, if I shut my eyes, would this realm of tiny things consume the rooms around me, and would I, like Gulliver, awake to discover myself bound hand and foot, an unwelcome giant? I had a vision of houses made for Claudia in whose garden mice would be monsters, and tiny carriages, and flowery shrubbery become trees. Mortals would be so entranced, and drop to their knees to look into the small windows. Like the spider's web, it would attract.

"I *was* bound hand and foot here. Not only by that fairy beauty—that exquisite secret of Claudia's white shoulders and the rich luster of pearls, bewitching languor, a tiny bottle of perfume, now a decanter, from which a spell is released that promises Eden—I was bound by fear. That outside these rooms, where I supposedly presided over the education of Madeleine —erratic conversations about killing and vampire nature in which Claudia could have instructed so much more easily than I, if she had ever showed the desire to take the lead—that outside these rooms, where nightly I was reassured with soft kisses and contented looks that the hateful passion which Claudia had shown once and once only would not return— that outside these rooms, I would find that I was, according to my own hasty admission, truly changed: the mortal part of me was that part which had loved, I was certain. So what did I feel then for Armand, the creature for whom I'd transformed Madeleine, the creature for whom I had wanted to be free? A curious and disturbing distance? A dull pain? A nameless tremor? Even in this worldly clutter, I saw Armand in his monkish cell, saw his dark-brown eyes, and felt that eerie magnetism.

"And yet I did not move to go to him. I did not dare discover the extent of what I might have lost. Nor try to separate that loss from some other oppressive realization: that in Europe I'd found no truths to lessen loneliness, transform despair. Rather, I'd found only the inner workings of my own small soul, the pain of Claudia's, and a passion for a vampire who was perhaps more evil than Lestat, for whom I became as evil as Lestat, but in whom I saw the only promise of good in evil of which I could conceive.

"It was all beyond me, finally. And so the clock ticked on the mantel; and Madeleine begged to see the performances of the Théâtres des Vampires and swore to defend Claudia against any vampire who dared insult her; and Claudia spoke of strategy and said, 'Not yet, not now,' and I lay back observing with some measure of relief Madeleine's love for Claudia, her blind covetous passion. Oh, I have so little compassion in my heart or memory for Madeleine. I thought she had only seen the first vein of suffering, she had no understanding of death. She was so easily sharpened, so easily driven to wanton violence. I supposed in my colossal conceit and self-deception that my own grief for my dead brother was the only true emotion. I allowed myself to forget how totally I had fallen in love with Lestat's iridescent eyes, that I'd sold my soul for a many-colored and luminescent thing, thinking that a highly reflective surface conveyed the power to walk on water.

"What would Christ need have done to make me follow him like Matthew or Peter? Dress well, to begin with. And have a luxurious head of pampered yellow hair.

"I hated myself. And it seemed, lulled half to sleep as I was so often by their conversation—Claudia whispering of killing and speed and vampire craft, Madeleine bent over her singing needle—it seemed then the only emotion of which I was still capable: hatred of self. I love them. I hate them. I do not care if they are there. Claudia puts her hands on my hair as if she wants to tell me with the old familiarity that her heart's at peace. I do not care. And there is the apparition of Armand, that power, that heartbreaking clarity. Beyond a glass, it seems. And taking Claudia's playful hand, I understand for the first time in my life what she feels when she forgives me for being myself whom she says she hates and loves: *she feels almost nothing.*"

IT WAS A WEEK before we accompanied Madeleine on her errand, to torch a universe of dolls behind a plate-glass window. I remember wandering up the street away from it, round a turn into a narrow cavern of darkness where the falling rain was the only sound. But then I saw the red glare against the clouds. Bells clanged and men shouted, and Claudia beside me was talking softly of the nature of fire. The thick smoke rising in that flickering glare unnerved me. I was feeling fear. Not a wild, mortal fear, but something cold like a hook in my side. This fear—it was the old town house burning in the Rue Royale, Lestat in the attitude of sleep on the burning floor.

" 'Fire purifies . . .' Claudia said. And I said, 'No, fire merely destroys. . . .'

"Madeleine had gone past us and was roaming at the top of the street, a phantom in the rain, her white hands whipping the air, beckoning to us, white arcs of white fireflies. And I remember Claudia leaving me for her. The sight of wilted, writhing yellow hair as she told me to follow. A ribbon fallen underfoot, flapping and floating in a swirl of black water. It seemed they were gone. And I bent to retrieve that ribbon. But another hand reached out for it. It was Armand who gave it to me now.

"I was shocked to see him there, so near, the figure of Gentleman Death in a doorway, marvellously real in his black cape and silk tie, yet ethereal as the shadows in his stillness. There was the faintest glimmer of the fire in his eyes, red warming the blackness there to the richer brown.

"And I woke suddenly as if I'd been dreaming, woke to the sense of him, to his hand enclosing mine, to his head inclined as if to let me know he wanted me to follow—awoke to my own excited experience of his presence, which consumed me as surely as it had consumed me in his cell. We were walking together now, fast, nearing the Seine, moving so swiftly and artfully through a gathering of men that they scarce saw us, that we scarce saw them. That I could keep up with him easily amazed me. He was forcing me into some acknowledgment of my powers, that the paths I'd normally chosen were human paths I no longer need follow.

"I wanted desperately to talk to him, to stop him with both my hands on his shoulders, merely to look into his eyes again as I'd done that last night, to fix him in some time and place, so that I could deal with the excitement inside me. There was so much I wanted to tell him, so much I wanted to explain. And yet I didn't know what to say or why I would say it, only that the fullness of the feeling continued to relieve me almost to tears. This was what I'd feared lost.

"I didn't know where we were now, only that in my wanderings I'd passed here before: a street of ancient mansions, of garden walls and carriage doors and towers overhead and windows of leaded glass beneath stone arches. Houses of other centuries, gnarled trees, that sudden thick and silent tranquillity which means that the masses are shut out; a handful of mortals inhabit this vast region of highceilinged rooms; stone absorbs the sound of breathing, the space of whole lives.

"Armand was atop a wall now, his arm against the overhanging bough of a tree, his hand reaching for me; and in an instant I stood beside him, the wet foliage brushing my face. Above, I could see story after story rising to a lone tower that barely emerged from the dark, teeming rain. 'Listen to me; we are going to climb to the tower,' Armand was saying.

" 'I cannot . . . it's impossible . . . !'

" 'You don't begin to know your own powers. You can climb easily. Remember, if you fall you will not be injured. Do as I do. But note this. The inhabitants of this house have known me for a hundred years and think me a spirit; so if by chance they see you, or you see them through those windows, remember what they believe you to be and show no consciousness of them lest you disappoint them or confuse them. Do you hear? You are perfectly safe.'

"I wasn't sure what frightened me more, the climb itself or the notion of being seen as a ghost; but I had no time for comforting witticisms, even to myself. Armand had begun, his boots finding the crack between the stones, his hands sure as claws in the crevices; and I was moving after him, tight to the wall, not daring to look down, clinging for a moment's rest to the thick, carved arch over a window, glimpsing inside, over a licking fire, a dark shoulder, a hand stroking with a poker, some figure that moved completely without knowledge that it was watched. Gone. Higher and higher we climbed, until we had reached the window of the tower itself, which Armand quickly wrenched open, his long legs disappearing over the sill; and I rose up after him, feeling his arm out around my shoulders.

"I sighed despite myself, as I stood in the room, rubbing the backs of my arms, looking around this wet, strange place. The rooftops were silver below, turrets rising here and there through the huge, rustling treetops; and far off glimmered the broken chain of a lighted boulevard. The room seemed as damp as the night outside. Armand was making a fire.

"From a molding pile of furniture he was picking chairs, breaking them into wood easily despite the thickness of their rungs. There was something grotesque about him, sharpened by his grace and the imperturbable calm of his white face. He did what any vampire could do, cracking these thick pieces of wood into splinters, yet he did what only a vampire could do. And there seemed nothing human about him; even his handsome features and dark hair became the attributes of a terrible angel who shared with the rest of us only a superficial resemblance. The tailored coat was a mirage. And though I felt drawn to him, more strongly perhaps than I'd ever been drawn to any living creature save Claudia, he excited me in other ways which resembled fear. I was not surprised that, when he finished, he set a heavy oak chair down for me, but retired himself to the marble mantelpiece and sat there warming his hands over the fire, the flames throwing red shadows into his face.

" 'I can hear the inhabitants of the house,' I said to him. The warmth was good. I could feel the leather of my boots drying, feel the warmth in my fingers.

" 'Then you know that I can hear them,' he said softly; and though this didn't contain a hint of reproach, I realized the implications of my own words.

" 'And if they come?' I insisted, studying him.

" 'Can't you tell by my manner that they won't come?' he asked. 'We could sit here all night, and never speak of them. I want you to know that if we speak of them it is because you want to do so.' And when I said nothing, when perhaps I looked a little defeated, he said gently that they had long ago sealed off this tower and left it undisturbed; and if in fact they saw the smoke from the chimney or the light in the window, none of them would venture up until tomorrow.

"I could see now there were several shelves of books at one side of the fireplace, and a writing table. The pages on top were wilted, but there was an inkstand and several pens. I could imagine the room a very comfortable place when it was not storming, as it was now, or after the fire had dried out the air.

" 'You see,' Armand said, 'you really have no need of the rooms you have at the hotel. You really have need of very little. But each of us must decide how much he wants. These people in this house have a name for me; encounters with me cause talk for twenty years. They are only isolated instants in my time which mean nothing. They cannot hurt me, and I use their house to be alone. No one of the Théâtre des Vampires knows of my coming here. This is my secret.'

"I had watched him intently as he was speaking, and thoughts which had occurred to me in the cell at the theater occurred to me again. Vampires do not age, and I wondered how his youthful face and manner might differ now from what he had been a century before or a century before that; for his face, though not deepened by the lessons of maturity, was certainly no mask. It seemed powerfully expressive as was his unobtrusive voice, and I was at a loss finally to fully anatomize why. I knew only I was as powerfully drawn to him as before; and to some extent the words I spoke now were a subterfuge. 'But what holds you to the Théâtre des Vampires?' I asked.

" 'A need, naturally. But I've found what I need,' he said. 'Why do you shun me?'

" 'I never shunned you,' I said, trying to hide the excitement these words produced in me. 'You understand I have to protect Claudia, that she has no one but me. Or at least she had no one until . . .'

" 'Until Madeleine came to live with you. . . .'

" 'Yes . . .' I said.

" 'But now Claudia has released you, yet still you stay with her, and stay bound to her as your paramour,' he said.

" 'No, she's no paramour of mine; you don't understand,' I said. 'Rather, she's my child, and I don't know that she can release me. . . .' These were thoughts I'd gone over and over in my mind. 'I don't know if the child possesses the power to release the parent. I don't know that I won't be bound to her for as long as she . . .'

"I stopped. I was going to say, 'for as long as she lives.' But I realized it was a hollow mortal cliché. She would live forever, as I would live forever. But wasn't it so for mortal fathers? Their daughters live forever because these fathers die first. I was at a loss suddenly; but conscious all the while of how Armand listened; that he listened in the way that we dream of others listening, his face seeming to reflect on everything said. He did not start forward to seize on my slightest pause, to assert an understanding of something before the thought was finished, or to argue with a swift, irresistible impulse—the things which often make dialogue impossible.

"And after a long interval he said, 'I want you. I want you more than anything in the world.'

"For a moment I doubted what I'd heard. It struck me as unbelievable. And I was hopelessly disarmed by it, and the wordless vision of our living together expanded and obliterated every other consideration in my mind.

" 'I said that I want you. I want you more than anything in the world,' he repeated, with only a subtle change of expression. And then he sat waiting, watching. His face was as tranquil as always, his smooth, white forehead beneath the shock of his auburn hair without a trace of care, his large eyes reflecting on me, his lips still.

" 'You want this of me, yet you don't come to me,' he said. 'There are things you want to know, and you don't ask. You see Claudia slipping away from you, yet you seem powerless to prevent it, and then you would hasten it, and yet you do nothing.'

" 'I don't understand my own feelings. Perhaps they are clearer to you than they are to me. . . .'

" 'You don't begin to know what a mystery you are!' he said.

" 'But at least you know yourself thoroughly. I can't claim that,' I said. 'I love her, yet I am not close to her. I mean that when I am with you as I am now, I know that I know nothing of her, nothing of anyone.'

" 'She's an era for you, an era of your life. If and when you break with her, you break with the only one alive who has shared that time with you. You fear that, the isolation of it, the burden, the scope of eternal life.'

" 'Yes, that's true, but that's only a small part of it. The era, it doesn't mean much to me. She made it mean something. Other vampires must experience this and survive it, the passing of a hundred eras.'

" 'But they don't survive it,' he said. 'The world

would be choked with vampires if they survived it. How do you think I come to be the eldest here or anywhere?' he asked.

"I thought about this. And then I ventured, 'They die by violence?'

" 'No, almost never. It isn't necessary. How many vampires do you think have the stamina for immortality? They have the most dismal notions of immortality to begin with. For in becoming immortal they want all the forms of their life to be fixed as they are and incorruptible: carriages made in the same dependable fashion, clothing of the cut which suited their prime, men attired and speaking in the manner they have always understood and valued. When, in fact, all things change except the vampire himself; everything except the vampire is subject to constant corruption and distortion. Soon, with an inflexible mind, and often even with the most flexible mind, this immortality becomes a penitential sentence in a madhouse of figures and forms that are hopelessly unintelligible and without value. One evening a vampire rises and realizes what he has feared perhaps for decades, that he simply wants no more of life at any cost. That whatever style or fashion or shape of existence made immortality attractive to him has been swept off the face of the earth. And nothing remains to offer freedom from despair except the act of killing. And that vampire goes out to die. No one will find his remains. No one will know where he has gone. And often no one around him—should he still seek the company of other vampires—no one will know that he is in despair. He will have ceased long ago to speak of himself or of anything. He will vanish.'

"I sat back impressed by the obvious truth of it, and yet at the same time, everything in me revolted against that prospect. I became aware of the depth of my hope and my terror; how very different those feelings were from the alienation that he described, how very different from that awful wasting despair. There was something outrageous and repulsive in that despair suddenly. I couldn't accept it.

" 'But you wouldn't allow such a state of mind in

yourself. Look at you,' I found myself answering. 'If there weren't one single work of art left in this world . . . and there are thousands . . . if there weren't a single natural beauty . . . if the world were reduced to one empty cell and one fragile candle, I can't help but see you studying that candle, absorbed in the flicker of its light, the change of its colors . . . how long could that sustain you . . . what possibilities would it create? Am I wrong? Am I such a crazed idealist?'

" 'No,' he said. There was a brief smile on his lips, an evanescent flush of pleasure. But then he went on simply. 'But you feel an obligation to a world you love because that world for you is still intact. It is conceivable your own sensitivity might become the instrument of madness. You speak of works of art and natural beauty. I wish I had the artist's power to bring alive for you the Venice of the fifteenth century, my master's palace there, the love I felt for him when I was a mortal boy, and the love he felt for me when he made me a vampire. Oh, if I could make those times come alive for either you or me . . . for only an instant! What would that be worth? And what a sadness it is to me that time doesn't dim the memory of that period, that it becomes all the richer and more magical in light of the world I see today.'

" 'Love?' I asked. 'There was love between you and the vampire who made you?' I leaned forward.

" 'Yes,' he said. 'A love so strong he couldn't allow me to grow old and die. A love that waited patiently until I was strong enough to be born to darkness. Do you mean to tell me there was no bond of love between you and the vampire who made you?'

" 'None,' I said quickly. I couldn't repress a bitter smile.

"He studied me. 'Why then did he give you these powers?' he asked.

"I sat back. 'You see these powers as a gift!' I said. 'Of course you do. Forgive me, but it amazes me, how in your complexity you are so profoundly simple.' I laughed.

" 'Should I be insulted?" he smiled. And his whole manner only confirmed me in what I'd just said. He seemed so innocent. I was only beginning to understand him.

" 'No, not by me,' I said, my pulse quickening as I looked at him. 'You're everything I dreamed of when I became a vampire. You see these powers as a gift!' I repeated it. 'But tell me . . . do you now feel love for this vampire who gave you eternal life? Do you feel this now?'

"He appeared to be thinking, and then he said slowly, 'Why does this matter?' But went on: 'I don't think I've been fortunate in feeling love for many people or many things. But yes, I love him. Perhaps I do not love him as you mean. It seems you confuse me, rather effortlessly. You are a mystery. I do not need him, this vampire, anymore.'

" 'I was gifted with eternal life, with heightened perception, and with the need to kill,' I quickly explained, 'because the vampire who made me wanted the house I owned and my money. Do you understand such a thing?' I asked. 'Ah, but there is so much else behind what I say. It makes itself known to me so slowly, so incompletely! You see, it's as if you've cracked a door for me, and light is streaming from that door and I'm yearning to get to it, to push it back, to enter the region you say exists beyond it! When, in fact, I don't believe it! The vampire who made me was everything that I truly believed evil to be: he was as dismal, as literal, as barren, as inevitably eternally disappointing as I believed evil had to be! I know that now. But you, you are something totally beyond that conception! Open the door for me, push it back all the way. Tell me about this palace in Venice, this love affair with damnation. I want to understand it.'

" 'You trick yourself. The palace means nothing to you,' he said. 'The doorway you see leads to me, now. To your coming to live with me as I am. I am evil with infinite gradations and without guilt.'

" 'Yes, exactly,' I murmured.

" 'And this makes you unhappy,' he said. 'You, who came to me in my cell and said there was only one sin left, the willful taking of an innocent human life.'

" 'Yes . . .' I said. 'How you must have been laughing at me. . . .'

" 'I never laughed at you,' he said. 'I cannot afford to laugh at you. It is through you that I can save myself from the despair which I've described to you as our death. It is through you that I must make my link with this nineteenth century and come to understand it in a way that will revitalize me, which I so desperately need. It is for you that I've been waiting at the Théâtre des Vampires. If I knew a mortal of that sensitivity, that pain, that focus, I would make him a vampire in an instant. But such can rarely be done. No, I've had to wait and watch for you. And now I'll fight for you. Do you see how ruthless I am in love? Is this what you meant by love?'

" 'Oh, but you'd be making a terrible mistake,' I said, looking him in the eyes. His words were only slowly sinking in. Never had I felt my all-consuming frustration to be so clear. I could not conceivably satisfy him. I could not satisfy Claudia. I'd never been able to satisfy Lestat. And my own mortal brother, Paul: how dismally, mortally I had disappointed him!

" 'No. I must make contact with the age,' he said to me calmly. 'And I can do this through you . . . not to learn things from you which I can see in a moment in an art gallery or read in an hour in the thickest books . . . you are the spirit, you are the heart,' he persisted.

" 'No, no.' I threw up my hands. I was on the point of a bitter, hysterical laughter. 'Don't you see? I'm not the spirit of any age. I'm at odds with everything and always have been! I have never belonged anywhere with anyone at any time!' It was too painful, too perfectly true.

"But his face only brightened with an irresistible smile. He seemed on the verge of laughing at me, and then his shoulders began to move with this laughter. 'But Louis,' he said softly. 'This is the very spirit of your age. Don't you see that? Everyone else feels as you feel. Your fall from grace and faith has been the fall of a century.'

"I was so stunned by this, that for a long time

I sat there staring into the fire. It had all but consumed the wood and was a wasteland of smoldering ash, a gray and red landscape that would have collapsed at the touch of the poker. Yet it was very warm, and still gave off powerful light. I saw my life in complete perspective.

" 'And the vampires of the Théâtre . . .' I asked softly.

" 'They reflect the age in cynicism which cannot comprehend the death of possibilities, fatuous sophisticated indulgence in the parody of the miraculous, decadence whose last refuge is self-ridicule, a mannered helplessness. You saw them; you've known them all your life. You reflect your age differently. You reflect its broken heart.'

" 'This is unhappiness. Unhappiness you don't begin to understand.'

" 'I don't doubt it. Tell me what you feel now, what makes you unhappy. Tell me why for a period of seven days you haven't come to me, though you were burning to come. Tell me what holds you still to Claudia and the other woman.'

"I shook my head. 'You don't know what you ask. You see, it was immensely difficult for me to perform the act of making Madeleine into a vampire. I broke a promise to myself that I would never do this, that my own loneliness would never drive me to do it. I don't see our life as powers and gifts. I see it as a curse. I haven't the courage to die. But to make another vampire! To bring this suffering on another, and to condemn to death all those men and women whom that vampire must subsequently kill! I broke a grave promise. And in so doing . . .'

" 'But if it's any consolation to you . . . surely you realize I had a hand in it.'

" 'That I did it to be free of Claudia, to be free to come to you . . . yes, I realize that. But the ultimate responsibility lies with me!' I said.

" 'No. I mean, directly. I made you do it! I was near you the night you did it. I exerted my strongest power to persuade you to do it. Didn't you know this?'

" 'No!'

"I bowed my head.

" 'I would have made this woman a vampire,' he said softly. 'But I thought it best you have a hand in it. Otherwise you would not give Claudia up. You must know you wanted it. . . .'

" 'I loathe what I did!' I said.

" 'Then loathe me, not yourself.'

" 'No. You don't understand. You nearly destroyed the thing you value in me when this happened! I resisted you with all my power when I didn't even know it was your force which was working on me. Something nearly died in me! Passion nearly died in me! I was all but destroyed when Madeleine was created!'

" 'But that thing is no longer dead, that passion, that humanity, whatever you wish to name it. If it were not alive there wouldn't be tears in your eyes now. There wouldn't be rage in your voice,' he said.

"For the moment, I couldn't answer. I only nodded. Then I struggled to speak again. 'You must never force me to do something against my will! You must never exert such power . . .' I stammered.

" 'No,' he said at once. 'I must not. My power stops somewhere inside you, at some threshold. There I am powerless. However . . . this creation of Madeleine is done. You are free.'

" 'And you are satisfied,' I said, gaining control of myself. 'I don't mean to be harsh. You have me. I love you. But I'm mystified. You're satisfied?'

" 'How could I not be?' he asked. 'I am satisfied, of course.'

"I stood up and went to the window. The last embers were dying. The light came from the gray sky. I heard Armand follow me to the window ledge. I could feel him beside me now, my eyes growing more and more accustomed to the luminosity of the sky, so that now I could see his profile and his eye on the falling rain. The sound of the rain was everywhere and different: flowing in the gutter along the roof, tapping the shingles, falling softly through the shimmering layers of tree branches, splattering on the sloped stone sill in front of my hands. A soft intermingling of sounds that drenched and colored all of the night.

" 'Do you forgive me . . . for forcing you with the woman?' he asked.

" 'You don't need my forgiveness.'

" 'You need it,' he said. 'Therefore, I need it.' His face was as always utterly calm.

" 'Will she care for Claudia? Will she endure?' I asked.

" 'She is perfect. Mad; but for these days that is perfect. She will care for Claudia. She has never lived a moment of life alone; it is natural to her that she be devoted to her companions. She need not have particular reasons for loving Claudia. Yet, in addition to her needs, she does have particular reasons. Claudia's beautiful surface, Claudia's quiet, Claudia's dominance and control. They are perfect together. But I think . . . that as soon as possible they should leave Paris.'

" 'Why?'

" 'You know why. Because Santiago and the other vampires watch them with suspicion. All the vampires have seen Madeleine. They fear her because she knows about them and they don't know her. They don't let others alone who know about them.'

" 'And the boy, Denis? What do you plan to do with him?'

" 'He's dead,' he answered.

"I was astonished. Both at his words and his calm. 'You killed him?' I gasped.

"He nodded. And said nothing. But his large, dark eyes seemed entranced with me, with the emotion, the shock I didn't try to conceal. His soft, subtle smile seemed to draw me close to him; his hand closed over mine on the wet window sill and I felt my body turning to face him, drawing nearer to him, as though I were being moved not by myself but by him. 'It was best,' he conceded to me gently. And then said, 'We must go now. . . .' And he glanced at the street below.

" 'Armand,' I said. 'I can't. . . .'

" 'Louis, come after me,' he whispered. And then on the ledge, he stopped. 'Even if you were to fall on the cobblestones there,' he said, 'you would only be hurt for a while. You would heal so rapidly and so perfectly that in days you would show no sign of it, your bones healing as your skin heals; so let this knowledge free you to do what you can so easily do already. Climb down, now.'

" 'What can kill me?' I asked.

"Again he stopped. 'The destruction of your remains,' he said. 'Don't you know this? Fire, dismemberment . . . the heat of the sun. Nothing else. You can be scarred, yes; but you are resilient. You are immortal.'

"I was looking down through the quiet silver rain into darkness. Then a light flickered beneath the shifting tree limbs, and the pale beams of the light made the street appear. Wet cobblestones, the iron hook of the carriage-house bell, the vines clinging to the top of the wall. The huge black hulk of a carriage brushed the vines, and then the light grew weak, the street went from yellow to silver and vanished altogether, as if the dark trees had swallowed it up. Or, rather, as if it had all been subtracted from the dark. I felt dizzy. I felt the building move. Armand was seated on the window sill looking down at me.

" 'Louis, come with me tonight,' he whispered suddenly, with an urgent inflection.

" 'No,' I said gently. 'It's too soon. I can't leave them yet.'

"I watched him turn away and look at the dark sky. He appeared to sigh, but I didn't hear it. I felt his hand close on mine on the window sill. 'Very well . . .' he said.

" 'A little more time . . .' I said. And he nodded and patted my hand as if to say it was all right. Then he swung his legs over and disappeared. For only a moment I hesitated, mocked by the pounding of my heart. But then I climbed over the sill and commenced to hurry after him, never daring to look down."

It was very near dawn when I put my key into the lock at the hotel. The gas light flared along the walls. And Madeleine, her needle and thread in her hands, had fallen asleep by the grate. Claudia stood still, looking at me from among the ferns at the window, in shadow. She had her hairbrush in her hands. Her hair was gleaming.

"I stood there absorbing some shock, as if all the sensual pleasures and confusions of these rooms were passing over me like waves and my body were being permeated with these things, so different from the spell of Armand and the tower room where we'd been. There was something comforting here, and it was disturbing. I was looking for my chair. I was sitting in it with my hands on my temples. And then I felt Claudia near me, and I felt her lips against my forehead.

" 'You've been with Armand,' she said. 'You want to go with him.'

"I looked up at her. How soft and beautiful her face was, and, suddenly, so much mine. I felt no compunction in yielding to my urge to touch her cheeks, to lightly touch her eyelids—familiarities, liberties I hadn't taken with her since the night of our quarrel. 'I'll see you again; not here, in other places. Always I'll know where you are!' I said.

"She put her arms around my neck. She held me tight, and I closed my eyes and buried my face in her hair. I was covering her neck with my kisses. I had hold of her round, firm little arms. I was kissing them, kissing the soft indentation of the flesh in the crooks of her arms, her wrists, her open palms. I felt her fingers stroking my hair, my face. 'Whatever you wish,' she vowed. 'Whatever you wish.'

" 'Are you happy? Do you have what you want?' I begged her.

" 'Yes, Louis.' She held me against her dress, her fingers clasping the back of my neck. 'I have all that I want. But do you truly know what you want?' She was lifting my face so I had to look into her eyes. 'It's you I fear for, you who might be making the mistake. Why don't you leave Paris with us!' she said suddenly. 'We have the world, come with us!'

" 'No.' I drew back from her. 'You want it to be as it was with Lestat. It can't be that way again, ever. It won't be.'

" 'It will be something new and different with Madeleine. I don't ask for that again. It was I who put an end to that,' she said. 'But do you truly understand what you are choosing in Armand?'

"I turned away from her. There was something stubborn and mysterious in her dislike of him, in her failure to understand him. She would say again that he wished her death, which I did not believe. She didn't realize what I realized: he could not want her death, because I didn't want it. But how could I explain this to her without sounding pompous and blind in my love of him. 'It's meant to be. It's almost that sort of direction,' I said, as if it were just coming clear to me under the pressure of her doubts. 'He alone can give me the strength to be what I am. I can't continue to live divided and consumed with misery. Either I go with him, or I die,' I said. 'And it's something else, which is irrational and unexplainable and which satisfies only me. . . .'

" '. . . which is?' she asked.

" 'That I love him,' I said.

" 'No doubt you do,' she mused. 'But then, you could love even me.'

" 'Claudia, Claudia.' I held her close to me, and felt her weight on my knee. She drew up close to my chest.

" 'I only hope that when you have need of me, you can find me . . .' she whispered. 'That I can get back to you . . . I've hurt you so often, I've caused you so much pain.' Her words trailed off. She was resting still against me. I felt her weight, thinking, In a little while, I won't have her anymore. I want now simply to hold her. There has always been such pleasure in that simple thing. Her weight against me, this hand resting against my neck.

"It seemed a lamp died somewhere. That from the cool, damp air that much light was suddenly, soundlessly subtracted. I was sitting on the verge of dream. Had I been mortal I would have been content to sleep there. And in that drowsy, comfortable state I had a strange, habitual mortal feeling, that the sun would wake me gently later and I would have that rich, habitual vision of the ferns in the sunshine and the sunshine in the droplets of rain. I indulged that feeling. I half closed my eyes.

"Often afterwards I tried to remember those moments. Tried over and over to recall just what it was in those rooms as we rested there, that began to disturb me, should have disturbed me. How, being off my guard, I was somehow insensible to the subtle changes which must have been taking place there. Long after, bruised and robbed and embittered beyond my wildest dreams, I sifted through those moments, those drowsy quiet early-hour moments when the clock ticked almost imperceptibly on the mantelpiece, and the sky grew paler and paler; and all I could remember—despite the desperation with which I lengthened and fixed that time, in which I held out my hands to stop the clock—all I could remember was the soft changing of light.

"On guard, I would never have let it pass. Deluded with larger concerns, I made no note of it. A lamp gone out, a candle extinguished by the shiver of its own hot pool of wax. My eyes half shut, I had the sense then of impending darkness, of being shut up in darkness.

"And then I opened my eyes, not thinking of lamps or candles. And it was too late. I remember standing upright, Claudia's hand slipping on my arm, and the vision of a host of black-dressed men and women moving through the rooms, their garments seeming to garner light from every gilt edge or lacquered surface, seeming to drain all light away. I shouted out against them, shouted for Madeleine, saw her wake with a start, terrified fledgling, clinging to the arm of the couch, then down on her knees as they reached out for her. There was Santiago and Celeste coming towards us, and behind them, Estelle and others whose names I didn't know filling the mirrors and crowding together to make walls of shifting, menacing shadow. I was shouting to Claudia to run, having pulled back the door. I was shoving her through it and then was stretched across it, kicking out at Santiago as he came.

"That weak defensive position I'd held against him in the Latin Quarter was nothing compared to my strength now. I was too flawed perhaps to ever fight with conviction for my own protection. But the instinct to protect Madeleine and Claudia was overpowering. I remember kicking Santiago backwards and then striking out at that powerful, beautiful Celeste, who sought to get by me. Claudia's feet sounded on the distant marble stairway. Celeste was reeling, clawing at me, catching hold of me and scratching my face so the blood ran down over my collar. I could see it blazing in the corner of my eye. I was on Santiago now, turning with him, aware of the awful strength of the arms that held me, the hands that sought to get a hold on my throat. 'Fight them, Madeleine,' I was shouting to her. But all I could hear was her sobbing. Then I saw her in the whirl, a fixed, frightened thing, surrounded by other vampires. They were laughing that hollow vampire laughter which is like tinsel or silver-bells. Santiago was clutching at his face. My teeth had drawn blood there. I struck at his chest, at his head, the pain searing through my arm, something enclosing my chest like two arms, which I shook off, hearing the crash of broken glass behind me. But something else, someone else had hold of my arm with two arms and was pulling me with tenacious strength.

"I don't remember weakening. I don't remember any turning point when anyone's strength overcame my own. I remember simply being outnumbered. Hopelessly, by sheer numbers and persistence, I was stilled, surrounded, and forced out of the rooms. In a press of vampires, I was being forced along the passageway;

and then I was falling down the steps, free for a moment before the narrow back doors of the hotel, only to be surrounded again and held tight. I could see Celeste's face very near me and, if I could have, I would have wounded her with my teeth. I was bleeding badly, and one of my wrists was held so tightly that there was no feeling in that hand. Madeleine was next to me sobbing still. And all of us were pressed into a carriage. Over and over I was struck, and still I did not lose consciousness. I remember clinging tenaciously to consciousness, feeling these blows on the back of my head, feeling the back of my head wet with blood that trickled down my neck as I lay on the carriage floor. I was thinking only, I can feel the carriage moving; I am alive; I am conscious.

"And as soon as we were dragged into the Théâtre des Vampires, I was crying out for Armand.

"I was let go, only to stagger on the cellar steps, the horde of them behind me and in front of me, pushing me with menacing hands. At one point I got hold of Celeste, and she screamed and someone struck me from behind.

"And then I saw Lestat—the blow that was more crippling than any blow. Lestat, standing there in the center of the ballroom, erect, his gray eyes sharp and focused, his mouth lengthening in a cunning smile. Impeccably dressed he was, as always, and as splendid in his rich black cloak and fine linen. But those scars still scored every inch of his white flesh. And how they distorted the taut, handsome face, the fine, hard threads cutting the delicate skin above his lip, the lids of his eyes, the smooth rise of his forehead. And the eyes, they burned with a silent rage that seemed infused with vanity, an awful relentless vanity that said, 'See what I am.'

" 'This is the one?' said Santiago, thrusting me forward.

"But Lestat turned sharply to him and said in a harsh low voice, 'I told you I wanted Claudia, the child! She was the one!' And now I saw his head moving involuntarily with his outburst, and his hand reaching out as if for the arm of a chair only to close as he drew himself up again, eyes to me.

" 'Lestat,' I began, seeing now the few straws left to me. 'You are alive! You have your life! Tell them how you treated us. . . .'

" 'No,' he shook his head furiously. 'You come back to me, Louis,' he said.

"For a moment I could not believe my ears. Some saner, more desperate part of me said, Reason with him, even as the sinister laughter erupted from my lips. 'Are you mad!'

" 'I'll give you back your life!' he said, his eyelids quivering with the stress of his words, his chest heaving, that hand going out again and closing impotently in the dark. 'You promised me,' he said to Santiago, 'I could take him back with me to New Orleans.' And then, as he looked from one to the other of them as they surrounded us, his breath became frantic, and he burst out, 'Claudia, where is she? She's the one who did it to me, I told you!'

" 'By and by,' said Santiago. And when he reached out for Lestat, Lestat drew back and almost lost his balance. He had found the chair arm he needed and stood holding fast to it, his eyes closed, regaining his control.

" 'But he helped her, aided her . . .' said Santiago, drawing nearer to him. Lestat looked up.

" 'No,' he said. 'Louis, you must come back to me. There's something I must tell you . . . about that night in the swamp.' But then he stopped and looked about again, as though he were caged, wounded, desperate.

" 'Listen to me, Lestat,' I began now. 'You let her go, you free her . . . and I will . . . I'll return to you,' I said, the words sounding hollow, metallic. I tried to take a step towards him, to make my eyes hard and unreadable, to feel my power emanating from them like two beams of light. He was looking at me, studying me, struggling all the while against his own fragility. And Celeste had her hand on my wrist. 'You must tell them,' I went on, 'how you treated us, that we didn't know the laws, that she didn't know of other vampires,' I said. And I was thinking steadily, as that mechanical voice came out of me: Armand must return tonight, Armand must come back. He will stop this, he won't let it go on.

"There was a sound then of something dragging across the floor. I could hear Madeleine's exhausted crying. I looked around and saw her in a chair, and when she saw my eyes on her, her terror seemed to increase. She tried to rise but they stopped her. 'Lestat,' I said. 'What do you want of me? I'll give it to you. . . .'

"And then I saw the thing that was making the noise. And Lestat had seen it too. It was a coffin with large iron locks on it that was being dragged into the room. I understood at once. 'Where is Armand?' I said desperately.

" 'She did it to me, Louis. She did it to me. You didn't! She has to die!' said Lestat, his voice becoming thin, rasping, as if it were an effort for him to speak. 'Get that thing away from here, he's coming home with me,' he said furiously to Santiago. And Santiago only laughed, and Celeste laughed, and the laughter seemed to infect them all.

" 'You promised me,' said Lestat to them.

" 'I promised you nothing,' said Santiago.

" 'They've made a fool of you,' I said to him bitterly as they were opening the coffin. 'A fool of you! You must reach Armand, Armand is the leader here,' I burst out. But he didn't seem to understand.

"What happened then was desperate and clouded and miserable, my kicking at them, struggling to free my arms, raging against them that Armand would stop what they were doing, that they dare not hurt Claudia. Yet they forced me down into the coffin, my frantic efforts serving no purpose against them except to take my mind off the sound of Madeleine's cries, her awful wailing cries, and the fear that at any moment Claudia's cries might be added to them. I remember rising against the crushing lid, holding it at bay for an instant before it was forced shut on me and the locks were being shut with the grinding of metal and keys. Words of long ago came back to me, a strident and smiling Lestat in that faraway, trouble-free place where the three of us had quarrelled together: 'A starving child is a frightful sight . . . a starving vampire even worse. They'd hear her screams in Paris.' And my wet and trembling body went limp in the suffocating coffin, and I said, Armand will not let it happen; there isn't a place secure enough for them to place us.

"The coffin was lifted, there was the scraping of boots, the swinging from side to side; my arms braced against the sides of the box, my eyes shut perhaps for a moment, I was uncertain. I told myself not to reach out for the sides, not to feel the thin margin of air between my face and the lid; and I felt the coffin swing and tilt as their steps found the stairs. Vainly I tried to make out Madeleine's cries, for it seemed that she was crying for Claudia, calling out to her as if she could help us all. Call for Armand; he must come home this night, I thought desperately. And only the thought of the awful humiliation of hearing my own cry closed in with me, flooding my ears, yet locked in with me, prevented me from calling out.

"But another thought had come over me even as I'd phrased those words: What if he did not come? What if somewhere in that mansion he had a coffin hidden to which he returned . . . ? And then it seemed my body broke suddenly, without warning, from the control of my mind, and I flailed at the wood around me, struggling to turn over and pit the strength of my back against the coffin lid. Yet I could not: it was too close; and my head fell back on the boards, and the sweat poured down my back and sides.

"Madeleine's cries were gone. All I heard were the boots, and my own breathing. Then, tomorrow night he will come—yes, tomorrow night—and they will tell him, and he will find us and release us. The coffin swayed. The smell of water filled my nostrils, its coolness palpable through the close heat of the coffin; and then with the smell of the water was the smell of the deep earth. The coffin was set down roughly, and my limbs ached and I rubbed the backs of my arms with my hands, struggling not to touch the coffin lid, not to sense how close it was, afraid of my own fear rising to panic, to terror.

"I thought they would leave me now, but they did

not. They were near at hand and busy, and another odor came to my nostrils which was raw and not known to me. But then, as I lay very still, I realized they were laying bricks and that the odor came from the mortar. Slowly, carefully, I brought my hand up to wipe my face. All right, then, tomorrow night, I reasoned with myself, even as my shoulders seemed to grow large against the coffin walls. All right, then, tomorrow night he will come; and until then this is merely the confines of my own coffin, the price I've paid for all of this, night after night after night.

"But the tears were welling in my eyes, and I could see myself flailing again at the wood; and my head was turning from side to side, my mind rushing on to tomorrow and the night after and the night after that. And then, as if to distract myself from this madness, I thought of Claudia—only to feel her arms around me in the dim light of those rooms in the Hôtel Saint-Gabriel, only to see the curve of her cheek in the light, the soft, languid flutter of her eyelashes, the silky touch of her lip. My body stiffened, my feet kicked at the boards. The sound of the bricks was gone, and the muffled steps were gone. And I cried out for her, 'Claudia,' until my neck was twisted with pain as I tossed, and my nails had dug into my palms; and slowly, like an icy stream, the paralysis of sleep came over me. I tried to call out to Armand—foolishly, desperately, only dimly aware as my lids grew heavy and my hands lay limp that the sleep was on him too somewhere, that he lay still in his resting place. One last time I struggled. My eyes saw the dark, my hands felt the wood. But I was weak. And then there was nothing."

1 AWOKE TO A VOICE. It was distant but distinct. It said my name twice. For an instant I didn't know where I was. I'd been dreaming, something desperate which was threatening to vanish completely without the slightest clue to what it had been, and something terrible which I was eager, willing to let go. Then I opened my eyes and felt the top of the coffin. I knew where I was at the same instant that, mercifully, I knew it was Armand who was calling me. I answered him, but my voice was locked in with me and it was deafening. In a moment of terror, I thought, He's searching for me, and I can't tell him that I am here. But then I heard him speaking to me, telling me not to be afraid. And I heard a loud noise. And another. And there was a cracking sound, and then the thunderous falling of the bricks. It seemed several of them struck the coffin. And then I heard them lifted off one by one. It sounded as though he were pulling off the locks by the nails.

"The hard wood of the top creaked. A pinpoint of light sparkled before my eyes. I drew breath from it, and felt the sweat break out on my face. The lid creaked open and for an instant I was blinded; then I was sitting up, seeing the bright light of a lamp through my fingers.

" 'Hurry,' he said to me. 'Don't make a sound.'

" 'But where are we going?' I asked. I could see a passage of rough bricks stretching out from the doorway he'd broken down. And all along that passage were doors which were sealed, as this door had been. I had a vision at once of coffins behind those bricks, of vampires starved and decayed there. But Armand was pulling me up, telling me again to make no sound; we were creeping along the passage. He stopped at a wooden door, and then he extinguished the lamp. It was completely black for an instant until the seam of light beneath the door brightened. He opened the door so gently the hinges did not make a sound. I could hear my own breathing now, and I tried to stop it. We were entering that lower passageway which led to his cell. But as I raced along behind him I became aware of one awful truth. He was rescuing me, but me alone. I put out my hand to stop him, but he only pulled me after him. Only when we stood in the alleyway beside the Théâtre des Vampires was I able to make him stop. And even then, he was on the verge of going on. He began shaking his head even before I spoke.

" 'I can't save her!' he said.

" 'You don't honestly expect me to leave without her! They have her in there!' I was horrified. 'Armand, you must save her! You have no choice!'

" 'Why do you say this?' he answered. 'I don't have the power, you must understand. They'll rise against me. There is no reason why they should not. Louis, I tell you, I cannot save her. I will only risk losing you. You can't go back.'

"I refused to admit this could be true. I had no hope other than Armand. But I can truthfully say that I was beyond being afraid. I knew only that I had to get Claudia back or die in the effort. It was really very simple; not a matter of courage at all. And I knew also, could tell in everything about Armand's passivity, the manner in which he spoke, that he would follow me if I returned, that he would not try to prevent me.

"I was right. I was rushing back into the passage and he was just behind me, heading for the stairway to the ballroom. I could hear the other vampires. I could hear all manner of sounds. The Paris traffic. What sounded very much like a congregation in the vault of the theater above. And then, as I reached the top of the steps, I saw Celeste in the door of the ballroom. She held one of those stage masks in her hand. She was merely looking at me. She did not appear alarmed. In fact, she appeared strangely indifferent.

"If she had rushed at me, if she had sounded a general alarm, these things I could have understood. But she did nothing. She stepped backwards into the ballroom; she turned, seeming to enjoy the subtle movement of her skirts, seeming to turn for the love of making her skirts flare out, and she drifted in a widening circle to the center of the room. She put the mask to her face, and said softly behind the painted skull, 'Lestat . . . it is your friend Louis come calling. Look sharp, Lestat!' She dropped the mask, and there was a ripple of laughter from somewhere. I saw they were all about the room, shadowy things, seated here and there, standing together. And Lestat, in an armchair, sat with his shoulders hunched and his face turned away from me. It seemed he was working something with his hands, something I couldn't see; and slowly he looked up, his full yellow hair falling into his eyes. There was fear in them. It was undeniable. Now he was looking at Armand. And Armand was moving silently through the room with slow, steady steps, and all of the vampires moved back away from him, watching him. 'Bonsoir, Monsieur,' Celeste bowed to him as he passed her, that mask in her hand like a scepter. He did not look at her in particular. He looked down at Lestat. 'Are you satisfied?' he asked him.

"Lestat's gray eyes seemed to regard Armand with wonder, and his lips struggled to form a word. I could see that his eyes were filling with tears. 'Yes . . .' he whispered now, his hand struggling with the thing he concealed beneath his black cloak. But then he looked at me, and the tears spilled down his face. 'Louis,' he said, his voice deep and rich now with what seemed an unbearable struggle. 'Please, you must listen to me. You must come back. . . .' And then, bowing his head, he grimaced with shame.

"Santiago was laughing somewhere. Armand was saying softly to Lestat that he must get out, leave Paris; he was outcast.

"And Lestat sat there with his eyes closed, his face transfigured with his pain. It seemed the double of Lestat, some wounded, feeling creature I'd never known. 'Please,' he said, the voice eloquent and gentle as he implored me.

" 'I can't talk to you here! I can't make you understand. You'll come with me . . . for only a little while . . . until I am myself again?'

" 'This is madness! . . .' I said, my hands rising suddenly to my temples. 'Where is she! Where is she!' I looked about me, at their still, passive faces, those inscrutable smiles. 'Lestat.' I turned him now, grabbing at the black wool of his lapels.

"And then I saw the thing in his hands. I knew what it was. And in an instant I'd ripped it from him and was staring at it, at the fragile silken thing that it was—Claudia's yellow dress. His hand rose to his lips, his face turned away. And the soft, subdued sobs broke from him as he sat back while I stared at him, while I stared at the dress. My fingers moved slowly over the tears in it, the stains of blood, my hands closing, trembling as I crushed it against my chest.

"For a long moment it seemed I simply stood there; time had no bearing upon me nor upon those shifting vampires with their light, ethereal laughter filling my ears. I remember thinking that I wanted to put my hands over my ears, but I wouldn't let go of the dress, couldn't stop trying to make it so small that it was hidden within my hands. I remember a row of candles burning, an uneven row coming to light one by one against the painted walls. A door stood open to the rain, and all the candles spluttered and blew on the wind as if the flames were being lifted from the wicks. But they clung to the wicks and were all right. I knew that Claudia was through the doorway. The candles moved. The vampires had hold of them. Santiago had a candle and was bowing to me and gesturing for me to pass through the door. I was barely aware of him. I didn't care about him or the others at all. Something in me said, If you care about them you will go mad. And they don't matter, really. She matters. Where is she? Find her. And their laughter was remote, and it seemed to have a color and a shape but to be part of nothing.

"Then I saw something through the open doorway

which was something I'd seen before, a long, long time ago. No one knew of this thing I'd seen years before except myself. No. Lestat knew. But it didn't matter. He wouldn't know now or understand. That he and I had seen this thing, standing at the door of that brick kitchen in the Rue Royale, two wet shrivelled things that had been alive, mother and daughter in one another's arms, the murdered pair on the kitchen floor. But these two lying under the gentle rain were Madeleine and Claudia, and Madeleine's lovely red hair mingled with the gold of Claudia's hair, which stirred and glistened in the wind that sucked through the open doorway. Only that which was living had been burnt away—not the hair, not the long, empty velvet dress, not the small bloodstained chemise with its eyelets of white lace. And the blackened, burnt, and drawn thing that was Madeleine still bore the stamp of her living face, and the hand that clutched at the child was whole like a mummy's hand. But the child, the ancient one, my Claudia, was ashes.

"A cry rose in me, a wild, consuming cry that came from the bowels of my being, rising up like the wind in that narrow place, the wind that swirled the rain teeming on those ashes, beating at the trace of a tiny hand against the bricks, that golden hair lifting, those loose strands rising, flying upwards. And a blow struck me even as I cried out; and I had hold of something that I believed to be Santiago, and I was pounding against him, destroying him, twisting that grinning white face around with hands from which he couldn't free himself, hands against which he railed, crying out, his cries mingling with my cries, his boots coming down into those ashes, as I threw him backwards away from them, my own eyes blinded with the rain, with my tears, until he lay back away from me, and I was reaching out for him even as he held out his hand. And the one I was struggling against was Armand. Armand, who was forcing me out of the tiny graveyard into the whirling colors of the ballroom, the cries, the mingling voices, that searing, silver laughter.

"And Lestat was calling out, 'Louis, wait for me; Louis, I must talk to you!'

"I could see Armand's rich, brown eye close to mine, and I felt weak all over and vaguely aware that Madeleine and Claudia were dead, his voice saying softly, perhaps soundlessly, 'I could not prevent it, I could not prevent it. . . .' And they were dead, simply dead. And I was losing consciousness. Santiago was near them somewhere there where they were still, that hair lifted on the wind, swept across those bricks, unravelling locks. But I was losing consciousness.

"I could not gather their bodies up with me, could not take them out. Armand had his arm around my back, his hand under my arm, and he was all but carrying me through some hollow wooden echoing place, and the smells of the street were rising, the fresh smell of the horses and the leather, and there were the gleaming carriages stopped there. And I could see myself clearly running down the Boulevard des Capucines with a small coffin under my arm and the people making way for me and dozens of people rising around the crowded tables of the open café and a man lifting his arm. It seemed I stumbled then, the Louis whom Armand held in his arm, and again I saw his brown eyes looking at me, and felt that drowsiness, that sinking. And yet I walked, I moved, I saw the gleam of my own boots on the pavement. 'Is he mad, that he says these things to me?' I was asking of Lestat, my voice shrill and angry, even the sound of it giving me some comfort. I was laughing, laughing loudly. 'He's stark-raving mad to speak to me in this manner! Did you hear him?' I demanded. And Armand's eye said, Sleep. I wanted to say something about Madeleine and Claudia, that we could not leave them there, and I felt that cry again rising inside of me, that cry that pushed everything else out of its way, my teeth clenched to keep it in, because it was so loud and so full it would destroy me if I let it go.

"And then I conceived of everything too clearly. We were walking now, a belligerent, blind sort of walking that men do when they are wildly drunk and filled with hatred for others, while at the same time they feel invincible. I was walking in such a manner through New Orleans the night I'd first encountered Lestat, that drunken walking which is a battering against things, which is miraculously sure-footed and finds its path. I saw a drunken man's hands fumbling miraculously with a match. Flame touched to the pipe, the smoke drawn in. I was standing at a café window. The man was drawing on his pipe. He was not at all drunk. Armand stood beside me waiting, and we were in the crowded Boulevard des Capucines. Or was it the Boulevard du Temple? I wasn't sure. I was outraged that their bodies remained there in that vile place. I saw Santiago's foot touching the blackened burned thing that had been my child! I was crying out through clenched teeth, and the man had risen from his table and steam spread out on the glass in front of his face. 'Get away from me,' I was saying to Armand. 'Damn you into hell, don't come near me. I warn you, don't come near me.' I was walking away from him up the boulevard, and I could see a man and a woman stepping aside for me, the man with his arm out to protect the woman.

"Then I was running. People saw me running. I wondered how it appeared to them, what wild, white thing they saw that moved too fast for their eyes. I remember that by the time I stopped, I was weak and sick, and my veins were burning as if I were starved. I thought of killing, and the thought filled me with revulsion. I was sitting on the stone steps beside a church, at one of those small side doors, carved into the stone, which was bolted and locked for the night. The rain had abated. Or so it seemed. And the street was dreary and quiet, though a man passed a long way off with a bright, black umbrella. Armand stood at a distance under the trees. Behind him it seemed there was a great expanse of trees and wet grasses and mist rising as if the ground were warm.

"By thinking of only one thing, the sickness in my stomach and head and the tightening in my throat, was I able to return to a state of calm. By the time these things had died away and I was feeling clear again, I was aware of all that had happened, the great distance we'd come from the theater, and that the remains of Madeleine and Claudia were still there.

Victims of a holocaust in each other's arms. And I felt resolute and very near to my own destruction.

" 'I could not prevent it,' Armand said softly to me. And I looked up to see his face unutterably sad. He looked away from me as if he felt it was futile to try to convince me of this, and I could feel his over-whelming sadness, his near defeat. I had the feeling that if I were to vent all my anger on him he would do little to resist me. And I could feel that detachment, that passivity in him as something pervasive which was at the root of what he insisted to me again, 'I could not have prevented it.'

" 'Oh, but you could have prevented it!' I said softly. 'You know full well that you could have. You were the leader! *You* were the only one who knew the limits of your own power. They didn't know. They didn't understand. Your understanding surpassed theirs.'

"He looked away still. But I could see the effect of my words on him. I could see the weariness in his face, the dull lusterless sadness of his eyes.

" 'You held sway over them. They feared you!' I went on. 'You could have stopped them if you'd been willing to use that power even beyond your own self-prescribed limits. It was your sense of yourself you would not violate. Your own precious conception of truth! I understand you perfectly. I see in you the reflection of myself!'

"His eyes moved gently to engage mine. But he said nothing. The pain of his face was terrible. It was softened and desperate with pain and on the verge of some terrible explicit emotion he would not be able to control. He was in fear of that emotion. I was not. He was feeling my pain with that great spellbinding power of his which surpassed mine. I was not feeling his pain. It did not matter to me.

" 'I understand you only too well . . .' I said. 'That passivity in me has been the core of it all, the real evil. That weakness, that refusal to compromise a fractured and stupid morality, that awful pride! For that, I let myself become the thing I am, when I knew it was wrong. For that, I let Claudia become the vampire she became, when I knew it was wrong. For that, I stood by and let her kill Lestat, when I knew that was wrong, the very thing that was her undoing. I lifted not a finger to prevent it. And Madeleine, Madeleine, I let her come to that, when I should never have made her a creature like ourselves. I knew that was wrong! Well, I tell you I am no longer that passive, weak creature that has spun evil from evil till the web is vast and thick while I remain its stultified victim. It's over! I know now what I must do. And I warn you, for whatever mercy you've shown me in digging me out of that grave tonight where I would have died: Do not seek your cell in the Théâtre des Vampires again. Do not go near it.' "

*   *   *

"I didn't wait to hear his answer. Perhaps he never attempted one. I don't know. I left him without looking back. If he followed me I was not conscious of it. I did not seek to know. I did not care.

"It was to the cemetery in Montmartre that I retreated. Why that place, I'm not certain, except that it wasn't far from the Boulevard des Capucines, and Montmartre was countryfied then, and dark and peaceful compared to the metropolis. Wandering among the low houses with their kitchen gardens, I killed without the slightest measure of satisfaction, and then sought out the coffin where I was to lie by day in the cemetery. I scraped the remains out of it with my bare hands and lay down to a bed of foulness, of damp, of the stench of death. I cannot say this gave me comfort. Rather, it gave me what I wanted. Closeted in that dark, smelling the earth, away from all humans and all living human forms, I gave myself over to everything that invaded and stifled my senses. And, in so doing, gave myself over to my grief.

"But that was short.

"When the cold, gray winter sun had set the next night, I was awake, feeling the tingling numbness leave me soon, as it does in winter, feeling the dark, living things that inhabited the coffin scurrying around me, fleeing my resurrection. I emerged slowly under the faint moon, savoring the coldness, the utter smooth-ness of the marble slab I shifted to escape. And, wandering out of the graves and out of the cemetery, I went over a plan in my mind, a plan on which I was willing to gamble my life with the powerful free-dom of a being who truly does not care for that life, who has the extraordinary strength of being willing to die.

"In a kitchen garden I saw something, something that had only been vague in my thoughts until I had my hands on it. It was a small scythe, its sharp curved blade still caked with green weeds from the last mowing. And once I'd wiped it clean and run my finger along the sharp blade, it was as if my plan came clear to me and I could move fast to my other errands: the getting of a carriage and a driver who could do my bidding for days—dazzled by the cash I gave him and the promises of more; the removing of my chest from the Hôtel Saint-Gabriel to the inside of that car-riage; and the procuring of all the other things which I needed. And then there were the long hours of the night, when I could pretend to drink with my driver and talk with him and obtain his expensive coopera-tion in driving me at dawn from Paris to Fontainebleau. I slept within the carriage, where my delicate health required I not be disturbed under any circumstances —this privacy being so important that I was more than willing to add a generous sum to the amount I was already paying him simply for his not touching even the door handle of the carriage until I emerged from it.

"And when I was convinced he was in agreement and quite drunk enough to be oblivious to almost everything but the gathering up of the reins for the journey for Fountainebleau, we drove slowly, cau-tiously, into the street of the Théâtre des Vampires and waited some distance away for the sky to begin to grow light.

"The theater was shut up and locked against the coming day. I crept towards it when the air and the light told me I had at most fifteen minutes to execute my plan. I knew that, closeted far within, the vampires of the theater were in their coffins already. And that even if one late vampire lingered on the verge of going to bed, he would not hear these first preparations. Quickly I put pieces of wood against the bolted doors. Quickly I drove in the nails, which then locked these doors from the outside. A passer-by took some note of what I did but went on, believing me perhaps to be boarding up the establishment with the authority of the owner. I didn't know. I did know, however, that before I was finished I might encounter those ticket-sellers, those ushers, those men who swept up after, and might well remain inside to guard the vampires in their daily sleep.

"It was of those men I was thinking as I led the carriage up to Armand's alley and left it there, taking with me two small barrels of kerosene to Armand's door.

"The key admitted me easily as I'd hoped, and once inside the lower passage, I opened the door of his cell to find he was not there. The coffin was gone. In fact, everything was gone but the furnishings, including the dead boy's enclosed bed. Hastily I opened one barrel and, rolling the other before me towards the stairs, I hurried along, splashing the exposed beams with kerosene and flinging it on the wooden doors of the other cells. The smell of it was strong, stronger and more powerful than any sound I might have made to alert anyone. And, though I stood stark still at the stairs with the barrels and the scythe, listening, I heard nothing, nothing of those guards I presumed to be there, nothing of the vampires themselves. And clutching the handle of the scythe I ventured slowly upwards until I stood in the door of the ballroom. No one was there to see me splash the kerosene on the horsehair chairs or on the draperies, or to see me hesitate just for an instant at that doorway of the small yard where Madeleine and Claudia had been killed. Oh, how I wanted to open that door. It so tempted me that for a minute I almost forgot my plan. I almost dropped the barrels and turned the knob. But I could see the light through the cracks of the old wood of the door. And I knew I had to go on. Madeleine and Claudia were not there. They were dead. And what would I have done had I opened that doorway, had I been confronted again with those remains, that matted, dishevelled golden hair? There was no time, no purpose. I was running through dark corridors I hadn't explored before, bathing old wooden doors with the kerosene, certain that the vampires lay closeted within, rushing on cat feet into the theater itself, where a cold, gray light, seeping from the bolted front entrance, sped me on to fling a dark stain across the great velvet stage curtain, the padded chairs, the draperies of the lobby doors.

"And finally the barrel was empty and thrown away, and I was pulling out the crude torch I'd made, putting my match to its kerosene-drenched rags, and setting the chairs alight, the flames licking their thick silk and padding as I ran towards the stage and sent the fire rushing up that dark curtain into a cold, sucking draft.

"In seconds the theater blazed as with the light of day, and the whole frame of it seemed to creak and groan as the fire roared up the walls, licking the great proscenium arch, the plaster curlicues of the overhanging boxes. But I had no time to admire it, to savor the smell and the sound of it, the sight of the nooks and crannies coming to light in the fierce illumination that would soon consume them. I was fleeing to the lower floor again, thrusting the torch into the horsehair couch of the ballroom, into the curtains, into anything that would burn.

"Someone thundered on the boards above—in rooms I'd never seen. And then I heard the unmistakable opening of a door. But it was too late, I told myself, gripping both the scythe and the torch. The building was alight. They would be destroyed. I ran for the stairs, a distant cry rising over the crackling and roaring of the flames, my torch scraping the kerosene-soaked rafters above me, the flames enveloping the old wood, curling against the damp ceiling. It was Santiago's cry, I was sure of it; and then, as I hit the lower floor, I saw him above, behind me, coming down the stairs, the smoke filling the stairwell around him, his eyes watering, his throat thickened with his choking, his hand out towards me as he stammered, 'You . . .

you . . . damn you!' And I froze, narrowing my eyes against the smoke, feeling the water rising in them, burning in them, but never letting go of his image for an instant, the vampire using all his power now to fly at me with such speed that he would become invisible. And as the dark thing that was his clothes rushed down, I swung the scythe and saw it strike his neck and felt the weight of his neck and saw him fall sideways, both hands reaching for the appalling wound. The air was full of cries, of screams, and a white face loomed above Santiago, a mask of terror. Some other vampire ran through the passage ahead of me towards that secret alleyway door. But I stood there poised, staring at Santiago, seeing him rise despite the wound. And I swung the scythe again, catching him easily. And there was no wound. Just two hands groping for a head that was no longer there.

"And the head, blood coursing from the torn neck, the eyes staring wild under the flaming rafters, the dark silky hair matted and wet with blood, fell at my feet. I struck it hard with my boot, I sent it flying along the passage. And I ran after it, the torch and the scythe thrown aside as my arms went up to protect me from the blaze of white light that flooded the stairs to the alley.

"The rain descended in shimmering needles into my eyes, eyes that squinted to see the dark outline of the carriage flicker against the sky. The slumped driver straightened at my hoarse command, his clumsy hand going instinctively for the whip, and the carriage lurched as I pulled open the door, the horses driving forward fast as I grappled with the lid of the chest, my body thrown roughly to one side, my burnt hands slipping down into the cold protecting silk, the lid coming down into concealing darkness.

"The pace of the horses increased driving away from the corner of the burning building. Yet I could still smell the smoke; it choked me; it burnt my eyes and my lungs, even as my hands were burnt and my forehead was burnt from the first diffused light of the sun.

"But we were driving on, away from the smoke and the cries. We were leaving Paris. I had done it.

The Théâtre des Vampires was burning to the ground.

"And as I felt my head fall back, I saw Claudia and Madeleine again in one another's arms in that grim yard, and I said to them softly, bending down to the soft heads of hair that glistened in the candlelight, 'I couldn't take you away. I couldn't take you. But they will lie ruined and dead all around you. If the fire doesn't consume them, it will be the sun. If they are not burnt out, then it will be the people who will come to fight the fire who will find them and expose them to the light of day. But I promise you, they will all die as you have died, everyone who was closeted there this dawn will die. And they are the only deaths I have caused in my long life which are both exquisite and good.' "

TWO NIGHTS LATER I returned. I had to see that rain-flooded cellar where every brick was scorched, crumbling, where a few skeletal rafters jabbed at the sky like stakes. Those monstrous murals that once enclosed the ballroom were blasted fragments in the rubble, a painted face here, a patch of angel's wing there, the only identifiable things that remained.

"With the evening newspapers, I pushed my way to the back of a crowded little theater café across the street; and there, under the cover of the dim gas lamps and thick cigarsmoke, I read the accounts of the holocaust. Few bodies were found in the burnt-out theater, but clothing and costumes had been scattered everywhere, as though the famous vampire mummers had in fact vacated the theater in haste long before the fire. In other words, only the younger vampires had left their bones; the ancient ones had suffered total obliteration. No mention of an eye-witness or a surviving victim. How could there have been?

"Yet something bothered me considerably. I did not fear any vampires who had escaped. I had no desire to hunt them out if they had. That most of the crew had died I was certain. But why had there been no human guards? I was certain Santiago had mentioned guards, and I'd supposed them to be the ushers and doormen who staffed the theater before the performance. And I had even been prepared to encounter them with my scythe. But they had not been there. It was strange. And my mind was not entirely comfortable with the strangeness.

"But, finally, when I put the papers aside and sat thinking these things over, the strangeness of it didn't matter. What mattered was that I was more utterly alone in the world than I had ever been in all my life. That Claudia was gone beyond reprieve. And I had less reason to live than I'd ever had, and less desire.

"And yet my sorrow did not overwhelm me, did not actually visit me, did not make of me the wracked and desperate creature I might have expected to become. Perhaps it was not possible to sustain the torment I'd experienced when I saw Claudia's burnt remains. Perhaps it was not possible to know that and exist over any period of time. I wondered vaguely, as the hours passed, as the smoke of the café grew thicker and the faded curtain of the little lamplit stage rose and fell, and robust women sang there, the light glittering on their paste jewels, their rich, soft voices often plaintive, exquisitely sad—I wondered vaguely what it would be to feel this loss, this outrage, and be justified in it, be deserving of sympathy, of solace. I would not have told my woe to a living creature. My own tears meant nothing to me.

"Where to go then, if not to die? It was strange how the answer came to me. Strange how I wandered out of the café then, circling the ruined theater, wandering finally towards the broad Avenue Napoléon and following it towards the palace of the Louvre. It was as if that place called to me, and yet I had never been inside its walls. I'd passed its long façade a thousand times, wishing that I could live as a mortal man for one day to move through those many rooms and see those many magnificent paintings. I was bent on it now, possessed only of some vague notion that in works of art I could find some solace while bringing nothing of death to what was inanimate and yet magnificently possessed of the spirit of life itself.

"Somewhere along the Avenue Napoléon, I heard the step behind me which I knew to be Armand's. He was signalling, letting me know that he was near. Yet I did nothing other than slow my pace and let him fall into step with me, and for a long while we walked, saying nothing. I dared not look at him. Of course, I'd been thinking of him all the while, and how if we were men and Claudia had been my love I might have fallen helpless in his arms finally, the need to share some common grief so strong, so consuming. The dam threatened to break now; and yet it did not break. I was numbed and I walked as one numbed.

" 'You know what I've done,' I said finally. We had turned off the avenue and I could see ahead of me the long row of double columns on the façade of the Royal Museum. 'You removed your coffin as I warned you. . . .'

" 'Yes,' he answered. There was a sudden, unmistakable comfort in the sound of his voice. It weakened me. But I was simply too remote from pain, too tired.

" 'And yet you are here with me now. Do you mean to avenge them?'

" 'No,' he said.

" 'They were your fellows, you were their leader,' I said. 'Yet you didn't warn them I was out for them, as I warned you?'

" 'No,' he said.

" 'But surely you despise me for it. Surely you respect some rule, some allegiance to your own kind.'

" 'No,' he said softly.

"It was amazing to me how logical his response was, even though I couldn't explain it or understand it.

"And something came clear to me out of the remote regions of my own relentless considerations. 'There were guards; there were those ushers who slept in the theater. Why weren't they there when I entered? Why weren't they there to protect the sleeping vampires?'

" 'Because they were in my employ and I discharged them. I sent them away,' Armand said.

"I stopped. He showed no concern at my facing him, and as soon as our eyes met I wished the world were not one black empty ruin of ashes and death. I wished it were fresh and beautiful, and that we were both living and had love to give each other. 'You did this, knowing what I planned to do?'

" 'Yes,' he said.

" 'But you were their leader! They trusted you. They believed in you. They lived with you!' I said. 'I don't understand you . . . why . . .?'

" 'Think of any answer you like,' he said calmly and sensitively, as if he didn't wish to bruise me with any accusation or disdain, but wanted me merely to consider this literally. 'I can think of many. Think of the one you need and believe it. It's as likely as any other. I shall give you the real reason for what I did, which is the least true: I was leaving Paris. The theater belonged to me. So I discharged them.'

" 'But with what you knew . . .'

" 'I told you, it was the actual reason and it was the least true,' he said patiently.

" 'Would you destroy me as easily as you let them be destroyed?' I demanded.

" 'Why should I?' he asked.

" 'My God,' I whispered.

" 'You're much changed,' he said. 'But in a way, you are much the same.'

"I walked on for a while and then, before the entrance to the Louvre, I stopped. At first it seemed to me that its many windows were dark and silver with the moonlight and the thin rain. But then I thought I saw a faint light moving within, as though a guard walked among the treasures. I envied him completely. And I fixed my thoughts on him obdurately, that guard, calculating how a vampire might get to him, how take his life and his lantern and his keys. The plan was confusion. I was incapable of plans. I had made only one real plan in my life, and it was finished.

"And then finally I surrendered. I turned to Armand again and let my eyes penetrate his eyes, and let him draw close to me as if he meant to make me his victim, and I bowed my head and felt his firm arm around my shoulder. And, remembering suddenly and keenly Claudia's words, what were very nearly her last words —that admission that she knew that I could love Armand because I had been able to love even her—those words struck me as rich and ironical, more filled with meaning than she could have guessed.

" 'Yes,' I said softly to him, 'that is the crowning evil, that we can even go so far as to love each other, you and I. And who else would show us a particle of love, a particle of compassion or mercy? Who else, knowing us as we know each other, could do anything but destroy us? Yet we can love each other.'

"And for a long moment, he stood there looking at me, drawing nearer, his head gradually inclining to one side, his lips parted as if he meant to speak. But then he only smiled and shook his head gently to confess he didn't understand.

"But I wasn't thinking of him anymore. I had one of those rare moments when it seemed I thought of nothing. My mind had no shape. I saw that the rain had stopped. I saw that the air was clear and cold. That the street was luminous. And I wanted to enter the Louvre. I formed words to tell Armand this, to ask him if he might help me do what was necessary to have the Louvre till dawn.

"He thought it a very simple request. He said only he wondered why I had waited so long."

WE LEFT PARIS very soon after that. I told Armand that I wanted to return to the Mediterranean—not to Greece, as I had so long dreamed. I wanted to go to Egypt. I wanted to see the desert there and, more importantly, I wanted to see the pyramids and the graves of the kings. I wanted to make contact with those grave-thieves who know more of the graves than do scholars, and I wanted to go down into the graves yet unopened and see the kings as they were buried, see those furnishings and works of art stored with them, and the paintings on their walls. Armand was more than willing. And we took leave of Paris early one evening by carriage without the slightest hint of ceremony.

"I had done one thing which I should note. I had gone back to my rooms in the Hôtel Saint-Gabriel. It was my purpose to take up some things of Claudia and Madeleine and put them into coffins and have graves prepared for them in the cemetery of Montmartre. I did not do this. I stayed a short while in the rooms, where all was neat and put right by the staff, so that it seemed Madeleine and Claudia might return at any time. Madeleine's embroidery ring lay with her bundles of thread on a chair-side table. I looked at that and at everything else, and my task seemed meaningless. So I left.

"But something had occurred to me there; or, rather, something I had already been aware of merely became clearer. I had gone to the Louvre that night to lay down my soul, to find some transcendent pleasure that would obliterate pain and make me utterly forget even myself. I'd been upheld in this. As I stood on the sidewalk before the doors of the hotel waiting for the carriage that would take me to meet Armand, I saw the people who walked there—the restless boulevard crowd of well-dressed ladies and gentlemen, the hawkers of papers, the carriers of luggage, the drivers of carriages—all these in a new light. Before, all art had held for me the promise of a deeper understanding of the human heart. Now the human heart meant nothing. I did not denigrate it. I simply forgot it. The magnificent paintings of the Louvre were not for me intimately connected with the hands that had painted them. They were cut loose and dead like children turned to stone. Like Claudia, severed from her mother, preserved for decades in pearl and hammered gold. Like Madeleine's dolls. And of course, like Claudia and Madeleine and myself, they could all be reduced to ashes."

PART IV

AND THAT IS THE END of the story, really.

"Of course, I know you wonder what happened to us afterwards. What became of Armand? Where did I go? What did I do? But I tell you nothing really happened. Nothing that wasn't merely inevitable. And my journey through the Louvre that last night I've described to you, that was merely prophetic.

"I never changed after that. I sought for nothing in the one great source of change which is humanity. And even in my love and absorption with the beauty of the world, I sought to learn nothing that could be given back to humanity. I drank of the beauty of the world as a vampire drinks. I was satisfied. I was filled to the brim. But I was dead. And I was changeless. The story ended in Paris, as I've said.

"For a long time I thought that Claudia's death had been the cause of the end of things. That if I had seen Madeleine and Claudia leave Paris safely, things might have been different with me and Armand. I might have loved again and desired again, and sought some semblance of mortal life which would have been rich and varied, though unnatural. But now I have come to see that was false. Even if Claudia had not died, even if I had not despised Armand for letting her die, it would have all turned out the same. Coming slowly to know his evil, or being catapulted into it . . . was all the same. I wanted none of it finally. And, deserving nothing better, I closed up like a spider in the flame of a match. And even Armand who was my constant companion, and my only companion, existed at a great distance from me, beyond that veil which separated me from all living things, a veil which was a form of shroud.

324

"But I know you are eager to hear what became of Armand. And the night is almost ended. I want to tell you this because it is very important. The story is incomplete without it.

"We travelled the world after we left Paris, as I've told you; first Egypt, then Greece, then Italy, Asia Minor—wherever I chose to lead us, really, and wherever my pursuit of art led me. Time ceased to exist on any meaningful basis during these years, and I was often absorbed in very simple things—a painting in a museum, a cathedral window, one single beautiful statue—for long periods of time.

"But all during these years I had a vague but persistent desire to return to New Orleans. I never forgot New Orleans. And when we were in tropical places and places of those flowers and trees that grow in Louisiana, I would think of it acutely and I would feel for my home the only glimmer of desire I felt for anything outside my endless pursuit of art. And, from time to time, Armand would ask me to take him there. And I, being aware in a gentlemanly manner that I did little to please him and often went for long periods without really speaking to him or seeking him out, wanted to do this because he asked me. It seemed his asking caused me to forget some vague fear that I might feel pain in New Orleans, that I might experience again the pale shadow of my former unhappiness and longing. But I put it off. Perhaps the fear was stronger than I knew. We came to America and lived in New York for a long time. I continued to put it off. Then, finally, Armand urged me in another way. He told me something he'd concealed from me since the time we were in Paris.

"Lestat had not died in the Théâtre des Vampires. I had believed him to be dead, and when I asked Armand about those vampires, he told me they all had perished. But he told me now that this wasn't so. Lestat had left the theater the night I had run away from Armand and sought out the cemetery in Montmartre. Two vampires who had been made with Lestat by the same master had assisted him in booking passage to New Orleans.

"I cannot convey to you the feeling that came over me when I heard this. Of course, Armand told me he had protected me from this knowledge, hoping that I would not undertake a long journey merely for revenge, a journey that would have caused me pain and grief at the time. But I didn't really care. I hadn't thought of Lestat at all the night I'd torched the theater. I'd thought of Santiago and Celeste and the others who had destroyed Claudia. Lestat, in fact, had aroused in me feelings which I hadn't wished to confide in anyone, feelings I'd wished to forget, despite Claudia's death. Hatred had not been one of them.

"But when I heard this now from Armand it was as if the veil that protected me were thin and transparent, and though it still hung between me and the world of feeling, I perceived through it Lestat, and that I wanted to see him again. And with that spurring me on, we returned to New Orleans.

"It was late spring of this year. And as soon as I emerged from the railway station, I knew that I had indeed come home. It was as if the very air were perfumed and peculiar there, and I felt an extraordinary ease walking on those warm, flat pavements, under those familiar oaks, and listening to the ceaseless vibrant living sounds of the night.

"Of course, New Orleans was changed. But far from lamenting those changes, I was grateful for what seemed still the same. I could find in the uptown Garden District, which had been in my time the Faubourg St.-Marie, one of the stately old mansions that dated back to those times, so removed from the quiet brick street that, walking out in the moonlight under its magnolia trees, I knew the same sweetness and peace I'd known in the old days; not only in the dark, narrow streets of the Vieux Carré but in the wilderness of Pointe du Lac. There were the honeysuckle and the roses, and the glimpse of Corinthian columns against the stars; and outside the gate were dreamy streets, other mansions . . . it was a citadel of grace.

"In the Rue Royale, where I took Armand past tourists and antique shops and the bright-lit entrances of fashionable restaurants, I was astonished to discover the town house where Lestat and Claudia and I had made our home, the façade little changed by fresh plaster and whatever repairs had been done within. Its two French windows still opened onto the small balconies over the shop below, and I could see in the soft brillance of the electric chandeliers an elegant wallpaper that would not have been unfamiliar in those days before the war. I had a strong sense of Lestat there, more of a sense of him than of Claudia, and I felt certain, though he was nowhere near this town house, that I'd find him in New Orleans.

"And I felt something else; it was a sadness that came over me then, after Armand had gone on his way. But this sadness was not painful, nor was it passionate. It was something rich, however, and almost sweet, like the fragrance of the jasmine and the roses that crowded the old courtyard garden which I saw through the iron gates. And this sadness gave a subtle satisfaction and held me a long time in that spot; and it held me to the city; and it didn't really leave me that night when I went away.

"I wonder now what might have come of this sadness, what it might have engendered in me that could have become stronger than itself. But I jump ahead of my story.

"Because shortly after that I saw a vampire in New Orleans, a sleek white-faced young man walking alone on the broad sidewalks of St. Charles Avenue in the early hours before dawn. And I was at once convinced that if Lestat still lived here that vampire might know him and might even lead me to him. Of course, the vampire didn't see me. I had long ago learned to spot my own kind in large cities without their having a chance to see me. Armand, in his brief visits with vampires in London and Rome, had learned that the burning of the Théâtre des Vampires was known throughout the world, and that both of us were considered outcasts. Battles over this meant nothing to me, and I have avoided them to this day. But I began to watch for this vampire in New Orleans and to follow him, though often he led me merely to theaters or other pastimes in which I had no interest. But one night, finally, things changed.

"It was a very warm evening, and I could tell as soon as I saw him on St. Charles that he had some-place to go. He was not only walking fast, but he seemed a little distressed. And when he turned off St. Charles finally on a narrow street which became at once shabby and dark, I felt sure he was headed for something that would interest me.

"But then he entered one side of a small wooden duplex and brought death to a woman there. This he did very fast, without a trace of pleasure; and after he was finished, he gathered her child up from the bas-sinet, wrapped it gently in a blue wool blanket, and came out again into the street.

"Only a block or two after that, he stopped before a vine-covered iron fence that enclosed a large overgrown yard. I could see an old house beyond the trees, dark, the paint peeling, the ornate iron railings of its long upper and lower galleries caked with orange rust. It seemed a doomed house, stranded here among the numerous small wooden houses, its high empty win-dows looking out on what must have been a dismal clutter of low roofs, a corner grocery, and a small adjacent bar. But the broad, dark grounds protected the house somewhat from these things, and I had to move along the fence quite a few feet before I finally spotted a faint glimmer in one of the lower windows through the thick branches of the trees. The vampire had gone through the gate. I could hear the baby wailing, and then nothing. And I followed, easily mounting the old fence and dropping down into the garden and coming up quietly onto the long front porch.

"It was an amazing sight I saw when I crept up to one of the long, floor-length windows. For despite the heat of this breezeless evening when the gallery, even with its warped and broken boards, might have been the only tolerable place for human or vampire, a fire blazed in the grate of the parlor and all its windows were shut, and the young vampire sat by that fire talk-ing to another vampire who hovered very near it, his slippered feet right up against the hot grate, his trembling fingers pulling over and over at the lapels of his shabby blue robe. And, though a frayed electric cord dangled from a plaster wreath of roses in the ceiling, only an oil lamp added its dim light to the fire, an oil lamp which stood by the wailing child on a nearby table.

"My eyes widened as I studied this stooped and shivering vampire whose rich blond hair hung down in loose waves covering his face. I longed to wipe away the dust on the window glass which would not let me be certain of what I suspected. 'You all leave me!' he whined now in a thin, high-pitched voice.

" 'You can't keep us with you!' said the stiff young vampire sharply. He sat with his legs crossed, his arms folded on his narrow chest, his eyes looking around the dusty, empty room disdainfully. 'Oh, hush!' he said to the baby, who let out a sharp cry. 'Stop it, stop it.'

" 'The wood, the wood,' said the blond vampire feebly, and, as he motioned to the other to hand him the fuel by his chair, I saw clearly, unmistakably, the profile of Lestat, that smooth skin now devoid of even the faintest trace of his old scars.

" 'If you'd just go out,' said the other angrily, heaving the chunk of wood into the blaze. 'If you'd just hunt something other than these miserable animals . . . .' And he looked about himself in disgust. I saw then, in the shadows, the small furry bodies of several cats, lying helter-skelter in the dust. A most remarkable thing, because a vampire can no more endure to be near his dead victims than any mammal can remain near any place where he has left his waste. 'Do you know that it's summer?' demanded the young one. Lestat merely rubbed his hands. The baby's howling died off, yet the young vampire added, 'Get on with it, take it so you'll be warm.'

" 'You might have brought me something else!' said Lestat bitterly. And, as he looked at the baby, I saw his eyes squinting against the dull light of the smoky lamp. I felt a shock of recognition at those eyes, even at the expression beneath the shadow of the deep wave of his yellow hair. And yet to hear that whining voice, to see that bent and quivering back! Almost without thinking I rapped hard on the glass. The young vampire was up at once affecting a hard, vicious expression; but I merely motioned for him to turn the latch. And Lestat, clutching his bathrobe to his throat, rose from the chair.

" 'It's Louis! Louis!' he said. 'Let him in.' And he gestured frantically, like an invalid, for the young 'nurse' to obey.

"As soon as the window opened I breathed the stench of the room and its sweltering heat. The swarming of the insects on the rotted animals scratched at my senses so that I recoiled despite myself, despite Lestat's desperate pleas for me to come to him. There, in the far corner, was the coffin where he slept, the lacquer peeling from the wood, half covered with piles of yellow newspapers. And bones lay in the corners, picked clean except for bits and tufts of fur. But Lestat had his dry hands on mine now, drawing me towards him and towards the warmth, and I could see the tears welling in his eyes; and only when his mouth was stretched in a strange smile of desperate happiness that was near to pain did I see the faint traces of the old scars. How baffling and awful it was, this smooth-faced, shimmering immortal man bent and rattled and whining like a crone.

" 'Yes, Lestat,' I said softly. 'I've come to see you.' I pushed his hand gently, slowly away and moved towards the baby, who was crying desperately now from fear as well as hunger. As soon as I lifted it up and loosened the covers, it quieted a little, and then I patted it and rocked it. Lestat was whispering to me now in quick, half-articulated words I couldn't understand, the tears streaming down his cheeks, the young vampire at the open window with a look of disgust on his face and one hand on the window latch, as if he meant at any minute to bolt.

" 'So you're Louis,' said the young vampire. This seemed to increase Lestat's inexpressible excitement, and he wiped frantically at his tears with the hem of his robe.

"A fly lit on the baby's forehead, and involuntarily

I gasped as I pressed it between two fingers and dropped it dead to the floor. The child was no longer crying. It was looking up at me with extraordinary blue eyes, dark-blue eyes, its round face glistening from the heat, and a smile played on its lips, a smile that grew brighter like a flame. I had never brought death to anything so young, so innocent, and I was aware of this now as I held the child with an odd feeling of sorrow, stronger even than that feeling which had come over me in the Rue Royale. And, rocking the child gently, I pulled the young vampire's chair to the fire and sat down.

" 'Don't try to speak . . . it's all right,' I said to Lestat, who dropped down gratefully into his chair and reached out to stroke the lapels of my coat with both hands.

" 'But I'm so glad to see you,' he stammered through his tears. 'I've dreamed of your coming . . . coming . . .' he said. And then he grimaced, as if he were feeling a pain he couldn't identify, and again the fine map of scars appeared for an instant. He was looking off, his hand up to his ear, as if he meant to cover it to defend himself from some terrible sound. 'I didn't . . .' he started; and then he shook his head, his eyes clouding as he opened them wide, strained to focus them. 'I didn't mean to let them do it, Louis . . . I mean that Santiago . . . that one, you know, he didn't tell me what they planned to do.'

" 'That's all past, Lestat,' I said.

" 'Yes, yes,' he nodded vigorously. 'Past. She should never . . . why, Louis, *you know*. . . .' And he was shaking his head, his voice seeming to gain in strength, to gain a little in resonance with his effort. 'She should have never been one of us, Louis.' And he rapped his sunken chest with his fist as he said 'Us' again softly.

"She. It seemed then that she had never existed. That she had been some illogical, fantastical dream that was too precious and too personal for me ever to confide in anyone. And too long gone. I looked at him. I stared at him. And tried to think, Yes, the three of us together.

" 'Don't fear me, Lestat,' I said, as though talking to myself. 'I bring you no harm.'

" 'You've come back to me, Louis,' he whispered in that thin, high-pitched voice. 'You've come home again to me, Louis, haven't you?' And again he bit his lip and looked at me desperately.

" 'No, Lestat.' I shook my head. He was frantic for a moment, and again he commenced one gesture and then another and finally sat there with his hands over his face in a paroxysm of distress. The other vampire, who was studying me coldly, asked:

" 'Are you . . . have you come back to him?'

" 'No, of course not,' I answered. And he smirked, as if this was as he expected, that everything fell to him again, and he walked out onto the porch. I could hear him there very near, waiting.

" 'I only wanted to see you, Lestat,' I said. But Lestat didn't seem to hear me. Something else had distracted him. And he was gazing off, his eyes wide, his hands hovering near his ears. Then I heard it also. It was a siren. And as it grew louder, his eyes shut tight against it and his fingers covered his ears. And it grew louder and louder, coming up the street from downtown. 'Lestat!' I said to him, over the baby's cries, which rose now in the same terrible fear of the siren. But his agony obliterated me. His lips were drawn back from his teeth in a terrible grimace of pain. 'Lestat, it's only a siren!' I said to him stupidly. And then he came forward out of the chair and took hold of me and held tight to me, and, despite myself, I took his hand. He bent down, pressing his head against my chest and holding my hand so tight that he caused me pain. The room was filled with the flashing red light of the siren, and then it was going away.

" 'Louis, I can't bear it, I can't bear it,' he growled through his tears. 'Help me, Louis, stay with me.'

" 'But why are you afraid?' I asked. 'Don't you know what these things are?' And as I looked down at him, as I saw his yellow hair pressed against my coat, I had a vision of him from long ago, that tall, stately gentleman in the swirling black cape, with his head thrown back, his rich, flawless voice singing the lilting air of the opera from which we'd only just come, his walking stick tapping the cobblestones in time with the music, his large, sparkling eye catching the young woman who stood by, enrapt, so that a smile spread over his face as the song died on his lips; and for one moment, that one moment when his eye met hers, all evil seemed obliterated in that flush of pleasure, that passion for merely being alive.

"Was this the price of that involvement? A sensibility shocked by change, shrivelling from fear? I thought quietly of all the things I might say to him, how I might remind him that he was immortal, that nothing condemned him to this retreat save himself, and that he was surrounded with the unmistakable signs of inevitable death. But I did not say these things, and I knew that I would not.

"It seemed the silence of the room rushed back around us, like a dark sea that the siren had driven away. The flies swarmed on the festering body of a rat, and the child looked quietly up at me as though my eyes were bright baubles, and its dimpled hand closed on the finger that I poised above its tiny petal mouth.

"Lestat had risen, straightened, but only to bend over and slink into the chair. 'You won't stay with me,' he sighed. But then he looked away and seemed suddenly absorbed.

" 'I wanted to talk to you so much,' he said. 'That night I came home in the Rue Royale I only wanted to talk to you!' He shuddered violently, eyes closed, his throat seeming to contract. It was as if the blows I'd struck him then were falling now. He stared blindly ahead, his tongue moistening his lip, his voice low, almost natural. 'I went to Paris after you. . . .'

" 'What was it you wanted to tell me?' I asked. 'What was it you wanted to talk about?'

"I could well remember his mad insistence in the Théâtre des Vampires. I hadn't thought of it in years. No, I had never thought of it. And I was aware that I spoke of it now with great reluctance.

"But he only smiled at me, and insipid, near apologetic smile. And shook his head. I watched his eyes fill with a soft, bleary despair.

"I felt a profound, undeniable relief.

" 'But you will stay!' he insisted.

" 'No,' I answered.

" 'And neither will I!' said that young vampire from the darkness outside. And he stood for a second in the open window looking at us. Lestat looked up at him and then sheepishly away, and his lower lip seemed to thicken and tremble. 'Close it, close it,' he said, waving his finger at the window. Then a sob burst from him and, covering his mouth with his hand, he put his head down and cried.

"The young vampire was gone. I heard his steps moving fast on the walk, heard the heavy chink of the iron gate. And I was alone with Lestat, and he was crying. It seemed a long time before he stopped, and during all that time I merely watched him. I was thinking of all the things that had passed between us. I was remembering things which I supposed I had completely forgotten. And I was conscious then of that same overwhelming sadness which I'd felt when I saw the place in the Rue Royale where we had lived. Only, it didn't seem to me to be a sadness for Lestat, for that smart, gay vampire who used to live there then. It seemed a sadness for something else, something beyond Lestat that only included him and was part of the great awful sadness of all the things I'd ever lost or loved or known. It seemed then I was in a different place, a different time. And this different place and time was very real, and it was a room where the insects had hummed as they were humming here and the air had been close and thick with death and with the spring perfume. And I was on the verge of knowing that place and knowing with it a terrible pain, a pain so terrible that my mind veered away from it, said, No, don't take me back to that place—and suddenly it was receding, and I was with Lestat here now. Astonished, I saw my own tear fall onto the face of the child. I saw it glisten on the child's cheek, and I saw the cheek become very plump with the child's smile. It must have been seeing the light in the tears.

I put my hand to my face and wiped at the tears that were in fact there and looked at them in amazement.

"'But Louis . . .' Lestat was saying softly. 'How can you be as you are, how can you stand it?' He was looking up at me, his mouth in that same grimace, his face wet with tears. 'Tell me, Louis, help me to understand! How can you understand it all, how can you endure?' And I could see by the desperation in his eyes and the deeper tone which his voice had taken that he, too, was pushing himself towards something that for him was very painful, towards a place where he hadn't ventured in a long time. But then, even as I looked at him, his eyes appeared to become misty, confused. And he pulled the robe up tight, and shaking his head, he looked at the fire. A shudder passed through him and he moaned.

"'I have to go now, Lestat,' I said to him. I felt weary, weary of him and weary of this sadness. And I longed again for the stillness outside, that perfect quiet to which I'd become so completely accustomed. But I realized, as I rose to my feet, that I was taking the little baby with me.

"Lestat looked up at me now with his large, agonized eyes and his smooth, ageless face. 'But you'll come back . . . you'll come to visit me . . . Louis?' he said.

"I turned away from him, hearing him calling after me, and quietly left the house. When I reached the street, I looked back and I could see him hovering at the window as if he were afraid to go out. I realized he had not gone out for a long, long time, and it occurred to me then that perhaps he would never go out again.

"I returned to the small house from which the vampire had taken the child, and left it there in its crib."

"Not very long after that I told Armand I'd seen Lestat. Perhaps it was a month, I'm not certain. Time meant little to me then, as it means little to me now. But it meant a great deal to Armand. He was amazed that I hadn't mentioned this before.

"We were walking that night uptown where the city

gives way to the Audubon Park and the levee is a
deserted, grassy slope that descends to a muddy beach
heaped here and there with driftwood, going out to
the lapping waves of the river. On the far bank were
the very dim lights of industries and river-front com-
panies, pinpoints of green or red that flickered in the
distance like stars. And the moon showed the broad,
strong current moving fast between the two shores;
and even the summer heat was gone here, with the
cool breeze coming off the water and gently lifting the
moss that hung from the twisted oak where we sat. I
was picking at the grass, and tasting it, though the
taste was bitter and unnatural. The gesture seemed
natural. I was feeling almost that I might never leave
New Orleans. But then, what are such thoughts when
you can live forever? Never leave New Orleans 'again?'
Again seemed a human word.

"'But didn't you feel any desire for revenge?'
Armand asked. He lay on the grass beside me, his
weight on his elbow, his eyes fixed on me.

"'Why?' I asked calmly. I was wishing, as I often
wished, that he was not there, that I was alone. Alone
with this powerful and cool river under the dim moon.
'He's met with his own perfect revenge. He's dying,
dying of rigidity, of fear. His mind cannot accept this
time. Nothing as serene and graceful as that vampire
death you once described to me in Paris. I think he is
dying as clumsily and grotesquely as humans often die
in this century . . . of old age.'

"'But you . . . what did you feel?' he insisted
softly. And I was struck by the personal quality of that
question, and how long it had been since either of us
had spoken to the other in that way. I had a strong
sense of him then, the separate being that he was, the
calm and collected creature with the straight auburn
hair and the large, sometimes melancholy eyes, eyes
that seemed often to be seeing nothing but their own
thoughts. Tonight they were lit with a dull fire that
was unusual.

"'Nothing,' I answered.

"'Nothing one way or the other?'

"I answered no. I remembered palpably that sorrow.

It was as if the sorrow hadn't left me suddenly, but had been near me all this time, hovering, saying, 'Come.' But I wouldn't tell this to Armand, wouldn't reveal this. And I had the strangest sensation of feeling his need for me to tell him this . . . this, or something . . . a need strangely akin to the need for living blood.

" 'But did he tell you anything, anything that made you feel the old hatred . . .' he murmured. And it was at this point that I became keenly aware of how distressed he was.

" 'What is it, Armand? Why do you ask this?' I said.

"But he lay back on the steep levee then, and for a long time he appeared to be looking at the stars. The stars brought back to me something far too specific, the ship that had carried Claudia and me to Europe, and those nights at sea when it seemed the stars came down to touch the waves.

" 'I thought perhaps he would tell you something about Paris . . .' Armand said.

" 'What should he say about Paris? That he didn't want Claudia to die?' I asked. Claudia again; the name sounded strange. Claudia spreading out that game of solitaire on the table that shifted with the shifting of the sea, the lantern creaking on its hook, the black porthole full of the stars. She had her head bent, her fingers poised above her ear as if about to loosen strands of her hair. And I had the most disconcerting sensation: that in my memory she would look up from that game of solitaire, and the sockets of her eyes would be empty.

" 'You could have told me anything you wanted about Paris, Armand,' I said. 'Long before now. It wouldn't have mattered.'

" 'Even that it was I who . . . ?'

"I turned to him as he lay there looking at the sky. And I saw the extraordinary pain in his face, in his eyes. It seemed his eyes were huge, too huge, and the white face that framed them too gaunt.

" 'That it was you who killed her? Who forced her out into that yard and locked her there?' I asked. I smiled. 'Don't tell me you have been feeling pain for it all these years, not you.'

"And then he closed his eyes and turned his face away, his hand resting on his chest as if I'd struck him an awful, sudden blow.

" 'You can't convince me you care about this,' I said to him coldly. And I looked out towards the water, and again that feeling came over me . . . that I wished to be alone. In a little while I knew I would get up and go off by myself. That is, if he didn't leave me first. Because I would have liked to remain there actually. It was a quiet, secluded place.

" 'You care about nothing . . .' he was saying. And then he sat up slowly and turned to me so again I could see that dark fire in his eyes. 'I thought you would at least care about that. I thought you would feel the old passion, the old anger if you were to see him again. I thought something would quicken and come alive in you if you saw him . . . if you returned to this place.'

" 'That I would come back to life?' I said softly. And I felt the cold metallic hardness of my words as I spoke, the modulation, the control. It was as if I were cold all over, made of metal, and he were fragile suddenly; fragile, as he had been, actually, for a long time.

" 'Yes!' he cried out. 'Yes, back to life!' And then he seemed puzzled, positively confused. And a strange thing occurred. He bowed his head at that moment as if he were defeated. And something in the way that he felt that defeat, something in the way his smooth white face reflected it only for an instant, reminded me of someone else I'd seen defeated in just that way. And it was amazing to me that it took me such a long moment to see Claudia's face in that attitude; Claudia, as she stood by the bed in the room at the Hôtel Saint-Gabriel pleading with me to transform Madeleine into one of us. That same helpless look, that defeat which seemed to be so heartfelt that everything beyond it was forgotten. And then he, like Claudia, seemed to rally, to pull on some reserve of strength. But he said softly to the air, 'I am dying!'

"And I, watching him, hearing him, the only creature under God who heard him, knowing completely that it was true, said nothing.

"A long sigh escaped his lips. His head was bowed. His right hand lay limp beside him in the grass. 'Hatred . . . that is passion,' he said. 'Revenge, that is passion. . . .'

" 'Not from me . . .' I murmured softly. 'Not now.'

"And then his eyes fixed on me and his face seemed very calm. 'I used to believe you would get over it—that when the pain of all of it left you, you would grow warm again and filled with love, and filled with that wild and insatiable curiosity with which you first came to me, that inveterate conscience, and that hunger for knowledge that brought you all the way to Paris to my cell. I thought it was a part of you that couldn't die. And I thought that when the pain was gone you would forgive me for what part I played in her death. She never loved you, you know. Not in the way that I loved you, and the way that you loved us both. I knew this! I understood it! And I believed I would gather you to me and hold you. And time would open to us, and we would be the teachers of one another. All the things that gave you happiness would give me happiness; and I would be the protector of your pain. My power would be your power. My strength the same. But you're dead inside to me, you're cold and beyond my reach! It is as if I'm not here, beside you. And, not being here with you, I have the dreadful feeling that I don't exist at all. And you are as cold and distant from me as those strange modern paintings of lines and hard forms that I cannot love or comprehend, as alien as those hard mechanical sculptures of this age which have no human form. I shudder when I'm near you. I look into your eyes and my reflection isn't there. . . .'

" 'What you asked was impossible!' I said quickly. 'Don't you see? What I asked was impossible, too, from the start.'

"He protested, the negation barely forming on his lips, his hand rising as if to thrust it away.

" 'I wanted love and goodness in this which is living death,' I said. 'It was impossible from the beginning, because you cannot have love and goodness when you do what you know to be evil, what you know to be wrong. You can only have the desperate confusion and longing and the chasing of phantom goodness in its human form. I knew the real answer to my quest before I ever reached Paris. I knew it when I first took a human life to feed my craving. It was my death. And yet I would not accept it, could not accept it, because like all creatures I don't wish to die! And so I sought for other vampires, for God, for the devil, for a hundred things under a hundred names. And it was all the same, all evil. And all wrong. Because no one could in any guise convince me of what I myself knew to be true, that I was damned in my own mind and soul. And when I came to Paris I thought you were powerful and beautiful and without regret, and I wanted that desperately. But you were a destroyer just as I was a destroyer, more ruthless and cunning even than I. You showed me the only thing that I could really hope to become, what depth of evil, what degree of coldness I would have to attain to end my pain. And I accepted that. And so that passion, that love you saw in me, was extinguished. And you see now simply a mirror of yourself.'

"A very long time passed before he spoke. He'd risen to his feet, and he stood with his back to me looking down the river, head bowed as before, his hands at his sides. I was looking at the river also. I was thinking quietly, There is nothing more I can say, nothing more I can do.

" 'Louis,' he said now, lifting his head, his voice very thick and unlike itself.

" 'Yes, Armand,' I said.

" 'Is there anything else you want of me, anything else you require?'

" 'No,' I said. 'What do you mean?'

"He didn't answer this. He began to slowly walk away. I think at first I thought he only meant to walk a few paces, perhaps to wander by himself along the muddy beach below. And by the time I realized that he was leaving me, he was a mere speck down there against the occasional flickering in the water under the moon. I never saw him again.

"Of course, it was several nights later before I realized he was gone. His coffin remained. But he did not return to it. And it was several months before I had that coffin taken to the St. Louis cemetery and put into the crypt beside my own. The grave, long neglected because my family was gone, received the only thing he'd left behind. But then I began to be uncomfortable with that. I thought of it on waking, and again at dawn right before I closed my eyes. And I went downtown one night and took the coffin out, and broke it into pieces and left it in the narrow aisle of the cemetery in the tall grass.

"That vampire who was Lestat's latest child accosted me one evening not long after. He begged me to tell him all I knew of the world, to become his companion and his teacher. I remember telling him that what I chiefly knew was that I'd destroy him if I ever saw him again. 'You see, someone must die every night that I walk, until I've the courage to end it,' I told him. 'And you're an admirable choice for that victim, a killer as evil as myself.'

"And I left New Orleans the next night because the sorrow wasn't leaving me. And I didn't want to think of that old house where Lestat was dying. Or that sharp, modern vampire who'd fled me. Or of Armand.

"I wanted to be where there was nothing familiar to me. And nothing mattered.

"And that's the end of it. There's nothing else."

THE BOY SAT MUTE, staring at the vampire. And the vampire sat collected, his hands folded on the table, his narrow, red-rimmed eyes fixed on the turning tapes. His face was so gaunt now that the veins of his temples showed as if carved out of stone. And he sat so still that only his green eyes evinced life, and that life was a dull fascination with the turning of the tapes.

Then the boy drew back and ran the fingers of his right hand loosely through his hair. "No," he said with a short intake of breath. Then he said it again louder, "No!"

The vampire didn't appear to hear him. His eyes moved away from the tapes towards the window, towards the dark, gray sky.

"It didn't have to end like that!" said the boy, leaning forward.

The vampire, who continued to look at the sky, uttered a short, dry laugh.

"All the things you felt in Paris!" said the boy, his voice increasing in volume. "The love of Claudia, the feeling, even the feeling for Lestat! It didn't have to end, not in this, not in despair! Because that's what it is, isn't it? Despair!"

"Stop," said the vampire abruptly, lifting his right hand. His eyes shifted almost mechanically to the boy's face. "I tell you and I have told you, that it could not have ended any other way."

"I don't accept it," said the boy, and he folded his arms across his chest, shaking his head emphatically. "I can't!" And the emotion seemed to build in him, so that without meaning to, he scraped his chair back on the bare boards and rose to pace the floor. But then, when he turned and looked at the vampire's face again, the words he was about to speak died in his throat. The vampire was merely staring at him, and his face had that long drawn expression of both outrage and bitter amusement.

"Don't you see how you made it sound? It was an adventure like I'll never know in my whole life! You talk about passion, you talk about longing! You talk about things that millions of us won't ever taste or come to understand. And then you tell me it ends like that. I tell you . . ." And he stood over the vampire now, his hands outstretched before him. "If you were to give me that power! The power to see and feel and live forever!"

The vampire's eyes slowly began to widen, his lips parting. "What!" he demanded softly. *"What!"*

"Give it to me!" said the boy, his right hand tightening in a fist, the fist pounding his chest. "Make me a vampire now!" he said as the vampire stared aghast.

What happened then was swift and confused, but it ended abruptly with the vampire on his feet holding the boy by the shoulders, the boy's moist face contorted with fear, the vampire glaring at him in rage. "This is what you want?" he whispered, his pale lips manifesting only the barest trace of movement. "This . . . after all I've told you . . . is what you ask for?"

A small cry escaped the boy's lips, and he began to tremble all over, the sweat breaking out on his forehead and on the skin above his upper lip. His hand reached gingerly for the vampire's arm. "You don't know what human life is like!" he said, on the edge of breaking into tears. "You've forgotten. You don't even understand the meaning of your own story, what it means to a human being like me." And then a choked sob interrupted his words, and his fingers clung to the vampire's arm.

"God," the vampire uttered and, turning away from him, almost pushed the boy off-balance against the wall. He stood with his back to the boy, staring at the gray window.

"I beg you . . . give it all one more chance. One more chance in me!" said the boy.

The vampire turned to him, his face as twisted with anger as before. And then, gradually, it began to become smooth. The lids came down slowly over his eyes and his lips lengthened in a smile. He looked again at the boy. "I've failed," he sighed, smiling still. "I have completely failed. . . ."

"No . . ." the boy protested.

"Don't say any more," said the vampire emphatically. "I have but one chance left. Do you see the reels? They still turn. I have but one way to show you the meaning of what I've said." And then he reached out for the boy so fast that the boy found himself grasping for something, pushing against something that was not there, so his hand was outstretched still when the vampire had him pressed to his chest, the boy's neck bent beneath his lips. "Do you see?" whispered the vampire, and the long, silky lips drew up over his teeth and two long fangs came down into the boy's flesh. The boy stuttered, a low guttural sound coming out of his throat, his hand struggling to close on something, his eyes widening only to become dull and gray as the vampire drank. And the vampire meantime looked as tranquil as someone in sleep. His narrow chest heaved so subtly with his sigh that he seemed to be rising slowly from the floor and then settling again with that same somnambulistic grace. There was a whine coming from the boy, and when the vampire let him go he held him out with both hands and looked at the damp white face, the limp hands, the eyes half closed.

The boy was moaning, his lower lip loose and trembling as if in nausea. He moaned again louder, and his head fell back and his eyes rolled up into his head. The vampire set him down gently in the chair. The boy was struggling to speak, and the tears which sprang now to his eyes seemed to come as much from that effort to speak as from anything else. His head fell forward, heavily, drunkenly, and his hand rested on the table. The vampire stood looking down at him, and his white skin became a soft luminous pink. It was as if a pink light were shining on him and his entire being seemed to give back that light. The flesh of his lips was dark, almost rose in color, and the veins of his temples and his hands were mere traces on his skin, and his face was youthful and smooth.

"Will I . . . die?" the boy whispered as he looked up slowly, his mouth wet and slack. "Will I die?" he groaned, his lip trembling.

"I don't know," the vampire said, and he smiled.

The boy seemed on the verge of saying something more, but the hand that rested on the table slid forward on the boards, and his head lay down beside it as he lost consciousness.

When next he opened his eyes, the boy saw the sun. It filled the dirty, undressed window and was hot on the side of his face and his hand. For a moment, he lay there, his face against the table and then with a great effort, he straightened, took a long deep breath and closing his eyes, pressed his hand to that place where the vampire had drawn blood. When his other hand accidentally touched a band of metal on the top of the tape recorder, he let out a sudden cry because the metal was hot.

Then he rose, moving clumsily, almost falling, until he rested both his hands on the white wash basin. Quickly he turned on the tap, splashed his face with cold water, and wiped it with a soiled towel that hung there on a nail. He was breathing regularly now and he stood still, looking into the mirror without any support. Then he looked at his watch. It was as if the watch shocked him, brought him more to life than the sun or the water. And he made a quick search of the room, of the hallway, and, finding nothing and no one, he settled again into the chair. Then, drawing a small white pad out of his pocket, and a pen, he set these on the table and touched the button of the recorder. The tape spun fast backwards until he shut it off. When he heard the vampire's voice, he leaned forward, listening very carefully, then hit the button again for another place, and, hearing that, still another. But then at last his face brightened, as the reels turned and the voice spoke in an even modulated tone: "It was a very warm evening, and I could tell as soon as I saw him on St. Charles that he had someplace to go . . ."

And quickly the boy noted:

"Lestat . . . off St. Charles Avenue. Old house crumbling . . . shabby neighborhood. Look for rusted railings."

And then, stuffing the notebook quickly in his pocket, he gathered the tapes into his brief case, along with the small recorder, and hurried down the long hallway and down the stairs to the street, where in front of the corner bar his car was parked.